作者：A.J.爱伦斯坦

主译：方华文

译者：张伟华　郑黎明

英汉对照

Fascinating Myths & Legends

50+1个令人入胜的传奇故事

and the love
of one woman,

he fought to
uphold justice

by breaking
the law.

KEVIN
COSTNER

安徽科学技术出版社
Encouragement Press, LLC

U0595789

图书在版编目(CIP)数据

50+1个最引人入胜的传奇故事 / (美) 爱伦斯坦
(Alenstein, A.J.) 著；方华文译. -- 合肥：安徽科学
技术出版社，2009.06
(50+1系列)
ISBN 978-7-5337-4435-9

Ⅰ. ①5… Ⅱ. ①爱… ②方… Ⅲ. ①故事－作品集－
世界 Ⅳ. ①I14

中国版本图书馆CIP数据核字(2009)第079292号

50+1个最引人入胜的传奇故事
(美) 爱伦斯坦(Alenstein,A.J.) 著 方华文 译

出 版 人：黄和平
责任编辑：姚敏淑 孙立凯
封面设计：朱 婧
出版发行：安徽科学技术出版社(合肥市政务文化新区圣泉路1118号
　　　　　出版传媒广场，邮编：230071)
网　　址：www.ahstp.net
E - mail：yougoubu@sina.com
经　　销：新华书店
排　　版：安徽事达科技贸易有限公司
印　　刷：合肥瑞丰印务有限公司
开　　本：787×1092　1/16
印　　张：14.5
字　　数：400千
版　　次：2009年6月第1版　2022年1月第2次印刷
定　　价：39.00元

(本书如有印装质量问题,影响阅读,请向本社市场营销部调换)

译　者　序

我们的生活扑朔迷离，千奇百怪的现象构成了一个个无法解答或难于解答的谜。这恐怕就是产生"神话"的原因之一吧。有的时候，"神话"与"现实"纠缠在一起，连最智慧的人都分不清。那么，"神话"中的"迷信"成分有多少呢？我的童年是在一个繁华的城市度过的，那儿是"科学的中心"，可有些现象却让当时的人费解。街头卖艺的说他们"刀枪不入"，甚至还现场示范……据传：位于西安市中心的钟楼地下锁着一条龙，它一旦出来就会洪水泛滥……街坊流传着一种说法：大山里有"神水"，可以医治百病。这样的"神水"谁不想喝一口！于是，都市里的人们蜂拥至荒山，每户抢回几瓶"神水"，全家受用。数万居民都喝了"神水"，可是没见哪个人因此而解除了病痛。一些"神话"破灭了，而另一些仍在影响着人类……

你相信UFO(不明飞行物)之说吗？20世纪以前较完整的目击报告有350件以上。据目击者说：不明飞行物外形多呈圆盘状(碟状)、球状和雪茄状。20世纪40年代末起，不明飞行物目击事件急剧增多，引起了科学界的争论。到80年代为止，全世界共有目击报告约10万件。不明飞行物目击事件与目击报告可分为4类：白天目击事件；夜晚目击事件；雷达显像；近距离接触和有关物证。UFO是外星人发射的吗？……

据说，在大洪灾之前，有一块闪烁着人类文明曙光的陆地，古希腊哲学家柏拉图称它为亚特兰蒂斯。根据柏拉图的描述，当时亚特兰蒂斯的生活非常奢华，因为根本无需用劳力赚取生活，一切都是自动化的，百姓享尽便利。大多数人面貌非常俊美，衣服由珠宝点缀，人们跳舞、聚会、服用迷幻药物。亚特兰蒂斯人最初诚实善良，具有超凡脱俗的智慧，过着无忧无虑的生活。然而随着时间的流逝，亚特兰蒂斯人的野心开始膨胀，他们开始派出军队，征服周边的国家。他们的生活也变得越来越腐化，无休止的极尽奢华和道德沦丧，终于激怒了众神。于是，众神之王宙斯一夜之间将地震和洪水降临在这块陆地上。亚特兰蒂斯最终被大海吞没，从此消失在深不可测的大海之中。这种传说属实吗？……

百慕大三角的怪现象你知道吗？百慕大群岛、佛罗里达半岛和波多黎各岛这三点连线形成一片三角地带，叫"百慕大三角"，面积达40万平方英里。这里气候温和，四季如春，各岛上绿树常青，鲜花怒放。不过，此地区出名，并非由于它风光旖旎，而是由于这儿发生过一些恐怖而神秘的事件。自从1854年起，在百慕大三角有50多艘船只和20多架飞机神秘失踪。有人认为这些失踪事件非常离奇，因为几乎从没有船员或飞行员发出遇险信号。而且，搜救人员未能找到幸存者或发现受难者的尸体，就是连一点船舶和飞机的残骸碎片也找不到。最有经验的海员或飞行员通过这里时，都无心欣赏那美丽如画的海上风光，而是战战兢兢、提心吊胆，唯恐碰上厄运，不明不白地葬身鱼腹。难道有魔鬼在作祟？……

一提到"尼斯湖水怪",你很可能会联想到美国大片中那个从水里突然冒出来袭击船只的像恐龙一样的庞然大物。真的有这种水怪吗？公元565年，亚当曼在《哥伦布的一生》这部传记中提到了尼斯湖水怪，这是关于它的最早记录。在这本书中，哥伦布当时去拜访苏格兰的一个部落首领，驻足于尼斯湖边，看到一个巨大的动物袭击游泳者。他情急之下大喝一声，那怪物马上掉头潜入水底，游泳者获救了。1934年4月，伦敦医生威尔逊途经尼斯湖，正好发现水怪在湖中游动。威尔逊连忙用相机拍下了水怪的照片，照片虽不十分清晰，但还是明确地显出了水怪的特征：长长的脖子和扁小的头部，看上去完全不像任何一种水生动物，而很像早在7 000多万年前灭绝的巨大爬行动物蛇颈龙。难道恐龙并没有彻底灭绝？……科学界沸腾了，考察的浪潮此起彼伏。结果如何呢？

巨石阵、麦田怪圈、吸血鬼、雪山野人……一个个怪现象、一件件怪事情搅扰着人类。这本书将给诸位提供一份休闲、探索的乐趣！

方华文

2009年5月于苏州大学

方华文简介

方华文，男，1955年6月生于西安，现任苏州大学外国语学院英语教授，著名学者、文学翻译家及翻译理论家，被联合国教科文组织国际译联誉为"the most productive literary translator in contemporary China"（中国当代最多产的文学翻译家，Babel.54:2, 2008, 145–158）。发表的著、译作品达1 000余万字，其中包括专著《20世纪中国翻译史》等，计200余万字；译著《雾都孤儿》《无名的裘德》《傲慢与偏见》《蝴蝶梦》《魂断英伦》《儿子与情人》《少年维特之烦恼》《红字》《从巅峰到低谷》《马丁·伊登》《套向月亮的绳索》《君主论》《社会契约论》以及改写本的《飘》《汤姆叔叔的小屋》《查特莱夫人的情人》《大卫·科波菲尔》《苔丝》《高老头》《三个火枪手》《悲惨世界》等；主编的译作包括《基督山伯爵》《红与黑》《简·爱》《汤姆·索亚历险记》《茶花女》《金银岛》《鲁滨孙漂流记》《巴黎圣母院》《莎士比亚戏剧故事集》《精神分析引论》《论法的精神》和《国富论》等；并主编了多部英汉对照读物。以上均为单行本著作，所发表文章不计在内。

Does the Easter Bunny Really Lay Eggs?

From the beginning of time human beings have surrounded themselves with myths and legends to explain the world around them. Many myths and legends may have grown out of the need to understand the unfathomable or to give a tangible presence to something that defied definition.

As humans become more educated and informed, many long-told myths are explained and therefore, are no longer myths. Yet one of the biggest mysteries surrounding myths and legends is their tenacity—no matter how well they are explained, debunked or replaced with facts, many seem to capture our imaginations. They linger on as superstitions, traditions or just good stories.

Many people still follow the story of the Loch Ness Monster, for example. Or search for the lost continent Atlantis. Or think certain numbers are lucky or unlucky. Superstitions abound in our modern world: Is Friday the 13th really unlucky? And is the unlucky part the day Friday or the number 13? Breaking a mirror lead to 7 years of bad luck? Or what about religious or festival traditions? Why is the Easter Bunny a symbol of a religious holiday? And does a bunny really lay eggs?

Old wives' tales have been a part of folk wisdom from ancient times. Supposedly passed down by old wives to young wives, these gems of wisdom are often warnings to discourage undesirable behavior or habits. Many are fun and hard to resist passing on: Eating carrots improves night vision or makes hair curly. If you smell dandelions, you will wet the bed.

Our modern age contributes its share of myths and legends, too. Urban myths, often rumors thought to be true by those who circulate them, spring up and persist. Their name notwithstanding, urban legends do not necessarily occur in an urban environment. Rather, they are called urban to distinguish them from traditional folk-based legends. And, in keeping with their modern origin, their circulation today can be instantaneous.

Looking over the wide range of myths and legends that has persisted so long—and continues to intrigue us—we may conclude that the uncertainty about the supernatural or the questions about what cannot be explained only partly explain the tenacity of myths. Myths and legends are just plain fun. Even when we can explain what we had thought was a mythical phenomenon, it is more interesting to continue to recite—and even embellish—the myth.

This book looks at common myths, legends, superstitions and old wives' tales and attempts to explain their origins as well as their veracity.

复活节彩蛋真是兔子下的吗？

自古以来人类就编造了神话和传说来解释身边的这个世界。很多神话和传说的出现也许是因为人类想要理解那些无法解释的景象或者弄懂那些无可名状的现象。

随着教育水平的提高和见识范围的扩大，人类已经能够解释许多长期流传的神话，于是这些神话便不再神奇。可是神话和传说之所以神秘，恰恰在于它们经得起时间的考验。无论人们怎样解释、澄清它们，或者摆出事实的真相，很多神话传说依然能够吸引我们的幻想。它们流传下来，成为迷信、传统，或者仅仅是个精彩的故事。

比如，很多人依然相信尼斯湖水怪的故事，或者还在寻找消失的大陆亚特兰蒂斯，或者认为有的数字给人带来幸运而有的数字则伴随厄运。迷信充斥着我们的现代世界：13号星期五果真给人们带来不幸吗？那么不幸到底来自于星期五这一天抑或是13这个数字？摔碎一面镜子能惹来7年的厄运吗？还有，宗教和节日传统又是什么情况？为什么复活节兔子是宗教节日的象征？复活节彩蛋真是兔子下的吗？

从古时候起，老妇人们的故事已成为民间智慧的一部分。想来是由老妇人向晚辈传授的，这些智慧的财富通常警示人们不要做出不受欢迎的举动，不要养成恶习。其中很多故事相当有趣，必然代代流传下去：吃胡萝卜能提高夜视力，或者长出卷发来。如果你闻蒲公英，就会尿床。

当今的时代也为神话传说贡献了一分力量。都市神话其实只是一些谣言，通常只有散播的人才会相信是真的。虽然名为都市神话，却未必发生在都市。之所以叫都市神话，只是为了区别于传统的来自民间的传说。而且，正因为都市神话出自现代，其传播速度也是相当惊人。

历史悠久的神话和传说至今还在吸引我们的兴趣，审视其内容的广泛，我们可以得出这样一个结论：变幻莫测的超自然或者无法作出解释的那些问题只不过部分说明了神话流传的原因。神话和传说是平常人家的乐事。哪怕已经能够解释那些曾经以为奇幻的现象，我们依旧继续传诵这些神话，甚至还会添油加醋，真是其乐无穷。

本书涵盖了常见的神话、传说、迷信和老妇人们的故事，试图解释他们的起源及其真实度。这些神话当中，有很多本身就是精彩的故事，也有很多

Many of these myths are good stories and many even have a kernel of truth to them. Some will be so good, in fact, that you may prefer to believe them rather than forgo the pleasure of repeating them in their original forms.

Is It a Myth or a Legend?

While the words myth and legend are commonly used in the same context, there are differences. As an author, I myself am guilty of confusing the two as I do not try to separate which of the chapters are about myths and which are about legends. I will let you decide for yourself. But to help you, consider what follows.

All about Myths

Coming from Greek (mythos) meaning word or story, in its simplest dictionary form, the word myth means a traditional story dealing with supernatural beings, ancestors or heroes who shape the worldview of a people. (For example, the entire Greek, and later Roman worlds, were shaped by their gods, heroes and men—all myths in their own right.) It is only much later that the word evolves to mean a fiction or half–truth or even a fictitious story. In their purest forms, myths are often sacred stories concerning either the origins of the world or major changes in the world order that have bought us to the present time.

Many scholars and researchers would say that myths have a sacred quality to them, often religious and just as frequently explaining how the world came to be or how men were created. Believers assume that myths are true; scholars do not care one way or the other, as it is not the truth behind the myth that fascinates them as much as how they started, developed and are now interpreted.

Myths are often symbolic, tales from the distant or primordial past; they connect the present to the origins of belief systems, of rituals and may even been a means to direct social action and values. Myths often involve heroic characters, many of them greater than life or normal humans. Myth characters can intervene in human affairs, even establishing patterns for life and living.

The one great difficulty contemporary men and women have is that we are so ingrained in a scientific world that we fail to see any basis for and value in myths. Myths certainly are not anti–science. In fact, both have existed side by side for centuries. For us to understand and even appreciate myths, it is necessary to try to put them in their historical context. Because of their rich symbolic and narrative appeal, many scholars believe that classical movies, books and music are the

甚至具备真实的本质。事实上,有些神话故事精彩绝伦,你情愿相信这是真的,也不愿错失那种乐趣,以其固有的形式回味它们,转述它们。

这是个神话,还是个传说?

虽然神话和传说常常用在相同的语境,两者之间却的确存在区别。

作为本书作者,我自己是把两者混为一谈的,并没有清楚说明哪些章节是神话哪些章节是传说,这种做法也许不太妥当。我想让读者自己作判断。不过仔细斟酌下文,应该会不无裨益。

关于神话

神话(myth)这个词汇来源于希腊语mythos,意为单词或者故事;神话出现在字典中最简单的形式时,指的是一个传统的故事,讲述超自然的事、人类的祖先或者修正人们世界观的英雄们。(例如,整个希腊民族和后来的罗马世界,都是受到了其神灵、英雄和人物的影响——而所有这些都源于他们自己的神话。)此后很久,这个词的含义演变成小说或半真实的故事甚至是虚构的故事。神话通常以最单纯的形式描述关于世界起源或世界格局重大变化的神圣故事。

很多学者和研究人员认为神话对他们来讲有着一种神圣的特质,这种特质通常带有宗教色彩,常常涉及世界如何产生、人类如何起源。信徒们认为神话是真实的;而学者们则不在意是否真实,因为让他们着迷的并非神话背后的真相,而是神话的起源、发展以及当代对其的解释。

神话作为从遥远的远古流传至今的故事,通常带有某种象征意义;神话把现代连接到了信仰体系和传统仪式的源头,也成了社会活动和社会评价的指导方法。神话中常常涉及英雄人物,他们当中多数比普通人来得更伟大。神话人物能够干涉人类的事情,甚至为人类构建生活的模式。

当代人的一大困难就是我们对科学世界坚信不疑,很难看清神话的基础和价值。神话当然不是反科学。事实上,神话和科学已经并存了几个世纪。对我们来说,要理解神话、欣赏神话,就必须把神话放到历史的背景中去。鉴于神话丰富的象征性和引人的叙事性,不少学者坚信,当代社会中经典的电影、书籍和音乐可以替代神话。

contemporary substitutes for myths.

Finally, myths have high drama. Involving super-human heroes and heroines, the plot is often complicated and involves interplay between different worlds (Mt. Olympus and Ancient Greece, for example). There is mystery and the action defies or breaks natural laws. But most of all, they are supposed to help us understand why we are here.

All about Legend

First and foremost, legends are not myths; nor are they folklore. The word comes from the Latin (legenda) for things to be read. In its simplest form, a legend is an unverified story handed down from one generation to another; it is popularly believed to be historically true. Unlike myths or folklore, legends are possible in reality; they are not outside of the realm of possibility.

A variation on the theme, in contemporary society, is a class of legends called urban. Whether they are specifically urban or even legends at all in the truest and strictest sense of the word, the phrase and its use continues to cloud the true meaning of a legend. Furthermore, the word legend is often applied to an exceptional contemporary person —a musician, singer, athlete or scientist —whose reputation is expected to be enduring and remain prominent for future generations.

For a legend to be a true legend, it will be fiercely defended as true by some. No matter what is said, no matter the extent of the so-called evidence, it happened as reported. Legends can be people (King Arthur, Robin Hood); they can be events (Paul Revere's ride); they can be places (Shangri-La, Atlantis); or they can even be animals or creatures (Loch Ness Monster, Yeti).

Finally, to separate the difference between myth and legend, one scholar uses the example of the Gordian Knot. As remembered from our school days, many men tried to unravel the knot that secured the pole of the sacred ox cart at Gordium. Great fame, fortune and promise went to the individual who could do so. In contemporary terms, Alexander the Great solved the problem by thinking outside of the box: Everyone else tried to untying it; he simply slashed it with his sword. The legend is the story of Alexander solving the knot problem forever; the myth of the Gordian Knot is the founding of Gordium itself, thus justifying the authenticity of a line of kings and Alexander's succession to that line.

Enjoy!

A.J. Alenstein

最后,神话还有很强的戏剧效果。由于牵涉到超人类的男女主人公,情节常常复杂离奇,多重世界交织在一起(如奥林匹斯山和古希腊)。其中有神秘的事件,有打破自然法则的活动。但是最为显著的是,神话应该帮助人类理解自身生存的原因。

关于传说

首先,传说既不是神话,也不是民间故事。传说(legend)这个词汇来自拉丁文legenda,意为读物。在其最基本的形式时,这个单词指的是一代代流传下来但是未经考证的故事,很多人相信这样的故事在历史上是的确发生过的。传说不像神话或者民间故事,它在现实中是有可能存在的,并非完全不可能的事。

在当代社会,传说的主题略有变动,出现了一种都市传说。这种都市传说,无论是专门的都市题材,还是从严格意义上来讲根本就是传说而已,都已给"传说"的真实含义笼上了一层迷雾。而且,"传说"这个词汇常常用在出色的当代人物身上——音乐家、歌唱家、运动员或者科学家——他们的荣誉经久不衰,一直照耀到数辈以后。

有的传说被认为是真的,自然有人强烈地维护其真实性。不管讲的什么内容,不管所谓的真凭实据到底有多少可信度,这种传说应该如报道所述那样发生过。这种传说的内容可能是人物(如亚瑟王、罗宾汉),可能是事件(如骑手保罗),可能是地方(如香格里拉、亚特兰蒂斯),甚至可能是动物(如尼斯湖水怪、夜帝)。

最后提一下,为了区分神话和传说,有位学者举了"戈耳迪之结"作为例证。从学生时代起我们就知道,在戈耳迪这个小国家,有很多人用尽办法想把固定圣牛车车辕的结打开。因为只要有人把这个结打开,他就能得到荣誉、财富和福佑。据当时的说法,亚历山大大帝独辟蹊径解决了这个难题:每个人都努力地想打开这个结,而他则当机立断地挥剑将它斩断。这个传说,讲述了亚历山大大帝一劳永逸地解决难题的故事;而这个神话,则描绘了戈耳迪的建国史,进一步确立了一代代国王及其后人们的王室身份。

祝您阅读愉快!
A.J.爱伦斯坦

Table of Contents

目 录

1

Table of Contents
目　录

2

Table of Contents

目　录

3

Table of Contents
目　录

4

50+1 个最引人入胜的传奇故事

plus one
Roswell, New Mexico

The summer of 1947 was the season of UFO sightings in the United States. One of the most notable incidents occurred during the first week of July in Roswell, New Mexico.

Roswell is a desert town located in southeast New Mexico. In 1947 it was the home to a United States Army Air Field and the station of the 509th Bomb Group of the Eighth Air Force. During that first week of July in 1947, a rancher in the area, Mack Brazel, decided to tour his land to check on his livestock after a severe thunderstorm the night before. During that tour he found several pieces of what appeared to be metal debris as well as a long, shallow trench gouged into the soil.

After conferring with neighbors who speculated that the debris might be remnants of an UFO, Brazel reported his findings to the local sheriff who, in turn, contacted the intelligence officer of the 509th Bomb Group, Major Jesse Marcel. Marcel relayed the information to his commander, Colonel William Blanchard, who closed the area while clearing away the debris.

On July 8, 1947, the Army's public information officer released a statement that the Army had recovered debris from a fallen UFO. Within hours, however, he rescinded the first statement and issued a correction that the Army had been mistaken in identifying the wreckage as debris from an UFO and that it was really debris from a weather balloon.

From the Army's point of view, the issue was closed. However, citizens of Roswell continued to hear rumors about alien bodies, debris with strange markings and UFOs showing up on radar in southern New Mexico. There were also stories that the strange debris and other artifacts supposedly from the wreckage were removed or hidden whenever anyone tried to investigate.

The term flying saucer was coined in 1947 when a newspaper quoted an eyewitness who said the flying objects he saw *flew like a saucer if you skip it across water.*

The Story Revisited

Thirty years later in 1978 the story reappeared when a reporter interviewed Jesse Marcel who alleged that the Army had covered up the UFO story with the weather balloon theory in 1947. This prompted numerous other stories and much speculation about the original incident. Finally,the Secretary of the Air Force conducted an investigation into the matter.

The first report in 1995 prepared for Congressman Steven Schiff concluded that the debris was probably material from a secret project called Project Mogul, a research program designed to assess the feasibility of detecting Soviet nuclear tests by using high-altitude balloon launches to monitor low-frequency acoustics in the upper atmosphere. Based on evidence gathered from archives, a second report in 1997 concluded that the 1947 incident was the fallout of activity that was focused on the Soviet Union since that year marked the beginning of the Cold War.

An engineer involved with the project claimed that Army researchers used makeshift radar

外加 1

新墨西哥罗斯威尔

1947年的夏天,美国举国上下都在谈论不明飞行物(UFO)。最有名的当属7月份的第一周发生在新墨西哥州的罗斯威尔事件。

罗斯威尔是新墨西哥州东南部的一个沙漠地带小镇。当时,罗斯威尔既是美国陆军航空部队基地,也是空军第8军第509轰炸小组的驻地。1947年7月份的第一周,当地的一个牧场主马可·布莱索决定去查看牧场上养的家畜,因为前一晚下了场大暴雨。正当他巡视的时候,他发现了几块似乎是金属的碎片,泥地里还有一条长长的浅沟。

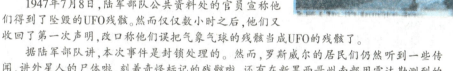

布莱索的邻居认为那些碎片是UFO的残骸,和他们商量之后,布莱索向镇长报告了他的发现。随后,镇长联系了509轰炸小组的情报局官员杰西·马瑟尔少校。马瑟尔少校将消息上报给指挥官威廉姆·布兰查得上校。而布兰查得上校派人封锁了这片牧场并清理这些碎片。

1947年7月8日,陆军部队公共资料处的官员宣称他们得到了坠毁的UFO残骸。然而仅仅数小时之后,他们又收回了第一次声明,改口称他们误把气象气球的残骸当成UFO的残骸了。

据陆军部队讲,本次事件是封锁处理的。然而,罗斯威尔的居民们仍然听到一些传闻,讲外星人的尸体啦,刻着奇怪标记的残骸啦,还有在新墨西哥州南部用雷达勘测到的UFO等。有些传闻猜测那些奇怪的残骸和人工制品是从UFO中跌落出来的,可是一旦有人想去调查,那些东西就被转移或者掩藏掉了。

> 飞碟这个提法产生于1947年,当时一家报纸引用了一位目击者的原话,他说看到的飞行物体"飞起来就像把碟子从水面上劈过去。"

旧事重提

30年之后,到了1978年,有记者访问杰西·马瑟尔少校,后者声称1947年陆军部队利用气象气球掩盖了UFO事件,于是这个事件又被提起。最终,为了回应人们的推测和好奇,空军部长组织人员对这一事件展开调查。

1995年第一份为国会议员史帝文·席夫准备的报告显示,那些碎片可能出自一项名为"莫古儿"的机密计划。这项计划的目的是判断是否有可能利用升至高空的气球监视高层大气中的低频声波,进而侦察苏联的核试验。从记载的相关文件来看,1997年的第二份报告显示1947年的那次事件其实是针对苏联的行动所泄露的一些端倪,因为那一年正标志着冷战的开端。

一位曾参与该计划的工程师透露,陆军部队的研究人员利用临时的雷达目标来追踪

targets for tracking the balloons because they did not have all the components necessary to make the targets. Instead, they commissioned a toy and novelty company to make the targets from tin foil and balsa wood strengthened by water-soluble glue and reinforced with tapes printed with symbols. At this point, everyone pointed out that the description of debris and of the objects at the original site was consistent with weather balloon material. Information from 1947 was not refuted point by point because personnel and evidence had changed or been lost.

Therefore, the Roswell incident was not considered a UFO event but rather the aftermath of the Mogul Project. Nevertheless, some believed the Air Force covered up the balloon testing by allowing the UFO story to grow.

A New Myth

Yet another myth about the incident as Roswell, New Mexico, has sprung up in recent years. This myth states that in March, 1948, 9 months after the UFO and alien sightings at Roswell, several currently prominent politicians were born—presumably offspring of the aliens who stepped from the UFO at Roswell. The babies born at that time are all well-known Democrats, so most people have assumed that this is a joke perpetrated by Republicans. This explanation is as good as any, since research indicates that only one of these politicians was born approximately 9 months after the Roswell landing. The politicians in question are listed below in the order of their birth dates:

Bill Clinton, former U.S. President: August 19, 1946

Howard Dean, former Governor of Vermont and Chairman of the Democratic Party: November 17, 1948

Charles E. Schumer, U.S. Senator from New York: November 23, 1950

Hillary Rodham Clinton, U.S. Senator from New York: October 26, 1947

Only Al Gore, Jr., former U.S. Vice President, was actually born within the approximate time frame on March 31, 1948.

This myth may have begun as a little fun mudslinging during Gore's campaign for president and then blossomed into a comment about all of the above Democratic politicians.

UFO Museum

So great is the fascination with incidents and events in and near Roswell, New Mexico that a group of enterprising locals created the UFO Museum. It is important to remember that Roswell is 200 or more miles away from any larger cities: Amarillo, Lubbock and El Paso in Texas and Las Cruces in New Mexico.

Founded as a non-profit educational institution in the fall of 1991, the museum opened for business in 1992. The goal of the institution is to educate the public on all aspects of UFO phenomenon, not just Roswell events. The exhibits cover a wide variety of topics, including events at Roswell, crop circles, UFO sightings in other locations, ancient astronauts and abductions.

So successful is this museum, that the Board of Directors has authorized management to acquire a new, larger site for the museum—which will be its fourth! Some 150,000 people come to Roswell and its museum each year; it is now the largest tourist attraction in the state of New Mexico. The fact is that the museum has been a huge catalyst to new business development in the area including new hotels, shops, restaurants and of course, the ever-present big box stores such as Wal-Mart. Amazing what a little myth and a bit more legend

气球，因为他们当时没有制造雷达目标必备的所有部件。因而，他们委托一家玩具公司用锡纸和热带美洲轻木来制作雷达目标，并且用可溶解于水的胶水和印有标志的带子来加固。就这一点来说，人人都指出，对于现场碎片的描述是和气象气球的材质相吻合的。1947年传出的信息没有被逐项反驳，原因在于人证和物证有的改变了而有的已经不在了。

因此，罗斯威尔事件并非UFO，而被看成是莫古儿计划的余波。不过，也有人相信美国空军是为了掩盖气球勘测的真相，而故意让UFO的说法流传开来。

新的神话

然而近些年，关于新墨西哥州罗斯威尔事件的另一个神话又出现了。据说1948年3月，也就是在罗斯威尔出现UFO和外星人的9个月之后，数位当今颇有影响力的政治家诞生了——他们有可能是从UFO里来到罗斯威尔的外星人的后代。当时出生的孩子现在都是鼎鼎大名的民主党员，因此有人怀疑这是共和党人的玩笑。这种说法和其他说法一样不太可信，因为研究显示这些政治家们只有一位是在罗斯威尔事件之后大约9个月出生的。涉及的民主党员按出生日期如下列所示：

比尔·克林顿，美国前总统：1946年8月19日
霍华德·迪安，前佛蒙特州州长兼民主党主席：1948年11月17日
查尔斯·舒莫，美国纽约州参议员：1950年11月23日
希拉里·克林顿，美国纽约州参议员：1947年10月26日
唯有美国前副总统阿尔·戈尔真正是出生在那个时间段的1948年3月31日。

这个神话可能是在戈尔竞选总统期间竞争对手的故意中伤，后来就发展成为针对上述民主党派政治家的评论。

UFO博物馆

在新墨西哥州罗斯威尔及其附近发生的事件有着巨大的魔力，因而一些富有商业头脑的当地人建造了UFO博物馆。人们必须记住罗斯威尔离附近的这些稍大点的城市最起码200英里远：得克萨斯州的阿莫里罗、拉伯克和艾尔帕索，以及新墨西哥州的拉斯库鲁斯。

UFO博物馆建于1991年秋季，当时是作为一个非赢利性质的教育机构，到1992年就变为商业性质了。该馆的建成是为了让大众了解UFO现象的方方面面，而不仅仅限于罗斯威尔事件。其展品涉及主题的范围极广，包括罗斯威尔事件、麦田里的怪圈、其他地方人亲眼目睹的UFO、古代宇航员和外星人的诱拐事件。

由于该馆一举成功，董事会委任管理部门寻找更大的场所来建立一个新馆——而这个新馆将是他们所建的第四个UFO博物馆。每年，大约有15万人来到罗斯威尔和这个博物馆；这已经成为新墨西哥州最大的旅游胜地。事实上，该博物馆已经成为了一个巨大的催化剂，催化该地区新的商业发展——包括新宾馆、商店、饭店，当然还有无处不在的"大盒子"商店如沃尔玛。一则小小的神话加上一点点传说居然引发了这般让人吃惊的后果！

will provide!

The new museum will be located about eight blocks north of its present location. It will take up an entire city block, across the street from a McDonald's—the only one in the world with a UFO theme. Ground breaking took place in July of 2007 but no opening date for the facility is provided.

Can You Really Believe in UFOs?

Many people associated with and who have investigated Roswell, New Mexico say that, yes, you can and should believe because this is just one of thousands of incidents and reports of sightings.

To start with, many accept a very broad definition of a UFO: A real or apparent flying object which cannot be identified.Many experts will say that 1947 in Roswell is the beginning of the modern history of UFOs and related phenomena. On the other hand, history is replete with writings and commentaries about some very unusual happenings in the sky—the problem is trying to discern whether they are anything out of the ordinary or common phenomena such as comets or meteorites. A few examples:

1. 1868: Reports document the first modern sighting of UFOs in Chile.

2. 1887: Mystery airships are seen and reported in New England.

3. 1917: The Fatima incident was reported by thousands in Portugal.

One of the great difficulties in trying to discern the credibility of much of what has been sighted is that UFOs and similar phenomena are often related to and victims of all kinds of religious, parapyschological, political and social movements and organizations.

However, there are some interesting and very believable events and physical phenomena which may be worthwhile as you weigh the evidence, pro or con, for yourself. Consider the following:

·Radar contact and tracking seems to be one of the strongest indicators that something is going on. This support is particularly good in that it often comes from trained military personnel or control tower operators.

·Physical trace evidence is common and includes such changes in an area as ground impressions, burned ground, felled trees and shrubs, higher than expected radiation and metal fragments. There are whole archives of this kind of data that support the conclusion that the experiences at Roswell are not so unusual.

·In addition, physiological changes in people and even animals have been routinely documented. Reports of temporary paralysis, burns and rashes on the skin have been recorded.

·Farmers and ranchers use experiences like crop circles and strange changes in crop behavior such as increased or decreased plant germination or growth as proof that something unusual has happened.

·And finally, researchers point out a whole host of indicators like stalled cars, power blackouts, interference with TV and radio signals and problems with aircraft navigation as the ultimate proof that Roswell is not unique—and is to believed.

Resources

www.roswellufomuseum.com. This Website describes the exhibits in the Roswell, New Mexico, museum that contains the most important information and resources pertaining to the UFO incident.

The Roswell Legacy, Big Sky Press, the 60th Anniversary Edition, 2007. This book, commemorating the 60th anniversary of the UFO crash, offers new information about the incident, much of which is from the viewpoint of those directly involved.

新馆将被建在现址以北大约8个街区处,届时将占据一个完整的街区,从世界上唯一一家以UFO为主题的麦当劳起横跨街道。2007年7月破土动工,但新馆的开馆时间还没有公布。

你真的相信UFO吗?

很多相关人员和那些曾经调查过罗斯威尔的人会说,是的,你可以相信也应该相信,因为这只是成千上万桩目击事件和报告当中的一次。

首先,对于UFO,很多人采纳一个非常宽泛的定义:一个真实的或是表面上看起来是那样的飞行物体,人们无法对其作出明确识别。很多专家会认为1947年在罗斯威尔发生的事就是现代UFO及其相关现象历史的开端。换句话说,历史上曾有众多的文章和评论,是关于空中出现的奇怪物体的——这个问题试图认清那些物体到底是非比寻常的东西呢,还是普通的现象就如彗星或者陨星。下面是一些例子:

1.1868年:报告记录了近代在智利第一次看到UFO。

2.1887年:在新英格兰有人看到神秘的飞船并就此做了报道。

3.1917年:在葡萄牙,成千上万的人报告了法蒂玛事件。

要弄清大部分目击的景象是否属实,最困难的一点就是,UFO及其相似现象总是和各种宗教的、超心理的、政治的和社会的活动以及组织联系在一起,并且成为其受害者。

然而,如果你要自己考虑证据的可信度,那么不管你持赞成还是反对的意见,一些非常有趣而且十分可信的事件和物理现象还是值得一提的。请斟酌以下内容:

·要证实某物的存在,雷达捕捉和雷达跟踪似乎是最强有力的证据。如果是来自受过训练的军事人员或指挥塔的控制人员,则这种支持更有说服力。

·物理示踪的证据非常普遍,包括在一个区域内出现的变化,如地上的印记、烧焦的土地、倒下的树木、高频的辐射、还有金属的碎片等。很多归档的这种数据都支撑着一个结论,即发生在罗斯威尔的事情并非如此异常。

·此外,人类的生理变化甚至动物的生理变化也常常有所记录。曾见报道上有短暂的瘫痪、烧伤、皮疹等。

·麦田里出现怪圈,庄稼出现奇怪的现象,发芽或生长的庄稼有时候多了有时候少了。牧场主们会把这些当做证据,证明不寻常的事情发生了。

·最后,研究人员指出了一系列的最终证据:汽车抛锚、无端停电、电视和电台收到干扰信号、飞机航行出现问题,等等——都可以证明罗斯威尔事件并非世间唯一,而且的确切实可信。

相关资源

www.roswellufomuseum.com 新墨西哥州罗斯威尔 UFO 博物馆收藏了关于 UFO 事件最重要的信息和资源,本网址对该馆内的展品进行了描述。

《罗斯威尔遗产》,大天空出版社,60周年版,2007年。该书是为纪念UFO坠毁60周年而出版,提供了很多坠毁事件的新信息,其中大部分来自当年事件的亲身经历者。

One

April Fools' Day

April Fools' Day, also known as All Fools' Day, has been celebrated for centuries in many parts of the world. Occurring on the first day of April, it has become the customary day to play pranks on unsuspecting individuals.

One of the earliest references to April Fools' Day appeared in *Poor Robin's Almanack*, a British almanac published between 1662 and 1828 and often attributed to the poet Robert (Robin) Herrick. In 1790 the following poem appeared in Poor Robin's Almanack:

The First of April, some do say
Is set apart for All Fools' Day.
But why the people call it so,
Nor I, nor they themselves do know.
But on this day are people sent
On purpose for pure merriment.

Origins of April Fools' Day

Although the exact origin of April Fools' Day is unknown, there are several theories about how the holiday came about. It is generally believed that the holiday developed in several countries and cultures around the same time during celebrations of the first day of spring. The time of year may be relevant because there is some evidence that in certain parts of the world April Fools'Day was part of the celebration of the spring equinox. The spring equinox, usually around March 21, is 1 of 2 days in the year (the other is the autumnal equinox around September 22) when the sun is directly above the equator and the length of day and night is exactly the same all over the earth. In keeping with this same line of speculation, the holiday may also represent the changing weather of late March and early April, when balmy seemingly spring like weather can suddenly become a winter storm. Nature, in essence, is teasing and fooling human beings.

Other people speculate that the origin of April Fools' Day arises from ancient myths and celebrations. The most likely theory is the one related to the change in the 1500s from the Julian calendar to the Gregorian calendar. In France, April 1 was at one time the end of the New Year's celebration. The French began their New Year's Day festivities on March 25 and ended on April 1. In 1582, however, Pope Gregory XIII devised his Gregorian calendar to replace the Julian calendar, introduced by Julius Caesar in 46 B.C.. The Gregorian calendar, which also had 365 days and the same months as the Julian calendar, corrected the Julian calendar by providing for a leap year of 366 days every fourth even year.

King Charles IX of France then mandated the adoption of the Gregorian calendar and announced that New Year's Day would become January 1 instead of April 1.It took some time for this change to reach the entire population of France and many, therefore, continued to celebrate the New Year in April. In addition, many citizens resisted the arbitrary change and clung to their old traditions. Eventually,those people who either resisted or were unaware of the new calendar became known as April fools. April fools were ridiculed and became the victims of pranks and

愚 人 节

    愚人节,也称为大家愚人节,在世界上很多地方已经庆祝了好几百年。四月份的第一天,对毫无防范的人开开玩笑已经成了一种风俗。

    关于愚人节最早的参考资料可以在《穷罗宾的历书》中找到。这是一本英国的历书,成书于 1662 年至 1828 年,该书的广为流传多亏了诗人罗伯特(罗宾)·赫里克。1790 年的时候书里面就出现了下面这样的诗歌:

    四月的第一天,有人说
    是专辟出来为愚人过。
    但为什么称为愚人节,
    我不清楚,他们自己也不晓得。
    可是这一天人们故意捉弄
    只是为了开怀一乐。

节日起源

    尽管愚人节确切的起源无人知晓,却流传着好几种说法。一般认为愚人节是在几个国家和文化环境中发展起来的,庆祝的时间也都差不多是在春季的第一天。一年当中的时段也许是互有关联的,因为有证据表明世界上一些地方的愚人节正是庆祝春分活动中的一部分。通常在 3 月 21 日前后的春分,和 9 月 22 日前后的秋分,是一年当中仅有的两天太阳位于赤道正上方,全球的白天黑夜时间相等。顺着这种思路,愚人节可能也代表了 3 月底到 4 月初的天气变化,此时芳香如春的天气可能刹那间就转成冬季的暴风雨。大自然,就其本质上来讲,总在揶揄和嘲弄人类。

    也有人认为愚人节是从古代的神话和庆典中演变而来的。最有可能的说法与 16 世纪时期法由罗马儒略历改为格里高利历有关。在法国,4 月 1 日曾经是新年的结尾。法国人从 3 月 25 日开始庆贺新年,直到 4 月 1 日才结束。然而 1582 年,教皇格里高利十三世制定出了格里高利历,替换了公元前 46 年由恺撒引进的儒略历。前者和后者一样,将一年分为 12 个月 365 天,但每过四年便出现一个闰年,有 366 天,这样就纠正了后者的一个错误。

    后来,法国国王查尔斯九世下令使用格里高利历,并宣布新年定在 1 月 1 日,而不再是 4 月 1 日。这个改变的过程过了很久才让所有的法国人接受,因此,很多人还继续在 4 月庆祝新年。而且,很多公民抵制这一恣意的更改,死守古老的传统。最终,那些人由于抵制或者不能清楚认识新历法,而被看成是四月里的傻瓜。他们总被揶揄或嘲弄,甚至被称为“四月的鱼”,象征着年幼的、缺乏经验的鱼,这种鱼非常容易捕获。一个常见捉弄方法

jokes. They were even called poisson d'avril, or April fish as a symbol of young, inexperienced fish that are easily caught. A common prank was to affix a paper fish to the back of someone to identify him or her as an April fool.

The Tradition Spreads

The customs surrounding April Fools' Day eventually spread from France to England and Scotland in the 18th century. As time went on, the holiday's tradition moved to other European countries and in the late 18th century was introduced to the American colonies by the English and French.

Because of the fun and frivolity associated with April Fools' Day, it has become an international festivity over the centuries, each country celebrating in its own unique way. In England, for example, April Fools' pranks are played only in the morning; it is considered bad luck to play a joke on someone after noon.Scotland, on the other hand, may celebrate for 2 days. In Scotland, April fools are known as gowks or cuckoos, a term of disrespect. Many of the jokes in Scotland involve the buttocks, so some people trace the origin of the Kick Me sign attached to a person's back to the April Fools' pranks of Scotland.

In Italy the holiday is called the Festival of Hilaria and is celebrated on March 25.In Portugal April Fools' Day falls on the Sunday and Monday before the beginning of Lent.

No matter where April Fools' Day is celebrated, however, the festivities are geared toward fun and lighthearted joking. Mean-spirited pranks are frowned upon across all cultures and gentle teasing and fun are the goal.

Pranks of Note

April Fools' pranks range from the simple to the complicated.Other pranks can be more elaborate and often media take the lead in perpetuating an April Fools' joke. For example, the British Broadcasting Company took the credit for a news report in 1957 lamenting that an early spring caused the annual spaghetti harvest to take place early as well. The reporter was careful to point out that the destructive spaghetti beetle was not responsible for the early harvest since the weevil had been eliminated in earlier years.

Even normally serious journalists look upon April fool as an opportunity to pull the public's leg. In 1993, for example, a reporter at a San Diego radio station announced that the space shuttle had been diverted from Edwards Air Force base and was making an emergency landing at a small local airport. In 2005 an official from NASA announced that the agency had pictures of water on Mars. The actual picture was a glass of water poised on top of a Mars candy bar. And during the year that the Canadian treasury introduced a two dollar coin, a Canadian radio station warned listeners that April 1 was the last day the treasury would honor the two dollar paper bills in circulation.

Resources

Proverbs, Riddles, Poems, Songs, Dances, Games, Play Folklore of American Holidays: A Compilation of More Than 600 Beliefs, Legends, Superstitions,Pageants and Foods, Thomson Gale, 1998. This book is a large reference book on 125 American holidays, including April Fools' Day.

*http://familyfun.go.com/arts-and-crafts/.*Click on Holiday and Seasonal, then click on April Fool's Day. This Website provides April Fools' prank suggestions for kids and adults, including classic pranks, food fun pranks and how-to videos.

就是把纸做的鱼粘在某人的背上，标志着那是一个四月傻瓜。

传统流传

18世纪的时候，愚人节前后的风俗活动最终从法国流传到了英格兰和苏格兰。随着时光流转，这个节日的传统也播散到了欧洲其他国家，18世纪末，英国人和法国人将其引入了美国殖民地。

愚人节充满了欢快和乐趣，因而数个世纪以来已成为国际性的节日。而且每个国家都以各自独特的方式来庆祝。比如，在英格兰，愚人节玩笑只能在上午开，一般认为如果下午开这种玩笑会带来厄运。而在苏格兰，愚人节要庆祝两天，四月傻瓜被看成郭公鸟或布谷鸟，得不到他人的尊敬。苏格兰的很多愚人节玩笑都与臀部有关，因此有人认为有的裤子后面贴有"踢我"的标志，就起源于苏格兰的愚人节恶作剧。

在意大利，愚人节是3月25日，这一天被称为"希拉里亚节"。在葡萄牙，愚人节则落在四旬斋开始前的星期一和星期二。

然而，无论是在何地庆祝愚人节，总是开些好玩的、让人心情轻松愉悦的玩笑。所有的文化都不欢迎趣味低劣的恶作剧，过愚人节的目标是轻微的打趣和逗乐。

著名恶作剧

愚人节的恶作剧有的简单，有的复杂。而有的恶作剧则经过精心准备，常常由媒体充当头领来把玩笑继续开下去。比如，1957年，英国广播公司就因为这样一则新闻报道而受到了公众好评：由于春天来临得过早，一年一度的意大利面大丰收也提前了。记者非常小心地指出，具有破坏性的意大利面甲虫不该为这次早到的丰收负责，因为它们早些年就已被消灭了。

哪怕是平时非常严肃的新闻工作者也把愚人节看做一个大好机会来捉弄大众。比如，1993年，圣地亚哥一家广播电台宣布，宇宙飞船脱离了爱德华空军基地，将紧急迫降在当地一家小机场。2005年，美国国家航空航天局的一位官员宣布他们拥有火星上的水的照片，那其实是一杯水放在糖果做的"火星"顶上的照片。加拿大财政部引进2元硬币的那一年，一家加拿大电台告诫听众，4月1日是加拿大财政部在流通中接受2元纸币的最后一天。

相关资源

《美国节日的谚语、谜语、诗歌、歌曲、舞蹈、游戏、民间戏剧：600多则信仰、传说、迷信、盛会和食物的汇编》，托马斯·盖尔，1998年。该书是一本内容丰富的参考书，涵盖了125个美国节日，包括愚人节。

http://familyfun.go.com/arts-and-crafts/ 点击"节日"，然后点击"愚人节"。该网址为大人小孩提供愚人节恶作剧的建议，包括经典的恶作剧、食品方面的恶作剧以及具体操作的视频。

Two

Atlantis

Atlantis is a legendary city—or possibly an island or a continent—that many people believe sank into the Atlantic Ocean thousands of years ago. The story originated with the Greek p hilosopher Plato (427 to 347 B.C.) in his works *Timaeus and Critias* written around 355 to 360 B.C.. In his first dialogue about Atlantis,Timaeus, Plato traced the history of Atlantis through the historian-politician Critias back to the original source, an Egyptian priest.

According to Plato, an advanced civilization once existed on Atlantis. Over the centuries the population of Atlantis accumulated great wealth because of the land's natural resources and the city was the center of trade and commerce,extending its influence throughout Europe and Asia. The people of Atlantis developed a rich culture and were said to possess secret wisdom and powers.

Plato identified Atlantis as the realm of Poseidon, god of the sea. Poseidon built a home at the top of a hill surrounded by rings of water and of land in the center of Atlantis. Poseidon created this fortress home to protect Cleito, a mortal woman with whom Poseidon had fallen in love. As time passed, Cleito and Poseidon became the parents of five sets of twin boys who became the first rulers of the city. The eldest son, Atlas, became the first king of Atlantis, controlling the central hill and surrounding rings. In the temple honoring Poseidon on the hill, the leaders of Atlantis gathered to discuss law and the rule of the city.

Plato portrays the area in great detail, beginning with a description of the water canal bisecting the rings of water and land leading to the central hill. The canal allowed travel to the temple on the hill from the surrounding city of Atlantis.Most of the populace lived in the densely populated area just outside the outer ring of water.

Beyond the immediate city, there was a large fertile plain whose outer edge bordered on mountains, which were homes to small villages, meadows, lakes and rivers. An irrigation canal collected water from the mountains' waterways, which enabled a second harvest each year. The land itself was rich with fruits, nuts and herbs and a large variety of animals roamed the plains.

After many years of living well-ordered lives and developing a superior culture,according to Plato, the people of Atlantis became greedy and corrupt. When Zeus, the ruler of the Greek gods, observed the immorality and corruption of the people of Atlantis, he and the other gods decided to inflict a punishment on the settlement. Great explosions shook the island and it disappeared into the sea.

Theories about Plato's Story

Plato's story of the mystical land fascinated generations of readers. Many decided it was a fable, a story of a civilization far ahead of any other ancient cultures while at the same time a basis for all advanced cultures to come. Others called it a morality tale that served as a warning to societies with a potential for becoming corrupt. Still others predicted that it did not exist at all.

One of the more believable theories of the origin of Atlantis was that it was part of the Minoan culture, destroyed during the Bronze Age by an overwhelming volcanic eruption, the effects of which may have reached as far as Southeast Asia. The Minoan civilization existed on the

12

亚特兰蒂斯

亚特兰蒂斯是个传说中的城市——也许是座岛屿也许是块大陆——很多人相信它在几千年前就沉到了大西洋底。这个故事源自希腊哲学家柏拉图（公元前427年至公元前347年）在其公元前360至前355年的作品《蒂迈欧》和《克里蒂亚》。在他第一次谈论亚特兰蒂斯的对话，也就是《蒂迈欧》中，柏拉图将亚特兰蒂斯的历史穿越过历史学家和政客们常提到的克里蒂亚，一直追溯到最初的起源，即一位埃及的牧师。

据柏拉图说，在亚特兰蒂斯曾经存在过非常先进的人类文明。由于亚特兰蒂斯自然资源异常富饶，且位于商业和贸易的中心，其威力直逼欧亚，因而几百年来人民累积了巨大的财富。亚特兰蒂斯的居民打造了浓郁丰富的文化，而且据说他们掌握着秘密的智慧和神力。

柏拉图将亚特兰蒂斯定位为海王波塞冬的王国。在亚特兰蒂斯的中央，波塞冬选择水土环绕的一座山的山顶上建造了家园。波塞冬创立这个堡垒般的家园是为了保护柯雷托——那是波塞冬爱上的一个凡人女子。随着时光流转，柯雷托和波塞冬相继生下了五对双胞胎男孩，他们后来成为这个城市的首批统治者。大儿子亚特拉斯成为亚特兰蒂斯的第一位国王，控制着中央的山脉和周边的水土。这些统治者聚集在山上波塞冬的庙宇里面，商讨这座城市的法律和制度。

柏拉图非常仔细地描绘这块土地，首先是一条通向中央山脉的运河将主岛周围的环水和环岛一分为二。这条运河使得亚特兰蒂斯城外围的人可以通达山上的庙宇。大部分的平民居住在外环水以外，那儿人口密度很高。

中央城市之外还有一片巨大的肥沃的平原，其外层边缘以山脉为界。而这些山脉上有许多小村庄、草地、湖泊以及河流。一条专门用于灌溉的运河从山上的溪流带下水来，保证了每年的第二次丰收。岛上富产水果、坚果和草药，还有各种动物在平原上奔跑散步。

柏拉图继续描绘，亚特兰蒂斯人在良好的秩序下生活了很多年，并且建起了高端的文化，之后就变得贪婪和腐败起来。希腊众神之主宙斯察觉到亚特兰蒂斯人变得不讲道义、贪污腐败，和其他神祇商量之后，决定对这块地方加以惩罚。一场大爆炸震撼了这座岛屿，使之消失，没入了海底。

柏拉图故事解说

柏拉图的这个故事神奇而迷人，使一代又一代的读者沉醉其中。不少人认为那只是一个寓言，里面提到的文明远远高于其他任何古代文明，而同时它又是一切即将来临的先进文明的基底。也有人把它看成讲述道德的故事，告诫人们腐败的可能性。甚至有人坚信所谓的亚特兰蒂斯根本从未存在过。

说到亚特兰蒂斯的起源，最可信的一种解说就是，它是米诺文化的一部分，青铜时代毁于一次火山大爆发。那次火山爆发甚至影响到了东南亚那么远。米诺文明存在于古代的泰拉岛（即现在的桑托里尼，位于爱琴海中克里特岛以北）。考古学家们把桑托里尼看

ancient island Thera, now known as Santorini, just north of Crete in the Aegean Sea. Archeologists consider Santorini a well-known Minoan site and have researched the island as part of extensive Minoan studies. Several have concluded that the ancient island of Thera could have, indeed, been the original site of Atlantis.

Arguments supporting this conclusion conclude:

·The Minoan culture, like the one described by Plato, ended in a devastating eruption. A catastrophic volcanic eruption around 1470 B.C. created a large crater in the center of Thera and fractured the surrounding land into many islands. What was originally in the center of Thera sank to the sea floor, lending credence to Plato's sunken city theory.

·Ancient depictions of Thera indicate that the island's physical and topographical features in many ways mirror those described by Plato as characteristic of Atlantis.

·Minoan archeological findings show no evidence of weapons or war machines and Plato's story depicts Atlantis as a peaceable civilization.

On the other hand, others argue:

·Plato's dialogues were fictional.

·The dates do not match. Plato wrote that Atlantis had sunk 10,000 years earlier, yet research into the Minoan culture shows that the volcanic eruption occurred 1,000 years before Plato wrote his dialogue. To refute this, some historians have speculated that there could have been an error in translation of the numbers from Egyptian.

Other Explanations

Plato was only the first of many who have searched for Atlantis. Ancient Greek writers who succeeded Plato continued to speculate about the lost city. In addition, for centuries explorers have identified the Canary Islands, the Azores, Tunisia, Western Africa and even Sweden as the site of lost Atlantis. During the age of exploration in the 16th century, when America was discovered, many scholars, including Sir Francis Bacon, the English philosopher and statesman, proclaimed that Atlantis was either the newly discovered America or was located between Europe and America. There was even speculation that the sophisticated Mayan culture of Central America was actually transplanted from Atlantis.

More recently, in 2004 an American scientist reported locating a sunken city on the Mediterranean sea bed between Cyprus and Syria. Using sonar scanning, the American has discovered what appear to be manmade walls, trenches and paths around a central hill that match Plato's description of Atlantis.

While more research is needed to confirm that this is Atlantis, many scholars agree that some of the similarities are worth exploring. However, others are skeptical, noting that the location of this new discovery is not opposite the Pillars of Hercules (now Gibraltar) as pinpointed in Plato's dialogue. In addition, scientists are careful to point out that there are many sunken cities on the sea floor because of changing climate pattern over several thousand years. The actual sea level has changed over time as glaciers melted and covered the continental shelves. Scientists have calculated that when ice sheets melted from the northern continents more than 18,000 years ago, the melting water flooded the continental shelf of Europe to a depth of more than 360 feet below the current sea level. And at the time that Atlantis was presumed to exist, the sea level would have been between 30 and 60 feet below the present sea level. Thus, scientists conclude that there are many submerged cities and islands—some of which may be mistakenly assumed to be Atlantis—in the seas of the world.

成有名的米诺文明遗址,并且把该岛当做米诺文明的拓展进行了研究。部分研究得出结论,证实这座古老的泰拉岛的确可能是亚特兰蒂斯的遗址。

支持这一结论的论据包括:
· 米诺文化,正如柏拉图所描述,终结于一场摧毁性的火山爆发。发生于公元前 1470 年的那次火山大爆发在泰拉岛中央形成了一个巨大的火山口,并把四周的陆地震成了许许多多的岛屿。原本存在于泰拉岛中央的一切都沉到了海底,这个事实给柏拉图沉没城市的说法增加了可信度。
· 对于泰拉岛古有的描绘显示出,该岛的物理特征和地形风貌在很多方面和柏拉图对于亚特兰蒂斯特征的描述不谋而合。
· 米诺文明的考古发现,没有武器或战争机器的迹象,而柏拉图的故事也把亚特兰蒂斯描述为和平的文明。
另一方面,也有人持不同意见:
· 柏拉图的对话都是虚构的。
· 时间对不上。柏拉图写的亚特兰蒂斯于 1 万年前沉没,而米诺文化的研究显示那场火山爆发发生于柏拉图写下对话的 1000 年前。但一些历史学家认为从埃及文翻译过来时在数字上出了点差错,以此驳斥了这一观点。

其他解释
探寻亚特兰蒂斯的人不计其数,柏拉图只是最早的一个。古希腊的一些作家继承柏拉图,继续研究这个失踪的城市。此外,数百年以来,探险家们发现了诸多亚特兰蒂斯的遗址:加那利群岛、亚速尔群岛、突尼斯、西非,甚至瑞典。16 世纪探险时代期间,美洲被发现以后,很多学者,包括英国的哲学家兼政治家弗朗西斯·培根爵士,都宣称亚特兰蒂斯要么就是新近发现的美洲,要么位于欧洲和美洲之间。甚至有人猜测中美洲精密复杂的玛雅文化就是从亚特兰蒂斯移植而来。

更近一些,到 2004 年的时候,一位美国科学家报告说发现了一个沉没的城市,位于地中海海底,塞浦路斯和叙利亚之间。这位科学家利用声呐扫描,已经发现了一座中央山脉周围有一些东西看起来像人工围墙、沟渠和道路,而这些和柏拉图对于亚特兰蒂斯的描绘刚好吻合。

为了证实那就是亚特兰蒂斯,还有很多研究是必须的。许多学者一致认为部分吻合点值得探索;而其他的就值得怀疑,更别提这处新发现的地点还并非柏拉图在对话中精确指出的那样,在赫丘勒斯之柱(即现在的直布罗陀海峡一带)的对面。此外,科学家们很小心地指出,由于数千年以来气候的转型,海底存在着许多沉没的城市。随着时间的改变,冰川融化,覆盖了大陆架,海平面其实一直在变。科学家们计算出,1.8 万多年以前,北极的大陆上冰原融化,融化的水将欧洲大陆的大陆架淹没到现今海平面的 360 多英尺以下。而假想中亚特兰蒂斯存在的时候,海平面比现在低 30~60 英尺。因此,科学家们得出结论,世界上有很多城市和岛屿都没入了海中,其中有一些被误认为是亚特兰蒂斯。

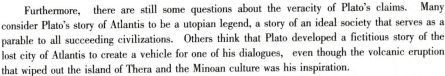

Furthermore, there are still some questions about the veracity of Plato's claims. Many consider Plato's story of Atlantis to be a utopian legend, a story of an ideal society that serves as a parable to all succeeding civilizations. Others think that Plato developed a fictitious story of the lost city of Atlantis to create a vehicle for one of his dialogues, even though the volcanic eruption that wiped out the island of Thera and the Minoan culture was his inspiration.

Despite the conflicting opinions about the existence of Atlantis, the quest to find the lost city/island/continent continues. The actual truth about Atlantis may never be known, but the legend continues to captivate explorers, scientists and researchers. The fact that such an advanced civilization could have possibly existed in the ancient world captivates readers and explorers alike because the legend feeds the need in human nature to seek and find paradise.

Resources

The Atlantis Encyclopedia, New Page Books, 2005. Written in an encyclopedic format, this book is a comprehensive discussion of Atlantis, its supposed location, its place in history and its impact on the modern world. The book includes 16 full-color illustrations.

The Atlantis Dialogue: Plato's Original Story of the Lost City, Continent, Empire, Civilization, Shepard Publications, 2003. The title of this book is self-explanatory: it contains Plato's dialogues relating the story of Atlantis. This is for the reader who wants to read about Atlantis from Plato's perspective.

http://theshadowlands.net/atlantis/index.html. The Shadowlands discusses the theories and claims regarding the lost continent of Atlantis and other mysteries of the unknown.

更进一步,柏拉图关于亚特兰蒂斯的故事,还有很多问题。很多人把这个故事看成一个乌托邦式的传说,讲述的是一个虚构的理想社会,是对此后一切文明的描绘。另外有些人则认为,尽管柏拉图的灵感来自那场摧毁泰拉岛的火山爆发和米诺文化,他构造这个虚幻的亚特兰蒂斯城失落之谜,只不过是为自己的一段对话创建一个载体。

亚特兰蒂斯是否真实存在过?大家的观点个个不一,可是找寻这座失落的城市、岛屿、大陆的探索仍在继续。亚特兰蒂斯的真相也许永远无法公开,可是这个传说不断吸引着探险家、科学家和研究人员。如此先进的文明在古老的世界可能存在过,这样的事实同样吸引着读者和探险家们,因为这个传说满足了人性中探寻天堂的需求。

相关资源
《亚特兰蒂斯百科全书》,新页图书,2005 年。以百科全书的格式编写,该书广泛讨论了关于亚特兰蒂斯的很多内容,包括其可能的位置、历史上的地位及其对现代社会的影响。内有 16 张彩色插图。

《亚特兰蒂斯的对话:柏拉图的原始故事——失落的城市、大陆、帝国、文明》,谢坡德出版社,2003 年。书名本身就作出了一定的解释:本书包括柏拉图就亚特兰蒂斯传说的对话。本书的读者希望从柏拉图的角度来了解亚特兰蒂斯。

http://theshadowlands.net/atlantis/index.html 该网址探讨失落的大陆亚特兰蒂斯和其他未知的神秘事件,及其相关猜测和解说。

Three

Bermuda Triangle

The Bermuda Triangle, also called the Devil's Triangle, is an area of the Atlantic Ocean located off the southeastern coast of the United States. It ranges from 500,000 to 1.5 million square miles. Because this area has been the site of the disappearance of many ships and aircraft, the Bermuda Triangle has been a source of speculation and concern for scientists, researchers and travelers for more than 150 years. Although not recognized as an authentic geographic name by the U.S.Board of Geographic Names, the Bermuda Triangle is nevertheless considered to be the name of a triangular area whose three points have unofficially been established as the island of Bermuda; Miami, Florida; and San Juan, Puerto Rico.

USS Cyclops

The first recorded disappearance of an American ship in the Bermuda Triangle was the incident involving the USS Cyclops.As part of the U.S. Navy's Atlantic fleet, the Cyclops served as a collier, a ship that refueled other maritime vessels, in the Baltic Sea. When the United States entered World War I in 1918, the Cyclops sailed to the Brazilian coast to service British ships in the south Atlantic. On February 16, 1918, the ship left Rio de Janeiro for the Barbados in the West Indies from which it was scheduled to sail to Baltimore, Maryland, with a cargo of more than 10,000 tons of manganese ore. After setting sail from the Barbados on March 4, the ship was never seen or heard from again. The ship's disappearance along with its 306 crew and passengers is one of the Bermuda Triangle's mysteries.

Over the years, there has been much speculation about the Cyclops' disappearance. Some attribute the disappearance to a boiler explosion that prevented the crew from sending a distress signal. There was even a story of a giant octopus that arose from the sea and dragged the Cyclops to the bottom.None of the theories about the cause of the disappearance was ever proved. In fact, no enemy crafts were in the area at the time.

Flight 19

The disappearance of Flight 19 may be the event most often associated with the Bermuda Triangle. On December 5, 1945, a squadron of five U.S. bombers carrying 14 fliers disappeared off the coast of Florida. On that afternoon the five bombers took off from the U.S. Naval Air Station, Fort Lauderdale, Florida, on an advanced over water navigational training flight. A senior qualified flight instructor was in charge of the exercise.By late afternoon on that December day, a message between the flight leader and one of the other pilots indicated that the instructor was uncertain of his position and of the way back to the Florida coast. At the same time, all the airplanes seemed to experience a malfunction of their compasses. Interference from Cuban broadcasting stations and other atmospheric static prevented clear communications from the flight members, and they lost all radio contact before their location could be pinpointed.

When the plight of Flight 19 became known, search aircraft were sent out. One search and rescue plane with a 13-man crew, launched early in the evening of December 5, was never seen or heard from again. Because a merchant ship saw and reported a burst of flame from that area, it was

百慕大
三角

百慕大三角，又叫魔鬼三角，是大西洋中的一块区域，距离美国东南海岸不远处，所覆盖的面积50万~150万平方英里。这个地方曾发生过多起轮船和飞机失踪事件，因而150多年以来一直是科学家、研究人员和旅行家们思考和关注的源头。百慕大三角尽管没有得到美国地名委员会的承认，却还是被认为是一块三角形地域的名称，它的三个"角"非官方地确认为百慕大岛、佛罗里达州的迈阿密和波多黎各的圣胡安。

"独眼巨人"号
首次记录在案的美国船只在百慕大三角失踪事件就是"独眼巨人"事件。这艘船作为美国海军大西洋舰队的成员，在波罗的海中为其他海军船只补充燃料。1918年美国参加第一次世界大战以后，"独眼巨人"向巴西海岸线航行，要到南大西洋去为英国舰队服务。1918年2月16日，该船驶离了里约热内卢，向西印度群岛的巴巴多斯航行，打算到了那儿后，装载1万多吨锰矿石再驶向马里兰州的巴尔的摩。3月4日，从巴巴多斯出发，这艘船就再也没有被人看到或听到过。"独眼巨人"连带船上的306名船员和乘客全都失踪，成为百慕大三角的一次神秘事件。

此后很多年，对于"独眼巨人"的失踪出现过很多猜测。有人认为此次失踪是因为锅炉爆炸阻止了船员们发送遇难信号。甚至有传闻说一只巨大的章鱼从海底浮出，把船拽了下去。但这些关于失踪原因的解说始终没有一个经过证实。事实上，当时附近海域没有任何敌军的船只或飞机。

第19飞行中队
第19飞行中队的失踪可能是最常和百慕大三角联系在一起的事件。1945年12月5日，一支由五架轰炸机组成的飞行中队，连同其14名飞行员全体从佛罗里达州海岸失踪。那天下午，五架轰炸机在先进的水上导航训练机导航下，从佛罗里达州劳德代堡的美国海军航空基地起飞。本次训练由一位资深的导航员负责。那天下午晚些的时候，训练机上的负责人和另外一位飞行员之间的通讯信息，就透露出当时机师已无法确定他的位置，也无法认清返回佛罗里达海岸的航线。同时，所有飞机上的指南针似乎都发生了故障。古巴广播站和其他大气层中的静电所产生的干扰，阻止了地面和飞机上的人员进行清晰的交流，在他们的方位得到确认之前他们失去了所有的无线电通讯。

得知第19飞行中队的境况后，地面派出了飞机前往搜寻，但是既没发现飞机的踪影，也没找到任何一名机员。搜救飞机上有13名机员，于12月5日傍晚起飞之后，就再也没人见过或听到过。恰巧当时有一艘商船看见并报告了海域上空有爆炸的火焰，因此

presumed that the search craft exploded and sank at sea.

Taking into consideration that Flight 19 was a training flight, thus presumably being conducted by inexperienced pilots, the disappearance could have resulted from an error in judgment or simple mistakes. In addition, if the planes were flying through a magnetic storm, which is a possibility, the compasses could possibly malfunction. And if the planes were lost and ran out of gas trying to find their way home, the resulting ditch into the cold Atlantic waters could have killed the crew.

USS Marine Sulphur Queen

Another mysterious disappearance is that of the naval tanker USS Marine Sulphur Queen, which radioed her position for the last time on February 3, 1963. En route to Norfolk, Virginia, from Beaumont, Texas, the Sulphur Queen's last radio message placed the ship in the Florida Straits near Key West, Florida. Even though the disappearance occurred within the boundaries of the Bermuda Triangle, the facts that the surrounding seas were populated by man-eating sharks and barracuda and that the ship carried 15,000 tons of molten sulphur that could have either exploded or poisoned the crew may explain the disappearance of this particular tanker.

Facts about the Bermuda Triangle

Beyond the information available to explain the disappearance of specific ships and aircraft, there are some natural factors present within the area known as the Bermuda Triangle that may account for some of its so-called mysteries.

First, many meteorologists believe that the Bermuda Triangle is notorious for unpredictable weather. A calm sea can suddenly develop a small thunderstorm that, without warning, can become a violent tornado or tropical cyclone that dissipates before reaching land. A ship or plane caught in one of these brief storms can be destroyed before the storm is detected.

The ocean floor also presents challenges. Most of the sea floor in the Bermuda Triangle is approximately 19,000 feet under the surface. Along the east coast of the United States, however, the continental shelf appears 50 to 100 feet under the surface. Farther south along the southern tip of the Bermuda Triangle lays the deepest point of the Atlantic Ocean, the Puerto Rico Trench, which is more than 27,000 feet below sea level. It is little wonder, then, that wide variations in water depth could have caused some of the mysterious disappearances in the Bermuda Triangle.

Yet another interesting factor is that the 80th meridian, a degree of longitude known as the agonic line, extends from Hudson Bay through the Bermuda Triangle. The agonic line is an imaginary line on the earth's surface along which true north and magnetic north are identical in perfect alignment and a compass needle makes no angle with the meridian. Thus, a navigator, even an experienced one, could veer off course by a degree or two and eventually become totally lost.

Many scientists do not consider the Bermuda Triangle mysterious or even real. Still, there will probably always be questions to answer and mysteries to solve about this particular region.

Resources

Into the Bermuda Triangle, International Marine/Ragged Mountain Press, 2005. The author turns to official reports from the National Transportation Safety Board and interviews with scientists and survivors to document the disappearances in the Bermuda Triangle.

www.history.navy.mil/faqs. Information about the Bermuda Triangle from the Department of the Navy-Naval Historical Center.

认为该搜救飞机发生了爆炸并沉到了海底。

有一点不得不考虑，第19飞行中队是一支正在训练的中队，因而控制飞机的可能都是些缺乏经验的飞行员；也许是判断上的失误或一个简单的小错误就导致了这次失踪事件。此外，假如飞机当时经过一场磁暴，所有的指南针可能都会失灵，这也是说不定的。再有，假如飞机已经迷途，而且在找寻归途的过程中燃油也用完了，那么最终坠入大西洋，冰冷的海水自然就冻死了所有的机员。

"海上硫黄女王"号
另一次神秘的失踪事件是美国海军油轮"海上硫黄女王"号。1963年2月3日该船最后一次通过无线电汇报了其位置，在从得克萨斯州的博蒙特前往弗吉尼亚州的诺福克途中，"海上硫黄女王"发出最后一次信号，告知该船当时在佛罗里达海峡靠近佛罗里达州基韦斯特的地方。尽管这次失踪事件发生在百慕大三角的边界以内，事实上，附近海域里有很多食人鲨和梭子鱼；而船上装载着1.5万吨熔化的硫黄，可能发生了爆炸，可能毒死了船上的水手——这些也许能够解释该油轮失踪的原因。

事实情况
一些资料的确可以解释某些船只和飞机的失踪，此外在百慕大三角这块海域中还有一些自然因素，也许可以说明一些所谓的神秘事件。

首先，不少气象学家认为百慕大三角气候不定、变化多端。平静的海面上，毫无征兆，突然就能刮起风暴下起雷雨，紧接着形成猛烈的龙卷风或者热带气旋，但到达陆地之前又倏然消失了。船只或飞机如果被卷入这些突如其来的风暴，也许还未来得及发觉，就已经被摧毁了。

海底也有巨大的挑战。百慕大三角的海底绝大部分都处于水下1.9万英尺左右。然而在美国东海岸，大陆架位于水下50~100英尺处。沿着百慕大三角南端再往南，就是大西洋的最深处，波多黎各海沟，在海平面下2.7万英尺处。这就不难理解，百慕大三角海水深度的巨大差异，完全有可能导致一些神秘的失踪事件。

另外还有一个有趣的因素：第80条经线，即被称为"零磁偏线"的经线，从哈得孙湾持续延伸到百慕大三角。零磁偏线是在地球上假想出来的一条线，沿着这条线，地球的真正北极和磁北极完全重合，因而指南针的指针和地球经线的磁偏角即为零。这样，航海员哪怕再有经验，也有可能驶离航线一到两度，而最终导致完全迷航。

很多科学家认为百慕大三角并不神秘，甚至根本并不真实。然而，这块特殊的地方总会有问题需要解决，总会有神秘需要探索。

相关资源
《走进百慕大三角》，国际海事山区出版社，2005年。作者研究美国国家运输安全委员会提供的官方报告以及对科学家和幸存者进行的采访，从而详细记录下了发生在百慕大三角的失踪事件。

www.history.navy.mil/faqs 该网址关于百慕大三角的信息都来自海军—海军历史中心。

Four

Blackbeard

Blackbeard

Blackbeard was one of the most notorious pirates in maritime history. Born in England around 1675, his real name was Edward Teach (sometimes spelled Thatch).

Although little is known about his early years as a sailor, there are records that Teach served on a British privateer based in the Caribbean island of Jamaica. At that time governments commissioned privately owned ships, known as privateers, during wartime to attack enemy ships. Teach began his career on a ship hired by Britain's Queen Anne to plunder French and Spanish ships during the War of the Spanish Succession. By the end of the war, Teach had become a seasoned, fearless pirate, capturing lightly armed merchant ships sailing in and out of the American colonies and seizing their cargo, including grain, molasses, rum, ammunition and tools.

Teach eventually centered his efforts on the southeastern Atlantic coast, creating a haven for his ships and pirates in North Carolina's Outer Banks because of its shallow sounds and inlets.

Origin of His Nickname

One of Teach's most fearful weapons was his appearance. He grew his dark hair and beard long and began to braid his beard, tying the ends with black ribbons. He also interlaced rope covered in gunpowder in his hair, lighting the ropes as he went into battle. He began to call himself Blackbeard.

With a bright red coat, at least two swords on his belt and bandoliers of pistols and knives across his chest, he was an imposing sight. When he set fire to the wicks in his hair, he frightened everyone he encountered.

Method of Operation

Blackbeard terrorized the coasts of the British colonies of Virginia and North and South Carolina during the years 1717 and 1718 in his ship Queen Anne's Revenge. He enjoyed superiority at sea because of the way he had rigged this ship—after he stole it. He added large c annons and reinforced the ship's sides while streamlining it so that it was swift, easily maneuvered and well equipped. Queen Anne's Revenge was large enough to accommodate up to 250 pirates.

Lurking in bends and behind sandbars in coastal rivers, Blackbeard ruthlessly attacked ships carrying both passengers and cargo in the dim light of early morning or evening when his own ship was hard to see. He and his crew often first determined the nationality of the victim ship and then raised that country's flag on the pirate ship in order to appear to be friendly. As soon as Blackbeard's ship was close to the target ship, he raised his own pirate flag, the sight of which caused the merchant crew to surrender immediately. If the ship refused to surrender, the pirates attacked the sailor manning the wheel, leaving the merchant ship to drift without its pilot. Snaring the drifting ship with grappling hooks, the pirates boarded the vessel, took the passengers and crew hostage and ransacked the ship for coins, gold, jewelry and other valuable cargo.

Blackbeard set up his base on the island of Ocracoke near the Outer Banks, a string of

黑　胡　子

黑胡子

黑胡子是海运史上一位臭名昭著的海盗。他于 1675 年左右出生在英国,本名叫做爱德华·蒂奇。

蒂奇早年当水手的经历很少为世人所知,但有记录显示他曾在一艘英国的私掠船上干过,其根据地就在牙买加加勒比海的一座岛上。当时英政府允许私人船只,也就是所谓的私掠船,在战时可以攻击敌方船只。西班牙内战期间,蒂奇当海员的那艘船,就受雇于英国安妮女王,奉命掠夺法国和西班牙的船只。战争结束时,蒂奇已经成为一个经验丰富无所畏惧的海盗,拦截进出美殖民地的那些略备武装的商船,抢夺他们的货物,包括谷物、糖浆、甜酒、军火以及工具。

蒂奇最终把劫掠的重点定位在大西洋东南海岸;并在北卡罗来纳州的东海岸为自己的船只和海盗建造了一个港口,因为那个港湾很安静,海水也较浅。

绰号来历

蒂奇最可怕的武器之一就是他的长相。他的黑头发和黑胡子都留得长长的,而且将胡子用黑色的丝带编成辫子。他还在头发间绑了敷上火药的绳子,每当参战时就点燃绳子。慢慢地他开始称自己为黑胡子。

他穿一件鲜红的外套,腰间至少挎两把剑,胸前佩戴着刀枪,这幅模样一看就叫人永生难忘。每次他点燃头发中的导火索,总能吓退遇到的所有对手。

劫掠手段

1717~1718 年间,黑胡子驾着那艘"安妮女王复仇"号,在弗吉尼亚、南北卡罗来纳等英国殖民地名震一时。他在海上占尽优势,因为他把船偷到手之后给好好地装备了一番。船上配备了大炮,船舷也加固了,船身处理成流线型。这样,这艘船行驶迅速,调遣灵敏,装备精良。而且"复仇"号船身巨大,足够容纳 250 名海盗。

常常是一大早或者是晚上光线昏暗的时候,黑胡子自己的船还很难被发现,他就带着人躲在河道绕弯的地方或者沿岸河流的沙洲后面,残忍地袭击装载乘客和货物的船只。他和手下的人通常先判断受袭船只的国籍,然后在自己的船上升起该国的国旗,让对方放松警惕。一旦靠近目标船只,他们立马挂出自己的海盗旗,商人们通常一看到就即刻投降了。如果遇到抵抗,海盗们就抓住掌舵的人,没了领航员,商船只能在海上漂游。而海盗们就利用钩锚将商船搁浅,抓住乘客和船员当人质,随后洗劫船上的钱币、黄金、珠宝和其他值钱的货物。

"东海岸"是离开英殖民地北卡罗来纳州海岸的一长串群岛,黑胡子后来就在那附近

islands off the coast of the British colony of North Carolina. This location allowed him to intercept ships traveling to the American coast. Although the colony was well established with a law enforcement policy, the local inhabitants tolerated Blackbeard and his pirates because they enjoyed purchasing the stolen goods he sold—including hard to come by items such as sugar and cloth. Because Blackbeard's stolen goods were usually less expensive than the imported English items, the colony's officials allowed Blackbeard to continue his import business.

Blackbeard's End

In the fall of 1718 Blackbeard arranged and hosted an enormous party for his crew and other pirate friends on Ocracoke Island. Alexander Spotswood, the governor of the colony of Virginia, heard about the festivities and decided the days of Blackbeard's blatant disregard for law and order had to end. Because he was dealing with a pirate with such a fierce reputation, Spotswood spent weeks planning Blackbeard's capture.

Spotswood decided to send two small, swift ships commanded by Lieutenant Robert Maynard of the British Royal Navy to Ocracoke Island. On the evening of November 21, 1718, Maynard and his ships approached Ocracoke Island. Although sandbars protected the pirate ship, Blackbeard, upon seeing the Royal Navy ships, realized that when the tide rose in the morning the navy's ships would slide over the submerged sandbars and attack the pirate ship.

To his men's surprise, Blackbeard appeared unconcerned about the approaching battle. They were even more puzzled in the morning when, rather than trying to outrun the naval ships, Blackbeard waited at his ship's wheel. As Maynard's ships began to move, Blackbeard steered his ship directly toward them, heading for a collision. Instead, however, Blackbeard slipped his ship through a narrow passageway between the beach and a barely visible sandbar. Giving chase, the navy ships smashed into the sandbar. As the naval ships stood stranded in the channel, Blackbeard and his crew bombarded them with cannons, destroying one navy ship. The second navy ship rested on the sandbar, seemingly deserted.

Maynard, however, ordered the crew of the stranded ship to toss supplies overboard to lighten the load. Slipping free from the sandbar, Maynard's remaining ship floated toward the pirate ship. Blackbeard and his men boarded what appeared to be a deserted ship when suddenly Maynard's sailors rushed onto the deck ready to fight. The stunned pirates were caught off guard and were soon overrun by the naval officers. Maynard ordered Blackbeard's head to be cut off and hung from the bow of Maynard's ship as a warning to other pirates.

History has romanticized Blackbeard, who in reality was nothing more than a ruthless thief and a daring pirate. After his death, no one was able to locate a treasure or a fortune. In fact, the sale of his ship and its cargo only netted around 2,500 pounds. And in the centuries that have passed since his death, no one has found any buried treasure on or around Ocracoke Island. Despite this, however, Blackbeard has become a legend, not only in the Carolinas but also in literature, films and music. Most of all, his daring feats and conquests have become a piece of history in the lore about colonial America.

Resources

Blackbeard: America's Most Notorious Pirate, Wiley, 2006. This book contains a detailed description of 18th century pirate life as well as a biography of Blackbeard.

*www.ocracoke-nc.com/blackbeard.*Website about Edward Teach, The Queen's Ann's Revenge, recovered treasures and artifacts as related by Ben Cherry "Blackbeard."

的奥克拉克岛建起了自己的基地。这样一个地段便于他拦截驶向美国海岸的船只。尽管该殖民地建立了法律强制执行的政策，当地居民还是忍受了黑胡子及其手下的行为，因为他们乐于购买这伙强盗抢来的货物，如糖和棉布等难以取得的物品。因为黑胡子他们所抢来的货品比从英国进口的东西要便宜一些，殖民地官员于是默许了黑胡子继续他的"进口交易"。

最终结局

1718年的秋天，黑胡子为他的手下和奥克拉克岛的"同道中人"举办了一次宴会，并亲自主持。弗吉尼亚的总督亚历山大·斯波茨伍德听说了这一场欢宴，横下决心——黑胡子藐视法规的日子该结束了。他知道这个海盗声名狼藉，让人闻风丧胆，特意花了好几个星期来部署这一次抓捕行动。

斯波茨伍德决定派出两艘小快艇，由英国皇家海军的中尉罗伯特·梅纳德指挥，驶向奥克拉克岛。1718 年 11 月 21 日晚，梅纳德指挥快艇到达目的地。尽管有沙洲护卫着海盗船，黑胡子看到皇家海军的快艇，就意识到只要清晨一涨潮，快艇就可以掠过没入水中的沙洲，继而攻打他的海盗船。

黑胡子对于即将面临的战事竟然显出一副漠不关心的样子，倒叫群盗吃了一惊。然而更让人想不通的是，凌晨的时候黑胡子不仅没有想法子逃脱海军船队的围堵，反而候在自己的方向盘边上。梅纳德的船开始活动，黑胡子驾着自己的船朝对方直撞过去。但是没有撞到，黑胡子的船从海滩和一条几乎看不见的沙洲之间的一条逼仄的通道滑了过去。梅纳德的船队紧追其后，却撞上了沙洲，于是搁浅了。黑胡子及其手下立刻对其进行炮轰，当场击毁了其中一艘。而另一艘搁浅在沙洲上，看来也起不了什么作用了。

但是梅纳德命令那艘船上的船员们把补给品扔出去，以减轻船身的重量。于是船又可以自由活动了，继续向着海盗船进发。黑胡子和他的手下以为那艘船上已经没人了，就爬了上去。梅纳德的士兵突然冲上了甲板，准备迎战。海盗们一下子懵了，被杀了个措手不及，很快就投降了。梅纳德命人将黑胡子的头颅砍下来挂在他们的船头，以儆效尤。

历史将黑胡子的故事演变为一个浪漫的传奇，其实他只是一个残忍的盗贼、恐怖的海盗。他死了之后，没有人知道他的藏宝之处。事实上，将他的海盗船以及船上的货物出售只得了大约 2500 英镑。数百年之后，在奥克拉克岛及其附近还是没有发现任何珍宝。然而黑胡子已经成为一个传奇，不仅限于南北卡罗来纳州，而且涉及文学、影视及音乐等领域。最值一提的是，他的"丰功伟绩"已经在殖民时期的美国传说中留下了浓重的一笔。

相关资源

《黑胡子：美洲最为声名狼藉的海盗》，威利，2006 年。本书详细描述了 18 世纪海盗的生活以及黑胡子的传记。

www.ocracoke-nc.com/blackbeard 该网址主要内容有爱德华·蒂奇、"安妮女王复仇"号、出土的珍宝和一些与另一个黑胡子本·切利有关的资料。

Five

Chupacabras

Chupacabra, whose name translates from Spanish to goat sucker, has been sighted most often in Puerto Rico, Mexico, Chile, Brazil and the United States. The first reported sighting in the United States was in Arizona in 1956 and the creature has supposedly been active in New Mexico, Florida, Arizona, Oregon, Michigan, Illinois and New Jersey. Nevertheless, most sightings have occurred in Puerto Rico and Chile.

Its popularity, or at least the frequency of reported sightings, peaked in the 1990s when in certain areas of Central and South America, particularly Puerto Rico and Chile, the chupacabra was identified as the culprit in cases of killed livestock. In most instances, the dead livestock were chickens and goats whose bodies were drained of all blood but remained otherwise intact. The dead animals' necks showed two or sometimes three puncture wounds. The discrepancy in the number of puncture marks were often attributed to the fact that some people reported the chupacabra as having two large fangs while others indicated that the creature had three large claws on each hand and foot.

Appearance and Characteristics

Although chupacabras have different appearances depending on who describes them, they share common traits across cultures and times. Many are at least three Chupacabras to four feet in height and stand and hop in an upright position similar to that of kangaroos. Other reports state that although they use their strong rear legs to jump rather than walk, they have been seen running on all four legs like an ape. They have leathery, scaly skin and sharp spines or quills along the spine. They are known to hiss or screech when angered or alarmed and to emit a disagreeable sulfur smell. On the other hand, some observers report no odor at all.

Although the description of an upright, humanlike animal predominates, there have been sightings in which the chupacabra seemed to be canine in appearance yet unlike any other known dog. These reports talk about hairless, doglike animals that attack larger animals, such as cattle and tear apart the victims' carcasses as a wild dog might do. These animals also have a noticeable spinal ridge, large eyes, fangs and claws. In some cases, cryptozoologists have labeled these creatures as wild dogs of a heretofore unidentified species.

But the eyes are most often the most distinctive characteristic. Chupacabras are famous for large, glowing red eyes set into their oval-shaped heads. There have been claims that the Chupacabra's red eyes have the power to hypnotize and paralyze its prey, allowing the creature to suck out the victim's blood in a leisurely way. There have even been reports that the chupacabra's mesmerizing eyes stun human observers, revealing a glimpse into the innate evil of the creature.

The chupacabra seems to have its own likes and dislikes. It likes goats, chickens, dogs, cats, ducks and cattle. Obviously, it likes blood and some observers have noted a visible engorgement of its abdomen after a chupacabra has been feeding on a victim. It is believed that an internal sac-like receptacle fills with the victim's blood as the chupacabra's hollow fangs extract it.

The chupacabra dislikes bright lights. For this reason, most attack only at night. One story of

丘帕卡布拉

　　丘帕卡布拉的名字是从西班牙语翻译过来的,意为山羊吸血鬼。在波多黎各、墨西哥、智利、巴西和美国,丘帕卡布拉最为多见。美国的首例目击报告于1956年发生在亚利桑那州,一般认为丘帕卡布拉常常活跃在新墨西哥、佛罗里达、亚利桑那、俄勒冈、密歇根、伊利诺伊和新泽西等州。不过绝大部分的目击还是发生在波多黎各和智利。

　　丘帕卡布拉的攻击事件,或者起码是有人报告的目击事件,于20世纪90年代达到最高峰。当时中美洲和南美洲的一些地区,特别是波多黎各和智利,发生了多起家畜被害的事件,被认定是丘帕卡布拉所为。死掉的家畜多半是鸡或者山羊,尸体的血被吸干,但其他部分丝毫未动;脖子上有两到三个伤口。之所以出现戳刺伤口数目的不一致,是因为有人报告丘帕卡布拉长有两颗巨大的獠牙,而另外有人则指认丘帕卡布拉的手脚上都长着三只巨型的利爪。

长相特征

　　尽管每个人描述的丘帕卡布拉在外形上都有差异,但是在任何文化任何时间,丘帕卡布拉都有着共同的特征。身高大多至少在三到四英尺,直立或者跳跃时身体处于垂直状态,跟袋鼠十分相像。另外有报告显示,尽管他们利用结实的后腿跳跃而非走路,却有人曾见他们用四条腿跑步,就像类人猿那样。他们强韧的皮肤上长有鳞片和尖刺,沿着脊柱则长满了羽毛。据说他们发怒或者示威时会发出刺耳的声音,还伴随着一种难闻的和硫黄差不多的气味。不过也有目击者说根本没有气味。

　　虽然大部分的描述都是直立的,和人类比较接近,但也有目击者称,丘帕卡布拉的长相看起来像犬,不过和别的已知的狗并不一样。据这些目击者说,丘帕卡布拉长得像狗,常常袭击大型的动物,如牛,把它们的尸体撕成碎块,就像野狗的做法一般。这样的丘帕卡布拉脊背上长着尖刺,眼睛很大,也有獠牙和利爪。有时候,神秘动物学家把他们归于暂未分类的野狗。

　　但是眼睛恐怕是最明显的特征。丘帕卡布拉椭圆形的脑袋上长着一对硕大的红眼睛,闪闪发光,这是很多人都知道的。有人声称,丘帕卡布拉的红眼睛有一种魔力,能够使它的猎物精神恍惚,麻痹瘫痪,这样它就可以悠闲自在地吸血了。还有报告说,人们只要看到丘帕卡布拉的魔眼,就会头晕目眩,通过这一点,就可以看出其恶魔的本质。

　　丘帕卡布拉看来也有它自己的好恶。它喜欢山羊、鸡、狗、猫、鸭和牛。显然它喜欢吸血,有人观察到它吸完血之后,腹部就明显地充盈起来。很可能是在它用中空的獠牙插入猎物身体的时候,猎物的血液就被吸到了它肚子里面一个像液囊的容器中。

　　丘帕卡布拉不喜欢强光。就因为这个原因,绝大多数的袭击事件都发生在夜里。有一

an attack in northern Chile reported that when police detectives swept the area with night vision equipment, they heard blood-curdling screeches and howls.

Theories

Many of the theories about the origin of the chupacabra are as bizarre and wide-ranging as the descriptions of the animal. While most of these theories are subject to debate, nevertheless, the theories below have become common explanations for the existence of the chupacabra:

• Because chupacabras resemble gargoyles of medieval Europe, they may have been brought to South America on Spanish ships exploring the New World.

• Some cryptozoologists speculate that chupacabras are from outer space and are alien creatures. They may be escaped pets of alien visitors to Earth. These theories have been reinforced by sightings of UFOs in areas where chupacabras have appeared.

• Some citizens of Puerto Rico where there have been many sightings think that the chupacabra was the result of a genetic experiment of a U.S. government agency in its laboratory in El Yunque, a mountain on the eastern section of the island.

• Some veterinarians in South America claim that the chupacabra is a genetically changed form of a vampire bat.

Myth or Real?

No one can say with any degree of certainty that chupacabras are, in fact, real animals, nor can anyone definitively disprove that they are not. What can be said is whether or not this creature is a hoax, it has appeared real to many observers.

Much of the information about chupacabras has grown out of the work of cryptozoologists, who study unidentified animals. Since cryptozoologists often rely on hearsay and circumstantial evidence based on alleged sightings by native inhabitants and travelers alike, many scholars dismiss the findings of cryptozoologists.

Many scientists, however, believe that the chupacabra is related to the aye-aye, a nocturnal primate native to Madagascar with shaggy fur, long claws and large eyes and ears. Resembling the North American raccoon, the aye-aye appears to be a close relative to the chupacabra. The blood-sucking characteristic of the chupacabra is explained as a process during which the chupacabra has evolved to feed on the blood of other animals, somewhat similar to that of the vampire bat.

If someone does eventually prove the existence of a specific animal or breed of animal that fits all the characteristics of a chupacabra, then scientific analysis will replace hearsay and rumor. Until that happens, however, the chupacabra will remain a frightening mystery.

Resources

Chupacabras: And Other Mysteries, Greenleaf Publications, 1997. This is a nonfiction work with information about the chupacabra and its impact in countries near the Gulf of Mexico, including Puerto Rico. The author covers stories about the animal, UFOs, government plots and other mysteries. The book includes photos, a bibliography and an index.

Cryptozoology A to Z: The Encyclopedia of Loch Monsters, Sasquatch, Chupacabras and Other Authentic Mysteries, Fireside, 1999. This book discusses chupacabaras as well as other mysteries in an encyclopedic format. Encompassing almost 200 entries, this book provides definitions, descriptions, drawings and photographs of eyewitnesses' accounts. The book also examines the relatively new field of cryptozoology and its study of unknown animals as well as the evolution of the field of cryptozoology.

个报导说在智利北边曾发生袭击事件,当警探用夜间可视设备搜索该片区域时,听到了尖叫声和咆哮声,简直令血液都为之凝固。

各种说法

关于丘帕卡布拉的来历,提法众多,但都和它的长相一样奇特而多种多样。这些说法大部分都存在争议,不过以下这些说法,是对于丘帕卡布拉的存在的公认解释:

· 丘帕卡布拉与中世纪欧洲的石像鬼十分相像,因而他们可能是在西班牙人探索新大陆的船上被带到南美的。

· 一些神秘动物学家猜测丘帕卡布拉来自外太空,是外星生物。他们可能是外星人的宠物,当外星人来到地球时他们逃了出来。在丘帕卡布拉出没的地方曾有人见到过UFO,于是这种说法就更令人信服了。

· 波多黎各一些地方曾有人多次目击丘帕卡布拉,当地一些居民认为它是美国政府部门在爱尔洋奎(位于该岛国东部的一片山区)的实验室里进行基因实验的结果。

· 南美洲一些兽医断定,丘帕卡布拉是吸血蝙蝠的一种基因变种。

是神话还是事实?

没有人能够断言丘帕卡布拉事实上的确存在,同样也没有人能够彻底地证实它们并不存在。可以确定的是,不管这种生物是否只是一场骗局,对于众多目击者来说,它就是真实的。

丘帕卡布拉的资料相当一部分都来自那些研究不明生物的神秘动物学家。由于他们的研究常常依赖于一些传闻和环境证据,都是以当地居民或游客的叙述为基础的,因而很多学者对于他们的发现不以为然。

然而,很多科学家相信丘帕卡布拉和狐猴有所关联。狐猴是一种夜行的灵长类动物,生长地为马达加斯加,长着蓬松的毛发、长长的利爪、硕大的眼睛和耳朵,外形和北美的浣熊十分相似。狐猴看起来和丘帕卡布拉有着较为亲近的关系。至于丘帕卡布拉的吸血行为,则是这样解释的:在其发展过程中,丘帕卡布拉逐渐演化为靠其他动物的血液为生,有点类似于吸血蝙蝠。

如果有人最终证实了一只或一种特殊的动物完全符合丘帕卡布拉的所有特征,那么科学的分析就将代替传闻和谣言。不过在那以前,丘帕卡布拉仍然只是一个骇人听闻的神秘故事。

相关资源

《丘帕卡布拉及其他神秘故事》,绿叶出版社,1997年。本书并非小说,记录了关于丘帕卡布拉的一些资料及其对墨西哥湾各国造成的影响,包括波多黎各在内。作者涵盖了丘帕卡布拉、UFO、政府阴谋及其他神秘故事。本书附有照片、一份参考书目和一份索引。

《神秘动物学A到Z:尼斯湖水怪、北美野人、丘帕卡布拉及其他真实神秘故事的百科全书》,飞赛德出版社,1999年。本书以百科全书的格式探讨丘帕卡布拉及其他神秘故事。收录了大约200个词条,内容有定义、描述、图片及目击者提供的照片。此外本书还详细讲述了一个比较新兴的领域——神秘动物学,及其对不明生物的研究和该领域的发展演变。

 *Six*

Crop Circles

Crop circles have captured the imagination of the public from the first reports of the phenomena in the mid-1970s until the present day. Are they human art forms or the work of extraterrestrial beings? Are they the handiwork of forces of nature?

What Are Crop Circles?

Crop circles are large circular areas or depressions that appear in geometric patterns in fields of grain (primarily wheat and corn) when the crops are tall. Crop circles even have a season—approximately April to September harvest, although the best time to create a crop circle is thought to be mid to late June. This is because the stems of grain crops—wheat in particular—are still young enough in June to rise partially back toward the sun, leaving a brushed rather than flattened effect in the crop circle.

Crop circles have ranged in size from 10 feet to more than 300 feet in diameter. They appear overnight and there are no tracks or other disturbances leading up to them. The grain stems are usually partially flattened or tangled and all bend the same direction, either clockwise or counterclockwise. There are never any signs of damaged, broken or forced stems.

Where Are Crop Circles Found?

Most crop circles have been found in the southeastern part of the United Kingdom. Wiltshire is acknowledged to be the center of crop circles and it may be no coincidence that Wiltshire county is also the location of some of England's most sacred Neolithic sites, including Stonehenge, Avebury, Silbury Hill and West Kennett Long Barrow burial grounds. Some researchers believe that crop circles have appeared near ley lines, which is the term given to alignments of ancient sites stretching across an area. Ley lines may be seen as an alignment of site markers or as a remnant of old walls or tracks identifying a sacred site.

About 10,000 crop circles have been reported throughout the world since documentation of the phenomena began in the late 1970s. Many of these circles have also been found in the same areas of ancient sacred sites.

The History of Crop Circles

Although crop circles commanded the attention of the public in the 1970s, there are earlier references. A 17th century woodcut depicts the devil mowing a circular pattern in a field. Later an article in the journal *Nature* in 1880 described a field with several crop circles, attributing the circles to a possible cyclonic wind.

In 1991 two Englishmen, Doug Bower and Dave Chorley, stepped forward and claimed responsibility for the crop circles that had been appearing since the late 1970s. They admitted that they were trying to play a joke to make people think that UFOs and extraterrestrial aliens were landing in southern England.

The only one to reveal itself is an organization called the Circlemakers. Led by John

麦田怪圈

自从20世纪70年代中期,首批麦田怪圈被报道后,这一现象就引发人们的想象,直到今天。那些怪圈到底是人类的艺术形式还是外星人的杰作? 或者是自然力量的作品呢?

何为麦田怪圈?

麦田怪圈指的是谷物长高后,在种植谷物的田地里(主要是小麦和玉米地)以几何图案出现的大块圆形面积。麦田怪圈甚至有其自身的季节——在4~9月的收获季节,不过一般认为制造怪圈的最佳时节在6月的中下旬。此时庄稼的茎——尤其是小麦的茎——还比较幼嫩,能够在一定程度上背向太阳生长,这样田地里的庄稼就显现出拂弯的效果,而不是压平的效果。

怪圈的直径从10英尺到300英尺大小不等。他们都是在一夜之间出现,而且附近没有人为痕迹。麦秆一般都出现一定程度的弯曲或纠结,而且都是朝着同一个方向,有的顺时针,有的逆时针;但从来也没有破坏、折断或强压的迹象。

麦田怪圈是在哪里发现的?

迄今为止大部分的麦田怪圈都是在英国的东南部发现的。威尔特郡被认为是怪圈的中心地带,当地也拥有英国的大部分新石器时代遗址,包括史前巨石阵、埃夫伯里石圈、西尔布利人造山和长冢墓地,这应该不是巧合。一些研究人员相信,麦田怪圈通常都出现在史前地貌线附近。史前地貌线是一个术语,指穿越过一片区域的古代遗址所连成的假想线,可以看成是遗址创建人的定位,也可以看成是古代圣地留下的残垣或其他踪迹。

自20世纪70年代末该现象被记录以来, 全世界已有大约1万例麦田怪圈被报告。其中有很多是在古代圣地被发现的。

麦田怪圈的历史

20世纪70年代时,麦田怪圈吸引了大众的注意,不过该现象其实古已有之。17世纪的一副木刻就描绘了恶魔在田地里割刈出圆形图案的场景。到1880年的时候,《自然》杂志上刊登的一篇文章描述了一片田地里呈现的几个怪圈,并认定旋风为怪圈形成的原因。

1991年, 两个英国人达格·鲍尔和戴夫·柯莱站出来招认,20世纪70年代末以来出现的麦田怪圈都是出自他们之手。他们承认只是想开个玩笑,让人们以为UFO和外星人曾降落在英国南部。

唯一进行自我公开的是一个叫"怪圈制造人"的组织。该组织的领导人约翰·兰伯格

Lundburg, a graphic designer, the Circlemakers has completed a few commercial formations, including a TV ad for Mitsubishi and a TV program for the History Channel. Other than these endeavors, the group will not reveal any other circles they have completed or undertake to construct a formation in front of eyewitnesses. Circlemakers wants to preserve the mystery of the art form.

In the past 25 years, crop circle formations have evolved from simple circles to large complex designs that are developed using complex mathematical principles. The largest crop circle formation so far contains 409 circles, covering more than 800 feet in a field in Wiltshire.

This evolving art form has intrigued the public so much in recent years that crop circle enthusiasts and artists have been dubbed cereologists, from Ceres, the ancient Roman goddess of agriculture and vegetation. This is also the root of the English word cereal.

Theories about Crop Circles

Despite the claims of present and past crop circle artists, these skeptics have developed several theories:

· The crop circles are the results of small whirlwinds (artists countered this by creating formations with straight lines).

· The crop circles appear on ley lines that are really lines of cosmic energy that connect to magnetic forces in the earth to create an electromagnetic current that flattens crops.

· The crop circles are the circular landing sites of UFOs, which create swirling patterns in grass or grain fields. This theory answers the question of why there seem to be no footprints or other tracks of humans left behind after building a circle design. Modern circle makers refute the latter by pointing out that the artist used the paths and ruts left by the tractor during the original plowing and planting of the field.

Most scholars believe that crop circles are manmade. They base their conclusions on the recent revelations about how circles are created as well as the fact that most of the crop circle activity occurs in one place—southern England—and that all of the unanswered questions about whirlwinds, electromagnetic fields and human tracks have been explained. Nevertheless, crop circles have a mysterious aura about them and despite scientific research, will always evoke the speculation that human beings are not the creators of these phenomena.

How to Make Crop Circles

According to modern circle makers, although a crop circle can be created overnight, it usually requires a week of preplanning and designing. Once the plan is ready, the crop circle can be constructed following these steps:

· Hammer a stake into the field at the predetermined center of the circle.

· Tie a rope to the stake and stretch it to the outside edge or circumference of the planned circle.

· Create the circle's perimeter by walking in a circle around the stake while holding the rope taut.

· Drag boards or metal pipes over the crop to flatten the stems within the circumscribed circle.

Resources

Secrets in the Fields: The Science and Mysticism of Crop Circles, Hampton Roads Publishing Company, 2002. This book examines the history of crop circles, their possible implications, human reactions to them and their authenticity. There are footnotes documenting the work and an extensive bibliography for further study.

www.cropcircleconnector.com. The Crop Circle Connector is the leading Website on the phenomenon of crop circles.

是一位美术设计人员。该组织业已完成了好几个商业图案,包括一次三菱的电视广告和历史频道的一次电视节目。除了上述成果,该组织拒绝透露他们完成的任何其他怪圈,也不愿在众目睽睽之下建造一个怪圈图案。他们说要保持该项艺术形式的神秘感。

在过去的 25 年间,麦田怪圈的形式已经从最初的简单圆圈发展成为大型的复杂的设计图,并且要用到复杂的数学原理。迄今为止最大的怪圈出现在威尔特郡的一块田地里,包含了 409 个圆环,覆盖了 800 多英尺的土地。

此项艺术发展如此迅猛,激发了公众极大的兴趣。最近几年,人们受到古罗马掌管农业和植物的谷物女神赛尔斯(Ceres)的启发,把热衷于怪圈的人和研究怪圈艺术的人戏称为"谷物学家"(cereologist)。

麦田怪圈的理论

无论是过去还是现在,都有怪圈艺术家们宣称可以制造怪圈,这些持怀疑态度的人提出了以下理论:

· 麦田怪圈是由小型旋风造成的(艺术家们为了反击,用直线就造出了图案)。

· 麦田怪圈沿着史前地貌线出现,但史前地貌线其实是宇宙能量的线。宇宙能量和地球内部的磁力息息相关,能够产生电磁流迫使谷物倒向一边。

· 麦田怪圈是 UFO 的圆环形着陆点,着陆时在草地上或者麦田里就产生了漩涡似的图形。该理论解释了为什么新的怪圈形成后没有脚印或其他人类迹象遗留下来。现代的怪圈制造者们则对前者进行了反驳:田地里耕种时拖拉机总会留下小路和车辙,而艺术家们正是利用了这一点。

大部分学者相信麦田怪圈是人造的。他们得出这一结论,是因为近些年来有人揭露了如何制造怪圈,而且大部分的怪圈都集中在英国南部,此外,关于旋风、电磁场和人类踪迹等原先未解的谜题都已解开。尽管科学研究已经能够作出解释,然而麦田怪圈自身有一种神秘的特质,终将吸引人们进行思考:人类也许并非这一现象的制造人。

如何造怪圈

据现代的怪圈制造者们说,虽然怪圈可以一夜做成,但是需要花上一个礼拜来提前准备和设计。定好计划后,按照以下步骤就可以建造出怪圈来:

· 在预先设定好的怪圈中心打下一个木桩。

· 在木桩上系上一根绳子,走到绳子的另一端,或者走到计划好的怪圈边缘处。

· 将绳子拉直,绕木桩走一圈,就形成了怪圈的外边。

· 在限定的圆环范围内,将木板或金属管从庄稼上方拖过去,这样就迫使茎部弯曲了。

相关资源

《田里的秘密:麦田怪圈的科学观和神秘论》,汉普顿·柔姿出版公司,2002 年。本书回顾了麦田怪圈的历史,推测其可能的含义,讲述人类对怪圈的反应以及怪圈到底是否真实;书内有脚注,还有一份内容广泛的参考书目,以供进一步研究。

www.cropcircleconnector.com 麦田怪圈联结网是研究怪圈现象的领军网址。

Seven

Crows & Ravens

For centuries human beings have been fascinated by crows and ravens, often in a negative way. In many cultures the crow and raven are considered bad omens, yet often for different reasons. Crows are negatively associated with the spiritual aspect of death whereas ravens tend to symbolize the physical aspect of death.

Belonging to the Corvidae family of birds, which includes not only crows and ravens but also rooks, magpies and jays, crows and ravens are large, nonmigratory birds that sport glossy black plumage and harsh voices. These two physical characteristics alone may be the basis of the fear of these birds. The color black is often associated with evil and even death, and among early superstitious cultures, the crow and raven were categorized with witches and black cats. Their raucous harsh calls did not enhance their image, either; the eerie cries of crows or ravens seem to forewarn of impending doom.

Physical features aside, crows and ravens are natural scavengers, and because they are often found on dead corpses, they have been associated with death, carnage, war and pestilence. This dietary practice did not endear the birds to the general populace.

To add to the negative perception of crows and ravens, they are omnivores, meaning they will eat anything including decaying flesh, rotting food or dung. This has given them a well-deserved reputation for spreading filth and disease. They also have a reputation for consuming crops at harvest time, angering farmers who depend on a bountiful harvest for their livelihood.

Positive Characteristics of Crows and Ravens

In spite of their negative connotations, crows and ravens have some positive characteristics. In addition to being intelligent, crows and ravens are large, strong and long-lived. Many can live for more than 30 years. They live in nests built high off the ground in trees, on cliffs or on power-line poles. They are monogamous when they pair off and return to the same nest every year. While they are not migratory birds, they do move in widening circles when looking for food.

These birds are skilled flyers, diving, flying upside down, performing somersaults or showing off other flying tricks. Their intelligence permits them to imitate sounds, including animal calls, human words or wind sounds.

Superstitions about Crows and Ravens

In most parts of the world the crow and the raven are considered omens of bad luck or worse. The following lists highlight the folklore that has been perpetuated about these birds for centuries.

Evil Symbols

Clearly, crows and ravens have been associated with evil symbols and portents of doom:

· Crows and ravens foretell death. This probably grew out of the supposition that because they eat carrion, these birds can smell the scent of death even before a person or animal dies.

· Ravens in particular are symbols of sin, especially stealing, lying and gluttony. Ancient

乌鸦与渡鸦

数个世纪以来，人类对于乌鸦和渡鸦，一直都感到十分好奇，但是主要体现在一些不好的方面。很多文化里面，乌鸦和渡鸦被看成是凶兆，不过原因倒是各不相同的。乌鸦通常和死亡的精神方面联系起来，而渡鸦则象征着死亡的肉体方面。

乌鸦与渡鸦和白嘴鸦、喜鹊、樫鸟同属于鸦类，但相对来说，体型比较大，不迁移，长着黑色光鲜的翅膀，声音刺耳难听。而黑色翅膀和难听的声音，可能正是它们令敌人望而却步的武器。黑颜色常令人联想起邪恶甚至死亡，而在早期的迷信文化中，乌鸦与渡鸦常常和巫婆与黑猫归为一类。粗粝刺耳的叫声也没能提升它们的形象，那叫声似乎可以提前预示命运的降临。

除了外表的特征，乌鸦和渡鸦还是天生的食腐动物，而且正因为它们常常出现在尸体上，所以总跟死亡、屠杀、战争及瘟疫联系起来。这种食腐习惯当然不会让人们喜欢上它们。

还有一点更增加了乌鸦和渡鸦的负面印象，就是他们什么都吃，包括腐败变质的肉类、烂掉的食物或粪便。这样说来，它们传播污秽和疾病的名声真是当之无愧。它们还有另一项"荣誉"，就是在丰收的时节破坏庄稼，惹得靠收获庄稼谋生的农夫们愤怒不已。

乌鸦和渡鸦的正面特征

乌鸦和渡鸦有很多负面含义，但同时也有一些正面特征：不但聪明、体型又大又强壮，而且很长寿，很多可以超过30年。它们把巢建筑在离地面很远的大树、悬崖或者电线杆上。每年成双成对地飞离鸟巢，然后又飞回来，实行着"一夫一妻制"。尽管不是迁移的鸟类，他们仍然在逐渐扩大的圆形范围内寻找食物。

它们精通飞翔，能够俯冲、倒飞、翻跟斗，还乐于展示飞翔技术。它们的智慧赋予他们模仿声音的能力，包括动物的叫声、人类的说话声或者风声。

涉及乌鸦和渡鸦的迷信

世界上绝大多数的地方都将乌鸦和渡鸦看成凶兆或者更甚。以下文字就突显了几个世纪以来有关这两种鸟的民间传说。

邪恶的象征

显然，乌鸦和渡鸦长期以来都是和凶兆、厄运联系在一起的：

·乌鸦和渡鸦能够预知死亡。这可能是因为它们吃腐肉，能够闻到死亡的气息，哪怕那个人或者动物还未曾死亡。

Greeks believed the god Apollo turned the raven black when the bird told him of his lover's unfaithfulness. This perpetuated the raven's image as a spy and a tattletale. According to the Bible, Noah sent a raven out to test the flood waters. The raven never returned, leading to the belief that the raven was seeking decaying flesh to eat rather than looking for dry land. A Jewish legend proclaims that Noah's raven was punished for its failure to return by being blackened and condemned to eat carrion forever.

· A lone crow above a house means bad news, most often death for someone within the house.

· It is unlucky to have a crow cross your path.

· If crows seemed unusually quiet during their annual molting, medieval European peasants believed they were preparing to take their discarded black feathers to the devil as a tribute.

· The medieval French believed that evil priests became crows and sinning nuns became magpies.

· Ravens eating in the streets of a town means a severe storm is coming.

· Ravens have lived in the Tower of London for more than 900 years and an old saying predicts that if the ravens leave the Tower, the Tower will fall and thus England, symbolized by the Tower, will fall.

Good Symbols

On the other hand, crows and ravens have positive meanings in some cultures:

· The crow has long been associated with motherly love and spiritual strength. In addition, at one time in Egypt two crows were an emblem of monogamy.

· In some African and Native American cultures, the raven is a kind guide who issues warnings to the living and guides the dead on their final journey.

· North American Eskimos interpret the crow or raven's harsh cry as a symbol of hope for a better time.

· Native Americans of the Pacific Northwest view the raven as a hero and believe the bird taught the first humans how to care for themselves and construct shelters. The raven is considered a benevolent caretaker who brought light, vegetation and animals into the world to help humankind. The flood story is interpreted as a raven leading the animals in pairs onto a raft, in the manner of Noah, to save them from a flood. In addition, Native Americans believe that the world was populated when the raven brought light into the world, frightening humans and causing them to flee to all corners of the world.

· In Norse mythology a pair of ravens led the god Odin.

· In some cultures the raven is a symbol of light or the sun. In ancient Greece Apollo, the god of light, considered the raven sacred. In certain Chinese traditions, the raven symbolizes light.

Resources

In the Company of Crows and Ravens, Yale University Press, 2007. This book examines the characteristics of ravens and crows as well as the other birds in their family. Blending science, art and folklore tales, the author reveals the intelligence, adaptability and memory of these birds. Crows, in particular, imitate human activity to solve problems (using moving cars as nutcrackers, for example) and quickly adapt to shifts in the world around them. Black and white illustrations highlight the book's stories of the ingenuity of the members of the Corvidae family of birds.

· 渡鸦专门就是罪恶的象征,尤以偷窃、撒谎和贪食为代表。古希腊人相信,渡鸦告诉阿波罗神,他的爱人对他不忠,阿波罗神大怒之下把渡鸦变成了黑色。这就将渡鸦的形象定位于间谍和告密者。据圣经上说,诺亚派出一只渡鸦去查看洪水是否已经退去。但是渡鸦再也没有回来,不免让人怀疑,它是寻找腐肉吃去了,并没有真正去寻找露出水面的陆地。一个犹太传说则认定,诺亚派出去的那只渡鸦由于未能返回而受到惩罚,被变成了黑色,而且永远要吃腐肉。

· 如果单只乌鸦盘旋在屋子上方,表示有坏消息,最常见的是屋子里有人要去世了。

· 如果在路上看见一只乌鸦,表示厄运降临。

· 在中世纪的欧洲,如果乌鸦在每年一度的换毛期间显得格外安静,农民们就会认为他们正准备将换下来的黑色羽毛当贡品献给恶魔。

· 中世纪时,法国人相信邪恶的牧师变成了乌鸦,而犯罪的修女则变成了喜鹊。

· 如果渡鸦在一个城市的街上吃东西,预示着一场大风暴即将来临。

· 渡鸦在伦敦塔上已经居住了900多年,一个古老的谚语曾经预测,如果渡鸦离开伦敦塔,那么塔就要倒塌,而它所象征的英国,也会跟着毁灭。

美好的象征

另一方面,乌鸦和渡鸦在某些文化里,也有积极的正面意义。

· 长久以来,乌鸦总让人联想到母爱和精神力量。另外,在埃及,两只乌鸦曾经是一夫一妻制的标志。

· 在一些非洲和土著美洲的文化里,渡鸦是一名善良的向导,它向活着的人提出警告,将死去的人引向最终的行程。

· 北美的爱斯基摩人将乌鸦或渡鸦粗粝的叫声解释为美好生活的新希望。

· 太平洋西北部的土著美洲人把渡鸦看成英雄,而且相信是渡鸦教会了最早的人类如何照顾自己,如何建造居住的场所。渡鸦成了一位慈悲为怀的守护者,给人类带来了光明、植物和动物。大洪水的故事是这样解说的:大洪水泛滥的时候,渡鸦以诺亚的形象出现,带领着各种动物,一双双一对对地走上了救生筏,得到了拯救。另外,土著美洲人还相信,渡鸦把光带到了人世间,使人们受到惊吓,迫使他们向世界的各个角落逃亡,这样人口才得以分布到世界各地。

· 在挪威的神话中,一对渡鸦为欧丁神引路。

· 在一些文化中,渡鸦是光明或太阳的象征。在古希腊,光明之神阿波罗认为渡鸦是神圣的。在中国的一些传统观念中,渡鸦象征着光明。

相关资源

《与乌鸦和渡鸦相伴》,耶鲁大学出版社,2007年。本书细述了乌鸦和渡鸦以及其他鸦类的特征。作者利用科学、艺术和民间故事,揭示了这些鸦类的聪明才智、适应能力和记忆能力。尤其是乌鸦,能够模仿人类活动去解决很多问题(比如利用开动的汽车来压碎坚果),而且能够迅速地适应周遭世界的变化。黑白插图凸显了书中故事所描绘的鸦类成员有多么聪明灵巧。

Curse of
King Tutankhamun

"They who enter this sacred tomb shall
swift be visited by wings of death."

Thus quoted an early 20th century newspaper, which reported the warning was inscribed on a tablet found in the newly discovered tomb of the Egyptian pharaoh Tutankhamun (also spelled Tutankhamen) in the Valley of the Kings at Luxor in November of 1922.

True or not, the actual story of King Tut's life and the discovery of his hidden tomb still capture the interest of Egyptologists, archeologists and ordinary people alike.

Who Was King Tut?

The story of the boy king Tutankhamun is shrouded in mystery, which has intrigued scholars for centuries. Pharaoh Tutankhamun succeeded Pharaoh Akhenaten to the throne and ruled Egypt for 9 years from 1347 to 1339 B.C.. When he was 18 years old, Tutankhamun died mysteriously and many speculated that he was assassinated. After his death his enemies tried to remove all traces of the boy king from official records, which added credence to the belief that he had been murdered.

Ancient Egyptians revered their pharaohs as deities and carefully preserved their bodies by embalming after death. They then placed the mummified corpses in elaborate tombs and surrounded the bodies with objects the royal beings would need in the next world, including great wealth and treasures. The tombs' architects then sealed the sites, blocking passageways, adding false doors and designing hidden rooms to confuse intruders. In some cases, they placed a curse on the entrance.

In most cases, these safeguards were ineffective. From early times grave robbers bypassed all the precautions and stole all the valuables from the dead royals. By the 19th century most if not all of the ancient tombs had been plundered. In the late 1800s European archeologists began to develop an interest in ancient Egypt and a number of expeditions set out to try to find any undiscovered tomb or unplundered crypt.

In 1890 the young English Egyptologist Howard Carter prepared to leave for Egypt. With his background and training he was prepared to conduct expeditions into ancient Egyptian sites and study ancient artifacts. During this time Carter became convinced that there was at least one undiscovered tomb—that of the little known Pharaoh Tutankhamun.

Discovering Tut's Tomb

Carter's team had been working in a secluded spot near the tomb of Ramses VI. In November , 1922 they uncovered a step hidden by debris from Ramse' tomb and digging farther found 15 more steps leading to a sealed doorway. On the doorway was the name Tutankhamun.

Inside the door Carter found a four-room tomb. Although modest by pharaoh standards, the tomb nevertheless contained more than 5,000 items including chariots, weapons, toy models, jars of oils, household items and magnificent jewelry. The mummy's head was covered with a lifelike

图坦卡门王
的诅咒

"任谁踏入这神圣的墓室，
随即接受死亡的双翼。"

20世纪初，一家报纸如是引用了刻在一个墓碑上的警告。这个墓碑位于1922年11月在路克索的帝王谷发现的埃及法老图坦卡门的墓地。

无论是真是假，图坦卡门王的生活史实，以及对他隐秘墓室的发掘，仍然吸引着众多的埃及学家和考古学家，也吸引着普通百姓。

图坦卡门王何许人也？

幼王图坦卡门的故事远离神奇，数个世纪以来学者们为之钻研不已。图坦卡门法老是继承阿肯那法斯法老登上了王位，在公元前1347~公元前1339年统治埃及共9年。图坦卡门18岁的时候，离奇去世，很多人揣测他是遭到了暗杀。在他去世之后，他的敌人们还设法将关于他的所有资料从国家的档案中抹掉，这样，就更让人相信他是被谋杀的。

古埃及人把他们的法老当成神灵一样敬畏，法老死后，他们会用香料来处理尸体，进行妥善保存。然后将制成木乃伊的尸体放入精巧的坟墓，并在尸体周围放满物品，包括大量的财产和珍宝，以供这些王室成员到了另一个世界继续享用。接着，坟墓的建造者就封闭墓地，阻断通道，安装假门，还设计了隐秘的墓室以迷惑入侵者。有些时候，他们会在入口处下一道诅咒。

绝大多数情况下，这些保护措施并不起效。很早的时候，盗墓者就绕开了所有的警戒，从王室墓地偷走了所有值钱的东西。到19世纪为止，不说是全部，最起码是绝大部分的古墓，都被洗劫过了。19世纪末，欧洲的考古学家们开始对古埃及产生兴趣，一些探险队出发去寻找尚未发现或者未遭劫掠的墓地。

1890年，英国一位年轻的埃及学家霍华德·卡特打算去埃及看看。他有这方面的知识，也接受过相关培训，他准备深入古埃及遗址去考察，去研究古代的文物。此时，卡特确信，起码有一所墓地是未经开发的，那就是鲜为人知的图坦卡门法老墓。

发现图坦卡门墓

卡特的挖掘队在拉姆西斯六世墓附近一个与世隔绝的地方继续工作着。1922年11月份，他们挖开拉姆西斯墓的残骸，发现隐藏其下的一个台阶，继续挖掘，又发现15级台阶，通向一个密封的入口。门上正是图坦卡门的名字。

进门以后，卡特发现，这座坟墓有四个墓室。尽管以法老的规格来看有点寒酸，但这座坟墓还是拥有5千多件陪葬品，包括二轮战车、武器、玩具模型、瓶装的油、居家用品和炫目的珠宝。图坦卡门木乃伊的脸上覆盖着一具栩栩如生的黄金面罩。此外还有成箱的

gold mask of Tutankhamun. In addition, there were chests of beautiful clothes, linens and musical instruments.

Carter, Lord Carnarvon and the excavation team celebrated the discovery. Everyone involved either ignored or dismissed the warnings about the curse of disturbing an unopened tomb.

The Curse

And then the legend about the curse began to form. Within only a few months of the opening of the tomb, Lord Carnarvon died. It was reported that at the time of Carnarvon's death, all the lights in Cairo went out and at the same instant in England, Carnarvon's dog howled and died. Even Sir Arthur Conan Doyle, creator of Sherlock Holmes and a believer of the occult, chimed in, stating that Lord Carnarvon's death could have been the result of the pharaoh's curse.

Five months after his death, Lord Carnarvon's younger brother suddenly died. And within a decade after the official opening of the tomb, six people associated with the discovery died. Suddenly, the curse of King Tut began to take on meaning.

The media, primarily newspapers, picked up on the curse story and sensationalized it. This was not the age of instant electronic coverage or televised investigative reporting. So newspapers were free to invent or exaggerate information to sell newspapers. No one bothered to report, for example, that Lord Carnarvon had been in poor health for more than 20 years following an automobile accident. Or that his cause of death was an infected mosquito bite that developed into life-threatening pneumonia that he could not overcome. Furthermore, while six people connected to King Tut's tomb died, most of the people involved in the discovery of the tomb lived for many years to ripe old ages. Howard Carter himself, obviously the prime target of a curse, lived for almost 17 years after entering the tomb, dying of natural causes just before his 65th birthday.

If Not a Curse, then What?

Most scholars believe that the facts show the number of deaths among those opening King Tut's tomb were the fabrications of a sensational media. Yet some think that there could be a scientific explanation for illness associated with ancient Egyptian tombs. In more recent times, doctors have noticed that museum employees who work with ancient artifacts and mummies often have symptoms consistent with exposure to certain fungi that can cause fever, fatigue and rashes. Other scientists have found mold spores on ancient mummies. Studies show that these spores can survive thousands of years in a dark, dry tomb, and scientists speculate that when a sealed tomb is opened, the spores swirl into the air propelled by the gust of fresh air from the outside. Since some of these organisms can be harmful or cause illness, museum workers now wear protective gear when handling ancient artifacts or examining mummies.

The ailments that accompany fungi or mold spores could possibly be the answers to any unexplained deaths of those who worked with Howard Carter and his team on the Tut project. It would appear that the legend of the curse of King Tutankhamun is just that—a legend.

Resources

The Complete Tutankhamun: The King, the Tomb, the Royal Treasure (King Tut), Thames & Hudson, reprint edition, 1995. This is a comprehensive study of King Tut's life and background, the structure of the tomb and the artifacts and objects found in the tomb.

www.egyptologyonline.com/tutankhamum.htm. Egyptology Online provides news, study aids, recommended book lists and a wealth of information concerning this fascinating subject.

华丽服装、亚麻布和乐器。

卡特、卡纳冯爵士和整个挖掘队都欢庆这一发现。谁也没有把对侵扰密室的诅咒放在心上。

诅咒

接下来，关于诅咒的传说开始应验了。图坦卡门墓打开后仅仅数月之内，卡纳冯爵士离世。据报道，卡纳冯死时开罗所有的灯霎时熄灭，同时，在英国，卡纳冯养的一条狗狂吠起来，随即也死了。《神探福尔摩斯》的作者阿瑟·柯南·道尔爵士相信有神秘事件的存在，连他也发表言论，认为卡纳冯爵士的死可能是法老诅咒的结果。

卡纳冯爵士去世5个月之后，他的弟弟突然也死了。图坦卡门墓被正式发掘的10年之内，前后有六个相关人员都去世了。一时之间，图坦卡门王的诅咒开始显现威力。

当时的媒体，主要是报纸，抓住了这诅咒的故事，对其进行大肆渲染。因为当时既没有即时电子通讯设备，也不能直播调查报告。于是为了增加报纸销售量，报社就毫无顾忌地捏造或者夸大新闻。没有人站出来澄清一些事实情况，比如卡纳冯爵士自从一场车祸后，20多年来健康状况一直欠佳。还有，他的死因是蚊子叮咬感染了导致威胁生命的肺炎，而他最终没能挺过去。此外，虽然与坟墓发掘工作相关的人员有6个去世了，但其他大部分的人都活了很多年，直到高寿而终。就说霍华德·卡特，他自己显然是诅咒首当其冲的目标，却在进入墓室后还活了近17年，直至65岁生日前不久才自然死去。

若非诅咒，那是什么？

大部分学者认为，说到那些打开图坦卡门墓的人员中死了有多少多少，只不过是媒体制造出来的噱头。然而也有部分学者考虑到，针对古埃及墓葬所引起的疾病，应该会有科学的解释。后来，医生们注意到，博物馆里经常接触古代文物或者木乃伊的工作人员常常会有一些症状，状如接触了某些导致发热、疲劳和皮疹的真菌。另有科学家在古代木乃伊身上发现了霉菌孢子。研究显示，这些孢子在阴暗、干燥的墓室内可以存活数千年。科学家们推测，密封的坟墓打开时，从墓室外吹进一阵新鲜空气，孢子就漂到了空气当中。由于这些有机生物中一些是对身体有害的，可能造成疾病，目前，博物馆的工作人员处理文物或者检查木乃伊时，都要穿上防护服。

伴随真菌或霉菌孢子而来的疾病，可能就是霍华德·卡特挖掘队一些未明死因的真相。关于图坦卡门王诅咒的传说，只不过就是一个传说而已。

相关资源

《完整的图坦卡门：法老王、坟墓、王室珍宝》，泰晤士和哈得孙出版社，重印版，1995年。本书是对图坦卡门王生活和背景、墓室构造、墓内发现的文物等的综合研究。

www.egyptologyonline.com/tutankhamum.htm 在线古埃及学网址提供关于此项令人着迷的主题的新闻、研究帮助、推荐书目和丰富的信息。

Nine

Disappearing Blonde Gene

Natural blondes are going to die out within the next 200 years. To put it another way, the gene for natural blondes will become extinct in fewer than 200 years and the last natural blonde will be born in Finland in 2202.

So reported several British newspapers, including *The Sun, The Express, The Daily Star of London and the Sunday Times,* in September of 2002. Within days the story was repeated on the British Broadcasting Company (BBC), on American TV news broadcasts and in other international newspapers.

The various media accounts carried some credence because in tracing the origins of the story, sources pinpointed an account on a German wire service that cited an anthropologist from the World Health Organization (WHO). Consequently, subsequent media sources began to credit WHO as the source of the study on the disappearing blonde gene. Finland was identified as the country in which the last natural blonde will be born in approximately 200 years because Finland claims to be the country with the highest proportion of natural blondes.

In October of 2002 the *New York Times* reported that the WHO had no knowledge of any study, had not conducted or planned any study and had no record of an anthropologist on its staff who had supposedly spoken to the original German reporter. At this point the WHO officially confirmed that the story was false.

The story began to die out. In 2006, however, the report of the disappearing blonde gene resurfaced in a few media sources and began to circulate again. This time the story appeared on the Internet and spread almost instantaneously around the world. It even became an item on the U.S. TV show, *The Colbert Report,* prompting Stephen Colbert to suggest a selective breeding program to save blondes.

The Disappearing Gene

What is the basis for the prediction that natural blondes will die out within 200 years?

This hypothesis rests on how recessive genes work. And to understand that, it is important to understand human genes and how they determine a person's characteristics.

Genes are the parts of living cells that specify the traits human beings inherit from their parents. These traits include such features as gender, height, physique and color of eyes and hair.

Genes are considered the units of heredity that are located on the threadlike structures called chromosomes in each cell's nucleus, the command center of cells. Each human cell nucleus contains 23 pairs of chromosomes, for a total of 46. One of each pair of chromosomes is inherited from each parent and 22 of the 23 pairs appear identical while the remaining pair, the sex chromosomes, identifies the sex of the child. Each pair of chromosomes contains thousands of genes. As a rule, specific genes occupy specific places on certain chromosomes, and scientists can perform tests to determine the locations and properties of each gene. Genes are made up of deoxyribonucleic acid (DNA) and each gene is a link of DNA in a chromosome. Because they are the carriers of DNA, genes influence the chemical and physical processes during growth and

金发基因正
在消失

天然的金发将在接下来的 200 年内渐渐绝种。换句话说,在不到 200 年的时间里,天然的金发基因将彻底灭绝。最后一位长着天然金发的人将于 2202 年出生在芬兰。

2002 年 9 月,英国的好几家报纸如是报道,包括太阳报、快报、伦敦每日星报和太阳时报。几天之内这样的报道在英国广播公司(BBC)、美国电视新闻广播和其他国际报纸也得以播报。

这诸多媒体的报道都有几分让人信服之处,因为追溯该报道的

根源,有资料明确显示,德国一家通讯社发表的一篇报告,正是引用了一位来自世界卫生组织(WHO)的人类学家的发言。自然而然,随后的媒体开始相信,WHO 正是此项研究的根源。该研究认定,大约 200 年之后,最后一位金发人就将出生在芬兰,因为在全世界,芬兰的天然金发比例最高。

2002 年 10 月,纽约时报声明,WHO 根本不知道什么金发研究,根本没有进行过、也没有计划过这样的研究,而且,人员档案中也从来没有那样一位人类学家去对德国的记者发言。在这一点上,WHO 正式确认,该报道纯属无中生有。

于是该报道渐渐淡出人们的视线。然而到了 2006 年,金发基因正在消失的报告又一次在几家媒体出现了,而且重新开始得以流传。这一次,这样的报道上了网,几乎在瞬间就传遍了全球。甚至连美国的电视脱口秀"科尔伯特报告"也出现了这样的内容,促使史蒂夫·科尔伯特建议开发一个选择育种的项目,以拯救金发种群。

正在消失的基因

是什么导致人们作出预言,说天然的金发种群将在 200 年内灭绝呢?

这一假说基于隐性基因的工作原理。要理解这一原理,就必须先弄清楚人类基因,以及基因是如何决定一个人的特征的。

基因是生命细胞的一部分,决定了人类从父母身上遗传而来的特征。这些特征包括性别、身高、体格和眼睛、头发的颜色,等等。

基因被认为是遗传单位,位于染色体上。细胞核是每一个细胞的命令中枢,里面有一些线状结构的物质,就是染色体。人类细胞核内有 23 对染色体,共计 46 条。每对染色体中,有一条来自父亲,一条来自母亲。23 对染色体中,有 22 对呈现出相同的性状,而剩下的一对叫做性染色体,就决定了孩子的性别。每对染色体都包含着几千个基因。基因有其自身的规律,特定的基因在染色体上占有特定的位置,科学家们可以通过实验确认每个基因的位置和特性。基因由脱氧核糖核酸(DNA)构成,每个基因就是染色体中的一组 DNA 序列。因为基因是 DNA 的载体,所以在生长过程中,基因就会对化学进程和物理进程产生影响。

aging.

Genes are classified as dominant or recessive. A dominant gene prevails over a recessive gene and the trait it possesses will be evident in the child. A recessive gene is a gene hidden by the dominant gene. In order for the trait carried on the recessive gene to appear in the child, the recessive gene must be present on both chromosomes in a pair, that is, the person must inherit the recessive trait from both parents. For example, brown or black hair and brown eyes are dominant traits while blonde hair and blue eyes are recessive. This means that a blue-eyed blonde must have a gene for these traits from both parents in order to have blue eyes or blonde hair.

The theory behind the disappearing blonde gene is that because the blonde gene is recessive, it will eventually be overwhelmed or outnumbered by the growing population of brown-haired people with the dominant gene. This belief is further supported by the fact that in this modern age, migration across geographical and cultural boundaries is common, so blonde people no longer live in an isolated area with other blondes with whom they conceive blonde children.

Adding to this explanation of the diminishing population of blondes is the theory that because blondes are considered to be more attractive, many brunettes dye their hair. Thus, many apparent blondes are really brunettes and carry the dominant gene for dark hair. This tends to mask the actual number of people who carry the recessive natural blonde gene.

Fact or Fiction?

Are natural blondes really going to disappear? Scientists are clear about the permanency of recessive genes. Unless a gene is associated with a danger to survival or to reproduction, it does not die out but is passed on to future generations. Since being a natural blonde does not constitute a danger to the propagation of the species, it does not appear that natural blondes or their recessive genes are going to disappear. In addition, even if racial intermixing reduces the number of people who demonstrate the recessive blonde gene, scientists stress that this does not reduce the prevalence of the gene. Unless the recessive blonde gene is passed onto offspring from both parents, it will not result in a natural blonde child, but that does not mean the recessive gene no longer exists.

Resources

*www.answers.com/topic/recessive-gene-2.*This Website explains the recessive gene and includes examples relating to humans and to Gregor Mendel's heredity experiments with pea plants.

*Chance in the House of Fate: A Natural History of Heredity,*Houghton Mifflin, 2001. This book is a series of natural history essays concerning the continuity and discontinuity of cellular and molecular life. The author includes descriptions of genetic determination and the effects of dominant and recessive genes on human development.

Welcome to the Genome: A User's Guide to the Genetic Past, Present, and Future, Wiley, 2004. Illustrated in full color, this book is an easy-to-read description of human genetic components and the blueprint of human DNA.

Albino Animals, Darby Creek Publishing, 2004. This is a children's book, aimed at young readers aged 9 to 12, who are interested in the role of the genetic recessive gene for albinism in animals. The book includes a glossary and bibliography for young readers who want to learn the basic science underlying genetic traits.

基因分为显性和隐性两种。显性基因凌驾于隐性基因之上,其性状特征能在孩子身上体现出来。隐性基因则隐没在显性基因之下。要显示隐性基因所携带的特征,必须在一组的两条染色体上都有该隐性基因的存在。也就是说,孩子必须从父母双方那里遗传该隐性基因。比如,棕色或黑色的头发、棕色的眼睛都是显性特征,而金发碧眼则是隐性特征。这就意味着,孩子出生要金发碧眼,就必须从父母双方那里都获得携带这些特征的基因。

金发基因正在消失,这种说法背后隐藏的理论,就在于金发基因是隐性的,最终将被越来越多的棕发人群的显性基因所压倒。在当今现代的社会,跨越地理和文化疆界的移民越见普遍,因而金发人群再也不能够生活在孤立的区域去和金发伴侣生下金发宝宝,这一事实情况更加支持了金发正在消失的观点。

除了这样解释金发变少的原因,另外还有一个说法,就是因为人们总认为金发非常有吸引力,很多长着棕黑色头发的人将自己的头发染成了金色。这样,很多看起来是金发的人其实是黑发,他们携带的是黑发的显性基因。这样就模糊了携带隐性金发基因的实际人数。

是事实还是虚构?

天然的金发真会消失吗?科学家们非常清楚,隐性基因将会长期存在。除非一种基因能阻止人类的生存或者繁衍,不然基因是不可能消亡的,只会一代代传下去。金发基因当然不存在威胁种族繁衍的危险,因而天然的金发或者金发基因也不可能消失。而且,即便不同人种间的通婚减少了表现出金发基因的人数,科学家们还是强调,这并没有减少该基因的存在。除非隐性的金发基因由父母双方传给下一代,不然出生的孩子不可能长出天然的金发,但是这并不意味着金发基因不再存在。

相关资源

www.answers.com/topic/recessive-gene-2 该网址解释了隐性基因,还包括针对人类的举例,以及孟德尔的豌豆遗传实验。

《命运之屋里的机遇:遗传的自然进程》,霍顿·米夫林,2001 年。本书包含一系列自然进程的文章,关于细胞生物和分子生物的连续和中断。作者描述了遗传性测定,以及显性基因、隐性基因分别对人类发展造成的影响。

《欢迎来到基因组:基因的过去、现在和将来之读者指南》,威利出版社,2004 年。本书有彩色插图,简单易懂,描绘了人类基因的成分和人类 DNA 的蓝图。

《白化病的动物》,达比·克里克出版社,2004 年。这是一本儿童读物,适合于 9~12 岁的小读者,他们想了解在白化病的动物身上,隐性基因起到了什么作用。本书包括一张词汇表,还有一些参考书目供孩子们学习隐藏在遗传特征背后的基础科学。

Easter Bunny

The Easter Bunny, an enduring symbol of the Christian holiday of Easter, has its origins in the old pagan celebrations of the arrival of spring. Early Christian missionaries noted that the pagan celebrations of spring occurred at the same time as the resurrection of Christ, so they incorporated the pagan beliefs into the Christian holiday to foster conversions to Christianity.

The Symbol of the Hare

Depending on the local tradition or beliefs of individual tribes, the spring festivals included different, although similar, rituals. The rites of spring were often joyous raucous festivals celebrating the rejuvenation of plants and vegetation as well as the conception and birth of both animals and human babies. The animal symbol of fertility, the hare, was considered sacred to the spring goddess in many cultures. In other tribes, it was believed that the goddess Eastre had the ability to change into a hare because fertility symbols were so sacred to her. Anglo-Saxon mythology states that Eastre changed her pet bird into a hare, and the hare, retaining some of its bird-like characteristics, laid brightly colored eggs to entertain the children.

Other stories claim that the awakening wild birds of the forest laid colorful eggs, and during the spring festivals people would hunt the eggs, bringing them back in baskets as offerings to the spring goddess.

The Symbol of the Egg

The egg symbol begins even earlier than the hare tradition. In fact, the egg has been associated with fertility and other rites accompanying the vernal equinox for so long that it is difficult to pinpoint the actual roots of the tradition. Ancient Romans and Greeks looked upon eggs as symbols of fertility, birth and abundance and the Romans believed that all life began with an egg. Even today Greeks dye Easter eggs red to symbolize the renewal of life in the spring (and the blood of Christ) and green to represent the new foliage appearing after the dormant winter season. In addition, in more recent times, some people dye their eggs in pastel colors, perhaps to signify the rainbow, another sign of hope and rebirth. To complete the ritual, many celebrants view the eating of the colored eggs during the holiday as a visible wish for increased fertility and prosperity in the coming year.

Regardless of the individual customs, the two universal symbols for spring for pre-Christian Europeans were the hare and the egg. This leads to the modern concept of the Easter Bunny.

The Modern Easter Bunny
United States

The Easter Bunny as it is known today in the United States is a direct descendant of an Easter tradition that appeared around the beginning of the 16th century in Germany. This story, first described in German literature in the 1500s, describes the Oschter Haws (Easter Hare) who would lay colored eggs. Children would make nests in their hats or bonnets before Easter, but only

复活节兔子

复活节兔子,是长期以来基督教复活节的一个象征,起源于古代异教徒对于春天到来的庆祝。早期的基督传教士注意到,异教徒是在基督复活的同一时间庆祝春天,因此他们将异教徒的信仰融合进复活节,以使他们改而信仰基督。

兔子的象征

基于各部落的当地传统和信仰,同为庆祝春天的节日却有着相似但不完全相同的仪式。这个欢腾的节日不但庆祝各种植物复苏,而且也庆祝动物和人类的受精及宝宝的出世。兔子作为多产的动物象征,在很多文化中被看成是春天女神的圣物。而在其他部落,人们则相信,女神伊斯特拥有一种魔力,可以变幻为一只兔子,因为对她来说,这多产的象征真的太神圣了。盎格鲁撒克逊的神话则认为,伊斯特把自己的宠物鸟变成了兔子,因而还保留一些鸟的特性,能够产下明亮的彩蛋,让孩子们高兴。

另外有些故事则强调,是森林中醒来的野鸟下了彩蛋。在节日期间,人们找寻这些彩蛋,把它们装在篮子里带回家,作为献给春天女神的贡品。

彩蛋的象征

彩蛋作为节日的象征,比兔子开始得更早。事实上,彩蛋长期以来就让人联想起旺盛的繁殖力以及伴随春分而来的其他仪式,因此,想要明确指认出这项传统的根源是非常困难的。古罗马人和古希腊人把蛋看成是生命繁殖、出生和丰收的象征,而且罗马人则认为所有的生命皆始于一只蛋。直至今日,希腊人还把复活节蛋染成红色,以象征春天里生命的轮回(也象征耶稣所留下的鲜血);染成绿色,以展现萧条的冬季过后新叶再现的生机。不但如此,近年来一些人用彩色颜料绘制彩蛋,也许是为了表现象征着希望和重生的彩虹。一些主持礼仪的教士认为,为了让礼节完整,在节日期间把彩蛋吃掉,就是亲眼能见的一种希望,希望来年更加繁荣兴旺。

尽管各地有各地的风俗,基督教创立之前,在欧洲两样东西是春天最常见的象征,那就是兔子和彩蛋。这就形成了现代人对复活兔的观念。

现代复活兔

在美国

在德国,大约16世纪初就出现了复活兔,传到美国后流传至今,仍然作为复活节的一项传统内容。16世纪德国的文学作品中首先出现了这样的故事,描述的复活兔能够下彩蛋。复活节来临之前,孩子们在帽子里做窝,但复活节早上,只有好孩子的帽子里才能发现彩蛋。想来复活兔是等孩子们不注意或者睡着了,才跑出来下蛋的。复活兔的光临,

good children would find colored eggs in their nests on Easter morning. Supposedly, the Easter Hare would lay the eggs when the children were not looking or were asleep. The arrival of the Easter Hare began to assume the same significance as the arrival of the Christkindl (Santa Claus) on Christmas Eve.

German settlers brought the legend of Oschter Haws with them when they arrived in the 1700s in what is now Pennsylvania Dutch country.

By the 1800s the Easter Hare had become the Easter Rabbit and had spread beyond the German settlements into the rest of the nation. The simple nests prepared by children in their hats or bonnets gave way to elaborate Easter baskets and as the Easter Rabbit became a soft fluffy Easter Bunny, families began to include chocolates, candies and money in the baskets. In Germany, too, the original home of the Easter Rabbit, edible Easter bunnies made of pastry and sugar began to appear in the mid-1800s.

Although not widely celebrated in the United States until after the Civil War in the 1860s, the Easter Bunny and Easter basket tradition have now grown into a major children's holiday ritual, comparable to that of Santa Claus and his Christmas gifts. Some children leave out carrots for the Easter Bunny similar to leaving milk and cookies for Santa Claus on Christmas Eve. Many families have expanded the Easter basket treats to include small gifts—sometimes even a live baby bunny—along with candy and other goodies. The notion of finding a basket filled with colored eggs has been replaced by an Easter egg hunt, in which the children search for colored Easter eggs, wrapped candy and small ornaments that have been hidden ahead of time.

There are also Easter egg rolls, races in which children run in parallel lanes, pushing an egg through the grass with a long-handled spoon. Easter egg rolls are often conducted by community groups and civic organizations, but the most famous one in the United States takes place on the South Lawn of the White House sponsored by the President and First Lady of the United States. Originally, the egg roll was held on the grounds of the United States Capitol, but after the roll in 1876 damaged the Capitol grounds, President Rutherford B. Hayes moved the festivity to the White House lawn.

The Easter Bunny in Other Countries

Australians do not view rabbits in a positive light. When rabbits were introduced into Australia, they quickly created an ecological disaster and are, therefore, considered pests. For this reason, the Australians have replaced the Easter Bunny with the Easter Bilby, a native marsupial. Australians sell chocolate Easter Bilbies and feature Easter Bilbies in ads for the holiday.

In France and Belgium, Easter eggs are an integral part of the holiday, but they are not laid by bunnies. Rather, the eggs are dropped from the sky by Easter bells. This derives from the Christian Easter tradition of silencing the church bells on Good Friday in deference to Christ's death and then ringing the bells again on Easter morning to signify the resurrection. The silent church bells are portrayed as flying bells that travel to Rome on Good Friday and then fly back on Easter morning, filled with eggs to be dropped.

Resources

www.easterbunny.com. This site provides information on commercial and religious aspects of the Easter Bunny and the Easter holiday.

www.professorshouse.com/family/holidays/history-easter-bunny.aspx. Website provides the history of the Easter Bunny.

就像圣诞前夕圣诞老人的光临一样,意义重大。

18世纪一些德国人移居到现在的宾夕法尼亚州荷兰郡,带来了复活兔的传说。

到19世纪为止,复活兔已经声名远扬,不仅限于德国移民,而且传播到了美国的其他地方。孩子们在帽子里建造的简陋小窝,被精致的复活篮取代;复活兔几经发展已经成为毛茸茸蓬松松的复活兔;大人们开始把巧克力、糖果和零钱也放进复活篮。同样的,在德国这个复活兔的故乡,19世纪中叶,出现了用面粉和糖制作的、可供食用的复活兔。

尽管在19世纪60年代的内战发生以前,复活兔和复活篮的传统并没有在美国广泛庆祝,但如今还是发展成为孩子们的一个重要节日庆典,堪与圣诞老人和圣诞礼物媲美。一些孩子会给复活兔留下些胡萝卜,这种做法和在圣诞前夕给圣诞老人留下些牛奶和曲奇饼简直异曲同工。有的人家在复活篮里放进更多的好东西,范围扩大到包括一些小礼品——有时甚至是一只活的兔宝宝——还有糖果,等等。以前孩子们乐于发现满满的一篮彩蛋,但是后来又发展成自己找寻彩蛋。孩子们自己搜寻预先藏好的彩蛋、包装好的糖果还有一些小巧的装饰品。

还有一项复活节"滚蛋"游戏,就是孩子们并排赛跑,用一把长柄勺子将一只彩蛋推过草地。滚蛋游戏经常都是社区和市政组织的,但是全国最有名的当属在白宫的南草坪上举行的滚蛋游戏。该游戏由美国总统和第一夫人赞助。起初,这项游戏是在美国国会大厦的地面举行,但是1876年的那场游戏破坏了地板,此后,拉瑟福德·伯查德·海斯总统就将这项传统游戏移到了白宫的草坪上。

复活兔在其他国家

澳大利亚人并不认为兔子带有积极的意义。兔子被引进澳大利亚后,很快就造成了一场生态灾难,因而澳洲人觉得兔子有害无益。正是由于这个原因,澳洲人将复活兔换成了复活比尔贝,这是当地一种有袋的动物。澳洲人出售巧克力制成的复活比尔贝,并用比尔贝来做节日的广告宣传。

在法国和比利时,彩蛋是复活节内在的一部分,不过不是复活兔下的,而是从天空中的复活钟里面落下的。这种说法起源于基督教复活节的一个传统:耶稣受难日,为了哀悼基督的死亡,教堂的钟声都沉默了,到了复活节早上,钟声才再次响起,以纪念基督的复活。根据人们的描述,在耶稣受难日,沉默的钟飞向罗马,而到了复活节早上,又飞了回来,里面装满的彩蛋,便从空中落下。

相关资源

www.easterbunny.com 该网址提供复活兔和复活节商业、宗教方面的信息。

www.professorshouse.com/family/holidays/history-easter-bunny.aspx 该网址提供复活兔的发展历史。

Eleven

Flowers in the Sick Room

There are many negative superstitions that persist about flowers in the sick room, even when scientific facts disprove these beliefs. Many of these stories are cultural or indigenous to certain nationalities and have been retold for so long they have become traditions.

Common Negative Beliefs about Flowers

Probably the most common superstition about flowers in the sick room is the belief that the flowers, either cut or growing as a plant, deplete the oxygen in the room, thereby depriving the patient of necessary oxygen to recover from illness. While this is an old superstition that has been proven to be erroneous, many people still believe that this is true.

In addition to the air quality question, there are also beliefs about taking flowers home or leaving them behind in the hospital. Many believe that when ill or injured patients are well enough to go home, they should leave all flower arrangements and potted plants behind rather than take them home. By taking plants home, the patients are making themselves vulnerable to a relapse and a subsequent return to the hospital in a short period of time.

Flower Color Taboos

In the United Kingdom, some people object to mixing red and white flowers in a bouquet to be delivered to an ill patient. This combination of colors supposedly may cause the death of a patient in the same or a nearby room, although not Flowers in the Sick Room necessarily the patient for whom the flowers are intended. As a rule, red flowers are believed to be lucky in that the color red signifies blood that, in turn, symbolizes life. However, combining red and white flowers symbolizes blood and bandages, which carry a negative connotation. Therefore, many well-wishers refuse to send a bouquet of red and white blooms and many patients refuse to accept an arrangement using these two colors.

Allergic Reactions

Despite the long-held views about the negative effects of flowers and plants in the sick room, there really is no reason to fear an adverse impact of flowers and plants on someone who is ill. There is one exception to this, however: if a patient is known to be allergic to a plant or flower or exhibits allergic symptoms-sneezing, coughing, breathing difficulties, rash—then placing flowers in his or her sick room is indeed detrimental. When this happens, the plants are usually sent home with a family member or disposed of in some other way.

Positive Effects of Flowers in the Sick Room

There has been research into the link between flowers or plants and positive effects on persons who are ill or recovering from illness or injury. In short, flowers make people happy, which, in turn, translates into a faster recovery. It is a well-known fact that anxiety, depression and agitation inhibit recovery from illness, and flowers seem to reduce all of these negative responses to illness.

Flowers also promote a positive mood among people in a room and thus increase a sense of sharing. Studies have shown that a warm, friendly interaction among patients, medical staff and visitors is conducive to recovery. Flowers promote a sense of satisfaction and boost emotional well

病房里的
鲜花

关于病房里的鲜花，长期以来就存在着很多负面的迷信观点，尽管科学事实已对其提出反证。很多故事对于一些民族来说是属于本土文化的，一直以来反复提起，就成了传说。

关于鲜花常见的负面观点

针对病房里的鲜花，最普遍的迷信观点，可能就是认为，无论是剪下来的花枝还是正在生长的植物，都能耗用房间里的氧气，进而致使病人缺乏身体复原所必需的氧气。当然这只是个古老的观点，如今已经证实是有误的，然而很多人仍然宁可信其有。

除了空气质量的问题，还有一些观点，追究到底应该把花带回家，还是留在医院里。很多人相信，病人痊愈以后，他们应该把鲜花和盆栽留在医院，而不该带着回家。如果带回家去，病人很快就容易旧病复发，接着重返医院。

鲜花颜色的禁忌

在英国，一些人反对将红色和白色的花扎成一束送给病人。这样的搭配也许会导致同室或者附近的某个病人死亡，而未必是接受鲜花的那个人。普遍认同的观点是，红花能带来好运，因为红色象征着血液，也就象征着生命。不过，把红花和白花包在一起，却象征着血和绷带，这让人感觉很不好。因此，满心祝福的人们是不愿送出一束红白相间的鲜花的，同样，很多病人也不愿收到由这两种颜色构成的花束。

过敏反应

尽管长期以来，病房里的鲜花和植物在人们看来具有负面效应，事实上并没有理由担心鲜花和植物会对病人产生不良影响。不过有个特例：如果知道病人对某种植物或鲜花过敏，或者表现出过敏症状——打喷嚏、咳嗽、呼吸困难、出疹子——那么在这个病人的房间里摆放鲜花就的确不好。发生这种情况的话，病房的植物通常由家人送回去，或者以其他的方式处理掉。

鲜花的正面效果

正在生病或者还未完全康复的人，他们会受到鲜花或植物的正面影响吗？简而言之，鲜花使人感到愉悦，这样就加速了病情的复原。众所周知，焦虑、沮丧或者过于激动能够减缓病情恢复，而鲜花似乎能够减少这些不利因素。

而且鲜花还能够改良病房里的气氛，这样就增强了病人之间的相互认同感。研究显示，病患者、医护者和探病者之间，如果相互交往得温暖而友好，非常有利于病情恢复。鲜

being, both of which contribute to a speedier recovery.

Colors that Improve Health

There have also been studies that show the positive health effects of different colors. Chinese practitioners, in particular, believe that flowers of certain colors affect different parts of the body. For example, red roses boost energy because red has the longest wavelength, which stimulates the adrenal glands to increase energy. The yellow lightwaves of sunflowers stimulate the brain, increasing alertness. The purple shades of irises affect the part of the brain that regulates sleep patterns and eliminates worries and fear. One component of purple, blue, triggers the release of melatonin in the brain, which promotes sound sleep, and thyroxin, a thyroid hormone that regulates metabolism. The green color of plants is relaxing, slowing the respiratory mechanism and the beating of the heart. The violet of lilacs curbs hunger, improves metabolism and triggers the secretion of endorphins, natural substances in the brain that promote relaxation and reduce stress. And the color orange strengthens the immune system, preventing allergic reactions and the digestive system, promoting healthful digestion.

Many cultures attach significance to flower bouquets and plants that incorporate colors that promote health and well-being. And while this may appear to be a myth, research and eyewitness accounts substantiate the fact that flowers and even certain colors, have a positive effect on health.

Flowers and Seniors's Health

In a study conducted in 2000, researchers at Rutgers University discovered that senior citizens who receive fresh flowers or flowering plants show a distinct improvement in their health. Specifically, flowers decrease depression and increase happy moods in senior citizens. In addition, flowers improve the memory and recall ability of seniors who tend to be forgetful. More than three quarters of seniors who received flowers during an illness scored high on a memory test compared to those who did not receive flowers. And finally, flowers encouraged sharing and companionship: Seniors who received flowers reached out to visitors and medical staff to share their flowers and to express their pleasure.

Air Purifiers

Finally, there is evidence that flowers can improve a room's atmosphere by purifying the air. A hospital room, in particular, often contains air pollutants introduced by the use of chemical cleaners and sanitizers. However, certain houseplants or flowers can filter out different toxins and improve the air quality in the room. Plant leaves absorb and destroy airborne chemicals, and a plant's roots break down air pollutants and use them for food and energy. By producing cells that are resistant to the air pollutants, plant roots clean the air in a natural way.

The best houseplants for cleaning the air the green way:

peace lily	English ivy	Boston fern	rubber plant
corn plant	bamboo palm	gerbera daisy	chrysanthemum

Resources

The Encyclopedia of Bach Flower Therapy, Healing Arts Press, 2001. This book describes the Bach flower therapy developed by the English physician Edward Bach more than 60 years ago. Bach therapy identifies 38 individual distilled flower essences that affect mental and emotional health. This book covers the history, philosophy and background of the therapy and then provides a detailed discussion of each essence.

The Essential Flower Essence Handbook: Remedies for Inner Well-Being, Hay House, 1998. This book discusses ways in which flowers and their essences can be instrumental in achieving emotional and mental health.

花让人产生满足感,激发幸福感,而这些情感对疾病的加速痊愈功不可没。

促进健康的颜色

也有研究显示出不同颜色对健康的正面影响。尤其是中国的医生相信,鲜花的各种特殊颜色对人体不同的部位产生作用。例如,红玫瑰能激发能量,因为红色波长最长,能够刺激肾上腺增强能量。向日葵发出的黄色光波能刺激大脑提高警觉。鸢尾植物紫色的阴影能对一部分大脑产生影响,这部分大脑调节睡眠,消除不安和恐惧。蓝色是紫色的组成成分,能够激发大脑释放褪黑素和甲状腺素。褪黑素可以改善睡眠,而甲状腺素可以调节新陈代谢。植物的绿色能让人放松,减缓呼吸的代谢和心跳。丁香花的紫色抑制饥饿感,加强新陈代谢,促使内啡肽的分泌。内啡肽是大脑中的一种天然物质,使人放松心情,减轻压力。而橘色能够加强免疫系统,预防过敏反应;也能够加强消化系统,促进饮食健康消化。

不少文化认为,花束和植物,如果颜色搭配得当,能够促进健康、改善心情,就非常有意义。尽管听起来也许有点神乎其神,但研究和亲历者的报告恰恰证实了鲜花,甚至一些颜色,对健康就是能起到积极的作用。

鲜花与老年人的健康

2000年进行的一项研究中,罗格斯大学的研究人员发现,老年人如果收到鲜花或者开花的植物,身体状况就会明显改善。尤为显著的是,鲜花让他们减轻了沮丧感,增加了快乐的心情。而且,老年人通常是很健忘的,鲜花却能够增强他们的记忆力。假如在病中收到鲜花,超过3/4的老年人,记忆测试会比没有收到鲜花的人得分高。最后一点,鲜花还能使人乐于分享、结交朋友:老年人一旦收到了鲜花,就更愿意和来访者及医护人员交流,请他们欣赏自己的花,也向他们表达自己的快乐。

空气净化剂

最后,有证据显示,鲜花还能够净化空气,改善室内的空气质量。尤其是在医院里,由于使用含有化学成分的清洁剂和消毒剂,空气中存在大量污染源。不过,一些盆栽植物或鲜花可以过滤掉各种有毒物质,改善室内的空气质量。植物的叶子能够吸收或分解空气中的化学物质,而植物的根部能够分解空气中的污染源,利用其当肥料。而且根部会产生一种细胞,能够抵御空气中的污染源,这样自然就净化了空气。

用绿色途径净化空气的最佳盆栽:

和平莲(白掌)	英国长春藤	波士顿肾蕨	印度橡胶树
玉米秧	雪佛里椰子	非洲雏菊	菊花

相关资源

《贝曲花疗法百科全书》,医术出版社,2001年。本书描述了英国内科医生贝曲在60多年前发明的花疗法。该疗法明确指出38种鲜花所蒸馏出来的香精可以对精神健康和情感健康产生影响。本书讲述了有关该疗法的历史、哲学和背景,接着提供了每种香精的详细讨论。

《鲜花香精要方手册:维护内在健康》,千草出版社,1998年。本书探讨了在得到情感健康和心理健康的过程中,鲜花和香精起到辅助作用的方式。

Fountain
of Youth

The story of the search for the Fountain of Youth is proof of the claim that human nature never changes. More than 500 years ago, the Spanish explorer Juan Ponce de Leon (1474 to1521) led an expedition to the New World to search for the Fountain of Youth just as modern-day seekers pursue their quest for the ever-elusive prolongation of youthful attributes.

Ponce de Leon never found the Fountain of Youth, but he did find what is now Florida and claimed it for Spain. He also conquered what is now Puerto Rico and governed that island for 3 years.

The Promise of the Fountain of Youth

Half a millennium ago there were many legends about the Fountain of Youth in both Europe and the New World. Its waters supposedly had properties that would restore youth to old people and heal all kinds of illnesses of those who bathed in it or drank it.

Alexander the Great had purportedly heard of a Fountain of Youth and had searched for it— to no avail—in the Himalayas in eastern Asia. There were also fables about a similar legend among the Polynesians whose tradition placed the Fountain of Youth in Hawaii.

European medieval folklore described a wonderful spring that contained the Water of Life in the Garden of Eden. These legends placed the Fountain of Youth in the Far East, so later explorers decided to search there for the special spring. And, as history showed, the early Spanish explorers thought the New World was the Far East.

Indian tribes in Central America and the West Indies thought the fountain was in the Bahamas. The Spanish King Ferdinand and other Europeans had heard that the Fountain was on the Bahamian island of Bimini, located just off the Florida coast near what is Miami today. So that is the area where the Spanish explorers, most notably Ponce de Leon, focused their search. Contrary to popular belief, Ponce de Leon was not searching only for the Fountain of Youth to restore his youth. Rather, like most European explorers of his time, he was equally interested in amassing gold, wealth and riches.

Ponce de Leon's Quest

As he searched for the Fountain of Youth, Ponce de Leon had several adventures along the way. Born into a noble family in Santervas de Campos in Spain, Ponce de Leon served in the court of King Ferdinand V and Queen Isabella I, the Spanish monarchs who sponsored Christopher Columbus'expeditions to the New World. In 1493 Ponce de Leon sailed on Columbus's second expedition to America and landed on Hispaniola, an island in the West Indies between Cuba and Puerto Rico and now partitioned into the countries of Haiti and Dominican Republic. Ponce de Leon left Hispaniola in 1508 to explore what is now Puerto Rico where he discovered gold. By 1509 he was governor of Puerto Rico and one of the wealthiest and most powerful Spaniards in the New World.

Having heard from the Caribe Indians, a tribe living in the West Indies, that the Fountain of Youth could be found in on the Bahamian island of Bimini, Ponce de Leon, under the auspices of King Ferdinand yet at his own expense, equipped an expedition to search for Bimini. In 1513 he

青春泉

寻找青春泉的传说证实了人类的本质从未发生改变。500多年以前,西班牙探险家庞斯·德·里昂(1474~1521年)远征到了新大陆,去搜寻青春泉,正如当代的谋求者寻觅那隐于迷雾中永葆青春的方法。

庞斯·德·里昂最终也没能够找到青春泉,但他确确实实发现了现在的佛罗里达州,当时就宣布其属于西班牙。他还征服了现在的波多黎各,并统治该岛长达3年。

青春泉的预言

大约500年前,在欧洲和新大陆上有很多关于青春泉的传说。泉水似乎有着某种神奇的魔力,只要在里面洗个澡,或者喝点泉水,就可以让老人回复青春,还能够包治百病。

据说,亚历山大大帝听说了这个青春泉,就派人到东亚的喜马拉雅山去搜寻——结果是白费工夫。波利尼西亚人也有相似的传说故事,不过他们一直认为青春泉在夏威夷。

欧洲中世纪的民间传说描绘了伊甸园中一眼奇妙的清泉,里面都是生命之水。这些传说认为青春泉在远东,因此后来的探险家们决定到远东地区寻找这眼特殊的泉水。而根据历史记载,早期的西班牙探险家们把新大陆当成了远东。

中美洲和西印度群岛的印第安部落认为青春泉应该在巴哈马群岛。西班牙国王斐迪南以及其他欧洲人听说青春泉就在巴哈马群岛的比米尼岛上,位置离佛罗里达的海岸不远,靠近现在的迈阿密。于是那儿就成了西班牙探险家们锁定的目标,其中最为著名的当属庞斯·德·里昂。与主流观点相左的是,庞斯·德·里昂并不仅仅探求使人返老还童的青春泉。和当时大多数欧洲探险家一样,他同时致力于搜集黄金等财富。

庞斯·德·里昂的探索

在搜寻青春泉的过程中,庞斯·德·里昂曾几次遇险。他出生在西班牙桑特瓦斯草原上的一个贵族家庭,曾在国王斐迪南五世和女王伊莎贝拉一世的宫廷伺奉。这两位是西班牙的元首,曾赞助哥伦布去新大陆探险。1493年,庞斯·德·里昂就曾随哥伦布的第二次探险,来到了美洲,在伊斯帕尼奥拉岛登陆。该岛位于西印度群岛,夹在古巴和波多黎各当中,现在已分属海地和多米尼加共和国。1508年,他离开该岛前往现在的波多黎各,并在那儿发现了黄金。1509年,他就成了波多黎各的统治者,同时也是新大陆上最有钱有权的西班牙人。

西印度群岛居住着克里比印第安人。庞斯·德·里昂从他们口中听到,青春泉就在巴哈马群岛的比米尼岛上。于是他在斐迪南国王的授意之下准备了一次向比米尼岛的远足,不过所有费用都是靠他自己解决。1513年,他登上了好几个岛屿,最终从佛罗里达州

visited several islands and eventually landed on the Florida coast. Thinking Florida was an island, Ponce de Leon claimed it for Spain and gave the land its name, which means many flowers in Spanish. Ponce de Leon continued to search for the Fountain of Youth in Florida, but never found it. Nevertheless, a spring in St. Augustine, Florida, is identified today as one that Ponce de Leon discovered in his quest for the Fountain of Youth.

St. Augustine

In April of 1513 the expedition of Ponce de Leon sighted and landed on the coast of Florida in the vicinity of what is today St. Augustine. His claim to this land was the beginning of the 300-year struggle between England and Spain for domination of the New World. At the time, however, Ponce de Leon and his crew were looking for riches and a Fountain of Youth.

Today in St. Augustine there is a tourist site labeled the Fountain of Youth located only a few hundred yards from the spot where Ponce de Leon actually stepped onto the beach. Fortunately for St. Augustine's tourist industry, there is a natural spring at this site.

Visitors to the Fountain of Youth in St. Augustine can study the exhibits depicting the history of the area, read about the discovery of the Fountain of Youth and buy bottles of the famous water from the Fountain.

Modern Fountains of Youth

As further proof of the allure of the promise of the Fountain of Youth, in 2006 master illusionist David Copperfield claimed he found the Fountain of Youth on one of the four tiny islands he purchased in the Exhuma chain of the Bahamas. Copperfield stated that dead foliage and dying insects are restored to full life and vigor after coming in contact with the water in his island's Fountain of Youth. So far he has made no claims about the restorative qualities of the water for humans, but he supposedly has hired biologists and other scientists to study the water's effect on human life.

On the other hand, today's Fountains of Youth reach into the realms of biology and chemistry to offer youthful reinvigoration. Clinics and spas all over the world offer hormonal treatment and cellular therapy to restore youth and health. Growth and sex hormones promise a return to the vigor and well-being of youth. Starting with a basic unit of life, the cell, many scientists are trying to reinvent perpetual youth. Whether or not these options work cannot be yet known; there have not been adequate studies of long-term use or possible adverse effects to judge safety and effectiveness. The most anyone can say at this point is that some of these regimens are helpful, many are merely cosmetic, but all reflect the intense interest in remaining perpetually young.

Resources

*www.fountainofyouthflorida.com/history.html.*This Website provides a history of Florida's Fountain of Youth as well as details about the early history of Florida. The information is arranged by centuries.

Juan Ponce de Leon: And the Search for the Fountain of Youth, Chelsea House Publication, 2000. This book, aimed at children aged 9 to 12 years old, describes the political, economic and social forces that inspired early explorers. Focused on Ponce de Leon, the book includes lively, engaging writing, illustrations, maps and historical documents.

www.newworldexplorersinc.org/fountainofyouth.pdf. Misconceptions and myths related to the Fountain of Youth and Juan Ponce de Leon's 1513 Exploration Voyage by Douglas T. Peck.

的海岸登陆。他以为佛罗里达是个岛,就宣布该岛为西班牙所有,并且给它起了佛罗里达这个名字,在西班牙语中意思是很多花。接下来,他就在佛罗里达寻找青春泉,可惜始终未能如愿。不过,在佛罗里达的圣奥古斯丁有一眼清泉,被确认是当年庞斯·德·里昂在搜寻青春泉的过程中发现的。

圣奥古斯丁

1513年4月,庞斯·德·里昂的探险队发现了佛罗里达州,并从其海岸登陆,登陆的地方就在现在的圣奥古斯丁附近。他宣布了这块土地属于西班牙,从此英国和西班牙之间为了争夺新大陆的统治权,展开了长达300年的斗争。而当时,庞斯·德·里昂及其手下要寻找的不过是财富和青春泉。

今天,圣奥古斯丁有一个旅游景点就打着青春泉的旗号,位置和当年庞斯·德·里昂踏上海滩的地方仅距几百码。这个地段竟然有一眼天然的清泉,这对圣奥古斯丁的旅游业来说,简直走运极了。

如果你到圣奥古斯丁的青春泉去游玩,陈列的展品会向你倾诉当地的历史。你可以阅读青春泉探索的相关资料,还可以购买几瓶闻名遐迩的青春泉水。

现代的青春泉

青春泉的希望到底有多吸引人,更进一步的证据就是:2006年,魔术大师大卫·科波菲尔宣布,他曾在巴哈马群岛艾克斯修玛一带购买了四个小岛,在其中的一座岛屿上,他就发现了青春泉。科波菲尔声称,枯死的树叶或濒死的昆虫只要碰到他岛上的青春泉水,就立刻重新焕发生命的光彩。目前他还没有说明这泉水对人类是否具有同样的魔力,不过估计他已经聘请了生物学家和其他科学家,研究泉水对人类生命的效用。

另一方面,现在说到青春泉,总会涉入生物和化学的研究领域,目的在于能够返老还童。为了恢复青春和健康,世界各地的诊所和温泉浴场都提供激素疗法或细胞疗法。生长激素和性激素都能使人重现活力,展示青春的最佳状态。很多科学家从细胞,也就是生命的基本单位出发,试图让人类永葆青春。以上提到的这些方法,到底能否起效还是个未知数。目前,针对这些方法的长期应用,或者可能存在的副作用,还没有充分的研究。因而无法断定是否安全,是否有效。关于这个方面,人们最多可以说,这些保养的方法中,一部分是确有裨益的,但大部分还是治标不治本。不过,这一切都折射出,永葆青春始终是人们强烈的愿望。

相关资源

www.fountainofyouthflorida.com/history.html 该网址提供了佛罗里达州的青春泉的历史,还有佛罗里达州的早期详尽的历史。网页内容按世纪先后排列。

《庞斯·德·里昂:寻找青春泉》,切尔西出版社,2000年。本书定位为9~12岁的小读者群,描述了激发探险家们外出探险的政治因素、经济因素以及社会力量。除了以庞斯·德·里昂为重点,还包括了生动传神的描写、插画、地图和历史文件。

www.newworldexplorersinc.org/fountainofyouth.pdf 这篇文章由道格拉斯·佩克撰写,内容包括人们对青春泉的错误观点和神话传说,以及庞斯·德·里昂在1513年经历的那次探险航程。

Thirteen

Four-Leaf Clovers

The four-leaf clover has traditionally been considered a sign of good luck. Many legends claim that each leaf is a symbol: the first leaf stands for hope; the second leaf represents faith; the third leaf symbolizes love; and the last leaf stands for luck. Other old traditions attribute different interpretations to the leaves of the clover: one leaf for fame; the second for wealth; the third for faithful love; and the fourth leaf for health. Despite their origins, all of the symbols point to some kind of good fortune.

History of the Four-Leaf Clover Legend

No one knows exactly when or why this myth started, but most scholars agree the first literary reference to the luck of the four-leaf clover occurred in the early 17th century. In 1620 The English writer, politician and merchant, Sir John Melton, wrote:"If a man walking in the fields find any four-leaved grass, he shall in a small while after find some good thing."

Yet there is almost universal agreement that references to the symbolism of the four-leaf clover began long before the 17th century.

Druids

The importance of the four-leaf clover predates Christianity, beginning in the pagan period when four-leaf clovers were Druid symbols. The Druids, dating to the 2nd century B.C. during the time of the ancient Celts of Gaul, Britain and Ireland, were members of the Celtic religious order of priests, soothsayers, judges and poets who dominated Ireland and most of Western Europe. The Druids elevated the four-leaf clover to the level of a religious charm that was supposedly powerful enough to ward off evil spirits and bad luck. Part of the significance of the four-leaf clover was the belief in its power to help its bearer spot and identify evil witches and demons. Those fortunate enough to see evil spirits thus had the opportunity to protect themselves.

These Celtic priests also believed that possessing a four-leaf clover helped them see good spirits, such as fairies and wood sprites. This captured the imagination of the people, especially children, who searched for four-leaf clovers so that they could see into the magical world of benevolent spirits.

The word Druid is of Celtic origin. Scholars believe that the word arises from the same linguistic source as the Greek word drus, meaning an oak. Combining drus with the Sanskrit word wid, meaning to know or see, produces the word Druid. Legend has it that the oak tree was sacred to the Druids and that the term Druid was bestowed on educated men and women possessing what was known as oak knowledge or oak wisdom.

There are Irish legends that tell of the meetings of Druids in sacred oak forests to conduct business, settle disputes and socialize. At the end of these gatherings, the Druids would perform the ritual of searching for four-leaf clovers and mistletoe, both of which they believed to be rare. The Druids believed that mistletoe would ensure a peaceful home and health and that four-leaf clovers would help them see otherwise hidden demons and evil spirits. The power of the lucky four-leaf clover would then allow them to prevent the demons from casting evil spells. Together with the mistletoe, the four-leaf clover would help ensure a harmonious home until the next

四叶幸运草

　　四叶草一直以来都被视作幸运的象征。很多传说都提到,每一片叶子分别具有其自身的含义:第一片代表希望,第二片标志信念,第三片象征爱情,最后一片代表运道。有些古老传说对于这四片叶子也有不同的解说:第一片是荣誉,第二片是财富,第三片是忠诚的爱情,第四片是健康。尽管源头各异,所有的标志都指向好运气。

四叶幸运草传说的历史

　　没人确切知道这个传说开始的时间和原因,但是大部分学者都认同,文学作品中最早出现四叶幸运草是在 17 世纪初期。17 世纪 20 年代英国作家、政治家兼商人约翰·梅尔顿爵士写道:"走在田间如果发现四片叶子的草,很快便有好运降临。"

　　不过人们普遍认为,四叶草作为幸运的象征,早在 17 世纪之前很久就已经开始了。

德鲁伊教徒

　　四叶草的重要象征比基督教开始得更早,异教徒的时候,四叶草是德鲁伊教的标志物。早在公元前 2 世纪,高卢、英国和爱尔兰都是古凯尔特人,德鲁伊教徒是凯尔特宗教中的传教士、占卜家、法官和诗人阶层,他们统治着爱尔兰和西欧的大部分地区。德鲁伊教徒将四叶草上升到宗教魅力的高度,说它具有足够的力量,能够避开恶魔和厄运。四叶草还有另外的魔力,可以帮助其拥有者指认出邪恶的女巫和魔鬼。人们如果足够幸运可以看到恶魔,自然就有机会保护自己。

　　这些凯尔特传教士同时还相信,只要拥有四叶草,就能够看到善良的神灵,比如仙女或者森林精灵。这一点让人们浮想联翩,尤其是孩子们,都想找到四叶草,看看仁慈的神灵住在怎样的一个魔法世界。

　　德鲁伊(Druid)这个单词起源于凯尔特语。学者们相信,这个单词和希腊语中的 drus(意为橡树)语源相同。Drus 和梵文中的 wid(意为知道或者看见)结合起来,就构成了 Druid。根据传说,对于德鲁伊教徒来说,橡树是神圣的,Druid 这个术语适用于受过教育的人,他们拥有所谓的橡树知识,或者说,橡树智慧。

　　爱尔兰有的传说描绘了德鲁伊教徒在橡树林里碰头,并商讨生意、解决纠纷或往来交际。在碰头会结束以后,他们通常会举行寻找四叶草和槲寄生的仪式。他们相信,这两种东西都非常罕见。他们也相信,拥有槲寄生,就能让家庭和睦、家人健康;拥有四叶草,则能够看到本来隐身的邪魔和恶鬼。这样,四叶草的魔力赋予他们力量,阻止魔鬼给他们下魔咒。如果同时拥有四叶草和槲寄生,家庭就能和睦团结,直到他们在神圣的橡树林里再一次碰头。

assembly in the sacred oak forest.

Irish and Christian Symbolism

The four-leaf clover did not diminish in significance with the advent of Christianity in Ireland and other Celtic strongholds.

Legend has it that Eve plucked one of the plentiful four-leaf clovers upon her eviction from the Garden of Eden as a memento of her days in Paradise. More common, however, was the association of the four-leaf clover with the Holy Trinity of Christianity. The Irish believed that one leaf each represented, respectively, the Father, the Son and the Holy Spirit. The fourth leaf represented God's grace.

The Four-Leaf Clover and the Shamrock

Is there a connection between the Irish shamrock and the four-leaf clover plant? The common four-leaf clover is a deviation from the usual three-leaf plant of the clover Trifolium repens. The normal three-leaf plant is the original shamrock plant of Ireland and the unofficial state symbol. Occasionally, the shamrock produces a fourth leaf and that rarity is considered lucky. In fact, botanists claim that only about one in ten thousand shamrock plants will naturally mutate to produce a four-leaf clover.

Therefore, there is, indeed, a direct connection between the Irish shamrock and the four-leaf clover in that the same clover species produces the shamrock and the plant that the rest of the world designates the lucky four-leaf clover. An additional tie between the shamrock and four-leaf clover plant is that the word shamrock originates from the old Gaelic (Irish) word seamrog, which means little clover.

Botanical Characteristics of the Four-Leaf Clover

Part of the luck associated with the four-leaf clover derives from some of the advantages it offers as a plant or crop.

There are approximately 300 different species of clover in the Trifolium family. The cultivation of clover started in Europe, but the plant has spread around the world, thriving in temperate climates. Farmers like to grow clover because livestock will readily eat it, either as it grows in the field or dried as hay. The plants themselves provide calcium, phosphorus and protein, all staples of a sound diet for animals.

In addition to its advantages as a diet staple for livestock, clover improves the soil in which it grows. The dense growth of clover slows erosion by holding the soil together. Clover also releases nitrogen into the soil and makes other nutrients more available to the next crops grown on that same plot of land. So clover's contribution to the soil as well as to the diet of domesticated animals is an additional piece of luck for farmers who plant clover in their fields.

Resources

The Four-Leaf Clover Kit (Mega Mini Kits), Running Press Book Publishers, 2003. This book/kit contains a 32-page book with facts and trivia about the four-leaf clover as well as seeds for growing clover so that the reader can search for his or her own four-leaf clover. The box containing the kit and book also serves as a planter.

Wishing: Shooting Stars, Four-Leaf Covers and Other Wonders to Wish Upon, Running Press Book Publishers, 1996. This book emphasizes the act of wishing on symbols and other mythical representations. It is a collection of stories about wishing customs, including, among others, wishing on a lucky four-leaf clover.

爱尔兰人和基督教徒的象征

在爱尔兰和其他凯尔特人集中居住的地方,基督教出现以后,四叶草的象征意义并没有消失。

传说夏娃被逐出伊甸园之时,从大量的四叶草中扯了一棵,以纪念在天堂度过的那些日子。不过,更为常见的说法是,四叶草和基督教义中的三位一体有所关联。爱尔兰人相信,每一片叶子分别代表圣父、圣子和圣灵。而第四片叶子则代表上帝的慈悲。

四叶幸运草和三叶浆草

爱尔兰的三叶浆草和四叶幸运草之间有着必然的联系吗?普通的四叶草是寻常的白三叶草的变种。而常见的三叶草则是最初的爱尔兰三叶浆草,并且是这个国家的非官方标志。三叶浆草偶尔会长出第四片叶子,正因为稀少,才被看成幸运。事实上,植物学家宣称,三叶浆草仅有万分之一的几率会自然变异,成为四叶草。

因此,爱尔兰的三叶浆草和四叶幸运草之间的确有着直接的联系——三叶浆草和世界上其他能够长出四叶草的植物,属于同一种苜蓿科。两者之间另外还有一层关联就是:三叶浆草(shamrock)这个单词就源自古爱尔兰语中的 seamrog(意为小四叶草)。

四叶草的植物学特征

四叶草能给人带来好运,与其植物特性的优势不无关联。

苜蓿科包括大约 300 种不同的四叶草。四叶草的培育始于欧洲,不过已经流传到全球,在温和的气候中蓬勃生长。农民都喜欢种植四叶草,因为不管是长在地里的还是加工成干草的,家畜都喜欢吃。四叶草自身能提供钙、磷和蛋白质,这些都是动物健康饲料的组成成分。

除了能给家畜提供上乘的饲料,四叶草还可以改善它所生长的田地里土壤的质量。如果密集种植四叶草,土壤能够相互靠拢,减缓侵蚀。四叶草还会向土壤释放氮元素,为这块土地上下一季的作物提供更多的养料。因此,四叶草对土地的贡献,及其对家畜饲料的贡献,在种植四叶草的农夫看来,无疑是额外的好处。

相关资源

《四叶草装备》,奔跑图书出版社,2003 年。本书(或装备)包括一本 32 页的图书,上面记载了关于四叶幸运草的事实情况和一些细微琐事,还有一些可种植的四叶草种子,这样,读者可以寻找到属于自己的四叶幸运草。包装书籍和装备的盒子,也可以当做花盆来用。

《心愿:流星、幸运草及其他可以许愿的奇妙场景》,奔跑图书出版社,1996 年。本书重点讲述了对象征物许愿的行为,以及其他一些神话传说。书中有很多描绘许愿习俗的故事,包括对四叶幸运草许愿。

Fourteen

Friday the 13th

To understand why so many people consider Friday the 13th to be an unlucky day, you have to understand the fears and superstitions surrounding both Friday and the number 13.

Myths about Friday

Friday is considered by many to be an inauspicious day to begin a new venture of any sort. The most popular reason for Friday's image of bad luck or misfortune dates to Christ's crucifixion, which took place on a Friday. However, the belief that Friday is an ill-fated day may also go back even farther to ancient Norse mythology and the practice of offering sacrifices to the goddess Friga (or Freya) from whom the day takes its name.

Over time there have been other reasons given to explain why Friday is such bad luck. Supposedly, Adam and Eve's eating the forbidden fruit in the Garden of Eden; Abel's murder; Noah's flood; the destruction of the Temple of Solomon; the confusion of tongues episode at the Tower of Babel; and Herod's massacre of innocent children all took place on a Friday. More recently, Western literature began to refer to Friday as an unlucky day in the 14th century when Chaucer stated in his *The Nun's Priest's Tale* that "on a Friday fell all this mischance."

Although many think that the beliefs about Friday's unlucky reputation began in pre-Christian times, in reality Friday was actually considered lucky by pre-Christian Germanic tribes. The Norse goddess Friga was the goddess of marriage and fertility and in this role became associated with happy events such as marriage and childbirth. However, as Christianity began to reach out to the Germanic peoples, Christian missionaries reformulated Friga as a pagan witch who perpetrated evil activities. One story even ties Friday to the unlucky number 13. Supposedly, the witches of the north observed their Sabbath on the sixth day of the week by gathering in a cemetery. On one occasion, Friga herself appeared before the group, which numbered 12 and gave them one of her sacred cats, which reformed the group into a pagan witches's coven of 13. Traditionally, every official coven since then has numbered exactly 13.

Despite how the legend of Friday's being unlucky developed, there are still unwritten constraints about what can be done on a Friday. Never embark on a journey, a marriage or a new venture on Friday. In particular, do not set sail— fishermen say: Friday's sail always fails. Do not move into a new home or start a new job. Do not get up from a sick bed on a Friday. Avoid butter churned and eggs laid on a Friday. Never turn a mattress on Friday. And the sad admonition: A child born on a Friday faces misfortune from the beginning.

Myths about the Number 13

People who suffer from triskaidekaphobia, the fear of the number 13, are numerous. Belief in the unlucky aspects of this number is one of the most tenacious superstitions.

The origins of the connections between the number 13 and bad luck are often unclear, but the most common connection is the Last Supper in which Judas Iscariot, who later betrayed Jesus, was the 13th person to sit down at the table. A slightly different interpretation states that Jesus was the 13th person to join the group at the Last Supper. This superstition, however, has been questioned by those who point out that Jesus was always the 13th person when he accompanied

13日星期五

要理解为什么那么多人认为 13 日星期五是不幸的一天，你就不得不先弄清楚围绕星期五和 13 这个数字的恐惧和迷信。

星期五的传说

很多人把星期五看成不吉利的一天，从这一天不管什么样的冒险都要开始了。星期五给人一种厄运来临的印象，最普遍认同的原因，可以追溯到耶稣的受难，因为那就发生在星期五。不过，人们相信星期五注定是倒霉的一天，这种观点也可以追溯到更早的古斯堪的纳维亚神话故事，以及向主司爱与美的女神弗蕾娅供奉牺牲品的做法。而弗蕾娅(Friga / Freya)正是星期五 (Friday)这个单词的词源。

当然在历史上，也有其他原因可以解释为什么星期五如此不幸。人们认为，亚当和夏娃在伊甸园里偷食禁果；该隐谋杀弟弟亚伯；"诺亚方舟"中的大洪水；所罗门圣殿的毁灭；巴别塔下语言的混乱；希律王屠杀无辜的孩子——所有这些事件都发生在星期五。时间推近一些，西方文学将星期五视作不幸的一天，始于 14 世纪。当时乔叟在他的《修女院教士的故事》中如此叙述："在一个星期五，所有的不幸降临了。"

很多人认为，人们早在基督教创立之前就把星期五和灾难联系在一起；但事实上，当时的日耳曼部落竟认为星期五能带来好运。斯堪的纳维亚的女神弗蕾娅主司婚姻和生殖，在这样一个角色中，她总是和幸福的事件关联着，比如结婚、生子。可是，基督教渗入日耳曼民族以后，基督传教士把弗蕾娅重新定位成一个异教徒的女巫，专门经营邪恶的勾当。有一个故事甚至把星期五和倒霉的数字 13 结合在一起。想来北方的女巫们就在一周中的第六天，聚集在墓地庆祝她们的午夜聚会。偶尔地，弗蕾娅自己也会出现在这 12 个女巫面前，拿出她的一顶圣帽交给她们，于是就构成了异教徒的"13 女巫聚会"。据说，从此，每一次正式的女巫聚会人数都是不多不少 13 个。

不去理会星期五厄运的这种传说是如何发展而来的，仍然有一些不成文的限定，哪些事情在星期五是做不得的。在星期五，绝不要开始一段行程、一个婚姻或者一次新的冒险。尤其不要航行——渔夫们说：星期五的航程永远不会成功。不要搬进新屋子，也不要开始新的工作。不要从病床上爬起来。还要避免星期五搅拌的黄油、星期五下的蛋。永远也不要在星期五翻床垫。还有个悲哀的警告：孩子如果出生在星期五，则从一开始就要面对不幸。

13 这个数字的传说

很多人对 13 这个数字非常恐惧。他们相信这个数字会给人带来厄运，这简直是最根深蒂固的迷信了。

人们把数字 13 和厄运联系在一起，究竟有着什么样的起源，并不十分清楚。不过最常见的解释就是，"最后的晚餐"中，背信弃义的犹大，是第 13 个在餐桌边坐下的人。他后来背叛了耶稣。还有一种版本，略微有些出入，说的是，最后的晚餐时，耶稣正是第 13 个

the 12 disciples and, therefore, must have eaten with them many times before the Last Supper.

Even earlier in pre-Christian times, a similar story is told about a banquet at Valhalla, the great hall of the Norse gods. Twelve gods were invited to dine, but Loki, the evil god of mischief, crashed the party, bringing the total number of the dinner guests to 13. Loki predictably created havoc and the Norse tribes decided that 13 dinner guests were bad luck.

This notion that 13 people sitting down together to dine was unlucky persisted and led to many superstitions. References in the early 18th century warned that 13 people sitting down together at a meal was an omen that one of them would die within a year. Many thought that the victim would be either the first person to rise from the table or the last person to sit down. Consequently, this led to a common practice of everyone sitting and standing at the same time before, during and after a meal.

The fear of the number 13 expanded beyond groups of 13 people to the number in general. Anything designated by the number 13 was avoided. Many hotels do not have rooms with the number 13 or even a 13th floor. Some municipalities shun street names containing the number 13. And having 13 letters in your name is considered unfortunate (think about Jack the Ripper, Charles Manson, Theodore Bundy and Jeffrey Dahmer).

Myths about Friday the 13th

Considering all the fears and superstitions about Friday and the number 13, what could be more fearful than a combination of both? Known as paraskevidekatriaphobia, or fear of Friday the 13th, this union of the sixth day of the week with the unlucky number 13 may be the most prevalent superstition in the United States, particularly since it can occur from one to three times a year. Some people refuse to go to work on Friday the 13th and many will not schedule a wedding on that day.

Irrational or not, this fear afflicts even normally sensible people. For example, both Herbert Hoover, an engineer by training and Franklin Delano Roosevelt, a well-educated person, suffered from triskaidekaphobia and paraskevidekatriaphobia. Roosevelt especially was superstitious about the number 13. There are reports that he summoned aides or staff members to fill in at the last moment if the guest list for a luncheon or dinner party fell to 13 people.

A Modern Legend?

Citations about Valhalla, pagan witches and the Last Supper notwithstanding, many scholars cannot document specific references for these superstitions before the late 19th or 20th century. In fact, the earliest mentions are generally considered citations in newspapers around 1908 and 1913. Consequently, many think this particular belief is a 20th century phenomenon that has been hyped by the media. Even so, many people still fear Friday the 13th and it just may be logical to stay at home, lock the doors and take no chances.

Resources

A Dictionary of Superstitions, Cassell, 1995.

www.urbanlegends.com. A compendium of urban legends, myths and folklore.

www.snopes.com. This urban legends reference page contains a list of the 25 hottest urban legends.

参与进来的人。不过，针对这样的说法，就有人提出问题了：耶稣和他的 12 个门徒在一起时，他不总是第 13 个人么？因此，在最后的晚餐之前，他应该已经无数次地和他们共同进餐过了。

甚至在更早的，基督教尚未创立之前，曾有个相似的故事，也是关于一次宴会，地点在斯堪的纳维亚众神的神堂，也就是瓦尔哈拉殿堂。12 位神灵受到邀请前往赴宴，但邪恶的火神洛基闯进了进去。这样，宾客的数目就成了 13 个。洛基不出所料地毁坏了这次宴会，因而斯堪的纳维亚部落认定，13 位宾客终将带来厄运。

13 个人坐在一起吃饭就会招致不幸，这样的观点不但一代代留存下来，而且还引出了很多迷信。18 世纪初，相关资料就警告说，如果 13 个人坐在一起吃饭，不出一年，其中有一个人就会死去。而且很多人认为，死掉的那个人，可能是第一个站起来的，也可能是最后一个坐下去的。自然而然，这就衍生出了一个普遍的做法：就餐前、进餐中或者就餐后，大家一起坐下，一起站起。

对于数字 13 的恐惧，渐渐超出了 13 个人组成的团体，扩大到 13 这个抽象的数字。任何事情，只要指向数字 13，人们就会避之不及。很多宾馆没有带 13 的房间号，甚至没有 13 楼。一些城市回避含有 13 的街道名。如果人名里面含有 13 个字母，也被看成是不吉利的——你想想，碎尸狂杰克（Jack the Ripper）、查理·曼森（Charles Manson）、连环杀手泰奥德·邦迪（Theodore Bundy）、变态杀人犯杰弗里·达马（Jeffrey Dahmer），这些人的名字可都是 13 个字母。

13 日星期五的传说

既然星期五和数字 13 都让人感到恐惧，那么还有什么比这二者结合更为恐怖呢？因此，13 日星期五，也就是一周的第 6 天刚好碰上倒霉的 13 号，就成了美国最普遍的迷信。更为火上浇油的是，这样的日子一年当中竟会出现 1~3 次。有的人在这样的日子不去上班，也有很多人不在这一天安排婚礼。

不管是不是毫无理由，即便是平时很理智的人也会受到这种恐惧的影响。例如，无论是训练有素的工程师赫伯特·胡佛，还是颇有教养的富兰克林·D.罗斯福，都害怕数字 13，更害怕 13 日星期五。罗斯福特别迷信于数字 13。有资料显示，如果他宴请的宾客正好是 13 个人，那么在最后一刻，他就会叫上副官或工作人员填补。

一则现代传说？

尽管引用了瓦尔哈拉殿堂、异教徒女巫和最后的晚餐等传说，在 19 世纪末或者 20 世纪，很多学者仍然无法用一定的资料来论证这些迷信。事实上，最早提到这些迷信的，普遍认为是在 1908~1913 年的报纸上。自然，很多人把这看成是一个 20 世纪的现象，遭到了媒体的炒作。即便如此，很多人依然害怕 13 日星期五。这一天，他们情愿留在家里，锁上门，什么事情也不干。

相关资源

《迷信辞典》，卡塞尔出版社，1995 年。

www.urbanlegends.com 简要描述了一些都市传说、神话和民间故事。

www.snopes.com 这是都市传说的参考网址，提供了 25 则最热门的都市传说。

Fifteen

Ghosts of Cornwall

Cornwall, the most southeastern tip of England on the English Channel, has been called one of the most haunted places in the British Isles. This designation seems appropriate, since many towns and villages in Cornwall boast about a ghost or supernatural event being an integral part of their history.

Whether or not any are true, they are such fascinating tales.

Wellington Hotel

The Wellington Hotel, a well-known old coaching inn at Boscastle, is the site of ghostly inhabitants. Several years ago the owner of the hotel looked up from his work at the reception desk to see a man walking past the desk. The hotelier was surprised to note that the man wore the boots, frock coat and ruffled shirt of an 18th century coachman and had tied his hair into an old-fashioned ponytail. The figure did not look ghostly or transparent, but the innkeeper was shocked to see the figure disappear into and through the wall. The hotelier was even more shocked to learn that an employee had also seen the same figure on several occasions.

The coachman is not the only ghost to frequent the Wellington Hotel. Another employee reported the sight of a ghostly apparition floating across a landing and disappearing through the wall of a guest room. Many believe that this is the ghost of a young woman who flung herself from the hotel's tower because of an unrequited love affair. Others have reported a dark figure drifting down the stairs and disappearing into the basement late at night. Perhaps he is the ghost of a man believed to be murdered at the site years ago.

Jamaica Inn

The Jamaica Inn at Bolventor purportedly has two ghosts. The first ghost is that of a murdered sailor who is reputed to sit on a wall outside Jamaica Inn. There have been several sightings, always in the same location.The second ghost is a man wearing a long coat or cloak and a tricorn hat, who was seen by a couple of guests as he walked toward them. Like the 18th century coachman of the Wellington Hotel, this man disappeared through the wall of a bedroom wardrobe.

Dozmary Pool

Dozmary Pool on Bodmin Moor in central Cornwall has a place in history as supposedly being the body of water into which Sir Bedivere threw the legendary sword Excalibur after King Arthur was mortally wounded. Dozmary Pool is also reputedly the home of the Lady of the Lake of Arthurian legend who gave Arthur the sword Excalibur and then became guardian of Excalibur after Arthur's death.

Dozmary Pool, the name of which means drop of sea, was said to be bottomless and connected to the sea by a tunnel. This has become impossible to prove, since Dozmary Pool dried up in 1869.

The Pool is also associated with the legend of Jan Tregeagle who supposedly was assigned to empty it.

Jan Tregeagle Legend

Jan Tregeagle, who actually existed as a 17th century magistrate who made his fortune by

---

66   www.ahstp.net

康沃耳郡的鬼魂

康沃耳郡位于英国最东南端，英吉利海峡之上。据说，整个不列颠群岛就属这个地方闹鬼最厉害。这一说法似乎并不为过，因为在康沃耳郡，有不少城镇或者乡村就曾经传出过鬼魂或者超自然事件。

不管是真是假，这些故事绝对引人入胜。

威灵顿宾馆

威灵顿宾馆位于博斯堡，是一座著名的历史悠久的马车旅馆。这儿就是鬼魂居住的地方。几年前，旅馆的老板正在前台忙碌着，不经意抬起头来，就看见一个人走过前台。他惊讶极了，因为那个人穿的靴子、长外衣以及饰有褶边的衬衫，都是18世纪马车夫的装束，而且他的头发还扎成了一个古老的马尾辫。那人看到起来并不像鬼，身体也不是透明的，但是旅馆老板看到他消失在墙面并且穿墙而过时，简直惊呆了。而且后来有一名员工说他曾好几次见到相同的身影，老板听后更是惊恐万分。

那个马车夫并不是唯一一个经常光顾威灵顿宾馆的鬼魂。另一名员工报告说，他曾看到一个幽灵漂浮过楼梯平台，穿过一间客房的墙壁就不见了。很多人认为那是一个年轻妇女的鬼魂，由于自己的爱情只有付出没有回报，她就从宾馆的楼顶上跳了下来。还有人汇报说，深夜有个黑色的人影从楼梯上飘荡下来，闪进了地下室。那可能是一个男人的鬼魂，人们相信，数年之前，他就在这个地方被谋杀了。

牙买加客栈

牙买加客栈位于博尔文特，据说有两个鬼魂。一个是被谋杀掉的水手，总是坐在客栈外的一堵墙上。曾有人好几次看到，每次都在同一个位置。另一个也是男的，穿着长长的外套或者斗篷，戴着一顶三角帽，曾有一对住店的夫妇看到他向他们走来。和威灵顿宾馆那18世纪的马车夫十分相像，这个男人也是穿过卧房里衣柜的墙壁，就不见了。

多姿玛丽湖

康沃耳郡中部的博德明高沼有一个多姿玛丽湖，里面有块地方据说曾是个贮水池，当年，亚瑟王受了致命伤，他身边的贝狄威尔骑士就在这里将传说中的"湖中剑"沉入了水底。在亚瑟王的传说中，多姿玛丽湖据说是湖中仙子的家园，她将"湖中剑"赠给了亚瑟王，而亚瑟王死去之后她又成了"湖中剑"的守护神。

多姿玛丽这个名字的意思是滴下的海水，据说这个湖深不可测，而且有一条隧道通向大海。不过自从1869年多姿玛丽湖干涸之后，这件事情就无法证实了。

多姿玛丽湖还和简·切基格尔的传说有所关联，他被指派的任务就是把湖水舀干。

简·切基格尔的传说

简·切基格尔是生活在17世纪的一个地方官员，据说他横行乡里，从博德明高沼

obtaining land illegally, is said to haunt Cornwall from the Bodmin Moor to Lands End at the southwestern tip of Cornwall.

Tregeagle's woes began after his death when a legal dispute arose about some land he had appropriated by forging some papers. During the trial, one of the parties called for Tregeagle to take the witness box. Among disbelieving laughter, a shadowy figure of Jan Tregeagle took the stand and testified that he had indeed deceived the defendant. The defendant won the case, but dealing with Tregeagle became an issue. The court decided to assign him a task to occupy him for all of eternity and he was charged with emptying the bottomless Dozmary Pool with a leaking shell.

Years later a storm blew in over Dozmary Pool and Tregeagle escaped pursued by demons. To ease his suffering at the hands of the demons, local priests and exorcists as well as several saints set him to new tasks, again to occupy him forever. Eventually, he was assigned the job of sweeping the sand from a cove into a bay at Lands End. Supposedly, he is still toiling at this task and his tormented cries can be heard in the winds from Bodmin Moor to Lands End.

The Ghost of Charlotte Dymond

Charlotte Dymond was found murdered near Camelford on April 14, 1844. Her lover, a disabled farmhand named Michael Weeks, was hanged at Bodmin for the murder, even though he was probably innocent.

Since that time, on the anniversary of her death Charlotte Dymond has been seen in the area, wearing a long gown, a red shawl and a silk bonnet. The story has become famous through The Ballad of Charlotte Dymond by the Cornish poet Charles Causley.

Flo at Duporth Manor

According to an old legend, the ancient manor house at Duport has been haunted for more than 100 years by a nun known as Flo. A century ago there were reports that she was striking matches and unlocking cabinets in various rooms at the manor.

The manor house has been torn down and the site is now the home of a local tourist attraction. Yet, according to employees at the site, Flo is still there. People staying there report that they have become aware of a presence in the rooms with them. The children's merry-go-round on the playground turns by itself even when there is no wind. Appliances and cooking equipment have been heard operating without any human assistance, only to stop when someone says, "Thanks, Flo, we do not need anything today."

Blackways Cove

A small inlet called Blackways Cove along the northern coast of Cornwall is said to be haunted either by the spirits of shipwrecked sailors or the ghost of a local man who thought he had been cheated. The man, a younger son of a farmer who had left his entire estate to his older son, had been so overwhelmed with anger that he determined to take revenge on his older brother. One night he slipped into the farm and set fire to the buildings, destroying the entire property. Only in the morning did he learn that his older brother had died the day before and had left the entire farm to him. The few stones remaining after the fire can still be seen in Blackways today.

Resources

Celtic Lore & Legend: Meet the Gods, Heroes, Kings, Fairies, Monsters and Ghosts of Yore, New Page Books, 2005. This book centers on tales and stories of the heroes, gods, ghosts, witches and fairies.

www.connexions.co.uk/html/ghosts.htm. Cultures, myths and legends of Cornwall.

到康沃耳郡西南端的天涯海角,无处不见他的踪影。他通过非法占有土地,牟取了大笔的财富。

有关切基格尔的灾难是从他去世后开始的。对于他伪造文书从而占用土地一事,当时就出现了法律纠纷。在审判过程中,一方提出要求,要切基格尔坐到证人席上去。伴随着一阵难以置信的狂笑,简·切基格尔模糊朦胧的身影出现在证人席上,承认自己的确欺骗了被告。被告赢得了这场官司,但是如何处置切基格尔却显得异常棘手。法官决定指派一项永远也无法完成的任务给他,就是让他用一只漏水的贝壳舀干深不可测的多姿玛丽湖。

数年之后,一场大风暴吹进了多姿玛丽湖,切基格尔趁机逃跑,后面跟着魔鬼。为了让他免于遭受魔鬼的折磨,当地的牧师和驱魔者,还有几名圣人派了新的任务给他,还是要让他永远无法完成。最终,他的任务是在天涯海角将沙子从一个小海湾扫进另一个海湾。据说,他至今仍在辛苦地干着活儿。从博德明高沼到天涯海角,刮风的时候,你还可以听到他的痛哭声。

夏洛特·戴蒙德的鬼魂

1844年4月14日,在卡姆尔福德附近,人们发现夏洛特·戴蒙德被人谋杀了。她的情人名叫迈克尔·维克斯,是个残疾人,在一个农场上打工。因为这起谋杀案,他被绞死在博德明,尽管他也许是无辜的。

从此以后,每到夏洛特·戴蒙德的周年祭日,就会有人看到她出没在这一带,穿着一件长袍,围着红色的披肩,戴着丝质的帽子。这个故事也通过康沃耳诗人查尔斯·考斯理的"夏洛特·戴蒙德民谣"而声名远扬了。

德泊施庄园的弗洛

根据一个古老的传说,德泊施的古老庄园里,100多年来一直在闹鬼。那是一个名叫弗洛的修女。一个世纪以前,就有人发现她在划火柴,或者打开各房间里的橱柜。

这座庄园已经废弃,现在是当地的一个旅游景点。不过,据那儿的工作人员说,弗洛还在。下榻于此的人也报告说,他们注意到房间里有什么东西和他们在一起。操场上,孩子们的旋转木马没风的时候也会自己转起来。厨房里,那些用具没有人使用也会发出声音,一定要有人说:"弗洛,谢谢你。今天我们什么也不要。"这种声音才会停止。

布拉克威士海湾

布拉克威士海湾是个小海湾,位于康沃耳郡的北海岸。据说那里闹鬼的不是沉船水手们的魂灵,就是当地一个男人的鬼魂。那个男人是一个农夫的小儿子,以为自己被欺骗了。农夫将所有的房产留给了大儿子,小儿子满怀愤怒,决心要报复哥哥。一天晚上,他溜进农场,一把火烧掉了所有的房屋,毁掉了整个农场。到了第二天早上,他才发现,哥哥已经在前一天就死了,并且将整个农场留给了他。至今,在布拉克威士,人们还可以看见寥寥几块火中剩下的石头。

相关资源

《凯尔特传说:与往昔的神灵、英雄、国王、仙女、怪物和鬼魂碰面》,新页图书,2005年。本书的重点是英雄、神灵、鬼魂、女巫和仙女的传说故事。

www.connexions.co.uk/html/ghosts.htm 康沃耳郡的文化、神话和传说。

Common
Health Myths

Everyone wants to do whatever it takes to improve or maintain his or her health, even when science and medical technology disprove long-held beliefs about health.

Following is only a sampling of commonly held beliefs about health.

Eating Chocolate Causes Acne

Anyone who has ever been a teenager has heard the admonition to avoid eating chocolate if he or she wants to avoid acne. This precaution, however, is unnecessary. A definitive study conducted more than 20 years ago disproved that chocolate causes acne.

What does cause acne then? The primary cause is hormones. That is why acne is such a problem for many teenagers—there is a normal surge of sex hormones during puberty. The increase in hormones causes an increase in oil produced by the oil glands in the skin. When the excess oil combines with dead skin cells and dirt, the skin's pores become clogged and attract bacteria, which cause pimples, blackheads and whiteheads. Pregnant women or women going through menopause may also develop acne temporarily when their level of hormones rises.

Eating chocolate then is not usually a factor at all. Some people are allergic to chocolate or to substances within chocolate or cocoa, which can cause breakouts. In these cases, avoiding chocolate is a prudent step. But except for those who are sensitive to chocolate, there is no reason to avoid eating chocolate in order to avoid acne.

Eating Carrots Improves Vision

Will eating more carrots really improve your vision? The simple answer is no. Studies have shown that carrots are rich in Vitamin A, which is important for eyesight, but a balanced diet, rich in all vitamins, provides enough nutrition for good vision.

There is some evidence, however, that a deficiency of Vitamin A and/or betacarotene, a nutrient that gives carrots their bright orange color and is used by the body to produce Vitamin A, may impair the ability to see in the dark. In this case, eating more carrots, or at least more foods with Vitamin A, may improve night vision.

The human body slows its conversion of beta-carotene to Vitamin A when it has enough Vitamin A for good health. When this happens, any extra beta-carotene consumed will more than likely turn the skin orange or yellow instead of improve vision. So eating more carrots will not be effective if the body's need for the vitamin is already being met.

Swallowing Chewing Gum Is Hazardous to Good Health

It takes 7 years for the body to digest swallowed chewing gum. Chewing gum is so sticky that, if swallowed, it causes the internal walls of the intestine to stick together. Fortunately, both of these beliefs are untrue.

Chewing gum is no different from anything else that is swallowed. It proceeds through the intestinal tract just as any other food would, eventually eliminated as waste in the same way as any other swallowed material. Granted, gum is indigestible, which means that the body cannot break it down into nutrients, so it passes through in the same condition as when swallowed.

In spite of this, some people may experience problems when they swallow gum. Chewing gum

健康神话

为了改善健康或永葆健康，每个人都愿意付出一切。尽管一些关于人体健康的观点长久以来为人们所相信，但科学和医技已经证实它们并不正确。

很多健康神话都为人们坚信，以下只是最常见的一小部分而已。

吃巧克力会长痤疮

任何人在十几岁的时候都会听到过劝诫：要是不想长痤疮，就不要吃巧克力了。可是，这样的警告，完全是空穴来风。一项20多年前的权威研究恰恰证实了，巧克力并不会导致痤疮。

那么，到底是什么引发痤疮的生长呢？最主要的原因就是激素。这就是为什么痤疮总是青少年的困扰——青春期，性激素通常会大量分泌。激素水平的增长就导致了皮脂腺分泌出大量的油。如果过多的油和死掉的皮肤细胞以及脏东西结合在一起，毛孔就会堵塞，就会滋长细菌，就引发了丘疹、白头和黑头。怀孕或更年期的妇女，如果激素水平升高，也会暂时生出痤疮。

因此，吃巧克力通常并不是引发痤疮的原因。有些人对巧克力过敏，或者对巧克力、可可里面含有的物质过敏，那样也能导致痤疮大量生长。在这种情况下，避免吃巧克力不失为谨慎的做法。但是除了对巧克力过敏的人，实在没有理由为了不长痤疮而不吃巧克力。

吃胡萝卜能改善视力

多吃胡萝卜真的能改善视力吗？答案很简单：不能。研究显示胡萝卜富含维生素A，而维生素A对视力非常重要。但是饮食均衡，全面吸收各种维生素，才能提供足够的营养，保持良好的视力。

然而，有证据显示，缺乏维生素A或β-胡萝卜素可能有损夜视力。β-胡萝卜素是一种营养成分，有了它，胡萝卜才显出鲜亮的橘黄色，人体也要利用它合成维生素A。缺乏这两种物质的话，多吃胡萝卜，或者至少多吃点含有维生素A的食物，就能改善夜视力。

一旦拥有足够的维生素A维持健康，人体就会减缓将β-胡萝卜素转化为维生素A。这时候，服用过多的β-胡萝卜素只能让皮肤泛出橘色或黄色，而无法改善视力。因此，如果人体所需的维生素已经足够，多吃胡萝卜并不能如你所愿。

吞入口香糖有害健康

口香糖如果吞入体内，完全消化要花7年时间。由于口香糖非常黏，如果吞入肚子，会将肠子的内壁粘连在一起。非常幸运，上面这两种观点都是错误的。

口香糖如果被吞到肚子里，和其他东西是没有什么分别的。它跟其他食物一样沿着肠道前进，最后也像其他被吞到肚子的东西一样作为粪便排出体外。人体无法消化口香糖，也就是说，人体不能将它分解成营养成分，因此它被排出体外时的状态还跟吞入体内时一样。

尽管如此，有些人吞下口香糖后，可能经历过一些麻烦。口香糖基本是由胶基（通常

basically consists of a gum base (usually a mix of natural and synthetic gums), softeners, flavors and sweeteners. The saliva dissolves everything but the gum base. However, some chewers may be allergic to the flavoring agents or the softeners. Even more common are reactions to the sweeteners, particularly sorbitol and mannitol, in sugarless gum. These ingredients can cause an upset stomach, gas or diarrhea in sensitive individuals.

Swimming after Eating Can Cause Cramps

Contrary to popular belief, waiting 30 minutes after eating before swimming is not necessary. The reason behind this admonition was that exercising after eating can cause possible stomach cramps that can lead to a decreased ability to swim and thus to possible drowning.

Some believe that digestion decreases the amount of blood flowing to the muscles because extra blood is needed in the intestinal tract to digest the food. While this may be true for those who eat a large, heavy meal and then engage in vigorous exercise, there seems to be little danger for those eating a normal meal and returning to the water. Most experts believe the body's blood and oxygen supply is sufficient for both muscles and digestion to function simultaneously.

Of course, it pays to be prudent. Sometimes swimming shortly after eating can cause heartburn or stomachache, in which case it is safer to rest before resuming the exercise. And, naturally, consuming large amounts of alcohol can impair both judgment and physical ability, so swimming may not be the best activity after drinking alcohol.

Basically, common sense should be the guideline for waiting or not waiting to swim after eating. If there are no problems, then the 30-minute waiting period is not necessary. And in fact, swimming or any exercise is not recommended on an empty stomach. Many health experts recommend a light snack before any exercise to boost the body's energy levels.

Wet Feet Can Cause a Cold

Cold are caused by germs—either viruses or bacteria. The germs are airborne, that is, they enter the body through the nose or mouth from the air. So wet feet cannot cause a cold.

There are many superstitions surrounding dangers leading to upper respiratory ailments, such as colds, flu or sinus infections. Some people believe going outdoors in cold weather without warm clothing can cause illness. Wet feet, wet hair and wet skin are often pinpointed as causes of pneumonia or respiratory infections, particularly in cold weather. How many mothers have wrapped their children in heavy coats, mufflers, hats with earflaps and boots in order to prevent colds and other illnesses? Yet they are not concerned about wet feet, hair or skin when the kids are swimming in the summertime.

The fact of the matter is that colds and other respiratory illnesses are caused by viruses and bacteria. While there may be some credence to the fact that enduring cold wet feet for a long period of time may lower the body's resistance to fighting off a germ or may reduce the body'temperature, wet feet do not cause colds.

Resources

www.cdc.gov/women/owh/myths. This Website from the U.S. government's Center for Disease Control (CDC) provides accurate and up-to-date information about health care and health care myths. The site provides several links, for example, to sites on cancer, diabetes, immunizations, smoking and reproductive health, that offer information on myths and facts.

www.ccohs.ca/headlines/text165.html. Canadian Health Network explores 10 myths about health.

是天然胶和合成胶的混合物)、软化剂、香精和甜味素构成的。唾液能溶解除了胶基以外的其他成分。但是,一些人可能对增味剂或软化剂过敏。更常见的情况是对甜味素有反应,尤其是无糖口香糖中的山梨醇或甘露醇。这些成分能让过敏的个体胃里不舒服,肠胃胀气,或者引起腹泻。

饭后游泳能导致抽筋

和人们普遍的想法恰恰相反,餐后等上 30 分钟再去游泳是不必要的。这一告诫背后的理由是:餐后锻炼可能导致胃部痉挛,这样游泳的能力下降,可能会溺水。

有些人相信,消化食物就减少了流向肌肉的血液,因为肠道需要额外的血液来进行消化。如果暴饮暴食了油腻腻的一餐,接下来又进行剧烈的运动,那么这种说法可能就是正确的了;但如果正常进餐,然后转回水中去游泳,则对身体没有害处。大部分专家认为,人体的血供和氧供可以同步保证肌肉活动和肠道消化。

当然,的确应该谨慎行事。有时候,刚吃完饭就去游泳可能导致胃灼热或胃疼。那样的情况下,稍事休息再开始锻炼会更加安全。另外,如果喝了很多酒,就会降低判断力和活动力,因此酒后游泳并非最佳选择。

基本上,一般的感觉应该是餐后是否立刻游泳的衡量标准。如果没有问题,就不需要等 30 分钟。而且事实上,专家们建议不要空腹游泳或进行其他锻炼。很多健康专家提议,在任何锻炼之前,吃一点点心,以提高身体的能量水平。

湿脚会引发感冒

感冒是由微生物引起的,可能是病毒,也可能是细菌。微生物可以在空气中传播,也就是说,微生物通过鼻子或嘴巴的呼吸就进入了人体。因此,湿脚是不可能引发感冒的。

按迷信观点,很多情况能引发上呼吸道疾病,比如感冒、流感或窦感染。有些人认为,冷天不穿保暖的衣服走到户外就会生病。湿脚、湿发、湿皮肤都被看成是肺炎或呼吸道感染的根源,特别是在冷天。为了防止感冒或其他疾病,有多少位母亲把自己的孩子包得严严实实的,厚外套、围巾、帽子、耳套、靴子,什么都用上了。不过夏天孩子们游泳的时候,母亲们并不在意他们的湿脚、湿发、湿皮肤。

事实情况是,感冒和其他呼吸道疾病都是病毒和细菌引起的。可能确有证据表明,双脚长时间又冷又湿,能够削弱机体对微生物的抵抗,也可能降低体温。但是湿脚本身并不会引发感冒。

相关资源

www.cdc.gov/women/owh/myths 该网址由美国政府的疾病控制中心提供精确、及时的卫生保健信息和健康神话方面的信息。该网址还提供了几个链接,比如,链接到癌症方面的、糖尿病方面的、免疫方面的、抽烟方面的和生育健康方面的网址,能够提供一些神话传说和事实情况。

www.ccohs.ca/headlines/text165.html 加拿大健康网,发掘了 10 个健康神话。

Seventeen

Holy Grail

The Holy Grail is best known in medieval legend as the cup used by Jesus at the Last Supper before his crucifixion and as the cup used to catch the blood flowing from Jesus during the crucifixion. Yet, despite this specific identification of the Grail, the Holy Grail embodies many ideas that are linked to ancient Celtic mythology and stories told by English, French and German authors.

Early History of the Grail

The Holy Grail has a different meaning each time it appears in mythology and literature. The story of the Grail begins with a tale related by early pagan Celts. The Celtic story tells of a cup or dish that endlessly provided food and drink for anyone who used it. Many scholars have identified parallels between medieval Welsh and Irish stories and tales of the Grail. There are old legends that describe magical plates or vessels that test the holder's worth or symbolize supernatural powers. In some of these stories, the Grail, whether it be a dish, platter or cup, has powers to create a never-ending supply of food or to raise the dead. Occasionally, a Grail story tells of the vessel's ability to determine the next king or ruler, simply because only a true monarch is capable of holding the Holy Grail.

On the other hand, some scholars think that the Holy Grail is solely a symbol of Christianity. In Christianity the Grail story begins with Joseph of Arimathea, a follower of Jesus Christ who used the Holy Grail as a cup to catch the blood flowing from Jesus during the crucifixion. Based on this legend of the Grail, these scholars link the Holy Grail to the Christian sacrament of Holy Communion.

Today the prevailing view is that the Holy Grail is a Christian symbol.

Joseph of Arimathea

Joseph of Arimathea, who caught the blood from Jesus' wounds during the crucifixion in the Grail, was later captured and imprisoned by the Roman occupation troops on the grounds that he was a follower of Jesus. According to the story, the Grail appeared to Joseph while he was in prison and, according to one version, fed Joseph for the 42 years of his imprisonment. After he was freed, Joseph and a group of Christians carried the Grail throughout the Holy Land, using it to serve the wine during communion services.

Later Joseph carried the Grail to Britain where he built a castle called Corbenic in which to store the Grail. Joseph and his descendants became guardians of the Holy Grail and served as overseers and rulers of Corbenic.

The Search for the Grail

The best-known legend of the Holy Grail centers on the search for the vessel, and the tales of the search revolve around the legends of King Arthur's Knights of the Round Table. According to the legend, the knights, gathered in the hall in King Arthur's castle for the feast of Pentecost, suddenly saw a vision of the Holy Grail suspended in midair. A group of knights then decided to search for the Grail throughout Britain.

During their search, the knights encountered danger and experienced exciting adventures,

圣　杯

在中世纪的传说中,关于圣杯最广为人知的,即是耶稣在最后的晚餐上使用了这个杯子,当他被钉死在十字架上时,也正是这个杯子盛接了从耶稣身上流出的鲜血。然而,尽管对于圣杯有着这样特定的认识,圣杯本身还体现着很多观点,这些观点联系着古代凯尔特神话和英国、法国以及德国的作家们所叙述的故事。

圣杯的早期历史

不同的时期圣杯出现在神话和文学作品中,代表着不同的含义。圣杯的故事始于早期凯尔特异教徒的一个传说。在这个凯尔特传说中,一个杯子或者是盘子吧,能够为任何使用它的人提供无穷无尽的饮食。很多学者认为,中世纪的威尔士和爱尔兰传说与圣杯的故事之间有着某种必然的联系。有些古老的传说描绘出神奇的杯盘,能够测试其主人的价值,或者象征着超自然的神力。在一些传说中,圣杯是盘子也好,碟子也好,杯子也好,总有魔力能够变化出无尽的食物,或者能够起死回生。偶尔还有这样的传说,讲述圣杯能够决定下一任的国王或统治者,仅仅因为唯有真正的君王才能够拥有它。

换一方面来说,一些学者认为,圣杯专门标志着基督教。在基督教义中,圣杯的故事起始于亚利马太的约瑟夫。他是耶稣基督的一个追随者,曾用圣杯作为容器盛接了耶稣受难时身上流出的鲜血。基于这个传说,这些学者就认为,圣杯和基督教的圣餐之间有所关联。

时至今日,最具影响力的观点认为,圣杯就是基督教的一个标志。

亚利马太的约瑟夫

亚利马太的约瑟夫,曾在耶稣受难时,用圣杯盛接了其伤口流出的鲜血。后来他受到了罗马占领军队的逮捕和关押,理由就是他信仰耶稣。根据这个传说,约瑟夫在狱中之时,圣杯就出现在他面前,而且有一个版本说,在他监禁期间,圣杯为他提供饮食长达42年之久。自由释放后,约瑟夫和一组基督教徒携带圣杯穿越圣地,圣餐的时候就用它提供美酒。

后来,约瑟夫带着圣杯来到了英国,并在那儿建了一座城堡,取名廓别涅克,就将圣杯保存在里面。约瑟夫和他的子孙后代从此就守卫着圣杯,同时也管理并统治着廓别涅克城堡。

寻找圣杯

有关圣杯的传说,最广为人知的,就集中在对它的寻找。而寻找圣杯的传说,则围绕亚瑟王的圆桌骑士传奇展开。根据这个传奇,圣灵降临节时,骑士们聚集在亚瑟王城堡的大厅中,突然就看到了圣杯的影像悬在半空中。于是一组骑士就决定踏遍英国去寻找圣杯。

在寻找圣杯的过程中,骑士们遭遇千难万险。以这样激动人心的经历为基础,就成就

which are the basis of the stories surrounding King Arthur and the Knights of the Round Table (see Chapter 22). During these events the knights discovered that only three knights—Galahad, Bors and Perceval—were morally suitable to complete the quest. These three, along with nine others from other countries, continued the search and finally entered Castle Corbenic. There they saw visions of Joseph of Arimathea as a priest and angels carrying the Grail and the spear that had pierced Jesus' side during the crucifixion. As the vision continued to emerge, a child appeared above the Grail and turned into bread. Simultaneously, Jesus emerged from the Grail and offered communion to the knights. The men interpreted the vision as proof that bread and wine were transformed into the body and blood of Christ. This became part of the Grail' legend and was referred to as the miracle of the Holy Grail.

The three knights then left Corbenic Castle and sailed away on a ship that also carried the Holy Grail. The ship carried the knights and the Grail to a distant city called Sarras and there, after Galahad died, Perceval and Bors watched the Grail ascend into Heaven. According to the legend, no one has seen the Holy Grail since that time.

The Grail In Literature

The legend of the Holy Grail was the inspiration for some of the best-known poetry and literature of the Middle Ages between approximately 1180 A.D. and 1240 A.D.. The earliest written account is generally acknowledged to be the French poem, *Conte del Graal*, translated as *The Story of the Grail*, by Chrétien de Troyes in the late 12th century.

For the next several years other versions of the story of the knights risking everything to acquire the Grail appeared in other Western European literature. Around the turn of the 13th century Robert de Boron wrote a verse entitled; *Joseph d'Arimathie*, which describes the story of the man who used the Grail to catch the blood from the crucified Christ. Another well-known piece was *Parzival* by Wolfram von Eschenbach written around 1220 A.D.. Two hundred years later the best-known of all the Grail legends in the English-speaking world, Sir Thomas Malory's *Morte DeArthur*, related the deeds of the Arthurian knights. While these tales differ in details and several points, all tell of the quest for the Grail by King Arthur's Knights of the Round Table.

In the 19th century, the story of the Grail reappeared in Alfred Tennyson's Arthurian cycle, *The Idylls of the King*. The German composer Richard Wagner produced his opera *Parsifal* based on the legend of the Holy Grail. And numerous modern books, movies and plays have turned to the ancient legend as their themes, including the movie *Python and the Holy Grail* in 1975.

Resources

The Grail Legend, Princeton University Press, 1998. The authors used the story of the Holy Grail to explain and illuminate the background of Christian culture. Beginning with the premise that the legend of the Holy Grail was based on an ancient Celtic symbol of redemption and eternal life, the authors show the Grail's relevance to modern life.

The Holy Grail: Imagination and Belief, Harvard University Press, 2005. The author of this book describes the history of the Holy Grail, beginning with Chrétien de Troyes's writings to the Catholic Church's interpretations to modern versions of the myth.

www.britannia.com/history/arthur/grail.html. Website containing information about Arthur and the Holy Grail.

了亚瑟王和圆桌骑士的传奇故事(参阅第22章)。经历了这些冒险事件,骑士们发现,他们当中只有3位——加勒哈德、博斯和帕西瓦尔——在道义上适合完成寻找圣杯的任务。他们3人,连同另外9个来自其他国家的人,继续寻找圣杯,最终进入了廊别涅克城堡。在城堡中,他们看到了一幅景象:亚利马太的约瑟夫是个牧师,天使们捧着圣杯,还有耶稣受难时刺入他侧身的长矛。这幅场景持续浮现,一个小孩出现在圣杯之上,并转化为一块面包。同时,耶稣从圣杯中浮现出来,向骑士们提供圣餐。骑士们看到这一幕,就确信面包和美酒已转变为基督的躯干和血液。这成了圣杯传说的一部分,也被看成圣杯的一个奇迹。

随后,这3位骑士离开廊别涅克城堡,携带圣杯乘船向远方航行。航船将骑士们和圣杯带到一个遥远的城市,名叫萨拉斯。在那儿,加勒哈德去世后,帕西瓦尔和博斯看守着圣杯升入天堂。根据传说,从此以后再也没人见过圣杯。

文学作品中的圣杯

圣杯的传说,是1180~1240年中世纪一些著名的诗歌等文学作品的灵感之源。大家所认可的最早书面记录,应该是12世纪末法国克雷蒂安·德·特罗亚的诗作 Conte del Graal,翻译过来就是《圣杯的故事》。

往后数年,骑士冒险为求圣杯的故事以其他版本出现在别的西欧文学作品中。大约13世纪初的时候,罗伯特·德·波龙撰写了一首诗作,名为《亚利马太的约瑟夫》,描写的是约瑟夫在耶稣受难时用圣杯承接他的鲜血。另一篇有名的作品是沃尔夫拉姆·封·埃申巴赫在1220年左右撰写的《帕西瓦尔》。200年之后,在英语国家中,有关圣杯的传说最为出名的,莫过于托马斯·马洛礼爵士的《亚瑟王之死》,它将亚瑟王骑士们的事迹串联了起来。所有这些传说故事,尽管在细节和一些情节点上有所差别,但都讲述了亚瑟王的圆桌骑士们是如何寻找圣杯的。

19世纪时,圣杯的故事又出现在丁尼生的亚瑟王系列《国王的叙事诗》中。德国作曲家理查德·瓦格纳,以圣杯传奇为蓝本,创作了歌剧《帕西瓦尔》。此外,无数现代著作、电影和戏剧都转向以古代传说为主题,包括1975年的影片《巨蟒和圣杯》。

相关资源

《圣杯传奇》,普林斯顿大学出版社,1998年。作者利用了圣杯的故事来解释说明基督文化的背景。故事的开端是这样一个前提:圣杯传奇乃基于古凯尔特一个赎罪和永生的标志,作者展示了圣杯和现代生活的关联。

《圣杯:想象和信仰》,哈佛大学出版社,2005年。本书作者描述了圣杯的历史,开头是克雷蒂安·德·特罗亚作品中所描述的天主教会对该神话现代版本的阐释。

www.britannia.com/history/arthur/grail.html 该网址包含了关于亚瑟王和圣杯的资料。

Eighteen

Hundredth Monkey Effect

The Hundredth Monkey Effect is a term that describes a phenomenon whereby a specific learned action spreads instantaneously from one group of animals to another, as soon as a certain number of participants accumulate. To put it another way, when enough individual members of a group accept and adopt a new thought or behavior, all individuals in the group adopt it because of a psychological phenomenon that allows the thought or behavior to be directly communicated from one mind to the next without the example of concrete experience.

The origin of the effect is attributed to studies of monkeys conducted in the 1950s and 1960s by Japanese researchers. While this interpretation of the monkey research has been discredited, the Hundredth Monkey Effect persists today as a parable or a metaphor of the possibility of producing positive change in human society.

Washing Potatoes

It all started with some dirty, gritty, sweet potatoes on the Japanese island of Koshima.

Japanese researchers decided to drop sweet potatoes in the sand near the home of a group of macaques, a type of monkey that includes the rhesus monkey and the Barbary ape and is native to Asia, Africa and the East Indies. The monkeys liked the taste of the sweet potatoes but objected to the gritty sand on the surface of the food.

Within a short time one of the monkeys, a young female named Imo, discovered that she could wash off the grit and dirt from the potatoes by swishing them in the sea. She taught this routine to her mother and to some of her siblings and playmates, who also taught their mothers the secret of clean sweet potatoes. Soon more and more of the young monkeys were washing their sweet potatoes in the water. Only the adults who had learned about cleaning the sweet potatoes from their children washed them in the sea. Other adults continued to eat the gritty sweet potatoes.

So far the story rings true in light of what the scientists expected to happen. And this is what the Japanese scientists documented in their findings. However, in 1979 Lyall Watson wrote a book, *Lifetide*, in which he claimed that once a critical number of monkeys who were washing their sweet potatoes was reached— supposedly the hundredth monkey—all of the animals in the region began washing their sweet potatoes. Watson even went so far as to claim that the new behavior of washing sweet potatoes spread immediately across the water to monkeys on nearby islands who began washing their sweet potatoes without ever being taught the practice. Watson's theory was that when enough individuals find something to be true, everyone automatically finds it to be true.

Years later Ken Keyes, Jr., revived the story in his book *The Hundredth Monkey*. Although he based his work on Watson's original story, he presented his idea as a parable, looking at Watson's story as an expression of the possibility of creating positive changes in human society.

Debunking the Myth

The story of the hundredth monkey as told by Watson and then expanded by Keyes does not fit the reports and documentation of the Japanese scientists. Watson even admitted to extrapolating his theory from the original scientific reports. Keyes's version is more accurate, but it, too, seems to have been manipulated to support its author's beliefs.

百猴效应

百猴效应是个术语，描绘一种现象：某个特殊的举动必须通过学习才能掌握，一旦一定数目的个体参与其中，瞬时就能从一组动物传播到另一组。换个角度来说，一个团体中，如果有足够数目的个体成员接受并采纳了新思想或新行为，团体中所有的个体成员也都会采纳，原因在于一种心理现象——思想或行为能够直接从一个人传达给另一个人，而不需要具体的经历。

百猴效应的起源归功于日本研究人员在 20 世纪 50 年代和 60 年代进行的对猴子的研究。这项研究的结论已经遭到质疑，但百猴效应延续至今，成了一个寓言故事，或者是一种隐喻，暗示在人类社会中引发积极转变的可能性。

清洗山芋

事情的起源要从日本的子岛上几只沾了沙砾的脏山芋说起。

岛上有一种猴子叫做短尾猴，包括猕猴和叟猴，原产于亚洲、非洲和东印度群岛。日本的研究人员在一群短尾猴家园的附近沙地里丢了一些山芋。猴子们很喜欢山芋的味道，但是讨厌山芋表面的沙砾。

时隔不久，一只名叫伊沫的幼年母猴就发现，她如果把山芋放到海水中滚动，就能够将沙砾和泥土洗去。她把这个方法教给了她的母亲、兄弟姐妹和玩伴们。而他们，也把洗干净山芋的秘密教给自己的母亲。很快，越来越多的幼年猴子都在水里清洗山芋了。而成年猴子，只有在跟自己的孩子学会这个方法后，才在海水里清洗山芋。其他的成年猴子，则继续食用沾了沙砾的山芋。

至此，根据科学家们所期待发生的事情，这个故事及其结论应该是正确的。而且，这正是日本科学家在他们的发现中所记录的内容。然而，1979 年，莱尔·华特森撰写了一本著作《生命之潮》。他在书中宣称，洗山芋的猴子一旦达到某个数目——假定就是第 100 只猴子——那么这片地域所有的猴子都开始清洗山芋。华特森进一步声明，洗山芋这一新行为即刻就穿越水面，传播到附近岛屿上的猴子。而它们，从未学习这个方法，却也开始清洗山芋了。华特森的理论是：如果足够的个体认为某件事是真的，那么所有个体都会自动认为那的确是真的。

数年之后，肯·凯埃斯在他的著作《第一百只猴子》中重新提起这个故事。尽管他的作品以华特森的原始故事为蓝本，他的观点呈现出来是寓言式的，将华特森的故事表达成在人类社会中引发积极转变的可能性。

解秘神话

百猴的故事先由华特森讲述，又由凯埃斯解释，但并不符合日本科学家所记录的报告和文档。华特森甚至承认，他是在原始科学报告的基础上进行推测的。凯埃斯的观点甚为精确，但是似乎也加入了一些操控，以支持他本人的看法。

First, not all of the young monkeys learned to wash their sweet potatoes. Many of the young monkeys did wash their sweet potatoes, but it was obvious that it was a learned behavior among young animals. Those who were older and had little contact with the younger monkeys ate their sweet potatoes complete with grit and dirt. Eventually, as with most learned behaviors, the younger monkeys who started the tradition grew up and taught their offspring, the next generation, the practice of washing sweet potatoes before eating them. Yet older adult monkeys who had not learned as youngsters to wash the potatoes never did wash the potatoes. In addition, the scientists did not report any evidence of potato washing in other groups of monkeys geographically separated from the original group. If there were such behavior on distant islands, more than likely it had developed in much the same way as it had in the original group: A young monkey accidentally discovered that water removed the grit from the sweet potatoes.

Cultural Interpretations

Disproving the story, however, does not mean that nothing can be learned from the story. The Hundredth Monkey Effect has become popular as a way of looking at social change. Several interpretations of the Effect point up the possibility of an optimistic future based on peace instead of war. That is, returning to Watson's theory, if enough individuals find something to be true, everyone automatically may find it to be true.

The story of the hundredth monkey also illustrates the way a paradigm shift might work. In most cultures fresh new ideas come from the generational group between childhood and adulthood. While creating new alternatives does not automatically replace older customs, it does provide more choices. The old continue to adhere to ideas they grew up with while the young adopt new ways. Old ways give way to new ways only when the older generation withdraws from status and power and the new young generation matures with a fresh point of view.

Finally, the story is an example of the way that simple innovations lead to cultural change: The monkeys began to use the ocean as new resource in their environment.

Today the theme of the Hundredth Monkey Effect—the idea of raising collective consciousness by reaching critical mass—is promoted by New Age spiritualists. The New Age is a contemporary cultural movement characterized by an interest in spiritual consciousness and a belief in reincarnation and astrology combined with meditation, vegetarianism and holistic medicine. The goal is serenity and peace for society.

Resources

The Hundredth Monkey and Other Paradigms of the Paranormal, Prometheus Books, 1991. This book is a collection of 44 essays that originally appeared in the *Skeptical Inquirer* published by the Committee for the Scientific Investigation of Claims of the Paranormal. The purpose of the book is an examination of unusual claims using an open scientific approach that combines intellectual curiosity and skepticism.

Why People Believe Weird Things: Pseudoscience, Superstition, and Other Confusions of Our Time, Owl Books, 2002. This book by the publisher of Skeptic magazine examines the way humans view odd and unusual phenomena. The author explores the human need to see patterns where no pattern exists. The book is indexed and contains a detailed bibliography. *The School Library Journal* recommends this book for young adults.

首先，并非所有的幼年猴子都学会了洗山芋。它们当中有很多，的确洗了山芋，但这明显是幼仔之间的一种学习行为。年长些的猴子与幼年猴子少有接触，它们带着沙砾和泥土就把山芋吃下去了。最终，就跟其他通过学习才能掌握的行为一样，初创这种行为的幼年猴子长大后，便将吃山芋前先清洗的方法教给后代。可是成年猴子如果没有像幼年猴子那样学习这个方法，则从不清洗山芋。此外，科学家们并没有报告任何证据能够证明在地域上和最初猴群分隔的其他猴群也清洗山芋。假如在遥远的岛屿上也有这样的行为，更可能的情况就是，这种行为的发展和最初实验猴群的发展是一样的模式——一只幼年猴子偶尔发现：水把山芋上的沙砾洗掉了。

文化解说

然而，反证了这个故事，并不意味着从这个故事中我们什么也学不到。百猴效应已经成为看待社会变迁的一种流行的方法。针对这种效应的几家阐释观点，都强调了基于和平而不是战争的乐观未来的可能性。也就是说，转回华特森的理论，如果足够的个体认为某件事是真的，那么所有人可能都会自动认为那的确是真的。

百猴的故事也解释了模式转换能够顺利进行的方法。在大多数的文化环境中，新的观点都出自幼年和成年之间的一代人。新创的另类方法不能够自动替代旧有的传统，但的确能够提供更多的选择。老年人继续坚持他们习以为常的观点，而年青一代则接纳了新方法。一旦老一代不再当道，青年一代的创新观点也逐渐成熟时，更新换代就完成了。

最后，这个故事本身还是一个很好的例子，说明了简单的创新能够引导文化转变，猴群在其自身环境中，开始将海水作为一样新资源来加以利用。

现在，百猴效应的主题——通过达到临界点来提升集体意识——已经受到"新世纪"唯心论者的推崇。"新世纪"是一场当代的文化运动，其特征为对精神意识极有兴趣，相信再生和占星术（结合了冥想、素食和整体疗法）；其目标是社会的宁静与和平。

相关资源

《第一百只猴子以及其他超自然范式》，普罗米修斯图书，1991年。本书收集了44篇文章，都出自"对声称超自然现象的科学调查委员会"出版的《怀疑的探索者》一书。本书的目标是使用公开的、结合了智慧的好奇心和怀疑论的科学方法，来检测那些超寻常的声明。

《为何人们相信怪事：当代的伪科学、迷信及其他困惑》，猫头鹰图书，2002年。本书由怀疑论杂志的出版社出版，检测人们看待罕见、怪诞现象的方式。作者探索到，没有模式存在的时候，人们需要找寻模式。本书编有索引，并包含一张详细的参考书目单。"学校图书馆期刊"向年轻的读者推荐此书。

Nineteen

Jack the Ripper

Jack the Ripper is the nickname of a serial killer who murdered prostitutes in London and the surrounding districts of Whitechapel, Aldgate and Spitalfields in 1888. Also known as the Whitechapel Murderer, Jack the Ripper got his nickname from the signature on a letter to a news agency from someone who claimed to be the murderer.

The Impact of Jack the Ripper

Over the years the story of Jack the Ripper has intrigued the public for a number of reasons above and beyond the fact that he was a serial killer. First, the culprit was never identified. Although there was speculation about several suspects, forensic science at that time was not sophisticated enough to pinpoint the identity of the killer. Criminal profiling, fingerprints and DNA analysis were unknown. The concept of trying to understand the motives or underlying rationale of a serial killer also was unknown, although every investigator involved in the Jack the Ripper case recognized the sexual element of the attacks.

Second, in 1888 when the murders occurred, the London press was enjoying a new upsurge in circulation among all classes of readers, so that the press coverage reached a wide audience throughout the metropolitan area. Feeding a growing demand for social change in the city, the press reported in great detail the viciousness of the attacks on poor, disadvantaged women. In addition, in order to increase circulation, the press exaggerated or twisted facts until a large body of folklore about the killer became part of the coverage.

Finally, the murderer appeared to be an attention-seeking exhibitionist who drew attention to himself by leaving his mutilated victims in plain sight and who supposedly wrote letters confessing to the crime. Even though most of the letters were disregarded as hoaxes, nevertheless they fed the sensationalism of the London press coverage.

The Crimes

Subsequent review of all the reports, however, revealed how Jack the Ripper killed his victims.

Autopsy reports indicated that all of the victims were strangled until they were unconscious or dead. The killer confronted the women from the front and review of the location of the bodies in relation to neighboring walls or fences revealed that they were attacked from the front in a standing position and then, after being strangled, were lowered to the ground, their heads turned to the murderer's left. Lack of bruising on the victims' heads indicated that they were lowered rather than thrown to the ground.

Despite the sexual aspect of the killings, the authorities never found any evidence that sexual intercourse had occurred. However, it is a common practice among sexual killers to take a trophy from the body and all of Jack the Ripper's victims had a piece or pieces of an internal organ missing. Most of the investigators thought this might be a clue to the killer's identity, since the trophies were removed so skillfully that it appeared to be the work of a surgeon or someone with extensive medical knowledge.

The murders were usually committed at night in a secluded yet publicly accessible site. And

碎尸狂杰克

"碎尸狂杰克"是一个连环杀手的别称,1888年他在伦敦以及周围的怀特查泊尔、阿尔捷特和斯毕塔菲尔德等区杀害了多名妓女,因此也称为"怀特查泊尔杀手"。"碎尸狂杰克"称号的由来,是因为有人声称自己就是作案者,并在寄给新闻机构的一封信上如此署名。

恶劣影响

多年以来,碎尸狂杰克的故事一直吸引着公众的注意,原因有很多,并不仅仅因为他是一个连环杀手。首先,凶手的身份未能确认。尽管曾经推断出几名嫌疑犯,但当时的法医学还不够发达,无法确认杀手的身份。犯罪心理画像、指纹检测和DNA分析都还不为人知。尽管涉及本案的每一名调查人员都意识到了袭击事件中的性因素,当时的人们还不懂得去探究连环杀手的犯罪动机或者隐藏在事实背后的逻辑依据。

其次,1888年谋杀案发生之时,伦敦报业的发行量正当急剧上升,读者遍布各个阶层,因而新闻报道的影响范围非常广阔,囊括了这个大都市的所有地区。为了满足市民对于社会变迁需求的增长,伦敦报业详尽地报道了对贫穷弱势的妇女的恶性攻击事件。此外,为了增加发行量,出版社常将事实夸大或者歪曲,乃至关于杀手的大量民间传说成为报道的内容。

再次,这个杀手似乎是一个爱出风头的人,他为了把公众注意力吸引到自己身上来,将被害者残碎的尸体丢在显眼的地方。据推断,写信承认犯下罪行的也是他。尽管大部分的信件都被看成是恶作剧,人们对此并不予理睬,然而这些信件倒是让伦敦的新闻报道引起哗然一片。

累累罪行

后人对所有的报告进行研究,揭示了碎尸狂杰克是如何杀人的。

验尸报告显示,所有的受害者在昏迷或者死亡之前都被掐。凶手是从前面走向被害妇女。研究一下尸体相对旁边墙壁的位置,就不难发现,她们是站立的时候受到了迎面而来的袭击,被掐窒息之后,又被放到地上,头部歪向凶手的左侧。受害者头部没有青肿的硬伤,表明她们是被放到地上的,而不是被摔到地上的。

尽管这些杀人事件含有性因素,但当局从未发现任何证据能证明有性交行为发生。然而,因性杀人的一贯做法都会从尸体上带走一样纪念品;而碎尸狂杰克的所有受害者,都有一块或者数块内脏组织不见了。多数调查人员认为,这可能是确定凶手身份的一条线索,因为取走的"纪念品"切割得非常娴熟,看来凶手是个外科医生,或者懂得丰富的医学知识。

凶杀的时间通常是晚上,而地点通常比较隐蔽但都是对公众开放的场所。而且杰克

the women who are considered to be the victims of Jack the Ripper were murdered within a few weeks of each other in the late summer and fall of 1888.

The Victims

Although no one really knows how many people Jack the Ripper killed, historians generally accept that he killed at least five women between August and November of 1888: Mary Ann Nicols, Annie Chapman, Elizabeth Stride, Catharine Eddowes and Mary Jane Kelly. They were of different ages and all were presumed drunk at the time of their deaths.

These five names come from the notes of a police inspector who did not join the force until after the murders and whose records were later found to contain errors. However, this information is presumed to be the most accurate. In reality, it was difficult at the time to determine who was a victim of Jack the Ripper because of the large number of vicious attacks on women in London during this time span.

The Jack the Ripper Letters

Over the course of the investigation into these murders, the police and the newspaper received thousands of letters about the case. Most of them were deemed useless and none was considered to be written by Jack the Ripper himself.

The police looked at three specific letters, namely, the Dear Boss letter, the From Hell letter and the Saucy Jack letter, but all were eventually dismissed as hoaxes. The letters mentioned specific details pertaining to one or more of the murders, but all were written after the details of each murder had been described in the press. The police attributed the letters to journalists who were looking to spice up their stories.

Suspects

There has been much speculation about the identity of Jack the Ripper. Unfortunately, nothing has been conclusive.

At the time, police investigators listed several suspects but were unable to substantiate the accusations. One was supposedly an attorney who committed suicide shortly after the last murder. Later, the man in question was identified as a physician who had no connection to the murders. Another suspect whose name was mentioned in the reports of a police officer in charge of the case was subsequently identified as a mentally ill but harmless man who was later confined to an institution.

Interest in Jack the Ripper continues to the present day. Through the latter part of the 20th century Jack the Ripper has often been identified as someone famous. Nothing has been verified, however, and his true identity remains hidden. Nevertheless, there are researchers who are interested in reviewing old records, reports and photos in an attempt to apply modern forensic methods in order to finally name the real Jack the Ripper.

Resources

The Complete History of Jack the Ripper, Constable and Robinson, 2002. This book is an exhaustive study of the facts behind the case of Jack the Ripper. One of the goals of the author is to dispel misinformation that grew out of police and press reports that fueled the rumors about the cases and the murderer.

Jack the Ripper: The Definitive History, Longman, 2004. This book is not just an attempt to identify the killer but rather a look at the murders in their historical context. The author is a leading authority on Jack the Ripper.

www.casebook.org. Website providing reviews, opinions and facts about the Jack the Ripper murders. This is the largest public repository of Ripper related information.

的那些女性受害者都是在 1888 年的夏末和秋天被杀害,前后相隔不超过数周。

被害人

虽然没人确切了解杰克到底杀了多少人,历史学家大致认同,他在 1888 年 8 月到 11 月间至少杀了 5 名妇女:玛丽·安·尼科尔斯、安妮·查浦曼、伊丽莎白·斯特莱德、凯瑟琳·埃得欧斯和玛丽·简·凯莉。她们年龄各异,而且据推断,在被害当时都喝醉了酒。

这 5 个人的名字出自一位警方调查人员的笔记。他是在谋杀案发生以后才进入警界的,而且后来发现他的记录有误。不过这份资料还是被看成是最精确的。事实上,在当时来说,要确认谋杀案是否为碎尸狂杰克所为是非常困难的,因为在这段时间内伦敦发生了大量的恶性攻击妇女事件。

碎尸狂杰克的书信

在案件的调查过程中,警方和报社收到了几千封关乎案子的信件。但大多数都被认定是毫无用处,而且这其中没有一封被认为是杰克亲自写的。

警方细查了其中的三封书信,即"亲爱的老板"、"来自地狱"和"傲慢的杰克",但最终都认为是恶作剧而已。这些信提到了一次或数次案件中的细节,但都是在这些细节于报纸上公布之后。警方认为之所以有这样的信件出现,是因为新闻记者想让他们的报道更加引人入胜。

嫌疑犯

对于碎尸狂杰克的身份确认,曾有诸多推测。遗憾的是,并没有得出明确的定论。

当时,警方调查人员列出了好几名嫌疑犯,但是均未能确立罪名。其中有一名被认为是个律师,它在最后一次谋杀案之后很快就自杀了。后来,经过确认他其实是个内科医生,和那些谋杀案并无关联。另一名嫌疑犯的名字曾出现在负责此案的警方官员报告中,紧接着被确认有精神疾患,但不会对他人造成伤害,后来被限制在某个机构中。

时至今日,仍有人对碎尸狂杰克饶有兴趣。20 世纪后半叶,杰克经常被指认为某个著名人物。然而,什么也没有查实,他的真实身世仍然是个谜。不过,有些研究人员着迷于重温古旧的记录、报告和相片,试图利用现代的法医学方法来最终揭开杰克之谜。

相关资源

《碎尸狂杰克的历史》,康斯塔布尔和罗宾森,2002 年。本书对杰克杀人案背后的真相进行详尽研究。作者的目的之一,就是要消除来自警方和新闻报道的错误信息,以免加大案件谣言的散布。

《碎尸狂杰克:权威历史》,朗文,2004 年。本书不仅仅试图确定凶手的身份,更是对历史环境下谋杀案的研究。作者是研究杰克的一名权威人士。

www.casebook.org 该网址提供杰克谋杀案的报道、评论和事实依据。这是杰克资料最大的公众收藏室。

Twenty

James Dean's Car

Was the Porsche Spyder in which James Dean died really cursed? It seemed to bring bad luck to whoever came in contact with it after Dean's death.

Many think that the car's mystique is an outgrowth of the iconic appeal of and mystery about its owner, James Dean. And much of the interest in Dean centers around his untimely death at age 24.

Life of James Dean

James Byron Dean was born in 1931 in Marion, Indiana, but moved at a young age with his family to Santa Monica, California.

When Dean was 9 years old, his mother died, which left a personal void in his life. In retrospect, many historians attribute his later antisocial behavior and personal problems to his mother's death. Unable to care for him after his wife's death, Dean's father sent him back to Indiana to be raised by an older sister. During his high school years, he began to develop interests in race car driving, bull fighting and acting. He also took drama classes and performed in high school productions.

Upon graduating from high school, Dean returned to California to live with his father and stepmother. During this time he enrolled in Santa Monica College and later UCLA where he majored in drama, and by 1951 had dropped out of college to become an actor.

Acting Career

His acting career began in an unremarkable manner. He landed several commercials and did behind-the-scene jobs on television shows, he decided to follow James Whitmore's advice and move to New York City to become a stage actor. Lee Strasberg accepted him into his famous Actors Studio and Dean began to take on some small roles in various TV shows. Already he was demonstrating the rebellious and angst-ridden persona he eventually became famous for.

His first big break was his selection by Elia Kazan to play the lead role of Cal in the film *East of Eden*, based on John Steinbeck's novel. Cal is the rebellious and misunderstood son of a faultfinding father and prostitute mother. Viewed along with his interpretation of the lead role of Jim Stark in the film *Rebel Without a Cause*, Dean seemed to become typecast as a misfit and dysfunctional young man.

Dean's last film was *Giant*, in which he starred with Elizabeth Taylor and Rock Hudson. His final on-screen appearance was a speech toward the end of this movie. The scene subsequently became known as The Last Supper, but the lines were later rerecorded because his mumbled words were unintelligible. The final lines were dubbed in because Dean had died before the film was edited.

Dean received a posthumous nomination for best actor in a leading role for his work in *East of Eden*. He was nominated, again posthumously, for an Academy Award for *Giant*. But he is best remembered for his portrayal of teenage confusion, anxiety and violence. His acting in *Rebel Without a Cause* is often cited as an illustration of the growing rebelliousness of teens in the 1950s—a movement that fostered the popularity of rock and roll music.

詹姆士·迪恩的
保时捷

那辆保时捷"霹雳马"——詹姆士·迪恩即死于其中——果真受了诅咒么？在迪恩死后，似乎凡是和它有所接触的人，都碰上了厄运。

很多人认为，这辆车之所以会有这样的魔力，是由其主人詹姆士·迪恩作为偶像的魅力造成，也和他的神秘身世有所关联。而且，人们对于他的关注焦点，正是集中在他24岁的英年早逝。

迪恩身世

詹姆士·拜伦·迪恩于1931年出生在印第安纳州的马里恩，在他很小的时候，他就随家人搬到了加利福尼亚州的圣莫尼卡。

迪恩9岁时，他的母亲去世了，这就给他的生活留下了一片空白。回顾这段情形，很多历史学家认为他后来的反叛举动和个人问题，源头都在于他母亲的去世。迪恩的父亲在妻子去世以后无法照顾孩子，就把他送回了印第安纳州，交给自己的一位姐姐抚养。在中学期间，他渐渐地对赛车驾驶、斗牛和演艺产生了兴趣。他还上了戏剧课，并参加了校园戏剧的演出。

中学一毕业，迪恩就回到加利福尼亚，和他的父亲及继母生活在一起。这段时间，他入学圣莫尼卡大学，后来还在加利福尼亚大学洛杉矶分校主修戏剧，1951年从大学辍学，成了一名演员。

演艺生涯

迪恩的演艺生涯刚开头并不顺利。他接拍了几个广告，在电视节目中做了一些幕后工作，但他还是听从詹姆士·惠特莫尔的忠告，前往纽约，成了一名舞台演员。李·斯特拉斯伯格接纳了他，让他进入自己声名显赫的演员工作室。从此，迪恩得以在各种电视节目中担当一些小角色。那时，他已经显露出反叛、动不动就焦躁苦恼的形象，那也正是他最终得以成名的形象。

伊利亚·卡赞挑中他出演电影《伊甸园之东》（改编自约翰·斯坦贝克的小说）的主角卡尔，这成就了他的第一次飞跃。影片中，卡尔的父亲吹毛求疵，母亲是个妓女，他们无法理解这个反叛的儿子。而在电影《无因反叛》中，他对主角吉姆·斯达克的演绎，则表明，他似乎已经成为一个青年人的经典角色——无法适应周遭的环境，也不能够履行自己的责任。

迪恩的最后一部影片叫做《巨人》，是他和伊丽莎白·泰勒以及罗克·哈德森的携手之作。而他最后一次出现在屏幕上，是在这部影片临近结尾之时所作的一次演说。这个场景随后被称为"最后的晚餐"，不过台词是后来重新录制的，因为他当时说话很模糊，根本听不清。最后几句台词还是别人配音的，因为影片还没最终制作好，迪恩已经离世了。

迪恩去世之后，凭着《伊甸园之东》的表演，获得了最佳男主角的提名。另外还凭借《巨人》获得了奥斯卡提名。不过人们最难以忘怀的，是他表现出的青少年那种迷茫、渴望以及暴力。他在《无因反叛》中的表演，常常被引用说明20世纪50年代时青少年的反叛行为日趋严重——那场运动促使摇滚乐大为流行。

Because of his acting presence on screen, his very short career and his untimely death, Dean became of cult figure who still elicits interest among young people as well as their parents who grew up during the rock and roll era.

His Death

While he was working on *Rebel Without a Cause*, he bought a Porsche 550 Spyder, which he raced after completing *Giant*.

Slated to race at Salinas, California, Dean asked his friend George Barris to customize the Porsche Spyder. When the car was ready, Dean and his mechanic set off on September 30, 1955, for Salinas. At the last minute, Dean decided to drive the Porsche himself rather than transport it to the race track on a trailer.

Later that afternoon Dean was driving west on U.S. Highway 46 when a car driven by a student named Donald Turnupseed made a turn and crossed into Dean's lane without seeing him. The resulting head-on collision of the two cars killed Dean and injured his passenger as well as Turnupseed. Turnupseed was not cited and it was later determined that, surprisingly, Dean was not speeding.

The Curse of the Spyder Death Car

Dean's Porsche Spyder has become notorious as a death car or a cursed car since Dean'death. Not only was the car the vehicle in which James Dean died, but also it was the car that either injured or killed others after his death.

George Barris, the one who customized the car for Dean, bought the wreckage of the automobile after Dean's death. During its transport, the car slid off a trailer and broke a mechanic's leg. Later Barris stripped the car of parts and sold them to other racers. One bought the engine only to be killed instantly in his first race using the Spyder's engine. Another buyer bought the Spyder's tires, which blew up simultaneously, causing the driver to go off the road. And the person who bought the Spyder's transmission was later injured in an auto accident.

Stealing parts from the car was hazardous as well. One thief cut his arm on sharp metal while trying to steal the steering wheel. Another man was injured stealing the car's front seat. Eventually Barris decided to store the car for safekeeping, but the California Highway Patrol convinced him to allow the car to be the main feature of a highway safety exhibit.

This project was not successful. First, the building where the car was stored caught on fire, demolishing everything except the actual car. Later at a safety display at a local high school, the car toppled over, breaking a student's hip. To add to the bad luck, every time the car was transported, there was a mishap. Once the car's transport trailer went out of control, throwing the driver clear, but he was crushed by the Porsche rolling off the transport. In two other instances, the car fell off the transport truck causing damage to nearby vehicles.

Finally in 1958 while being returned to George Barris, the car disappeared. So far there have been no reports that the Porsche Spyder has ever been found.

Resources

Live Fast, Die Young: The Wild Ride of Making Rebel Without a Cause, Touchstone, 2006. This book examines the making of the film *Rebel Without a Cause*, probably the best-known of James Dean's three films. The coverage includes casting, writing, history and symbolism within the plot and idiosyncrasies of the actors. The final chapters delve into the Dean cult and how it affected the film's popularity and endurance.

www.jamesdean.com/about/photos/car.htm. James Dean Website includes a historical gallery of photos of James Dean's car.

正是由于迪恩在屏幕上的演艺生涯短暂如昙花一现，还有他的英年早逝，使得他成为人们膜拜的偶像，至今还是吸引着青少年和从摇滚乐时代走过来的家长们。

迪恩之死

拍摄《无因反叛》期间，他购买了一辆保时捷550"霹雳马"，这辆车他在完成《巨人》的拍摄之后曾驾驶着参加比赛。

迪恩被选中参加加州萨利纳斯的赛车比赛，他请朋友乔治·巴利斯帮他对那辆保时捷"霹雳马"进行改装。车子改装好后，1955年9月30日，迪恩和他的机修师就要出发前往萨利纳斯。出发前的最后一刻，迪恩决定，不用拖车把这辆保时捷运送到比赛场地了，他要亲自驱车前往。

晚些时候，迪恩正在美国第46号公路上向西行驶。当时有一个名叫东纳尔德·特纳普斯彼得的学生正开着一辆轿车，他没看到迪恩，拐个弯就进入了迪恩的车道。两辆车迎面撞击，迪恩死亡，他车内的乘客和特纳普斯彼得两人受伤。特纳普斯彼得没有受到传讯，后来人们发现，当时迪恩并没有超速的，确令人惊讶。

车之诅咒

迪恩去世后，他的那辆保时捷"霹雳马"就成了死亡之车或者是诅咒之车，令人骇然。这辆车不仅仅让迪恩死于非命，而且在迪恩死后还让其他一些人受伤甚或送了命。

为迪恩对车进行了改装的乔治·巴利斯，在迪恩去世后，购买了车的残骸。运输过程中，车从拖车上滑落下来，压折了一名机修工的腿。后来，巴利斯从车上拆下一些部件，卖给了其他的赛车手。有个人买了引擎，结果在第一次使用这个引擎参加赛车时就死于非命。另一个买主买了轮胎，结果轮胎同时爆胎，车子也驶离了公路。还有一个人买了变速器，结果后来在一次车祸中受了伤。

从车上偷掉的零部件，也具有同样的杀伤力。有个小偷企图盗窃方向盘，手臂被尖锐的金属部件刺伤。另一个人在偷盗车前座时也受了伤。最后巴利斯决定妥善保存这辆车，但是加州公路巡逻队说服他同意让车作为一场公路安全展的特色展品。

这次计划并没有成功。首先，车子所在的大楼着了火，除了车子本身，其他什么都烧掉了。后来在当地一个中学的安全展出时，车子又翻了身，使一名学生臀骨骨折。更加糟糕的是，每次运送这辆车，总会出现灾难。有一次，运送的拖车失去控制，把驾驶员彻底甩了出去，随之这辆保时捷从拖车上滚落，将他碾个粉碎。另外两起事故中，车子从运送的卡车上跌落下来，导致附近的车子被撞坏。

最后，1958年，车子在返回给巴利斯的途中消失了。从此再也没人见到过这辆保时捷"霹雳马"。

相关资源

《快活地生，漂亮地死：<无因反叛>拍摄期间的疯狂驾驶》，试金石出版社，2006年。《无因反叛》也许是迪恩三部影片中最广为人知的，本书考证了该部影片的拍摄。内容包括演员挑选、剧本写作、拍摄历史、情节含义以及各位演员的个性气质。最后几章深入研究了影迷对迪恩的膜拜，以及在这种膜拜的影响下，影片是如何受到欢迎和持久不衰的。

www.jamesdean.com/about/photos/car.htm 这是詹姆士·迪恩的网址，收集了他那辆保时捷的诸多照片。

Twenty-one

Killer in the Back Seat

In its most succinct form, this legend claims that a good Samaritan warns an unsuspecting driver that a dangerous killer is hiding in the back seat of her car.

Although there are many variations of this legend, each one follows the same pattern and includes the same cast of characters: a male Good Samaritan, a female victim (driver) and a male killer in the back seat. And in each instance the victim interprets the act of warning as aggression and is unaware that the real danger is closer than she realized.

Origins of the Legend

The legend first appeared in the 1960s and has spread exponentially as the Internet grew and electronic communications expanded. This is truly an urban legend in the sense that its development and its variations are influenced by modern technology. It gained credence by appearing in a letter to Ann Landers's yndicated column in the early 1980s as a horrendous experience that had happened to a friend of the letter writer.

The Basic Story

A woman is visiting a friend for the evening and late in the evening or early morning hours she gets into her car to drive home. As she starts her car and moves away from her friend's home, she notices a car starting up behind her. Driving behind her toward the highway, the driver of the car will not pass her. She begins speeding to see if she can escape him.

When she arrives at her own home, the car is still directly behind her. Pulling into her driveway, she honks her horn to alert her husband in the house. By the time the husband comes out, the second car has pulled into the driveway directly behind her car. The driver in the car that has been following jumps out of his car, and in answer to the husband's question about his following the wife, says that he was trying to warn the wife about the man in the back seat of her car: "I was going to work as your wife left and when I turned my headlights on, I noticed a man duck down in the back seat of your wife's car. I followed her to warn her." Sure enough, when the husband opens the back door of his wife's car, there is a man crouched in the back seat.

Standard Variations of the Legend

The following versions have been told over and over. In most cases, the only differences in the stories are whether or not the killer is armed and, if so, with what kind of weapon. As a rule, the weapon is most often a knife, hatchet or meat cleaver and it is usually a sharp-edged implement rather than a blunt object.

Flashing Lights

A common variation of the car following the victim is the tale in which the pursuer flashes his headlights repeatedly as he follows the woman victim. He later reveals that this prevented the assailant from attacking the woman because his flashing lights illuminated and therefore intimidated the attacker every time he arose from the back seat to attack the woman driver.

Gas Station Attendant

Another common version of this story portrays a gas station attendant as the good Samaritan. A woman pulls into a gas station to fill up and pays at the pump with a credit card. The attendant

后座杀手

这个传说,简而言之,就是一位好心人告诫一名毫不设防的驾驶员,她的车后座下躲藏了一个危险的杀手。虽然有好多种不同的版本,但每一种的模式相同,都包括以下人物的阵容:一位男性的好心人,一名女性的受害者(驾驶员),还有车后座下的一个男性杀手。而且在每个版本中,受害者总是将人家的告诫反而当成是蓄意侵犯,却没有意识到真正的危险比自己预想的要更为接近。

传说起源

本传说始见于20世纪60年代,随着网络的发展和电子通讯的普及,迅速地广为流传。故事从成型到衍生出不同的版本,都受到了现代技术的影响,从这个意义上来说,这倒的确是个真正的都市传说。80年代初,有人给安·兰德斯辛迪加专栏来信,就提到自己的一个朋友曾有过这样可怕的经历,于是增加了这个传说的可信度。

基本情节

一名妇女整晚都在朋友家做客,深夜或者凌晨时分,她上车准备开车回家。汽车发动,从朋友家离开时,她注意到有一辆车紧贴在后面也发动了。那辆车就跟在她后面驶向公路,但并不超车。她开始加速,看看是否能够甩开后面的人。

回到家,那辆车仍然紧紧地尾随其后。她把车开进自家的车道,为了让屋里的丈夫有所警觉,不停地按响汽车喇叭。她丈夫从屋里出来的时候,那辆车也紧跟着进入了车道。驾驶员从车里跳下来,做丈夫的询问他为什么跟踪他的妻子,他回答说他是想告诉那个女的,她的车后座下藏了个男人:"你妻子驾车离开的时候,我正准备去上班,一打开车前灯,我就发现有个男人猫腰躲在你妻子的车后座下。我就跟着她,想警告她来着。"丈夫打开妻子的车后座,果不其然,还真有个男人蜷伏在后座下面。

通行版本

以下都是被人们重复、熟知的通行版本。在大多数版本中,仅有的区别就在于那个杀手是否带有凶器,如果有,那么又是带的何种凶器。一般来说,最常见的凶器是一把餐刀、一柄斧子或者是一把切肉刀,也就是说,通常是利器而非钝器。

车灯闪亮

一种常见的版本就是:尾随受害者的汽车不断地打开车前灯。他后来解释说,这样就能阻止杀手袭击前面的妇女,因为每次他从后座下面钻出来,车灯一闪就照亮一切,也就吓退了他的进攻。

加油站内

在另一种常见的版本里,则由一名加油站的服务员充当了好心人的角色。一名妇女驱车进入加油站加油,就在油泵边上拿出信用卡支付。服务员以信用卡有问题为由,喊她

calls out to her to get out of the car and come into the station because there is a problem with her credit card. If the woman resists entering the station (probably because it is late and there is no one else around at the station), the attendant insists. When the driver reluctantly goes into the station to argue with the attendant, he tells her that he has seen a man hiding in the back seat of her car and has already called the police. Depending on who is telling the story, the gas station attendant may or may not report having seen a weapon. As usual, the victim is a woman and both the good guy and the bad guy are men.

Latest Version of the Legend

The latest version does not differ from the original stories in its descriptions of the ways in which the good Samaritan warns the victim. It does, however, depict the methods used in the attack on the victim, identifies the attack as a gang ritual to be completed as a part of an initiation into a gang.

This ritual supposedly has specific rules that must be met in order for the assailant to become a member of a gang. First, the attack must take place in a well-lit area and at a gas station. Second, the wannabe gang members must leave the back seat and hide under the car (or, as an alternative, behind the gas pumps) without the victim becoming aware of their presence. When the driver attempts to get into her car, the gang members either slash at her ankles or, if they are behind gas pumps, grab her from behind. When the victim falls, the attackers kill her.

In some stories there is an alternative ritual required for gang initiation. This involves capturing a woman for the gang to rape.

Real or Hoax?

Despite this legend's persistent repetition and alternative variations, there is really no evidence that this legend has ever happened. Granted, there have been reports of rapes by attackers hiding in the back seat of a car, but the basic carjacking method described in these stories statistically does not happen very often. As a rule, most carjackings take place when the assailant opens the front door of the car and jumps in while the driver is behind the wheel. Police reports show that very few carjackers lurk in the back seat waiting for their opportunity.

On the other hand, these tales do serve one purpose: They alert everyone to be cautious and aware of his or her surroundings at all times. Whether or not such legends are true, it is only good common sense to:

· Always lock car doors, even if you are gone for only a minute or two to pay for your gas or pick something up;

· look underneath your car when approaching it from a distance and check the back seat (including the floor of the back seat) before entering; and

· be aware of your surroundings, other people and other vehicles whenever you are out alone, especially at night.

Resources

Be Afraid, Be Very Afraid; The Book of Scary Urban Legends, W.W. Norton, 2004. This is a compilation of some of the scariest legends or tales that have been passed on by word of mouth or via TV shows or movies. Included are contemporary tales that have gained prominence on the Internet. The author attempts to trace each legend to its roots and to either prove or disprove many of the more familiar ones.

www.snopes.com/horrors/madmen/backseat.asp. Variations of the Killer in the Backseat urban legend.

下车到加油站里面去。如果她不肯进去(可能因为时间太晚,而周围又没有其他人),服务员就会坚持要求她进去。她不情不愿地进去之后要跟服务员理论,这时候服务员告诉她,他看到有个男人躲在她车后座下面,而他已经联系过警察了。在不同的版本中,那个加油站服务员看到的杀手有的带有凶器,有的就没有。通常情况下,受害者是一名妇女,而好心人和那个坏蛋都是男性。

最新版本

最新版本和初始版本大同小异,都是一名好心人告诫受害者的故事。不过,新版描绘了袭击受害者的方法,指出这样的袭击是进入某犯罪团伙前必须完成的某种仪式。

这个仪式也许有着特别的规定,必须把它完成,才能成为团伙的成员。首先,这样的袭击必须发生在灯火通明的地方,比如加油站。其次,想要加入团伙的那个人必须离开车后座,躲到车子底下(或者另一种做法就是躲到加油泵后面),不能让受害者察觉。受害者即将上车的时候,那个人就砍伤她的脚踝,或者如果他是躲在加油泵后面的话,则从后面抓住她。受害者倒下后,他就将她杀死。

有些版本里面提到加入团伙的另一种仪式,就是抓一名妇女回去让团伙成员们强奸。

是真是假?

尽管这个传说被人反复提起,而且还有多种版本,事实上并没有证据能证明这样的事情的确发生过。即便有的报道中,强奸犯确实就躲在车后座下,但是从统计数字来看,这样的劫车方法并不常见。一般来说,大多数的劫车案件都是这样发生的:驾驶员坐在方向盘前,罪犯打开前门,跳进来。警方的报告显示,绝少有劫车犯潜伏在后座下面等待机会。

换个角度,这些故事都有着同一个目的:告诫每个人,在任何时候都要小心周围的环境。这个传说不管是真是假,以下几点必须当做常识牢记:
* 永远都要锁好车门,哪怕只离开一两分钟去付个油钱或者取个东西;

* 从远离汽车的地方回来时,先检视车子底下和车后座(包括后座下的地板),然后才上车;
* 孤身在外时要注意周围环境、其他人和其他车,尤其是晚上。

相关资源

《害怕,非常害怕——惊悚的都市传说》,W.W.诺顿公司,2004年。本书对很多最最惊悚的传说故事进行了编辑,这些故事经由口耳相传或者影视作品流传下来,包括网上盛传的当代传说。作者力图追溯每个传说的源头,对于更熟悉的故事,则要求证其真实性。

www.snopes.com/horrors/madmen/backseat.asp 都市传说"后座杀手"的各种版本。

Twenty-two

King Arthur & the Knights of the Round Table

King Arthur was a legendary king who became the main character in some of the most popular English literature from medieval times. The literature grew out of word-of-mouth stories of brave deeds and exciting adventures of a warrior king and his knights.

There is some evidence that the stories about Arthur began as Celtic folklore. Arthur's name alone suggests this. The name Arthur is possibly of Celtic origin from artos viros, meaning bear man. The Welsh version is arth gwyr. Both may have evolved into Arthur. In addition, the early Latin form of Arthur is Arcturus, also a derivation of the original Welsh. Since Rome invaded Britain in the 1st century A.D., the Latin language may have played some role in the final version of the name Arthur.

Arthur's Life

Since most of the information about Arthur's life comes from the accumulation of information and tales by medieval storytellers, it is difficult to describe his life with any historical accuracy. Even though Arthur was supposedly born around 465 A.D. and is referred to in legends and tales in the 6th and 7th centuries, almost everything known about Arthur is based on traditions appearing in stories of the 11th and 12th centuries.

Geoffrey of Monmouth, for example, outlines Arthur's life in his *Historia Regum Brittaniae (History of the Kings of Britain)* in the 12th century. Geoffrey relates that Arthur was the son of Uther (phonetically similar to the name Arthur) and was a fierce warrior against the Barbarians. Eventually, Arthur ruled over a vast empire but returned home from a battle when he learned his nephew had rebelled against his rule. His encounter with his nephew was Arthur's last battle.

Over many years the story of Arthur changed and grew, until Sir Thomas Malory wrote what many consider to be the definitive biography of Arthur in his *Le Morte De'Arthur* in 1485. Malory tells the story of how Arthur became king. After Uther''s death, there was no king of England, so Merlin, the court sorcerer, placed a sword in a stone, saying that whoever withdrew the sword from the stone would become king. Arthur pulled the sword out, was crowned king and married Guinevere whose dowry was the round table where Arthur's knights sat. The shape of the table was significant because it meant that there would be no quarrels over rank among the knights sitting at the table.

According to Malory, Arthur defeated the Roman emperor Lucius and became emperor himself. He and his knights then began the search for the Holy Grail (see Chapter 17), the cup that Christ had used at the Last Supper. Meanwhile, however, there was trouble in the kingdom. Arthur's greatest knight, Lancelot, fell in love with Guinevere. Lancelot fled the kingdom but returned to rescue Guinevere when he learned she had been sentenced to death. Placing his nephew in charge of his kingdom, Arthur followed Lancelot and his queen and declared war on his former knight. The nephew, however, rebelled and Arthur was forced to return to put down the rebellion. This was Arthur's last battle on the Salisbury Plain where he killed his nephew but was mortally wounded himself. Claiming he was going to Avalon, Arthur floated away on a barge. This inconclusive ending led to speculation that he never did die. However, his grave was allegedly

亚瑟王和圆桌骑士

亚瑟王是一位传奇式的君主,从中世纪起,他就成了一些最为流行的英语文学作品中的主要角色。这样的文学作品出自人们口述的故事,内容通常是骁勇的国王及其手下骑士们的英勇事迹和刺激冒险。

有证据表明,亚瑟的故事都起源于凯尔特民间传说。亚瑟这个名字本身就有所提示。这个名字应该是源于凯尔特语artos viros,意思是"熊人"。威尔士语为arth gwyr。这两个名字都演化为亚瑟(Arthur)。而且,亚瑟的早期拉丁语为Arcturus,也是由最初的威尔士语演化而来。公元1世纪,罗马人侵略了英国,因此拉丁语在亚瑟名字的最终版本中应该有所表现。

亚瑟生平

关于亚瑟的生平,大部分的信息都来自中世纪的传说故事,因此,要想以历史的精确性来描绘他的一生非常困难。尽管人们认为亚瑟出生在公元465年左右,而且提到他的传说故事也都是在6、7世纪,可是人们所知的亚瑟的事情,都是基于11、12世纪的故事中出现的。

例如,12世纪时,蒙茅斯的杰佛里在他的《不列颠国王史》中,就勾勒出了亚瑟的生平。杰佛里讲述,亚瑟是尤瑟(发音和亚瑟十分相似)的儿子,是一名激烈对抗蛮族的勇士。最终,亚瑟统治了一个巨大的王国。但有一次他在外作战时得知他的侄子造反,便赶回国内。亚瑟和侄子的这次战斗是他的最后一次作战。

多少年以来,亚瑟的故事改变着、成长着,直至1485年,托马斯·马洛礼爵士撰写了《亚瑟王之死》,书中内容被很多人看成是亚瑟的正传。马洛礼讲述了亚瑟如何成为一代国王。尤瑟去世之后,英国就没了国王,因而宫廷术士墨林将一把剑插入石头,声称任何人只要拔出这把剑,就将成为国王。亚瑟将剑拔了出来,于是被加冕为王,并和基内维尔结婚。基内维尔的嫁妆就是一个圆桌,后来亚瑟的骑士就坐在它的四周。圆桌的形状意义非凡,因为这就意味着所有的圆桌骑士之间没有等级之分,也无须因此而争吵。

根据马洛礼的描述,亚瑟打败了罗马皇帝卢修斯,自己当上了皇帝。他和他的骑士们开始寻找圣杯(参阅第17章),也就是基督在最后的晚餐中用过的杯子。然而同时,亚瑟自己的国度也出现了问题。亚瑟麾下的第一骑士兰斯洛特爱上了基内维尔。兰斯洛特逃离英国,然而当他得知基内维尔被判极刑,又返回来营救她。亚瑟安排侄子掌管国家大事,自己则追踪兰斯洛特和王后,并对他的前骑士宣战。可是亚瑟的侄子竟然造反,迫使亚瑟归国平息叛乱。这是亚瑟的最后一战,发生在索尔兹伯里平原,他杀死了自己的侄子,自身也遭受重创。接着,他宣布要前往阿瓦隆,乘着一艘驳船就漂走了。这个非定论的结尾不免让人猜测,亚瑟并未死亡。不过,据说,12世纪亨利二世统治期间,人们在格拉斯顿伯里发现了他的坟墓。

discovered in Glastonbury during the reign of Henry II in the 12th century.

Knights of the Round Table

The story of King Arthur is incomplete without a look at the Knights of the Round Table. The legend of the Knights of the Round Table grew out of medieval British literature rather than out of the pagan Celtic tales that first mentioned Arthur. This is shown by the description of King Arthur's knights who wear the armor and display the behavior of the knights of the Middle Ages who first appeared in medieval France.

The knights were men of honor, nobility, courtesy and courage. They were expected to protect women, honor the king and take on courageous quests. Supposedly, King Arthur bestowed a special emblem on the Knights of the Round Table when he chose them as his knights. The cross in the emblem reminded them to live pure lives in order to be chosen to search for the Grail. The dragon on the emblem represented loyalty to King Arthur and the Round Table symbolized the equality, unity and comradeship of the group. The charge from King Arthur to the Knights of the Round Table became well-known as the code of chivalry to which all honorable men aspired.

There are several different legends about the Round Table. One states that Merlin had the table built for Uther, Arthur's father, who gave it to King Leodegan, Guinevere's father. He, in turn, bestowed it upon Guinevere as her dowry when she married Arthur. Another story appearing around 1200 A.D. claimed that Arthur commissioned the table to seat 1,600 knights and yet fold to carry on horseback. Apparently, this occurred after the knights fought over the most prestigious seats at a feast. Still another tradition says the table was built to seat 12 knights, resembling the Last Supper, with an empty space representing Judas's seat. The empty seat was reserved for a knight so pure that one day he would find the Holy Grail. When Sir Galahad's name appeared on the seat one day, he occupied the seat from that time forward. Eventually, according to tradition, Galahad was one of the knights to find the Holy Grail.

Legend or Real?

For centuries scholars have debated about whether Arthur was a historic or a legendary figure. During the Renaissance the Tudor kings argued that Arthur was real, but then they had traced their lineage to Arthur and used that information to justify their succession to the throne. Others, however, cannot find more than tenuous connections between Arthur and real persons.

Many historians have concluded then that Arthur, while not a specific king with a band of knights, was eventually presented as a mythical figure based on minor warriors who had battled various invaders at different times in history. Whether or not Arthur was a historical figure, there is no question that the influence of the figure of Arthur on literature, art and history is immense.

Resources

Le Morte D'Arthur: King Arthur and the Legends of the Round Table, Signet Classics, 2001. This is Sir Thomas Malory's classic telling of the story of King Arthur's life and death. The emphasis is on Arthur's death and the dissolution of chivalry and the legend of Camelot.

The Story of King Arthur and His Knights, Kessinger Publishing, LLC, 2004. Aimed at readers aged 4 to 8, this is a reprint of the 1903 version of the story of King Arthur from Scribner's Publishers.

www.legendofkingarthur.co.uk/king-arthur-knights. Includes a list of Knights of the Roundtable and links to stories about the individual knights.

圆桌骑士

如果不提圆桌骑士，那么亚瑟王的故事就算不得完整。亚瑟王是在凯尔特异教徒的传说中首先出现的，而圆桌骑士的传说则出自中世纪的英国文学。亚瑟王的骑士们所穿的盔甲，还有他们的行为举动，都符合中世纪的骑士(初见于中世纪的法国)。

圆桌骑士是荣誉、高贵、谦恭和勇气的象征。骑士们尽职保卫妇女，并承担英勇的任务。据说，亚瑟王给选中的圆桌骑士每人授予了一枚特别的徽章。徽章上的十字提醒他们，想要寻找圣杯，生活必须要纯洁无瑕。徽章上的龙代表对亚瑟王的忠诚。圆桌则标志着平等、团结以及骑士间的友谊。亚瑟王指派给圆桌骑士的任务闻名遐迩，作为骑士精神的标志，让所有高贵人士艳羡不已。

关于圆桌，流传着好几种不同的传说。其中一种说是墨林派人为亚瑟的父亲尤瑟打造了圆桌，尤瑟又将圆桌赠与基内维尔的父亲列欧德根王。而他，在基内维尔嫁给亚瑟的时候又把圆桌当成嫁妆送给了女儿。另一种传说出现在公元1200年左右，宣称是亚瑟请人打造了这个圆桌，以容纳1600名骑士，但是折叠起来可以放置在马背上。显然，圆桌打造之前，骑士们曾为了争夺宴会中的最高位置而大打出手。另外还有一种传说则指出，圆桌只够坐下12名骑士，和最后的晚餐十分相似，留了个空位代表犹大的座位。空位为纯洁无瑕，终有一日能找到圣杯的骑士而保留。有一天，加勒哈德爵士的名字出现在那个位置上，从此以后他就一直坐这个座位。根据传说，加勒哈德最终就是找到圣杯的骑士之一。

传说还是现实？

亚瑟到底是个历史人物还是个传说角色，学者们为此争论了数个世纪。文艺复兴时期，都德王室争辩说亚瑟是个真实人物，不过他们随即追溯自己的血统到亚瑟王，并且以此证明自己对王位的继承权。然而，其他人却找不到强有力的证据，以证明亚瑟和真实世界的必然联系。

于是很多历史学家得出结论：亚瑟并非一个拥有一群骑士的君王，而是一个神话人物，其原型是在历史不同时期击退各种侵略者的无名英勇战士。但是不管亚瑟是否为真实的历史人物，毫无疑问，这一形象对文学、艺术和历史的影响都是无与伦比的。

相关资源

《亚瑟王之死：亚瑟王以及圆桌骑士的传说》，印章经典系列，2001年。这是托马斯·马洛礼爵士的经典小说，讲述亚瑟王的生平事迹。重点聚焦在亚瑟的死亡以及骑士团的分解和卡米洛城的传说。

《亚瑟王及其圆桌骑士的故事》，凯辛格出版社有限责任公司，2004年。本书以4至8岁的儿童为读者群，其实是Scribner出版社1903年的《亚瑟王故事》的再版。

www.legendofkingarthur.co.uk/king-arthur-knights 该网址列出圆桌骑士的名单，并可链接到每个骑士的生平事迹。

Twenty-three

Legend of Sleepy Hollow

The Legend of Sleepy Hollow is a short story written by an early American author, Washington Irving (1783~1859), who has the distinction of being the first American writer to earn his living only on his writing. This fact alone may be considered by some to be a legend. The actual legend of Sleepy Hollow tells of a headless horseman who wanders the countryside around Tarrytown, New York, in the early 19th century.

The Legend

The story, based on an old German folktale, takes place around 1790 in Sleepy Hollow, a part of the Dutch settlement of Tarrytown, New York, in the Catskill Mountains. Ichabod Crane, the local schoolmaster falls in love with Katrina Van Tassel, the daughter of a local farmer. Katrina, however, has another suitor as well: Brom Bones, a brawny troublemaker who brags about his exploits as a fighter.

The Van Tassels throw a party to which they invite both Crane and Bones. Crane borrows a horse named Gunpowder from his friend, Hans Van Ripper, to ride to the party. As usual, the party begins with a feast followed by music. The participants dance together and a disgruntled Bones watches Crane dance with Katrina. As the evening wears on, the storytelling starts and everyone regales one another with ghost stories and tales of haunted places. The favorite story of the evening is the oft repeated description of the headless horseman who haunts the cemetery at night. Supposedly, the local legend of the headless horseman relates the tale of the ghost of a mercenary Hessian soldier who lost his head during some nameless battle of the American Revolutionary War. According to the story, he rides nightly in search of his head.

When the party ends, Crane mounts his borrowed horse and heads home through the graveyard. Suddenly the headless horseman appears and chases him to a bridge where Crane perceives the horseman to throw his head at him.

The next morning Van Ripper's horse Gunpowder appears at his owner's barn without Ichabod Crane. The town begins a search for the schoolmaster, but when they arrive at the bridge, the townspeople find only Crane's hat and a smashed pumpkin a few yards away. Brom Bones wins the maiden Katrina and the reader is left with the impression that the headless horsemen who chased Crane after the party was really Bones in disguise.

The story is an example of the classic literary tradition of the conflict between city and countryside and between brains and brawn. In this case the countryside and brawn win, since the schoolteacher Crane disappears and the muscular Bones wins the damsel.

Literary Significance of the Author and the Work

During the late 1700s and the early 1800s New York City became a literary center. One of its notable writers was Washington Irving, born and reared in New York City, who began his career as a journalist for several periodicals in New York City. He wrote his first book, *A History of New York*, under the pen name of Dietrich Knickerbocher. Soon the word Knickerbocher became a humorous nickname for the city and residents of New York.

In 1815 Irving moved to Birmingham, England, to live with his sister and her family. While

睡谷传说

"睡谷传说"是早期美国作家华盛顿·欧文(1783~1859)的一则短篇小说。欧文是美国首位仅靠写作维生的作家,光凭这一事实情况,也构成了一个传奇。睡谷传说其实讲述了这样一个故事:19世纪初,一名无头骑士在纽约州塔利镇近郊徘徊。

睡谷传说

故事源于一个古老的德国民间传说,于1790年左右发生在卡兹奇山脉纽约州塔利镇的睡谷之中。这是一片荷兰人后裔的居住区。当地一名男教师伊卡博德·克莱恩爱上了一个农场主的女儿卡特琳娜·范·塔塞尔。可是另外有个叫布罗姆·伯恩斯的人也爱着卡特琳娜,那人四肢发达,爱惹麻烦,还总吹嘘自己是个斗士。

范·塔塞尔家举办了一场宴会,同时邀请了克莱恩和伯恩斯两人。克莱恩跟好朋友汉斯·范·瑞普尔借来一匹马,名叫"火药",骑着去参加宴会。按照惯例,宴会开始是酒席,接下来就奏起了音乐,众人一起跳舞。伯恩斯看到克莱恩和卡特琳娜共舞,心里十分恼火。夜幕降临,大家开始讲故事,每个人都兴致勃勃地讲起鬼故事或者某个地方的惊悚传闻。人们在夜间反复讲、也最喜欢听的,就是那个无头骑士半夜里在墓地徘徊的故事。当地的这则传说讲述的是一名德国赫塞雇佣兵的鬼魂,他在美国革命战争的某次无名之战中失去了头颅。传说中还提到,他总在半夜里骑着马寻找自己的头颅。

宴会结束之后,克莱恩骑着借来的马,穿过坟场径直回家。突然,无头骑士出现了,跟着他到了桥头,把自己的头颅向他扔过来。

第二天一早,范·瑞普尔的"火药"出现在自家的马厩里,但是没人看到伊卡博德·克莱恩。镇上的人四处搜寻,但在桥头,他们只找到了克莱恩的帽子,几码开外有一只摔碎的南瓜。布罗姆·伯恩斯抱得美人归。读者当然心领神会,宴会后追踪克莱恩的那个无头骑士,实则就是乔装的伯恩斯。

这个传说,是传统文学一个经典的例子,反映了城市和乡村、智慧和体力之间的冲突。本故事中,乡村和体力获得了胜利,克莱恩教师消失了,肌肉纠结的伯恩斯获取了姑娘的芳心。

作者及其作品的文学意义

18世纪末到19世纪初,纽约市已成为一个文学中心。声名鹊起的作家之一就是华盛顿·欧文,他生于此长于此,最初的写作生涯是在数家杂志担任记者。他用"迪德里希·尼克博克"这个笔名写出了第一部作品《纽约外史》。不久,"尼克博克"就成了纽约这个城市及其居民的戏称。

1815年,欧文移居英国的伯明翰,和他姐姐一家住在一起。在英期间,他撰写了第二

in England, he wrote his second book, *The Sketch Book of Geoffrey Crayon, Gent.* A huge success in both England and America, the book was a collection of short stories, including *The Legend of Sleepy Hollow*. The book was literarily significant in that Irving combined the styles of the essay and the sketch forms to create a new literary form, the short story.

Reader response to the book was instantly enthusiastic and the public particularly enjoyed *The Legend of Sleepy* Hollow and another tale from the book, *Rip Van Winkle*. *The Sketch Book of Geoffrey Crayon, Gent* was reviewed and widely read in both England and America and was the first book by an American author to become popular outside the United States. Because of this, American literature assumed its place in the world as an established art form.

Washington Irving's Later Adventures

Washington so enjoyed living in Europe that he stayed there for 17 years after his mother died in New York. He moved to Dresden for a couple of years, then to Paris for a year and finally to London. As he traveled throughout Europe he wrote about his experiences and the people he met. *Bracebridge Hall*, written in 1822, described typical daily life in England. Later when he settled for a while in Spain, he wrote *Columbus* (1828), *Conquest of Granada* (1829) and *the Companions of Columbus* (1831). The Spanish were so impressed with his scholarly research on these books about Columbus that they elected him to the Real Academia de la Historia.

Irving was happy exploring Europe, but after a while he missed his family and America. So he returned to America to live with his brother in upstate New York. He had enjoyed his travels in Europe so much, however, that he decided to venture forth in America and explore the frontier. So he set off for the west with two companions and traveled the frontier as far as Oklahoma. He wrote of these adventures in *The Cayon Miscellany and A Tour of the Prairies*, both in 1835.

In 1836 Irving returned to his brother's home where he lived until 1842 when he was appointed American ambassador to Spain. He eventually returned home to live with his brother and write until his death in 1859.

Sleepy Hollow and Rip Live on Today

As proof that ghost stories are eternally popular, there have been recent film adaptations of *The Legend of Sleepy Hollow*. *The Legend of Sleepy Hollow* starring Jeff Goldblum as Icabod Crane was produced in 1980 as a made-for-TV movie. And *Sleepy Hollow* came out in 1999, featuring Johnny Depp as Icabod Crane.

The film adaptations demonstrate that, in spite of his prolific writings and later work, what is remembered about Washington Irving are his two most popular stories. *The Legend of Sleepy Hollow* and *Rip Van Winkle*, became so well-known and loved within a few years of their first appearance in *The Sketch Book of Geoffrey Crayon, Gent* that they were later published separately in their own illustrated volumes. As time went on, most of Irving's other work has disappeared into obscurity, but *The Legend of Sleepy Hollow* lives on and is part of every school's curriculum.

Resources

The Complete Tales of Washington Irving, Da Capa Press, 1998. This book is a handy reference anthology for those who enjoy reading the tales of Washington Irving.

The Original Knickerbocker: The Life of Washington Irving, Basic Books, 2007. This biography by a well-known historian provides the important details of Washington Irving's life while at the same time emphasizing Irving's place in the birth of American literature.

Rip Van Winkle, Black Dome Press Corp., 2003. This is the story of Rip Van Winkle who drinks a magic brew that puts him to sleep for 20 years. When he awakes, he is faced with a world that has changed dramatically during the previous 2 decades.

www.hyland.ofrg/sleepyhollow. The first Website dedicated to the *Legend of Sleepy Hollow*.

部作品《见闻札记》——包括"睡谷传说"的短篇故事集。该书在英国和美国都获得了巨大的成功,具有非凡的文学价值。其关键在于欧文将散文的风格和随笔的形式结合起来,创立了一种新的文学体裁:短篇小说。

这部作品一经问世,立刻引起读者热烈的反响,公众尤其欣赏"睡谷传说"和书内另一篇传奇"瑞普·范·温克尔"。《见闻札记》在英美两国被广泛阅读,并受到众多评论。这也是美国作家的作品第一次在国外流行开来。正是有了欧文,美国文学从此在世界上被认定是一种成熟的艺术形式。

欧文的后续探险

华盛顿·欧文特别钟爱欧洲,母亲去世之后,他离开纽约,在欧洲定居了17年之久。他先是在德国的德累斯顿住了两三年,接着就搬到巴黎住了一年,最后又到伦敦。游历欧洲期间,他写了一些自己的所见所闻。1822年的《布雷斯勃列奇田庄》描绘了英国的典型日常生活。后来他又在西班牙居住一段时间,写了《哥伦布》(1828)、《攻克格拉纳达》(1829)和《哥伦布的伙伴们》(1831)。西班牙人震惊于他在这几本著作中对哥伦布的学术研究,推选他为"历史上真正的学者"。

游历欧洲,欧文始终兴致不减,但终有一日,他怀念家乡和祖国了。于是返回美国,和哥哥一起居住在纽约北部。可是他仍然醉心于游历,因而决定在国内继续探险,要前去考察边境。于是他带着两个同伴向西部出发,游历边境直至俄克拉何马州。一路上的险遇都被他写进了1835年的两部作品:《蜡笔杂集》和《草原游记》。

1836年,欧文回到哥哥家中居住下来,一直逗留到1842年,他被任命为美国驻西班牙大使。最终,他又归来,住在哥哥家里,并坚持写作,直至1859年去世。

睡谷和瑞普流传至今

最近有部影片改编自"睡谷传说",正好有力地说明了鬼怪故事永远受欢迎。由杰夫·构尔德布鲁姆扮演伊卡博德·克莱恩的《睡谷传奇》于1980年出品,这是专为电视拍摄的影片。而1999年出品的《睡谷》,则由约翰尼·德普扮演伊卡博德·克莱恩。

尽管欧文是个多产的作家,但人们牢记的还是那两篇最为出名的短篇故事,改编的电影恰恰就说明了这一点。"睡谷传说"和"瑞普·范·温克尔"最初出现在《见闻札记》后,短短数年之内,声名远扬,受到读者的钟爱,因此后来都分别出版了各自带有插图的专册。随着时间的流逝,欧文大部分其他作品都从读者眼前消失了,但是"睡谷传说"依然受欢迎,并且进入了各校的教科书。

相关资源

《华盛顿·欧文全集》,Da Capa出版社,1998年。本书是一册便携的欧文故事集。

《尼克博克起源:华盛顿·欧文生平》,基础图书,2007年。这本传记的作者是一位有名的历史学家,向人们提供了欧文生平的重要详情,同时重点强调了欧文在美国文学的创立过程中,所发挥的重要作用。

《瑞普·范·温克尔》,黑色穹顶出版社,2003年。故事讲述瑞普·范·温克尔喝了一种魔酒,致使他沉睡了20年。当他醒来,世界已经发生了戏剧性的变化。

www.hyland.ofrg/sleepyhollow 首家专门讲述"睡谷传说"的网址。

Twenty-four

Lemmings Suicide Myth

Is it really true that lemmings commit mass suicide? As a matter of fact, lemming suicide is a myth, based partly on an act of nature and partly on the perpetuation of a scene in a Disney film.

Characteristics of the Lemming

Lemmings are small animals that resemble mice. In fact, they belong to the rodent family, which includes voles, muskrats, rats, mice, hamsters and gerbils. They have long, soft gray or brown fur and, unlike mice and rats, very short stubby tails. And like many rodents, their teeth, particularly the incisors, grow continuously so that they can dig up and chew through tough foliage.

The natural habitat of lemmings is a cold northern climate, often in Scandinavia and the Arctic tundra. They are vegetarians, eating leaves, grasses, shoots and in colder months, roots and bulbs. Lemmings do not hibernate but remain active during the harsh Arctic winters, searching for remnants of grasses as well as roots and bulbs under the snow. They must also remain on the lookout for their predators, such as owls, stoats and foxes.

Like all rodents, lemmings have a high birth rate, reproducing rapidly and often. Lemmings are solitary animals, living and foraging alone until they meet to mate. As soon as they have mated, lemmings go their separate ways, so there are not family units as with other groups of animals.

Population Fluctuations and Migrations

While many members of the rodent family have population surges now and then, lemmings have the most regular fluctuations; they tend to experience a population explosion every 3 to 4 years. Their populations jump upward and then almost drop to extinction until the next population explosion. Scientists have studied such variables as food availability, stress of overcrowding, increase in predators, contagious diseases and changing weather conditions, but no one has been able to explain the periodic fluctuations of the lemming population.

What researchers have consistently found, however, is that these population explosions create lemming migrations away from the centers of dense population. As a rule, the migrations begin slowly and sporadically with a small initial group beginning to move at night and graduate to larger groups traveling during the day. In keeping with lemmings' characteristic preference for individual solitude, the overall migration does not move as a continual mass but in smaller groups with gaps of 10 or more minutes between each group. The groups tend to follow paths and roads and avoid bodies of water. However, if lemmings are forced to swim to survive, they will, but their swimming ability is poor and they are likely to drown if the weather is windy and the sea is choppy.

The Myth of the Lemming

Many people believe that lemmings commit mass suicide by leaping off cliffs into the sea during their mass migrations, which is their response to overcrowding. In reality, lemmings do not hurl themselves off cliffs into the sea. Rather, the migrating lemmings may accidentally fall off a cliff or drown while negotiating the crowd or unfamiliar territories. This is not a deliberate act of

旅鼠自杀

　　旅鼠真的集体自杀吗？事实上，旅鼠自杀只是个神话传说，它的依据部分来自自然现象，部分来自迪斯尼影片中的一个场景。

旅鼠特性

　　旅鼠是一种体型较小的动物，长得有点类似于家鼠。事实上，旅鼠属于啮齿类，这一类当中还包括鼹鼠、麝鼠、大鼠、家鼠、仓鼠和沙鼠。它们的皮毛又长又柔软，呈灰色或者棕色，尾巴和大鼠、家鼠不同，又短又粗硬。和其他众多啮齿类动物一样，旅鼠的牙齿不停地生长，尤其是门牙，这样他们才能刨地，才能将粗硬的叶子嚼烂。

　　旅鼠的自然栖息地要有寒冷的北方气候，通常是在斯堪的那维亚(指丹麦、挪威、瑞典和冰岛一带)和北极苔原地带。它们是天生的素食主义者，只吃树叶、青草、嫩枝，冷天的时候也吃植物的根茎。旅鼠从不冬眠，即使在北极的严冬中，照样活跃着寻找残草和雪底下的根茎。它们还必须保持警惕，以防天敌来犯，比如猫头鹰、黄鼠狼和北极狐。

　　和所有的啮齿类动物一样，旅鼠繁殖力极强，生殖幼崽的频度非常高。旅鼠是独居动物，独立居住，独立寻找食物，直至交配的时候才相聚。交配完成后，它们立刻分道扬镳，因此旅鼠不以家庭为单位，这一点和其他动物群是不一样的。

数量波动和迁徙

　　啮齿类动物大多都会时不时地出现数量激增现象，而旅鼠的数量波动最有规律；它们往往在3~4年的时间里就经历一次个体数目大爆炸。旅鼠的数量突然剧增，接着一下子减少到几乎灭绝，直至下一轮数量爆炸。科学家们分析了一些可变因素，比如能够寻找到的食物、过于拥挤带来的压力、天敌数目的增加、传染性的疾病以及天气环境的变化，但依然没人能够解释旅鼠数目为什么会有周期性波动。

　　不过，研究人员坚持不懈地研究，发现旅鼠数目的爆炸导致旅鼠迁离密集地。通常情况是，起初由一小支旅鼠队伍在晚间出发，速度很慢，时断时续；到后来，队伍越来越庞大，行程也改在了白天。由于旅鼠喜欢个体独居的特性，整个迁移队伍并非延绵不绝的整体，而是分成一个个小团队，相互之间间隔10多分钟的距离。这些小团队通常沿着小径和公路，避水前行。不过，如果逼得没有办法，为了生存它们也会游泳。但它们的游泳水平非常有限，如果风大起来，海面上波涛翻滚，它们多半会被淹死。

旅鼠神话

　　很多人相信，旅鼠在大规模迁移的过程中，会从悬崖跃入大海，集体自杀，这是它们解决数目过多的方法。事实上，旅鼠并不这样做。它们只不过是在穿越拥挤的或者不熟悉的区域时，可能偶尔会从悬崖跌落或者掉入水中。这可不是什么计划周密的自杀行动，而是由相互推搡、拥挤，或者在新的地方辨不清方向造成的。事实的真相恰恰完全相反：当食物和地界的竞争过于激烈时，旅鼠更可能做出的反应是相互残杀，而不是牺牲自我。总

suicide but a result of pushing and shoving and confusion in a new place. The truth of the matter is that when competition for food and space becomes overwhelming, lemmings are more likely to kill each other than to kill themselves. In general, lemmings, like most animals, place survival as their highest priority.

White Wilderness

The Walt Disney film *White Wilderness*, an Academy Award-winning nature documentary released in 1958, is considered to be the origin of the lemmings myth. Filmed in Alberta, Canada, which is neither a native habitat of lemmings nor does it boast a sea, the movie depicts a cliff plunge suicide scene of lemmings hurling themselves into the sea. The filmmakers bought a few dozen captured lemmings from Inuit children in Manitoba, Canada and imported them to Alberta for the filming. To film the suicide sequence, the filmmakers placed the lemmings on a snowcovered turntable and filmed them from different angles to simulate a mass migration. Afterward, the lemmings were transported to a cliff overlooking a river and herded off the cliff into the water. The entire scene used only a few lemmings to create the illusion of a large migration of animals forced to commit suicide because of overcrowded conditions.

No one knows if Walt Disney himself knew about the lemming scene, but it was characteristic of producers of nature documentaries at the time to capture exciting, dramatic footage to promote the films. The only difference between this particular documentary and others is that it became the basis for an enduring and widespread belief that lemmings commit suicide when their population grows too large.

This myth has become further entrenched in modern folklore as a metaphor for large groups of human beings who follow the crowd blindly regardless of consequences.

Lemmings and Global Warming

The greatest threat to lemming survival today is not the age-old problem of overcrowding and accidental death because of migrations; the bigger danger is global warming.

Lemmings need snow to insulate them from cold temperatures. This, in turn, contributes to their fertility, which affects their rate of reproduction. If they are able to reproduce, their numbers increase and they remain an important factor in the food chain of their habitat: The fewer number of lemmings, the fewer number of their predators that rely on lemmings for food. In addition, the warming of the Earth can potentially interfere with the lemmings' own food supply. Already, the tundra and other areas of their habitats are experiencing warmer temperatures, resulting in thawing and freezing that can coat the lemmings' food supply (shrubs and grasses) in ice.

Adapting to these changes is necessary for both lemmings and their predators to survive. Those who adapt will not only survive but also possibly dominate. This interference in the natural food chain is of concern to scientists and naturalists who are investigating the food web in Arctic regions for signs of significant change.People are becoming concerned about environmental changes that will affect the lemmings and other animals sharing their home.

Resources

Lemmings Don't Leap: 180 Myths, Misconceptions, and Urban Myths Exploded, Chambers, 2007. This reference book debunks common misconceptions and myths. Not only does the book provide information about the lemming myth, it examines beliefs and myths from all sorts of categories as well.

Lemmings (True Books), Children's Press, 2007. Aimed at reading levels of children aged 9 to 12, this title examines the lemming and its characteristics.

www.physorg.com/news96287811.html. This Website discusses a study by the Wildlife Conservation Society about how climate change affects lemmings.

而言之,旅鼠跟大部分动物一样,将生存问题摆在至高的地位。

《白色旷野》

沃尔特·迪斯尼的影片《白色旷野》于1958年出品,是一部获得了奥斯卡奖的自然纪录片,被人们认为是旅鼠传说的源头。这部影片的拍摄地是加拿大的阿尔伯达省,这个地方并非旅鼠的天然栖息地,也没有真正的大海。影片描绘了旅鼠从悬崖跃入海中自杀的场景。摄制组成员向马尼托巴省的因纽特小孩买了几十只旅鼠,放到阿尔伯达省用于拍摄。

为了拍摄自杀的整个过程,摄制组把买来的旅鼠放在一个覆盖着雪的转盘上,从各个角度拍摄,伪装成大迁移的情景。接着,又把旅鼠运到一个悬崖上,底下是一条河。随后把旅鼠成群赶下悬崖跃入水中。整个场景仅仅用了几十只旅鼠,但制作出来的视觉效果却是大规模的旅鼠迁移,并且由于数目过多而被迫集体自杀。

没有人知道沃尔特·迪斯尼本人是否了解旅鼠的自杀场景,但在当时,自然纪录片的制作人员都希望抓取激动人心、充满戏剧色彩的镜头以提高票房。该部影片和其他纪录片唯一的区分就在于,它为以后长期广泛流传的旅鼠因为数量过多而集体自杀的神话奠定了基础。

这一神话进一步渗入现代民间传说,成了一则隐喻,讽喻那些无视后果,盲目随大流的人。

旅鼠和全球变暖

时至今日,旅鼠最大的生存危机并非长久以来密度过大的问题,亦非迁移过程中意外的死亡;更大的危机在于全球气候变暖。

旅鼠需要雪的覆盖,以助它们隔开寒冷的气温。并且这也有助于他们的生殖,影响到它们的繁殖力。如果它们能够不断繁殖,数量就会增加,就能在栖息地的食物链中维持重要的作用:旅鼠的数量越少,以旅鼠为生的肉食动物就越少。同时,地球变暖也潜在的影响了旅鼠自身的食物供应。在苔原地带以及其他旅鼠栖息地,气温已经比原来偏高,导致可以覆盖旅鼠食物(灌木和草根)的冰雪融化。

为了生存,旅鼠和它的天敌都不得不适应这些变化。只有适应环境,才能存活下来,甚至有可能占统治地位。对自然界的食物链进行干涉,在科学家和自然学家们看来,非常有意义。他们在北极地区调查食物网,想探索出重大变化的标志。人们开始关注环境变化,因为这才真正影响了旅鼠及其附近动物们的生活。

相关资源

《旅鼠并不往下跳:180则传说、误解和都市神话大揭秘》,钱伯斯出版社,2007年。这本工具书揭开了一些常见的误解和神话之谜,不仅提供了旅鼠神话的相关信息,而且核查了各种类别的迷信和神话。

《旅鼠》,儿童出版社,2007年。本书以9~12岁的少年儿童为读者群,核查了旅鼠及其特性。

www.physorg.com/news96287811.html 该网址探讨了野生生物保护学会所作的一项研究:气候变化是如何对旅鼠产生影响的。

Twenty-five

Lincoln & Kennedy Connections

When what appears to be a senseless tragedy occurs, there is a tendency to search for meaning or patterns that can explain the event. Such is the case with the list of coincidences between the two United States presidents, Abraham Lincoln and John F. Kennedy, both of who were assassinated while in office.

The list of coincidences or connections between these two presidents first appeared in 1964, shortly after the 1963 assassination of John F. Kennedy during his visit to Dallas, Texas. While most of the items on the list—and similar lists—have been debunked by historians, the coincidences nevertheless are somewhat eerie, and for this reason have persisted for more than 40 years.

The List

The most common coincidences between the two presidents are as follows:

· Both Abraham Lincoln and John Kennedy have seven letters in their last names.

· Both Lincoln and Kennedy were second children and named for their grandfathers.

· Abraham Lincoln was elected to Congress in 1846; John Kennedy was elected to Congress in 1946.

· Abraham Lincoln was runner-up for his party's vice presidential nomination in 1856; John Kennedy was runner-up for his party's vice presidential nomination in 1956.

· Abraham Lincoln was elected president in 1860; John Kennedy was elected president in 1960.

· Lincoln had a secretary named Kennedy; Kennedy had a secretary named Lincoln. Both secretaries warned her boss not to go to, respectively, the theater and Dallas.

· Both were focused on civil rights, Lincoln facing the issue of slavery and Kennedy concerned with equal rights for all Americans, including African-Americans.

· Both were assassinated on a Friday in the presence of their wives.

· Both were shot in the head.

· Lincoln was killed in the Ford Theater; Kennedy was killed in a Lincoln limousine manufactured by Ford Motor Company.

· Both assassins were known by three names: Lincoln's assassin was John Wilkes Booth and Kennedy was shot by Lee Harvey Oswald.

· Both assassins have 15 letters in their names.

· Booth ran from the theater and was found by federal agents in a tobacco warehouse; Oswald ran from a warehouse and was found by the police in a movie theater.

· Both assassins were killed before they were put on trial.

· Both Lincoln and Kennedy were succeeded by southern Democrats and former senators named Johnson who were born 100 years apart. Andrew Johnson, who was Lincoln's vice president, was born in 1808, and Lyndon Johnson, Kennedy's successor, was born in 1908.

· Both Johnsons have 13 letters in their names.

Connecting distantly related facts and stretching information can yield even more similarities,

林肯与肯尼迪

　　当悲剧不知不觉发生时，人们总会寻找悲剧发生的原因。如:两位美国总统亚伯拉罕·林肯与约翰·弗·肯尼迪在任职期间都遭到刺杀，还有很多方面竟如此巧合。

　　约翰·弗·肯尼迪于1963年考察得克萨斯州达拉斯，在那里惨遭暗杀，随后就出现了两位总统之间的诸多相似之处。

　所列如下

　·亚伯拉罕·林肯和约翰·肯尼迪总统的姓都是7个字母。

　·林肯和肯尼迪他们在家中排行都是老二,名字都是他们祖父给取的。

　·亚伯拉罕·林肯于1846年当选国会议员，而约翰·肯尼迪却是在1946年当选为国会议员。

　·亚伯拉罕·林肯于1856年被提名为副总统，而约翰·肯尼迪于1956年被提名为副总统。

　·亚伯拉罕·林肯于1860年当选为总统，而约翰·肯尼迪于1960年当选为总统。

　·林肯的秘书名叫肯尼迪，而肯尼迪的秘书名叫林肯，两位都分别提醒他们不要去剧院和达拉斯。

　·两位总统都关注民权:林肯关注奴隶制度问题，而肯尼迪关心美国人包括美籍非洲人平等权的问题。

　·两位总统都是星期五遭刺杀，并且他们的妻子都在现场。

　·林肯是在福特剧院被杀，而肯尼迪却在福特汽车公司制造的林肯牌轿车里被杀害。

　·刺杀林肯的凶手叫约翰·威尔克思·布思，而枪杀肯尼迪的凶手叫李·哈维·奥斯瓦德，他们的名字都是3个单词。

　·刺杀两位总统凶手的名字都是15个字母。

　·事后，布恩从剧院逃走，后来被烟草仓库的一位代理商发现，而奥斯瓦尔德从仓库逃走，后来被电影院的警察发现。

　·两位凶手都在审判前自杀。

　·安德鲁·约翰逊，生于1808年，前任参议员，林肯在位时是副总统;而林肯·约翰逊，生于1908年，前任参议员，肯尼迪在位时是副总统，他们都是南方人，年龄却恰好相差100岁。

　·两位约翰逊的名字都是13个字母。

　　从以前的很多相关事实的信息中，人们还能发现更多的巧合。的确，上面的所说的一

which appear to be something of a reach. Indeed, many of the commonly accepted coincidences as listed above do not withstand close scrutiny. While some items on the list are true, others have been either refuted or dismissed.

Refuting the Folklore of the Connections

At first glance, the coincidences between the two presidents who served 100 years apart seem amazing, especially given that both men were assassinated while in office. However, several of the items on the list are either factually incorrect or have been misinterpreted to fit the list. For example, it is true that each man was elected to office—first Congress and then the presidency—100 years apart. Yet that is where the similarity between their respective political careers ends. Lincoln began as a state legislator who, after his single term in the House of Representatives, did not win any national political office until he was elected president in 1860. Kennedy, on the other hand, had been elected and re-elected to national office several times before he became president. He served in the House of Representatives for three terms before filling a Senate seat in 1952, to which he was re-elected in 1958 before running for president in 1960.

As far as the presidency is concerned, Lincoln was re-elected to a second term in 1864, but Kennedy never had the opportunity because he was killed in the third year of his first term as president.

Other minor coincidences are simply coincidental or incorrect. The number of letters in the names of each president as well as in the names of the assassins are simple coincidences. The stories about each man's secretaries, however, are wrong. Kennedy's secretary was indeed named Evelyn Lincoln, but there is no evidence that she did or did not urge Kennedy to forgo the Dallas trip. Historical research shows that Lincoln had two secretaries: John Nicolay and John Hay. There is no mention of anyone named Kennedy who served him as secretary.

The coincidence that both assassins were known by three names is also not exactly true. While both men had three names, they did not commonly use all three names and only became known by their full names after they appeared in newspaper accounts. Booth, an actor, was often called J. Wilkes Booth or John Wilkes to distinguish him from his brother, also an actor. Lee Harvey Oswald normally was called Lee Oswald.

Civil Rights

Both Abraham Lincoln and John Kennedy are portrayed as presidents with a deep interest in civil rights. In fact, neither man showed a particular concern about civil rights, although each man lived and served during a time when civil rights were an issue. Nevertheless, there is no evidence that either man would have changed the racial situation had political events not forced them to address the issue. Although Lincoln personally opposed slavery, he was concerned more with how slavery divided the Union rather than with how he could liberate the slaves. He also questioned whether white citizens would accept the end of slavery. Many historians even think that the Emancipation Proclamation was issued as a political expedient during wartime. The actual follow up—constitutional amendments ending slavery and extending the right to vote to all races—were not enacted until after Lincoln's death.

In Kennedy's case, he promoted civil rights and appropriate legislation only after several riots and crises, such as the University of Mississippi's refusal to accept a black student and the bombing of a black church in Birmingham, Alabama, made it imperative that something be done. Kennedy did not actively make civil rights a priority so the legislation languished in Congress. Only after his death in 1963 did the Civil Rights Act of 1965 and the Voting Rights Act of 1965 pass, championed by his successor, Lyndon Johnson.

系列巧合,许多人已普遍认同,但很多也经不起认真地推敲,因为其中一些是真实的,另一些也曾遭到质疑。

来自民间的驳斥

乍一看,百年来,两位总统之间的一系列巧合,特别是在任职期间均遭到暗杀一事,这似乎令人惊讶。但事实上,上述所说的很多方面要么是错误的,要么被曲解了。例如:两位总统第一次当选为国会议员和后来当选为总统,时间相差100年,这是事实。但是,林肯政治生涯是从州议员开始的,在众议院任职满一届后,直到1860年当选为总统前,都没有赢得任何的政府官员职位;而肯尼迪在成为总统前,多次当选政府官员,3次当选为众议院议员,1952年和1958年2次当选为参议院议员,1960年当选为总统。就总统职位而言,1864年林肯再次当选为总统;而肯尼迪在总统第一任期的第三年就遭到暗杀。

另外一些细微的巧合仅仅是巧合罢了,或者根本不属实。如:两位总统的姓都是7个字母及凶手的名字是15个字母,这纯属巧合。而有关两位总统的秘书的故事,则完全不正确。肯尼迪的秘书真名是爱维琳·林肯,她是否曾提醒肯尼迪不要去达拉斯访问则无从考证,历史研究表明林肯总统有两位秘书:一位是约翰·尼克拉,另一位叫约翰·海,没有人提到有一位叫肯尼迪的人做他的秘书。

两位凶手的名字都是3个单词,这根本不属实。两个凶手名字确实是3个单词,但是平时很少用,仅在报纸的报道材料中出现过。布思是一位演员,全名是吉·维尔克斯·布思,为了避免与他同样当演员的兄弟相混淆,也被称为约翰·维尔克斯;而李·哈维·奥斯瓦尔德平时被称为李·奥斯瓦尔德。

民权

许多报道说,亚伯拉罕·林肯与约翰·肯尼迪总统都关注民权问题,事实上,在两位总统生活的时代和任职期间,民权确实是一个热点问题,但两位总统都不太关注民权问题。尽管林肯总统反对奴隶制度,但他更关心的是奴隶制度会导致国家分裂而不是解放奴隶,是否当时的政治事件逼迫林肯关注奴隶制度问题,来改变种族歧视现状,这一点无法考证。甚至对白人是否同意接受废除奴隶制度这一问题,林肯自己也怀疑。许多历史学家甚至认为,林肯发表《解放奴隶宣言》,这是战争时期的一种政治手段,事实上,直到林肯去世后,才修改宪法,废除奴隶制度,使全体公民享有选举权。

至于肯尼迪总统,在其任职期间,爆发了许多动乱和危机,如:密西西比大学拒绝接收黑人学生,位于阿拉巴马州的伯明翰黑人教堂遭爆炸袭击,这些都迫使他着手改善民权,但进展缓慢。1963年,肯尼迪总统逝世后,林德·约翰逊继任总统,1965年《民权法案》和《1965年选举权法案》才得以通过。

Similarities of the Two Johnsons

The fact that both Lincoln and Kennedy were succeeded by southerners is logical given the political circumstances of each president. Lincoln was a northerner running for re-election in a country torn by civil war between the north and the south. He needed a southerner as a vice presidential running mate to balance the ticket. So he selected Andrew Johnson from Tennessee, a southerner who had remained loyal to the Union. Similarly, Kennedy was a northern New Englander, and he needed a southern vice presidential mate to appeal to the south and the west. Lyndon Johnson of Texas fit the bill. The coincidence that both vice presidents were named Johnson may be explained by the name's being so common in both Lincoln and Kennedy's eras.

Considering all of the facts behind the coincidences surrounding these two presidents, it would seem that connecting the two men may have originated in a national wish to make sense of two similarly troubled times. While some of the coincidences are actually true, many have been purposed as a way to show a pattern in analogous tragedies.

Resources

www.geocities.com/nephilimnot/coincidences_presidents.html. This Website lists numerous connections and coincidences between the Lincoln and Kennedy presidencies, many of which appear to be somewhat of a stretch.

History Is Repeating Itself: Through Coincidences in the American Presidency, Trafford Publishing, 2006. This book presents coincidences within the American presidency and among U.S. Presidents. It includes Lincoln and Kennedy among its descriptions of the presidents.

两位约翰逊的相似之处

从逻辑上看，林肯与肯尼迪两位总统所处的政治环境决定了其继任者是南方人士。林肯自身是北方人，在竞选第二任总统时，美国爆发内战，为了安抚选民，他需要一位来自南方的副总统。来自田纳西州的南方人安德鲁·约翰逊，长期以来忠于联邦政府，于是被他看中。类似地，肯尼迪来自北方的新英格兰州，为了吸引西南地区的选票，他也需要一位来自南方的副总统作为搭档，得克萨斯州的林德·约翰逊便是合适人选。两位约翰逊副总统有着一样的名字，这在当时其实是再普通不过的事情了。

纵观两位总统身处的时代，我们不难理解这些巧合背后的事实，其中一些是真实的，许多也是故意用来阐释这些相似悲剧的。

相关资源

www.geocities.com/nephilimnot/coincidences_presidents.html. 该网址提供了关于林肯与肯尼迪总统很多惊人巧合的事情。

《历史在重演：美国总统的巧合》，特拉福德出版社，2006年。本书记录了美国总统很多惊人巧合的事情，包括林肯与肯尼迪总统。

Twenty-six

Loch Ness Monster

The Loch Ness Monster, often referred to as Nessie, is an unidentified aquatic animal that supposedly lives in Loch Ness, a large, freshwater lake near the city of Inverness in northern Scotland.Today there are those who assert that Nessie is a myth while others equally fervently claim that the animal exists.

Early Sightings

The earliest reported sighting of Nessie was recorded in 565 A.D. by Adamnan in the *Life of St. Columba*, a biography of the man who is reputed to have introduced Christianity to Scotland.

Yet even before Adamnan's report, early Romans invading Scotland in the 1st century found stones around Loch Ness with picture carvings of animals. The inhabitants of northern Scotland at that time were the Picts, an ancient tribe of tattoo-covered people. The Picts' fascination with animals was revealed in their drawings and carvings and their artists took great care to depict the animal subjects realistically. Thus, all of the animals in the carvings were easily recognizable. That is, all but one unusual creature with a long beak, a head spout and flippers. Because it could not be compared to any known animal, many observers decided it could be some sort of swimming elephant.

It is interesting to note that Scottish folk tales tell of many large mythical beasts that are associated with waterways and lakes. Many of the stories ascribe magical powers to these animals. The tale of the Loch Ness Monster, on the other hand, was quite specific with details etched into stones surrounding the lake and the story persisted. In fact, its main impact was its effect on local folklore, because the Pictish stone carvings of this strange beast were the beginning of a story that has captured the imagination of people for more than 1,500 years.

Modern Legend

The modern version of the Loch Ness Monster legend began in 1933 on a warm spring afternoon. A new road that provided the first clear view of the lake from the north side had just been built along the shore. A local couple driving home on this road suddenly glimpsed what they described as "an enormous animal rolling and plunging on the surface"of the water. They described what they saw to a reporter for the *Inverness Courier* whose editor used the word monster for the first time in describing the animal. Thus began the modern media infatuation with the Loch Ness sighting.

Public interest began to build during that spring and then escalated quickly when another couple reported seeing the creature out of the water shambling across the shore road.

Excitement continued to grow when the *London Daily Mirror* hired a big game hunter, Marmaduke Wetherell, to investigate the area. Within a few days, the hunter found fresh footprints of a large, four-toed animal, which he estimated to be about 20 feet long. Wetherell immediately sent plaster casts of the footprints to London's Natural History Museum for analysis.

While waiting for the museum's report, hundreds of thrill seekers descended on Inverness and Loch Ness, filling the local hotels and creating massive traffic jams.

The news was disappointing. The specialists at the museum reported that the footprints were

尼斯湖水怪

尼斯湖水怪,也称"尼西"(意为尼斯湖里的有趣的小怪物),是水生动物,据说生活在苏格兰北部恩华利斯市附近的大淡水湖里。今天,一些人的确认为这种动物存在,而另一些认为尼斯湖水怪是一个神话故事。

早期发现

公元565年,亚当曼在《哥伦布的一生》(哥伦布曾把基督教带到苏格兰,从此他的名字家喻户晓)这部传记中提到尼斯湖水怪,这是关于尼斯湖水怪的最早记录。

在亚当曼之前,公元一世纪,早期入侵苏格兰的罗马人发现,尼斯湖周围的石头上刻有这些动物。那时皮克特人在苏格兰北部一带生活,他们是一支古老的文身部落。从那些艺术家的绘画和雕刻中可以知道皮克特人对那种动物很感兴趣。这种动物很特别,很长的钩形鼻子,像嘴一样的头及鳍状肢,不像一般的常见动物,许多人认为可能是某种会游泳的大象。

有趣的是苏格兰民间故事中叙述的很多巨大神奇的动物都与水域和湖泊有关。它们都有神奇的魔力。尼斯湖水怪这个民间故事,具体详细地描绘了湖边石头上刻画的动物形象,一千五百多年来,人们一直在想象尼斯湖水怪的模样。

现代传说

有关尼斯湖水怪的现代传说发生在1933年。那是一个温暖的春天下午,沿着湖边刚刚修建好一条新路,这样从北边可以清晰地看到湖的美景。那天,当地一对夫妇正驾车回家,突然看到湖面有一个巨大的动物从堤边侧身跃入湖中。后来这对夫妇经过认真冷静的回忆,写了一篇文章,在英国《长披风信使报》上发表,从此尼斯湖水怪为全世界所知。这便开始了尼斯湖水怪的现代传说。

在那个春天之后,又有一对夫妇说看到尼斯湖水怪在湖边马路上慢慢地走过,人们便开始更加关注它。

伦敦《每日镜报》派出大名鼎鼎的记者马尔马杜克·韦特雷尔来到此地,寻访水怪。几天后,他发现了庞大的、刚留下的四趾动物脚印,估计20英尺长,很快他将该脚印模型送往伦敦自然历史博物馆分析。在等待分析结果的几天里,几百名探求者纷纷涌到恩华利斯市和尼斯湖畔,造成当地旅馆爆满,交通阻塞。

结果令人失望,博物馆专家认定这些是河马留下的脚印。人们不知道是自己被韦特雷尔戏弄和欺骗,还是韦特雷尔自己也是受害者。但是这件事情确实降低了人们对尼斯

those of a hippopotamus—and not just any hippopotamus, but a stuffed hippo foot from the base of an umbrella stand or an ashtray stand. No one knew if Wetherell was the victim or perpetrator of the hoax, but the incident deflated the interest in the Loch Ness Monster and delayed serious study of the situation.

In 1934, however, interest was rekindled when the *Daily Mirror* published a striking photo of the monster that solidified the image of the Loch Ness Monster into the public's mind forever. The photo shows a slender neck topped by a small head emerging from the water. Because the photo appeared in a credible source, many people decided that the photo was proof of the existence of the monster.An animal with a small head, a long slender neck and one or more humps protruding above the water. Some also reported flippers. The Loch Ness Monster now had a specific visual image that has since become familiar to everyone.

Sixty years later in 1994, investigators reported that the 1934 photo was a fake, part of a scheme to scam the *Daily Mail*. The ruse was uncovered when Ian Wetherell, Marmaduke's son, revealed that his father, angry about the *Daily Mail's* treatment of him after the hippo foot incident, created a phony photograph using clay mounted on a toy submarine. The photo that was once considered evidence of the existence of the Loch Ness Monster was now looked upon as proof that the monster was not real.

Does Nessie Exist?

Some people think that the number of reported sightings should create circumstantial evidence that the monster does, indeed, exist. In addition, several sonar experts from both the United Kingdom and the United States have explored Loch Ness and have detected large moving objects deep under water. Some of these expeditions have also recorded chirp, click and swishing sounds in Loch Ness. Still others have obtained murky underwater photographs of objects that resemble animals.

On the other hand, a BBC team used sonar and satellite navigation techniques to search for Nessie but found no trace of the monster. They made a thorough examination of all sections and depths of the lake for a large moving object, but the team only found a buoy anchored several meters below the surface.

The BBC group, as well as many others, has put forth the idea that the Loch Ness Monster is really a plesiosaur, a marine reptile that became extinct about the same time as dinosaurs. Supporters of this idea cite the coelacanth, a 400 million-year-old fish that was once thought to have become extinct along with the dinosaurs 65 million years ago but was discovered alive and well in 1938. Others, however, point out Loch Ness is too small to support an animal as large as a plesiosaur, and the waters are too cold for a cold-blooded plesiosaur. Nevertheless, some scientists claim that animals adapt to survive and the conditions in Loch Ness could conceivably support a plesiosaur.

Yet observers'preconceived ideas seem to influence what they think they see. The BBC team even tested this by concealing a fence post below the surface of the lake and then raising it as a group of tourists passed by. Later most of the tourists said they had seen a square object, but several sketched Nessie's head when asked to draw what they saw.

The final answer may simply be that the Loch Ness Monster is too much fun to relinquish.

Resources

The Loch Ness Monster: The Evidence, Birlinn Publishers, 2004.

www.mysteriousbritian.co.uk/fortean/nessie.html. Website to guide you to mysterious places, legends and folklore within the British Isles.

湖水怪的关注度和研究热情。

然而，到了1934年，《每日邮报》在醒目的位置刊登了一张尼斯湖水怪的照片。在照片中，可以看到一个怪物伸长脖子，将小脑袋露出水面，再次激起了人们对尼斯湖水怪的关注。由于照片来源可靠，许多人说这张照片可以证明尼斯湖水怪确实存在。小小的脑袋，细长的脖子，露出两个驼峰似的脊背，有些还说有鳍状肢。如今，人们已熟悉了尼斯湖水怪，模样也清晰具体了。

60年后(1994年)，调查者说1934年刊的照片是假的。兰·韦特雷尔(马尔马杜克·韦特雷尔的儿子)揭露了其父亲的骗局，照片是用玩具动物塑造了河马脚，并对《每日邮报》刊登父亲照片一事很生气。这张假照片再次证明了尼斯湖水怪不存在。

尼斯湖水怪存在吗

人们认为，有关见到尼斯湖水怪的报道足以证明其确实存在。此外，许多来自英美两国的鱼群探测专家研究了尼斯湖，发现深水中有一种巨大的运动物体和吱吱沙沙等声音，有人还拍到了类似动物的水底运动物体的模糊照片。

相反，BBC考查队利用鱼群探测技术和超声波导航技术来探测尼斯湖，并没有发现怪物的迹象。他们全面而深入地研究了湖底巨大的运动物体，认为湖底深处的巨大运动物体是漂浮的锚状物罢了。

如许多其他人一样，BBC考查团认为尼斯湖水怪其实是一种蛇颈龙的水生爬行动物，它们已经灭绝了(在恐龙灭绝时期)。支持者认为，四亿年前的空棘鱼(早在6500年前已经灭绝，即恐龙灭绝时期)，于1938年又出现了。然而，也有人认为尼斯湖湖面太小，巨大的蛇颈龙无法生存，同时湖水太凉，冷血蛇颈龙不能适应。尽管如此，一些科学家认为，尼斯湖的生存环境完全适宜蛇颈龙的生存。

然而，科学家们怀疑人们的心理在作祟才导致一系列的"目击"证据。BBC考查队曾做过一个试验，他们将一个篱笆桩偷偷放入尼斯湖湖底，并在游客众多的地方将其浮出水面。结果显示，大多数游客说他们看到了一个方形物体，并且绘声绘色的描述出怪物的头，勾勒出尼斯湖水怪的模样。

最终答案或许是：尼斯湖水怪很有趣，继续关注。

相关资源

《尼斯湖水怪：证据》，Birlinn出版社，2004年。

www.mysteriousbritian.co.uk/fortean/nessie.html. 该网址主要介绍了不列颠岛上很多神秘地方，相关传说及民间故事。

Twenty-seven

Lost Dutchman's Gold Mine

The legend of the lost Dutchman's gold mine has all the ingredients of a fascinating story: Lost treasure, gold, sacred land, fierce Indians, the Wild West and a rugged mountain with an ominous name.

The Story of the Lost Mine

The story begins in the Superstition Mountain near what is today Apache Junction, approximately 30 miles east of Phoenix, Arizona. Around the year 1540, Spanish conquistadors, led by Francisco Vasquez Coronado searching for the legendary Seven Golden Cities of Cibola reported by earlier Spanish explorers, reached Superstition Mountain. The Apaches told Coronado about the vast gold reserves in the mountain but warned him that the Thunder God would destroy anyone who trespassed on the sacred ground.

Ignoring the warnings of the Indians, Coronado and his men searched for gold, but men began to disappear in the wilderness. Searching for their comrades, the Spanish found only bodies, many of which were decapitated. This was enough to deter the Spaniards, who fled the region. As he left, Coronado dubbed the mountain Superstition Mountain because of the mysteries surrounding it.

Peralta's Discovery

The first man to discover gold on Superstition Mountain was Don Miguel Peralta, a prominent rancher from Sonora, Mexico. In 1845 he found a rich deposit of gold and prepared to return to Mexico for men and supplies to mine the area. Before he left the mountain, he memorized the landmarks surrounding the site, one of which resembled a sombrero. He called his find the Sombrero Mine. Later, another explorer, P. Weaver, stumbled onto Sombrero Mine and decided it looked like a needle. After he carved his name at the base, the formation became known as Weaver's Needle, an important landmark for later explorers.

Peralta mined the site for a few years, sending vast quantities of gold back to Sonora. Meanwhile, the Apache, angry that the Mexicans were trespassing on sacred land, prepared to strike. Peralta learned about the attack and packed up his men, concealing the approach to the mine until he could return. He never made it; the Apaches massacred the entire group of Mexicans except for one Peralta cousin who lived to tell the story. Meanwhile, in 1848 the United States annexed the land as the Arizona Territory, and the Peralta family lost their land grant to the United States. They could no longer legally mine the site.

Jacob Waltz

A German immigrant named Jacob Waltz gave the legend its name of the lost Dutchman's mine. German immigrants were often called Dutchmen, a mispronunciation of the word Deutch, which means German in English. Waltz came to the United States in the 1840s and headed for California when the Gold Rush of 1849 began. In 1861 he became a citizen and could thereafter legally file claims. Moving to the Arizona Territory, he began to prospect around Superstition Mountain. Supposedly he met the Peralta survivor from the earlier Apache massacre, which led many to think that the mine Waltz claimed to find was the original Peralta mine.

失落的金矿

失落的金矿，一个神奇的故事:失去的财富、金子、神圣土地、残忍的印第安人以及西部荒凉地，还有不知道名称的崎岖山脉。

失落的金矿

故事发生在迷信山附近(今阿帕契附近)，位于亚利桑那州凤凰郡东部大约30英里处。大约1540年，弗朗西斯科·瓦斯奎兹·科罗拉多率领西班牙征服军到达这里，寻找早期西班牙探险家所说的西波拉市的七座传奇金矿。阿帕契人告诉科罗拉多，山上藏有很多金子，但警告说不要非法侵入这块神圣土地，否则会遭雷神惩罚。

没有理会印第安人的提醒，科罗拉多和他的人开始淘金，但所有人都消失了。后来，西班牙人寻找他们，只发现具具尸体，许多是无头尸，西班牙人害怕极了，便逃离此地，迷信山便由此得名。

佩拉塔的发现

佩拉塔，一位杰出的牧场主。来自墨西哥胡安·米格尔·佩拉塔，是第一个找到迷信山金矿的人。1845年，他发现了一块丰富的金矿储地，便准备返回墨西哥，叫人来开采金矿。在下山前，他记住了金矿周围的界标，其中一处像阔边帽，阔边帽金矿便由此而来。又一位探险家，皮·韦弗也找到了这块金矿，他认为这块地方像一根针，后来把自己的名字刻在山底，形状就像纺织的针。这也成为后继探险家探险的重要界标。

开采了几年金矿，佩拉塔带回了大量的金子。此时，阿帕契人痛恨墨西哥人(墨西哥人非法入侵神圣土地)，准备攻击他们，佩拉塔了解到情况，解雇了所有采矿人，偷偷返回家去，没有告诉任何人金矿的位置，因此也没有人知道通往金矿的道路。后来，阿帕契人屠杀了所有墨西哥采矿工人，只有佩拉塔的侄子活着回来，说起这件事情。1848年，美国人占领了亚利桑那地区，控制了这里的金矿，从此，佩拉塔家族失去了这块金地。

雅各·华尔兹

雅各·华尔兹，生于德国，19世纪40年代移民到美国，1849年淘金热兴起时，去了加利福尼亚州，1861年，成为合法的美国公民。德国移民也称Dutchmen，Dutchmen在英语里的含义是德国人，是由于单词Deutch发音错误引起的。华尔兹随后来到亚利桑那，开始勘探迷信山。据说，他曾碰见佩拉塔(阿帕契人大屠杀的幸存者)，因此，很多人认为华尔兹要找的金矿就是先前佩拉塔的金矿。

Waltz continued to live modestly in the Phoenix area, although he always seemed to have gold in his pockets. In 1887 an earthquake struck the area, rearranging the landscape on Superstition Mountain. There are reports that Waltz could no longer find the mine, because the earthquake had obliterated landmarks. In 1891 a flood devastated the Phoenix area and destroyed Waltz' s property. Concerned about him, a friend, Julia Thomas, found him struggling in his flooded house. She took him in and nursed him through a bout of pneumonia. During his illness, she questioned him about the location of his mine and after his death she sold her business and set out to find the mine.

She was unsuccessful. To recover her losses, she began to sell maps to lead prospectors to the mine site, but no one ever found it. It is possible that the maps were deliberately misleading, which only adds to the mystery of the legend.

Fact or Fiction?

There is documentary evidence—mining claims, census records and other public references—that Jacob Waltz did exist. But the question of whether or not he found a rich vein of ore and exactly where he found it has not really been answered.

According to the legend, Waltz's mine is located in Superstition Mountain near an outcrop known as Weaver's Needle. In nearby areas there are many gold mines that have yielded significant quantities of gold. Yet no one can say with any certainty that Jacob Waltz's mine is among them. So while it is clear that Waltz existed and that gold was found in areas near the site of his mine, many believe that it has not actually been proven that one of these mines is actually the lost Dutchman' s gold mine.

On the other hand, some explorers propose that the lost gold mine has, indeed, already been located. The Bull Dog Mine, discovered in November of 1892, matches the description and location of the lost Dutchman's mine. The ledge of gold in the Bull Dog Mine fits Waltz's exact description of the ledge of gold in the mine he found. Waltz also mentioned that his mine was in a location that was subject to attack from the Apache Indians. The Bull Dog Mine also is in a location that was the site of numerous Apache attacks. Therefore, many think that the lost mine of the Dutchman is no longer lost.

Therefore, many people are still looking for the lost Dutchman's mine. There is a Superstition wilderness area approximately 30 miles east of Phoenix, Arizona, just beyond Apache Junction near the old mining town of Goldfield. Explorers and treasure seekers camp in the campgrounds of Lost Dutchmen State Park at the foot of Superstition Mountain and search for the lost mine. Most visitors recommend visiting during the winter between late fall and early spring—when the temperatures are lower, thus making hiking and camping more enjoyable.

Resources

The Bible on the Lost Dutchman Gold Mine and Jacob Waltz: A Pioneer History of the Gold Rush (Prospecting and Treasure Hunting), Wolfe Publishing, 2002. This book is a pioneer history of the Arizona Territory and the West based on the journals of early settlers and prospectors in the West. The old journals have not been edited or modified and the book provides differing accounts of the same events written by different people.

www.superstitionmountainmuseum.org/LostDutchmanExhibit.htm. Website of the Superstition Mountain Museum, the Jacob Waltz "Lost Dutchman" exhibit.

华尔兹尽管很有钱(拥有很多金子),但从不张扬,在凤凰地区一带过着平静的生活。1887年,这里发生了大地震,迷信山地形完全改变,金矿周围的界标也消失了。据说,华尔兹再也没有找到那座金矿。1891年,这里爆发了洪水,淹没了华尔兹的房屋,他无家可归,还感染上了肺炎。这时,他的一位朋友——朱莉娅·詹姆斯,把他带回自己家,精心照料。华尔兹后来告诉詹姆斯金矿的具体位置。华尔兹死后,詹姆斯变卖了所有家产,去寻找那座金矿。

最终她也没能找到那座金矿。为了挽回原有的家业,她便开始将标有金矿位置的地图卖给探险家们,可能地图上的标志故意误导,以至于没有人找到过那座金矿,这样使得这座金矿变得更加神秘。

事实还是虚构

确实有文件材料——采矿证明,户籍调查证明,其他公共证明——证明有雅各·华尔兹这个人。但他是否找到了金矿矿脉,金矿的具体位置在哪,这些都不得而知。

据说,华尔兹找到的金矿位于皮·韦弗针形区尖头处附近,迷信山一带。这里曾有人采到过大量的金子。但是,无人知道华尔兹金矿的具体位置。也很明显,这一带已发现大量金子,华尔兹金矿确实存在,华尔兹金矿是否就是先前失落的金矿,这一点并不清楚。

一些探险家也认为失落的金矿确实存在。1892年11月,他们发现了叭喇狗金矿,这与传说中失落的金矿相吻合,如:叭喇狗金矿的周围地形与华尔兹金矿周围地形一致,都容易受到阿帕契人的攻击。因此,很多人认为失落的金矿又回来了。

总之,许多人仍在寻找失落的金矿,有人在古老的金矿区附近发现了神秘的荒凉地带,位于阿帕契附近,亚利桑那州凤凰地区东部大约30英里处。探险家和寻宝者们都纷纷来到迷信山山脚,在一座国家公园扎营,以便寻找失落的金矿。大多数参观者建议最好在冬季(深秋与早春之间)来这里,因为这时气温较低,更适合徒步旅行和露营。

相关资源

《失落的金矿与华尔兹:一部淘金热的开拓史》,沃尔夫出版社,2002年。本书讲述了美国西部及亚利桑那地区的开拓史,很多内容仍是基于早期定居者及勘探者的日记。本书提供了不同的人对同一事件的看法,并未对相关内容做任何修改。

www.superstitionmountainmuseum.org/LostDutchmanExhibit.htm 迷信山博物馆及雅各·华尔兹"失落的金矿"展览馆网址。

Twenty-eight

Lost Patrol

One of the most intriguing mysteries in the history of aviation was the disappearance of five U.S. Navy torpedo bombers—and later its rescue plane—while performing a routine training mission on a clear day off the coast of Florida. Known as Flight 19 or the Lost Patrol, the squadron vanished off the face of the Earth and remains one of the most perplexing mysteries in the history of aviation.

The Mission

At 2:10 p.m. on the afternoon of December 5, 1945, Flight 19 left the Naval Air Station at Fort Lauderdale, Florida. The squadron, consisting of five TBM Avenger Torpedo Bombers swung out eastward over the Atlantic Ocean on a routine 2-hour navigational training mission. Each plane carried three crew members, a pilot, radio operator and gunner for a total of 15 men. The flight leader, Lt. Charles Taylor, was an experienced combat pilot and a qualified flight instructor. The aircraft were the most powerful and efficient available and they had been checked out carefully in the preflight process.

At around 3:45 p.m. a radio message between the leader on Flight 19 and another pilot in the squadron indicated that the instructor was lost and uncertain of the direction of the Florida coast. In addition, the lost crew indicated their compasses were malfunctioning and that they could not see land. Radio communications became spotty because of static, atmospheric conditions and interference from Cuban broadcasting stations. Despite various confused radio transmissions, all radio contact was lost before the ground crew could determine the problem or pinpoint the squadron's location. Shortly after 4 p.m. all radio contact terminated, and the squadron was not heard from again.

Within minutes rescue craft set out to locate and rescue the lost patrol. A large flying boat called a Martin Mariner with a reinforced hull designed to withstand turbulent sea landings took off, carrying 13 crew members and specialized rescue equipment. Within 10 minutes, the land base lost all contact with the Mariner. The rescue ship and its crew disappeared for no apparent reason. Despite a massive search and rescue response, no wreckage from either the Flight 19 or the Mariner was ever found.

What Happened to Flight 19?

At the time and in subsequent investigations, no one has been able to discover with any certainty what exactly became of Flight 19 and its rescue team. One recurring, but unproven, reason for the squadron's disappearance is a speculation that somehow Flight 19 got caught in the strange area of what is known as the Bermuda Triangle, that stretch of the Atlantic Ocean that has become legendary for unexplained maritime disasters.

Many historians think that the planes became lost somewhere east of Florida in the area of the Bermuda Triangle, were unable to determine a return course to the base and were forced to land at sea after dark when they ran out of fuel.

Taking into consideration that Flight 19 was a training flight, thus presumably being flown by inexperienced pilots, the disappearance could have resulted from an error in judgment or simple

28

失踪的巡逻队

一个晴朗的下午,正在佛罗里达海岸执行常规训练任务的五架美国海军鱼雷轰炸机(也称第19巡逻队)失踪了,后来它的营救飞机也失踪了,这是美国飞行史上最神秘的事件之一。

使命

1945年12月5日下午两点十分, 由五架TBM复仇者鱼雷轰炸机组成的第19巡逻队从佛罗里达州的福特·劳德代尔堡空军机场起飞, 每架轰炸机有三组人员:飞行员,无线电话务员和机枪组人员(整个巡逻队总计15人),执行大西洋上空向东为期两个小时的常规飞行训练任务。LT.查理斯·泰勒,巡逻队队长,是一位有经验的战斗飞行员和合格的飞行指导员。起飞前,他们仔细检查过飞机,确保一切准备正常。然后带上飞行必备物品,投入到这次飞行任务中去。

下午三点四十五分左右,巡逻队长和其他飞行员之间的一次通讯信息显示导航员已迷失方向。此外,机组成员指出指南针也不正常,无法看到陆地。由于静电干扰,大气状况及无线电台干扰,通讯电波也时断时续,后来通讯中断,地面机组人员无法检测到舰队的具体方位和故障情况。四点整,巡逻队完全与地面失去联系。

几分钟后, 马丁水手号水上飞机带着13名营救人员和专门设备开始搜救巡逻队,十分钟后也与地面失去联系。然后,不知为何,马丁水手号飞机及其所有成员消失了,虽然组织了全面搜救,但最终没有找到第19巡逻队及水手号飞机的残骸。

第19巡逻队怎么了

经过当时及随后的调查研究,仍没有人知道第19巡逻队和它的营救飞机失踪的确切原因。人们猜测第19巡逻队的失踪可能是它闯入了大西洋的百慕大三角地区——大西洋中一系列令人无法解释的海事灾难的传说之源。

历史学家认为,飞机进入佛罗里达东部百慕大三角地带,由于无法辨别返航路线,天黑后,燃料用完,不得不强行着陆,坠入大海。

考虑到第19巡逻队是飞行训练中队,可能当时是由新手飞行员驾驶,飞行员方向判断错误或操作失误而导致飞机失踪。刚开始飞机电波传输正常,巡逻队队长的指令可以

mistakes. For example, one early radio transmission indicated that the original squadron leader transferred his command to another pilot, perhaps one less qualified. At another point, a pilot who had been flying missions out of Miami over the south Florida region for some time reportedly became confused about whether he was looking at the Florida Keys or the cays of the northern Bahamas. And there seemed to be confusion among the crew members about whether they were flying eastward or westward.

In addition, if the planes were flying through a magnetic storm, which is a possibility, the compasses could possibly malfunction. Toward the end of the training exercise when the radio transmissions began to fade, the weather changed; the daytime visibility was replaced by rain, air turbulence and darkness. If the planes were indeed lost and ran out of gas trying to find their way home, a forced landing after dark into the cold Atlantic waters meant little if any chance of survival, so the crew of Flight 19 were presumed to be lost at sea.

Even less is known about what happened to the rescue Mariner flying ship. Because a passing merchant ship saw and reported a burst of flame from that area during that time, some believe that the search craft exploded and sank at sea. To add credence to that theory, the rescue planes, designed to remain aloft for 24 hours, were known as flying gas tanks and therefore highly flammable.

The Navy spent five days searching and combing an ever-widening area for wreckage from either the torpedo bombers or the rescue craft. The in-flight explosion and fire—plus the film of oil on the water surface in the area where the rescue Mariner was presumed to have been—may confirm its fate, but no one can explain what happened to the original five planes of Flight 19.

Why Flight 19 got lost and where it got lost are the two big questions still unanswered. Subsequent explorations and searches have not yielded any more information than what was discovered during the initial search in 1945. While the Bermuda Triangle theory may or may not be true, there are those who find that explanation too simple. And as long as those kinds of questions remain, people will continue to wonder about the very strange disappearance of the Lost Patrol.

Resources

The Disappearance of Flight 19, Barnes & Noble Books, 1981. This book provides a detailed description of the Flight 19 story.

21st Century Mysteries: Bermuda Triangle and Flight 19, Progressive Management, 2006. This electronic book on CD-ROM contains information, including military documents, on the Bermuda Triangle and the disappearance of Flight 19. This book uses material from the Department of Defense, the U.S. Navy, the National Weather Service, Department of Energy, NASA, U.S. Coast Guard, and the Navy Undersea Warfare Center at Newport, Rhode Island, which is reproduced in a PDF format.

www.crystalinks.com/bermuda_triangle.html. Website that provides information about the Devil's Triangle, including maps.

www.byerly.org/bt.htm. A compilation of dates from 1492 to 2001 on over 170 disappearances of ships, boats, planes and other phenomena which have occurred in or near the area known as the Bermuda Triangle.

正常地传送到其他飞行员那儿,或许是某个飞行员缺乏经验,操作失误导致飞机失踪。另外,有一名飞行员一直在南佛罗里达地区迈阿密上空执行飞行任务,他分不清看到的是佛罗里达暗礁还是巴哈马群岛北部的珊瑚礁。似乎机组人员都有困惑,无法确定飞机是在朝东还是朝西飞行。

此外,如果飞机飞行时受磁暴干扰,这时指南针会失常,通讯信号微弱,天空一片漆黑,加上倾盆大雨,能见度低,这样飞机就无法辨别返航方向。天黑后,如果燃料用完,不得不强行着陆,最后坠入冰冷的大西洋水中,这意味着渺茫的生存机会。第19巡逻队可能就是这样失踪的。

但很少有人知道营救飞机为何失踪。当时,一艘商船恰好经过那块区域并报告说看到了爆炸的火光。有人相信搜救飞机爆炸并沉入海底。为了增加这一说法的可信性,有人说当时那架营救飞机被设计成可24小时连续飞行,因此以飞行的油箱著称,很容易着火。

飞机失事后,美国海军花了五天时间,在更广阔的海面上打捞鱼雷战斗机及营救飞机的残骸。当时水手号营救飞机着火爆炸,另外水面上还有一层油,飞机坠入大海,命运可想而知了,但是没有人知道第19巡逻队的5架飞机当时到底发生了什么。

为什么第19巡逻队会失踪?它在哪儿失踪?这两大问题至今没有找到答案。后来的很多说法都没有跳出1945年那时的框框。百慕大三角理论也不知道是真是假,毕竟相关的解释太简单了。第19巡逻队为何失踪?只要这样的问题还没有找到答案,人们还将继续关注它。

相关资源

《21世纪的神秘:百慕大三角和第19巡逻队》,前进管理出版社,2006年。这是一本CD版的电子图书,记录了百慕大三角及第19巡逻队失踪的事件。本书材料源于美国国防部、美国海军、国家气象局、能源部、美国航空航天局、美国海岸警备队及罗德岛州的纽波海军水下战中心,这些材料均以PDF格式重新编排。

www.crystalinks.com/bermuda_triangle.html. 有关魔鬼大三角的信息,附有地图。

www.byerly.org/bt.htm. 该网址收集了1492年~2001年期间发生在百慕大三角及其附近的170多艘(架)船只和飞机失踪事件及其他神秘现象的资料。

Twenty-nine

Lucky & Unlucky Numbers

The concept of lucky and unlucky numbers is universal across all cultures. Although especially strong in Asian cultures, the idea of attaching significance to numbers is nevertheless global in its appeal and prevalence.

Assigning meaning to numbers is the basis of the science or art of numerology. Numerology is a popular prediction system based on the mystical values assigned to numbers. In some cases, numbers are associated with letters and practitioners of numerology search for hidden meanings in words by converting their letters to numbers. In other instances, numerologists attach great significance to the numerical values of a person's name or birthplace. Combined with the numbers in the person's birth date, these values can be the foundation for determining each person's lucky number.

Although the interest in numbers began when humans learned to count, numerology is the product of folklore and as such each of its systems is unique to the region where the folk stories originated. That is why numbers assume more importance in some cultures than in others.

Which Numbers Are Lucky and Which Are Unlucky?

Every culture has its own set of lucky and unlucky numbers. And the way in which these numbers are interpreted often depends on ancient folkloric beliefs.

In Egyptian culture, the number 4,223 was considered unlucky because the pictograms (4,000, 200, 15 and 8) that represent the number depict a scene that could be construed to be the murder of the pharaoh. Greeks and Russians consider the number 2 to be lucky because each country had wise kings who were designated by that number. Conversely, the number 4 carries negative meaning to Russians who have not forgotten Ivan IV, better known as Ivan the Terrible.

In ancient times the Persian mathematician al-Kwarizmi thought the numbers 2, 3, 5, 7, 11, 13, 17, 19, 23, 29 and 31 were unlucky because they were prime numbers (a number that can be divided only by 1 or by itself). He considered the numbers 6, 28, 496 and 8,128 to be perfect numbers. (for example, 1 x 2 x 3=6, 1+2+3=6.)

The United States

In the United States two numbers stand out: 13 and 7.

People who suffer from triskaidekaphobia, the fear of the number 13, are numerous. The origins of the connections between the number 13 and bad luck are often unclear, but the most common connection is the Last Supper in which Judas Iscariot, who later betrayed Jesus, was the 13th person to sit down at the table. A slightly different interpretation states that Jesus was the 13th person to join the group at the Last Supper.

The fear of the number 13 expanded beyond groups of 13 people to the number in general. Anything designated by the number 13 was avoided. Many hotels do not have rooms with the number 13 or thirteenth floors. Some municipalities shun street names containing the number 13. And having 13 letters in your name is considered unfortunate.

The number 7, on the other hand, is considered to be lucky in the United States. Consider its designations: 7 days in a week, 7 sacraments, 7 sister colleges (Wellesley, Barnard, Mount

幸运数字和
不幸运数字

在世界各地的文化中,特别是亚洲,都有幸运数字和不幸运数字的说法。给数字附有一定的含义在世界上也是普遍的。

人们一般依据科学或数字命理学来给数字附有一定的含义。数字命理学是给某些数字附上一定的含义,使数字具有神秘的内涵。是一种人们普遍认可的与预测有关的学科体系。在某些方面,数字往往与字母密切相关,数字命理学的从事者往往将某个字母转换成数字,然后去寻找这些数字的内在意义。另外,数字学家也经常给某个人的姓名,出生地附有数字方面的意义,再加上人的出生日期。通过这些,数字学家可能就会推测某个人的幸运数字是什么。

从人类学会记数时,就对数字感兴趣。数字命理学是民间故事的产物,数字在不同的文化中有不同的地位。

幸运数字和不幸运数字

每种文化群体都有自己的一些幸运数字和不幸运数字。很多古老的民间故事都提到了不同数字的不同含义。

如:埃及人认为数字4223是不好的,因为在象形文字里(4000,200,15和8),它们组成的图形,恰好象法老遭谋杀的样子。希腊人和俄罗斯人认为2是幸运数字,因为在他们国家被称为2的国王都是明智的。相反俄罗斯人认为4是不幸运的数字,因为俄罗斯人不会忘记伊万四世(是个暴君)。

在古代波斯,数学家花拉子密认为2、3、5、7、11、13、17、19、23、29和31是幸运数字,因为它们是质数(只能被1和自身除尽),认为6、28、496和8128是幸运数字(例如:$1×2×3=6$,$1+2+3=6$)。

美国

在美国,人们不会忘记数字13和数字7。

有很多美国人都患有恐惧数字13症,害怕数字13。为什么美国人将数字13和厄运连在一起,原因不知,但人们普遍认为与"最后的晚餐"这个故事有关。传说,犹大(犹大后来出卖了耶稣)是第13个进来的人,也有人说在"最后的晚餐"宴会上,耶稣是第13个进来的人。

总之,恐数字13并不只是限于13人的群体活动中,只要是与数字13有关的东西都是不好的。如:很多宾馆没有13号房间,13层楼,一些城市街道名称中也避开数字13,如果你的名字有13个字母,也是不幸运的。

相反,数字7是幸运的。如:一周7天,7个圣礼,7姐妹大学。

很早以前旧有许多关于数字7的神话故事,一般都与宗教有关。如:传说上帝7天造了

Holyoke, Vassar, Smith, Radcliffe, Bryn Mawr).

Many of the myths about the number 7 go back to earlier times and cultures and are often rooted in religion. God supposedly created the world in 7 days and many religious holidays and festivals last 7 days. In another context, the Greek philosopher and mathematician Pythagorus thought that 7 was the perfect number in that 3 (represented by the triangle) and 4 (represented by the square) were the perfect figures. There were 7 ancient planets (Sun, Moon, Mercury, Venus, Mars, Jupiter and Saturn) and 7 Wonders of the Ancient World. There are 7 deadly sins and 7 seas. And 7 is the most likely roll of two dice.

The Far East

In the Chinese culture there is almost always a meaning behind a number. Numbers can be either lucky or unlucky and as a rule the distinction between the two is the pronunciation of the sound of the word. For instance, the Chinese view the number 8 as the luckiest number. This is because the pronunciation of the number sounds almost like the word that means good luck or becoming rich. This is a favorite number for telephone numbers and license plate tags.

The number 8 is also considered the ideal number for a wedding date. Many weddings are planned for August (the 8th month) 8, 18 or 28. There are recipe titles that incorporate the number 8: Eight Treasure Porridge or Eight Treasure Tea. And in keeping with the Chinese attitude toward the number 8, the Beijing Olympic Games will start on August 8 at 8 p.m. in 2008.

In addition to the number 8, the number 9 carries a positive meaning for the Chinese. The sound of the number 9 is the same as the sound of the pictogram meaning long lasting. As the largest single unit number before 10, the number 9 also represents male energy.

On the other hand, the Chinese consider the number 4 unlucky. Again, this belief is based on the sound of the word: The sound of 4 sounds like the word meaning death. Even more unlucky is the number 14, the sound of which corresponds to the phrase guaranteed death.

The Japanese also fear the number 4 because its pronunciation in Japanese sounds like the word for death. In contrast to the Chinese, however, the Japanese consider 9 to be an unlucky number because it has the same pronunciation as the words meaning agony or torture. Like the number 13 in the United States, the numbers 4 and 9 are often omitted as room, floor or seat numbers in Japan.

The Number 666

This number carries great significance in both eastern and western cultures. It is an unlucky number in the West and a lucky number in the East. According to the Christian Bible, the number 666 is synonymous with the devil and may well be considered the unluckiest number in western cultures. To far eastern ears, however, the number 666 sounds like the phrase everything going smoothly and thus it is considered to be very lucky.

No matter what the culture, it is clear that numbers are tied closely to good and/or bad luck. Whether or not a number is lucky or unlucky usually depends on its connotation within a cultural group. Within that structure most people can decide if numbers are lucky or unlucky depending on their own personal beliefs and circumstances.

Resources

From Zero to Ten: The Story of Numbers, Oxford University Press, 2002. Aimed at a reading level of 9 to 12 years, this children's book provides a history of numbers, including counting systems, money, measurement and lucky numbers.

世界万物,很多宗教节假日都是7天时间。另外,希腊哲学家和数学家毕达哥拉斯认为7是幸运数字,因为3(代表三角形),4(代表矩形),它们都是幸运数字。还有7大行星(太阳、月亮、水星、金星、火星、木星和土星)、世界7大奇迹、7大罪恶、7大海洋(全球)等说法。另外,在掷色子中,7点必须是两个色子同时滚动才行。

远东
在中国,数字也有幸运和不幸运之分,他们往往与汉字的发音紧密相关。如:数字8是幸运数字,因为8的发音类似于汉字"发"的音(发财),所以中国人总是喜欢电话号码和汽车牌照号含有数字8。

很多人也会选择带有"8"的日期举行婚礼,如8月8日,18日和28日。还有一些食谱名称含有数字"8",如八宝粥、八宝茶。北京奥运也定在2008年8月8日下午8时开幕,这都与中国人对数字8的态度有关。除了数字8外,9也是幸运数字,因为9的发音与象形文字"9"的发音一样,意味着"持久"。另外,9也是单个数字中最大的,9还有精力旺盛之意。

相反,中国人认为4是不幸运数字,因为数字4的发音很像汉字"死"的发音。更不幸运的是数字14,它的发音与汉字"逝世"相同。

日本人也害怕数字4,因为它的发音与日语汉字"死"的发音类似。与中国不同的是,日本人认为9也是不幸运数字,因为9的发音与日语汉字"折磨"发音相同。像数字13在美国一样,在日本,也没有带数字4和9的房间、楼层号和座位号。

数字666
某些数字在东西方文化中都一定的含义,但不完全相同。有些数字在西方文化认为是不幸运数字,在东方文化群体中却是幸运数字。如:《圣经》中认为数字666是不幸运的,因为"666"与恶鬼(Devil)是同义词。
所以666在西方文化中被认为是最不幸运的数字。而在远东,数字666往往被认为是非常幸运的数字,因为它的读音听起来像"六六大顺"。
虽然,无论在什么样的文化群体,某些数字总是与好运或厄运相联系起来。无论是幸运数字,还是不幸运数字,它的含义总是与文化有关。在某个文化群体中,哪些数字是幸运的哪些是不幸运的,这取决于某个人的个人信仰和生活环境。

相关资源:
《从0到10:数字的故事》,牛津大学出版社,2002年。这是一本儿童读物,适合9~12岁的小读者,介绍了数字的历史,包括计数体系、钱的计法、度量和幸运数字。

Mirror Myths

From ancient to modern times mirrors have been a subject of lore and folk tales. Before mirrors developed into the objects we recognize today—that is, before 16th century Venice when the technique for manufacturing mirrors into large wall hangings—anything reflective was considered magical and imbued with the power to look into the future. In ancient mythology there are stories of gods and goddesses gazing into still water to determine their futures. For example, there is the well–known Greek myth of Narcissus, the beautiful youth who, glimpsing his reflection in a forest pond, fell in love with himself. Since his beloved did not respond to his advances, he felt rejected and eventually pined away and died. According to the myth, Narcissus' rejection by the beautiful vision in the pond was really retaliation by the woodland nymphs whom Narcissus had earlier cruelly spurned.

The ancients also believed that reflective surfaces could be used by mere mortals to receive and interpret messages from the gods. Some people even considered mirrors symbols of luck in that they repelled evil and attracted good.

The Human Soul and 7 Years of Bad Luck

Many of the more common mirror myths originated with the idea that the human soul is trapped within a mirror, that is, the human soul projects out of the body and into a mirror to be perceived as a reflection. This is the underlying basis of the most widely known mirror superstition: Breaking a mirror brings 7 years of bad luck. Since early times many have believed that breaking a mirror also breaks the soul within the mirror, namely the soul of the person who breaks the mirror. The soul, angry that it has been injured or damaged, imposes 7 years of bad luck as punishment for such carelessness.

While many people accept this belief, not many know why the punishment is bad luck for 7 years. This goes back to the ancient Romans who believed that life renewed itself every 7 years. Thus, if you broke a mirror and therefore damaged your soul, you had to wait at least 7 years before the soul could renew or repair itself.

Overcoming the Curse of 7 Years of Bad Luck

Like many other myths based on human superstitions, the broken mirror curse was considered preventable if the right steps were taken. Eliminating the broken pieces of the mirror was one of the most important remedies, although the procedure for doing so varied among different groups of people. One method was to grind the broken pieces into dust so that shattered or distorted reflections could no longer be seen. Supposedly, this would lift the curse after only 1 year of bad luck.

There are also other methods of averting the bad luck of a broken mirror:

· Turn around counterclockwise three times immediately upon breaking a mirror.

· Light seven white candles on the first night after breaking the mirror and blow them out with one breath at midnight.

· Throw salt over your shoulder as soon as you break a mirror.

镜　　子

　　从古至今,很多民间故事、文学作品中都有对镜子的描写,镜子是获得知识的工具。16世纪前,人们对镜子的了解不像今天这么多。当时威尼斯掌握了玻璃镜的制作技术,镜子被作为墙上悬挂物而且能够反射物体,于是人们便把镜子看做具有魔力,能够预测命运。古代很多神话故事有这样的描写:神常常趴在河边,从水中反映出自己的真面目,这样可以预测自己的命运。例如:那可索斯是古希腊神话中的美少年,他偶然在森林的池塘看到自己的倒影,然后就爱上了自己。因为这种爱得不到回报,最后他憔悴而死。传说,那可索斯以前拒绝过一位美少女的爱,而当他爱上自己池塘里的倒影时,同样遭到拒绝,这就是报应。

　　古人相信镜子是神的意志体现。甚至一些人认为镜子是运气的象征,镜子可以避邪,镜子可以给人带来好运。

人的灵魂和七年厄运
　　很多有关镜子的神话有这样的描述:镜子反映人的灵魂,即人的影像会出现在镜子里,这种影像就是人的灵魂。人们常听到的迷信说法是:打碎一面镜子会带来7年的厄运。打碎镜子,就是打碎灵魂,因为灵魂被打碎了,受到了伤害或损坏,这样就会给人带来7年厄运,这是对人因粗心打碎镜子的惩罚。

　　很多人相信这种说法,但不知道为何是7年厄运。这种观点产生于古罗马,他们认为人的灵魂需要7年才能重生,如果你打碎了镜子,也就打碎了灵魂,这样你必须等7年,灵魂才能得到恢复重生。

克服7年厄运的诅咒
　　很多人相信打碎镜子会带来7年厄运的迷信说法,但是也有很多人相信如果采取恰当的措施,这种厄运会得到挽救。如:打碎镜子后,将镜子碎片消除;将镜子碎片碾成粉末状,这样就不能再看到自己的破碎的变形的影像。据说这样只会带来一年的厄运而不是7年。

　　还有其他一些办法来避免厄运:
　　· 镜子打碎后,自己逆时针转3圈。
　　· 镜子打碎后,当天晚上就点燃7支白蜡烛,在午夜时一口气吹灭。
　　· 镜子打碎后,在自己肩膀上洒点盐。

Other Mirror Superstitions

The broken mirror followed by 7 years of bad luck is the best known but by no means the only myth about mirrors. There are both negative and positive beliefs about mirrors.

Negative Beliefs about Mirrors

Mirrors have long been associated with death. In many cultures a broken mirror supposedly foretells a death in the family within the year. This association of death goes back to the idea that the human soul can become entrapped within a mirror, thereby leading to death. Therefore, in many cultures, infants were not permitted to look into the mirror until after their first birthday for fear their souls could become trapped and lead to death. Similarly, many people covered mirrors during sleep or illness so that a wandering soul could not be caught within a mirror, unable to return to its body.

In Southeast Asia there are people who refuse to look into mirrors in a home they are visiting for fear of leaving part of their soul in the mirror to be later manipulated by their host. There is also a cultural practice of waving mirrors before the image or icon of a death goddess to satisfy her need for a sacrifice by showing a person's reflection only.

Some people also believe:

· If you see your reflection in a mirror in a room in which someone recently died, you yourself will soon die.

· Some actors think it is bad luck to see their reflection while looking over the shoulder of another person.

· It is bad luck to see your reflection in a mirror in a candlelit room.

Positive Beliefs about Mirrors

Mirrors are not always associated with bad luck or death. Many people believe there are positive attributes of mirrors. For example:

· The mirror symbolizes money. Therefore, you should hang one in the dining room or kitchen to attract money and food to the household.

· Hanging many mirrors in a home is good luck, because of mirrors's ability to attract good luck and deflect evil.

· The couple who first sees each other in a mirror will have a long, happy marriage.

· A woman can see the image of her future husband by eating an apple while sitting in front of a mirror. An image of a man will appear behind her shoulder.

· Finally, if you are alone and feel sad or depressed, you can stand in front of a mirror and focus on your eyes to lift your mood.

Resources

The Mirror: A History, Routledge, 2002. This book, outlining the development of the mirror as well as its social and psychological implications throughout its history, reveals the significance of the mirror on Western culture. Beginning with the mirrors of antiquity, the author traces the development of the mirror through history. The book also explores the symbolism of the mirror as it pertains to religion, art, magic, philosophy and literature.

www.urbanlegendsonline.com/mirrors.html. Urban legends and superstitions pertaining to mirrors.

其他有关镜子的迷信

人们都知道,打碎镜子会带来7年厄运这一神话,但这并不是有关镜子的唯一神话故事。

不好的一面

人们经常把镜子与死亡联系起来,很多地方有这样的传说,破碎的镜子意味着一年内家里要死人。因为镜子反映着人的灵魂,镜子打碎了,灵魂也就碎了,这样人也就会死。还有很多地方有这样的说法:小孩出生后的第一年是不能看镜子的,因为这样的话,他的灵魂很容易被吸到镜子里去。同样,在睡觉或生病时,要把镜子盖起来,因为镜子可以把人的灵魂吸进去。

在东南亚,一些人拜访朋友时,不愿在朋友家里照镜子,因为他们害怕镜子会把他的灵魂吸进去。还有些地方,人们在死神的圣像面前挥舞镜子,这样表明他们在向神灵祭祀。

还有人认为:

· 如果你在死人房间的镜子里看到自己,那么你不久也会死。

· 一些演员认为,如果他从另外一个人身边经过时,看到他的影像,这会带来厄运。

· 在昏暗的房间里,如果你看到镜子中的自己,这会带来厄运。

好的一面

镜子并不总是与厄运和死亡有关,它也有许多好的一面:

· 镜子象征着金钱,如果你在餐厅或厨房里挂一面镜子则意味着招财进宝。

· 在家里挂上几面镜子会带来好运,因为镜子可以避邪,可以招来好运。

· 如果第一次是在镜子里看到对方的一对夫妻,则意味将来有一个幸福美满的婚姻。

· 如果一位女士坐在镜子前吃苹果,她就有可能见到她未来丈夫的模样。

· 如当你感到孤单,悲伤沮丧时,你可以站在镜子前,这样心情就会好很多。

相关资源

《镜子:历史》,Routedge 出版社,2002 年。本书讲述了镜子的起源与发展以及镜子的社会与心理意义,揭示了镜子在西方文化的作用。本书从古代镜子开始回顾了镜子的发展过程,作者还从宗教、艺术、魔法、哲学及文学的角度探讨了镜子的象征意义。

www.urbanlegendsonline.com/mirrors.html. 都市传奇及有关镜子的迷信。

Thirty-one

Moby Dick

Call me Ishmael, the first line of the novel *Moby Dick*, is one of the most famous quotes in American literature. Written in 1851 by Herman Melville, the novel was published first in Britain and then by Harper and Brothers in the United States. The novel received negative reviews on its publication but is now considered a classic in the tradition of American romanticism.

Although calling on his experience as a sailor on a whaling ship in the 1840s, Melville was possibly inspired by an article in The Knickerbocker magazine in 1839, which related the killing of an albino whale named Mocha Dick in the 1830s. Living near the coast of the island of Mocha off Chile's southern coast, Mocha Dick was famous for attacking ships and sporting numerous harpoons in his hide from various battles with whalers. How the name Mocha Dick translated into Moby Dick as the title of Melville's novel is unknown.

The Story of Moby Dick

The title of the book refers to an enormous mottled whale with a white hump who is notorious for ferociously attacking whaling ships and escaping capture. Captain Ahab, captain of the whaling ship Pequod, engages in a single-minded ruthless pursuit of Moby Dick. His driven quest to kill the white whale is his response to Moby Dick's amputation of one of Ahab's legs on an earlier whaling expedition. Thus, an overlying theme of the book becomes one of revenge and retribution, that of the man against the whale.

While telling the story of the hunt for the mysterious and elusive Moby Dick, Melville presents a vivid portrayal of the typical 19th century whaling expedition. Part of Melville's purpose in writing the book was to offer information about the whaling industry in a compelling and emotional way, rather than just as a prosaic documentary. Consequently, much of the book does not pertain to the plot or story line but rather to a detailed description of the whaling business.

The Symbolism of Moby Dick

More than just an adventure story, *Moby Dick* is symbolic, even allegorical. The white whale has been interpreted as representing evil, in contrast to the usual attributions of purity and good to the color white. At the same time, the whale is strong, mysterious and extremely powerful and can, therefore, be seen as representing a powerful, unknowable God. The novel conveys the idea that Ahab believes that Moby Dick is a symbol of all that is wrong in the world and that it is his destiny—in fact, duty—to eliminate this symbolic evil. The fact that Ahab cannot seem to conquer Moby Dick has led many scholars and readers to believe that the whale symbolizes fate, providence and perhaps God.

Ahab, too, is often seen as evil, because he admits that the sole purpose of his voyages is to take revenge on Moby Dick as retaliation for amputating his leg. His driven single-mindedness is highlighted in the episode in the book in which the Pequod encounters the ship Rachel whose captain asks Ahab's help in searching for a missing whaling crew. Ahab refuses to help, for fear he will miss his chance to kill Moby Dick.

Eventually, Pequod and Ahab come to a tragic end when, after battling for 3 days, Moby Dick shatters and sinks the ship. All except Ishmael, the story's narrator, drown.

白　鲸

"叫我伊希梅尔(Ishmael)"，这是小说《白鲸记》中的第一句。《白鲸记》是美国作家赫尔曼·麦尔维尔1851年写的一部小说，先后在英国和美国的伍德斯托克和哈珀出版。小说出版后，就曾一度被19世纪美国文学的大潮所淹没，后被认为是美国最有象征意义的经典小说。

伊希梅尔，捕鲸船上的一名水手，1839年，他看到《尼克博克杂志》上有一篇文章，写的是19世纪40年代人们捕杀一种叫摩卡·迪克的白鲸故事。摩卡·迪克白鲸生活在智利南部海岸的摩卡岛海岸附近，身上长有许多像渔叉一样的东西，它经常袭击捕鲸船只。伊希梅尔的小说原名是《Mocha Dick》，至于后人为何将它译为《Moby Dick (莫比迪克)》，原因并不清楚。

白鲸故事

莫比迪克是一条凶猛无比的白鲸，它横行海上多年，曾使无数捕鲸船和水手命丧大海。而亚哈，"裴廓德号"捕鲸船的船长，不幸在出海时被白鲸莫比·迪克咬掉一条腿，为了复仇，他专事搜捕莫比·狄克，追杀莫比·狄克。小说《白鲸》正是以船长亚哈复仇主题贯穿故事始末的。

《白鲸》是讲述船长亚哈追杀一条神奇白鲸的冒险故事。也是一部反映十九世纪捕鲸生活的作品。作者伊希梅尔不是简单地停留在故事情节和内容的描写上，而是详细描绘了当时捕鲸业的情况。

白鲸的象征意义

小说《白鲸》不仅仅是一部冒险故事，还是一部融冒险、哲理、象征意义于一体的鸿篇巨作。"白鲸"在这里成了一种庞大的、而又难以征服的神秘动物。"白鲸"是罪恶的象征，也是上帝神力的象征，而它的白色象征着纯洁和无辜。在船长亚哈的眼中，"白鲸"又被理解为世间一切"恶"的化身，因为亚哈本人根本无法征服白鲸，这样，也让许多读者和学者们认为白鲸是命运、上帝和无边神力的象征。

船长亚哈，在出海时被白鲸莫比·迪克咬掉一条腿，这次出海他的唯一目标就是报仇，誓死捕杀莫比·迪克。在小说中有这样一段描述：船长亚哈所在的"裴廓德号"捕鲸船曾遇到另一艘捕鲸船，那个船长请求亚哈救助失踪的捕鲸人员，遭到他的拒绝，因为他担心那样做，就有可能错过捕杀莫比·迪克的机会。从这个意义上说，他就是一个不折不扣的邪恶魔王的象征。

最后，亚哈终于遇到了莫比·狄克，在经过连续三天的恶战之后，它咬碎了小艇，也撞

The final questions seem to come down to who represents good or evil. Is the white whale a symbol of evil because it destroys a ship and its crew? Or is Ahab evil because of his obsession with revenge that overwhelms his better human nature? Conversely, is Ahab a symbol of good because he seeks to conquer and understand Nature and God? Does the fact that no one can understand the nature of Moby Dick imply limits to human knowledge? What does that mean to the notion of comprehending the nature of God? Is Melville saying that the ways of Moby Dick, like the ways of God, cannot be known by man and therefore trying to understand and interpret them, as Ahab does, is useless and perhaps even fatal?

Many answers to these questions come back to fate. The narrative contains numerous references to fate, particularly doomed fate. For example, the crew believes in prophecies and the ability to foresee the future. Yet Melville implies that the sailors, Ahab included, are deluding themselves when they think that fate exists and that they can have knowledge of it or control over it. The name of the ship, Pequod, too, is a symbol of doom. Pequod was the name of a Native American tribe in Massachusetts that was unable to survive the arrival of the colonists. In addition, the ship is black and decorated with bones and teeth of dead whales, a sailing symbol of violent death.

In addition to exploring such themes as fate, evil, good and the existence of God, the story of Moby Dick was also Melville's way of examining the social and political issues of mid-19th century America. The crew of the Pequod seems to be egalitarian and harmonious in an age when the country was struggling with issues of slavery, race and rigid social structure. The crew is made up of all sorts of men from around the world and the men are paid and promoted on the basis of their productivity and skill.

Yet this crew and the work of the Pequod symbolize the exploitative activities that characterized American and European territorial expansion at that time. For example, there are no restrictions on whaling; it is pursued for profit and even sport without regard for the possible extinction of the animal. In addition, the white men on the Pequod depend on nonwhite harpooners to do the most dangerous work during the whale hunt. Furthermore, nonwhites do all of the dirty work and there are references to black men having less value as a slave than the value of a whale.

Moby Dick, both the whale and the book, has symbolic meanings for various characters in the story as well as for the readers, then and now. Although the book is a detailed depiction of 19th century whaling, the story works on several intellectual and emotional levels as well. The whale can be seen as a symbol of human greed, revenge, good, evil and belief in a spiritual being. Its interpretation rests with each individual reader.

Resources

The Meaning of Moby Dick, Kessinger Publishing, LLC, 2006. This book delves into some of the symbolism and meaning behind the tale of Moby Dick.

The following list contains the most popular modern editions of Herman Melville's book:

Moby Dick, Penguin Popular Classics, 2007. The first half of this book is the Modern Language Association's approved text of the novel. The second half of this book contains historical notes, textual history, original publication information and background of the author and the novel. Available in hardcover, paperback and audio cassette versions.

Moby Dick, Barnes & Noble Classics, 2003. This book includes, along with the original novel, a biography of the author, other works inspired by the novel, study questions and a glossary of sea terminology.

沉了大船。船长亚哈、"裴廓德号"船和全体船员水手都与莫比•狄克同归于尽,只剩下一个幸存者伊希梅尔给人们讲述这个悲惨的故事。

白鲸的象征意义究竟是什么?是象征着恐怖邪恶吗?亚哈船长是白鲸的对立面,他又象征着什么?他到底是企图摧毁善与美的邪恶的化身,还是象征着人类的善与美?总之,没有人能够知道伊希梅尔这部小说蕴涵的真正意义。怎样去理解白鲸是命运、上帝和无边神力的象征,又如何理解船长亚哈,这些只有读者根据自己的经历和思考才能做出自己的评判。

所有这些问题答案归根结底是"命运"问题。这部小说有很多内容都是与"命运"有关,特别是宿命论。在赫尔曼•麦尔维尔的小说中,船员及船长亚哈,他们都是自欺欺人的,他们明明知道自己无法改变命运,却仍然与命运作斗争。"裴廓德号"捕鲸船也象征着死亡。"裴廓德"取自马萨诸塞的被灭绝的印第安部落之名,黑色的船体,加上鲸牙和鲸骨的装扮,因而它还象征着全体船员的最终灭亡。

除了命运主题外,罪恶、善与美及上帝神力是《白鲸》所要揭示的又一主题。这部小说详尽地描写了捕鲸工人在海上艰苦的生活及悲惨命运,揭示了19世纪美国社会的黑暗。"裴廓德号"捕鲸船全体船员,每当在困难危险关头,他们总是挺身而出,勇敢沉着地与鲸搏斗,最后转危为安,他们是人类平等、和谐的追求者,而他们却是被压在社会底层的奴隶。

小说描述了受歧视的黑人,印第安人受雇于"裴郭德号"出海捕鲸的故事,反映了捕鲸工人的危险而又艰辛的生活,揭露了资本主义社会财富的血腥来源,象征着当时资本主义的剥削制度。例如:当船长亚哈置船员的生死于不顾,无止境地追求利润,疯狂掠夺和榨取捕鲸工人用血汗和生命换来的财富。

《白鲸》是世界上伟大的小说之一,全书的焦点集中于一条名叫莫比迪克的白鲸。《白鲸》像一座象征意义的迷宫,这里面的很多人物几乎都有多层次的象征意义。《白鲸》首先是一部反映19世纪捕鲸生活的作品,也是一部融冒险、哲理于一体的巨作。白鲸象征着"恶"与"贪婪",也是"纯洁与正义"的化身,是上帝神力的象征。《白鲸》的意思不在书中,而在读者本身。

相关资源

《白鲸的意义》,Kessinger出版社,2006年。本书讨论了白鲸的象征意义。

有关伊西梅尔的现代流行作品还有:

《白鲸》,企鹅流行读物,2007年。本书前半部分已得到当代语言协会的认可,后半部分针对最初版小说的相关历史事件给出了注解,在最初版本基础上,还给出了小说及作者的背景介绍。该书平装版、精装版及磁带版均有售。

《白鲸》,巴诺出版社,2003年。本书在最初版本基础上,增加了作者传记,依据小说写的其他作品,思考题和海洋术语词汇表。

Thirty-two

Mythical Animals

Mythical animals have been a part of almost every culture in the world. A mythical animal has often been a symbol for a spiritual or religious belief from ancient times to the present and there are many examples of various types of imaginary animals depicted in art, literature and music.

Three of the most common mythical animals are the mermaid, the phoenix and the unicorn.

Mermaid

A mermaid is a water creature with the head and upper body of a human woman and the lower body of a fish. The male equivalent is known as a merman and the plural form is often the gender–neutral merpeople.

In myths mermaids usually live in homes under seas and lakes and are comfortable in the water or lying on rocks surrounding the sea or lake. Often accompanied by seals (there are myths that seals can transform themselves from seals into mermaids), mermaids sometimes foretell the future. The most common myth tells of mermaids luring sailors with their beautiful singing and music. Some stories relate that once the sailors succumb to the music, mermaids take them prisoner and carry them to their underwater homes, forgetting that the sailors cannot breathe underwater. Other myths tell of the mermaids' singing distracting sailors so that they fall overboard or shipwreck their vessels. Because of these myths, for centuries sailors feared mermaids and believed that sighting a mermaid was bad luck and predicted death by drowning or some other catastrophe.

Stories of mermaids are almost universal. The first known tales appeared in Assyria around 1000 B.C.. There were other Babylonian myths about mermaids, and Greek mythology tells of the Sirens who lured sailors with their seductive singing. The Arabian Nights includes several tales about sea people who are physically similar to humans except for their ability to breathe and live under water. In addition, the Apsara are beautiful water nymphs featured in myths and tales from India.

More recently mermaid–like creatures have been reported to have been discovered after the tsunami of December 2004. The photographs documenting the recent story appear to be the same photos displayed after a storm in the Philippine Islands a few years earlier. These creatures were supposedly constructed from animal parts, including monkeys and were similar to the creatures crafted for 19th century traveling circuses and carnivals.

Phoenix

The phoenix is a mythical bird in Egyptian and Greek mythology. Associated with the sun god Re (also called Ra) in Egyptian mythology and the god Apollo in Greek mythology, the phoenix is always male. Furthermore, folklore states that there is only one phoenix at any one time and each one lives approximately 500 years or as long as 1,500 or even 12,000 years, depending on the storyteller.

The phoenix has brilliant gold and red–purple plumage and is similar in size to a large eagle,

神话动物

很多文学作品、艺术及音乐都有对各种各样神话动物的描绘,而这些动物一般都是宗教和神灵的象征。

最常见的三种神话动物是美人鱼、凤凰和独角兽。

美人鱼

美人鱼是一种生活在海洋里的动物,按照传统说法,美人鱼以腰部为界限,上半身是女人人体,下半身是鱼。与其相对应的是男性人鱼,美人鱼这个单词的复数形式是merpeple,是个没有性别区分的中性词。

一些神话故事认为美人鱼是一种生活在海洋或湖泊里的动物,那里水温合适、周围多岩石、适合栖息,美人鱼常以海豹为伴(传说海豹后来演变成了美人鱼),有时可预言未来。关于美人鱼的神话有很多,大多是关于美人鱼的动听声音具有欺骗性这样的神话。

当听到美人鱼悦耳的叫声时,水手们注意力便分散,就会从船上跌入水中,或者导致船舶失事。这时,美人鱼趁机俘获他们,将其拖入水底,他们不知道水手们在水底不能呼吸,最后死去。几个世纪以来,有许多美人鱼与水手的传说故事。很多人相信如果水手在出海时看到美人鱼,厄运便会降临。

有很多关于美人鱼的故事,最早可以追溯到公元前1000年的王国。在巴比伦和希腊的神话故事里也有很多关于美人鱼用悦耳的歌声引诱水手们的说法,如:塞任(希腊女妖)用歌声引诱水手。在阿拉伯神话《天方夜谭》中也有许多这样类似人体的鱼的故事,这种鱼能够像海洋动物一样在水底生活。另外,在印度神话里也有关于美少女(Apsara)的许多故事。

2004年12月海啸结束后,有人发现了许多像美人鱼一样的动物,还拍下了它们的照片,这些照片与几年前菲律宾岛大地震后拍摄的美人鱼照片很相像。传说这些都是神秘的动物,类似于十九世纪马戏团或狂欢节上人们用来表演的奇怪动物。它的身体形态很奇怪,某个地方像这种动物,另一地方又像另一种动物(如猴子)。

凤凰

古埃及和希腊神话认为凤凰是一种雄性鸟。人们提到凤凰,就会联想到太阳神(埃及人称作Re或者Ra,希腊人称Apolle)。民间故事中有这样的说法,世界上只有一只凤凰,寿命大约为500年,最长可达1 500年至12 000年。

凤凰和鹰、苍鹭、鹈等动物一般大小,全身长有金色的羽毛,闪闪发光的翅膀,悦耳的鸣叫声。传说凤凰每天早上来到附近的井边沐浴并歌唱,以至太阳神经过时也会停下战

heron or stork, again depending on the folk story. Legend has it that each morning the phoenix would bathe in a nearby well and sing such a beautiful song that the sun god would stop his chariot to listen.

At the end of each life cycle, the phoenix constructs its own funeral pyre of aromatic wood and spices, sets it on fire and allows itself to be consumed by the flames. Another phoenix then rises from the ashes with renewed youth and beauty. The young phoenix carries the remains of its father to the alter of the sun god in the Egyptian city of Heliopolis (city of the sun). The bird's association with the sun may have come about because of the symbolism of the sun dying in the evening and reemerging in the morning.

The bird's longevity and its dramatic rebirth have made it a symbol of immortality and spiritual rebirth. The Egyptians associated the bird with the creation of life and the flooding of the Nile. The connection of the bird to the sun also led Egyptians to designate the bird as the god of time that determined the divisions of the day, month, week and year. Later after the 1st century A.D., Christians began to interpret the phoenix myth as an allegory of the resurrection of Christ and life after death.

Although most accounts state that the legend of the phoenix began in Babylonian and Greek mythology, the myth appears in many cultures at many times, including Chinese, Japanese, Russian, Native American and Caribbean civilizations. In each case, the bird is identified with the sun and is similar in appearance to the legendary bird of the Babylonian/Greek myths. In more modern times, the bird has appeared as a symbol on the Greek flag and today is part of the city flags and seals of both Atlanta, Georgia (to symbolize the rebirth of Atlanta after it was torched in the Civil War) and San Francisco, California (to commemorate its rebuilding after the earthquake and fire of 1906).

Unicorn

The unicorn is an imaginary animal with the head and body of a horse, the legs of a deer and the tail of a lion. It gets its name from the single horn (Latin unus means one and cornu means horn) that projects from the middle of its forehead. Unicorns are usually depicted as white and unlike other mythical animals that evoke fear, believed to symbolize purity and chastity. In fact, the prevailing legend is that a unicorn can be seen only by those who possess exceptional virtue and honesty.

During the Middles Ages in Europe, many thought that the single horn contained a substance to neutralize poison. Consequently, powders supposedly made from grinding the single horns of unicorns were in high demand and sold for exorbitant prices. No one really knows where the powders came from, but scholars believe that the image of the unicorn originated from word-of-mouth descriptions of rhinoceroses.

The legend of the unicorn is not confined to medieval Europe. The Chinese have believed in unicorns for thousands of years, although the Chinese unicorn has a body of a deer, the tail of an ox and the hooves of a horse. The only feature that is consistent with the western description of a unicorn is the single horn growing out of the middle of the forehead.

Like the western unicorn, however, the Chinese unicorn symbolizes goodness and is revered as an omen of good fortune and a representative of the basic elements of life. On the other hand, Japanese tradition tells of a unicorn that was a fearsome animal. With the body of a bull and a shaggy mane, the Japanese unicorn is supposedly able to detect guilt. Story has it that once the Japanese unicorn determines a person is guilty of a crime, the animal will pierce the criminal

车来聆听它的悦耳的歌声。

在临死之时，凤凰采集芳香植物的树枝、香草筑成一个巢，然后点火自焚，在熊熊火焰中，一只幼凤凰诞生了。新生的幼凤凰就将老凤凰的骨灰装进药蛋中，在上面涂上防腐的香料油，带着它飞到太阳神那里，由太阳神将它放在太阳庙的神坛上。这或许就是人们为什么将凤凰和太阳联系在一起的原因——太阳是傍晚落山，第二天早上又重新升起，这象征着重生和复苏。

凤凰代表着永生，象征重生和复苏。埃及人认为凤凰象征着重生，还象征着尼罗河泛滥。凤凰与太阳，这也使埃及人认为凤凰是太阳神，决定着年、月、日的划分。公元一世纪，基督教徒把凤凰看做是耶稣的复活。

尽管有关凤凰的传说是起源于巴比伦和希腊神话，但是在中国、日本、俄罗斯、美国及加勒比地区也有很多关于凤凰的神话故事，都认为凤凰与太阳有关，象征着再生，复活。这一点与巴比伦和希腊神话里的说法是一致的。现在希腊国旗上绘有凤凰的图案，在美国加利福尼亚州的洛杉矶市旗及印章上都绘有凤凰图案(纪念1906年地震后，城市得以重建)，在佐治亚州的亚特兰大的旗帜上也绘有凤凰的图案(纪念内战结束后，该市得以重建)。

独角兽

独角兽是传说中的一种神秘动物，体形像马，四肢像鹿，尾巴像狮子，额前有一螺旋角(拉丁语Unus是独角之意)。从大多数的描述看来，独角兽是一种全身雪白的动物，代表着纯洁，不像其他动物那样的可怕。事实上，很多流传故事中还有这样的说法：只有忠诚老实的人，才能看到独角兽这种动物。

在中世纪的欧洲，很多人认为独角兽的角有治疗疾病的作用，也可以解毒。独角兽的角磨制成粉可以制成解毒剂，因此这种粉末后来很畅销，价格也不菲。但没有人知道这种粉末来自哪儿。学者们认为在口头流传的故事中很多对独角兽的描述与对犀牛的描写差不多。

关于独角兽的传说并不只局限于中世纪的欧洲，几千年前在中国就有很多关于独角兽的故事。独角兽体形像鹿，尾巴像牛，四肢像马，这与西方的描述不一样，但额前长有一只角这点与西方独角兽的说法是一致的。

中国与西方的说法一样，独角兽象征着善与美，是好运的征兆。相反，日本人认为独角兽是一种凶猛的怪兽，体形像公牛，毛发蓬乱，令人恐惧。据说，在日本，独角兽可以被用来断定某人是否有罪，如果独角兽将角刺进罪犯的心脏，则证明他有罪。

在印度、阿拉伯半岛、亚洲部分地区还有关于独角兽的一些神话故事。传说成吉思汗在看到独角兽后，会在激烈的战斗中逐渐败退下来，这也意味着当看到独角兽，就应该停

through the heart with its single horn.

There are other tales of unicorns in other cultures as well, including India, Arabia and part of Asia. Allegedly, Genghis Khan backed away from a ferocious battle after seeing a unicorn and interpreting the sight as a sign that he should not attack his enemy.

Resources

Wonder Beasts: Tales and Lore of the Phoenix, the Griffin, the Unicorn, and the Dragon, Libraries Unlimited, 1995. This book is arranged in encyclopedic entries and includes excerpts from classic texts. Each entry traces the origins of the beast and discusses the different forms it has taken in various cultures. This book is especially informative about the phoenix, although it describes other creatures in great detail as well.

Mermaids: Magical Beings, Laughing Elephant, 1999. This book compiles extracts about mermaids from literature and art resources.

Mermaids: Sirens of the Seas, Running Press Publishers, 2003. This is an art book about mermaids with full–color paintings, sculptures and drawings by Gaugin and Klimt. The book also contains quotations about mermaids from literary sources, such as Ovid, Shakespeare, Goethe, Melville and Poe.

The Unicorn Treasury: Stories, Poems and Unicorn Lore, Magic Carpet Books, 2004. This book, aimed at children aged 9 to 12 years old, presents the most popular legends about unicorns and includes original poems and stories.

Dragons and Unicorns: A Natural History, St. Martin's Griffin, 1992. This book purports to present the first scientific look at unicorns and other creatures. Written in a whimsical way, the book contains drawings and other illustrations.

Book of the Unicorn, Overlook, 1998. This illustrated book charts the mythology of unicorns through the ages and different cultures and includes reports of documented sightings.

The Lore of the Unicorn, Dover Publications, 1993. This illustrated book follows the development of the unicorn legend in mythology, folklore, medicine, literature and art.

止攻击敌人了。

相关资源

《奇怪的动物：凤凰、狮鹫、独角兽和龙的传说故事》，书目文献出版社，1995 年。本书以百科全书的格式编排的，一部分内容摘自名作名篇。内容有动物的起源以及在不同文化中的不同象征意义。本书重点讲述了凤凰。

《美人鱼：神秘的动物》，Langhing Elephant 出版社，1999 年。本书搜集了有关美人鱼的很多资料，这些材料均源于文学和艺术作品。

《美人鱼：海洋女妖》，冉宁出版社，2003 年。该书是一本精美的艺术书籍，一些有关美人鱼的油画和绘画出自毕加索及克里姆特。此外，本书还引用了很多名家有关美人鱼的语录，如奥维德、莎士比亚、歌德、梅维尔和爱伦·坡。

《独角兽之宝：故事、诗歌和独角兽的传说》，魔毯出版社，2004 年。本书定位为 9~12 岁的小读者群，重点讲述了独角兽的传说故事，包括最早的一些诗歌和故事。

《龙与独角兽：自然史》，圣马丁出版社，1992 年。本出版物旨在成为第一本在科学证据基础上探讨独角兽及其他动物的书籍，书内附有插图。

《独角兽》，瞭望图书，1998 年。本书带你全面了解不同时期，不同文化中的独角兽神话故事，还包括相关的文献资料，书内附有插图。

《独角兽传说》，多佛尔出版社，1993 年。本书涵盖了神话故事、民间故事、医学、文学及艺术中很多有关独角兽的传说故事，书内附有插图。

Thirty-three

Poseidon

Poseidon was the Greek god of the sea and, as such, had dominion over the sea and over storms at sea as well as over earthquakes originating from beneath the sea. He was also the god of horses. Legend says he created the first horse by striking a rock with his trident, the three-pronged spear he carried.

Poseidon was primarily considered the god of the sea, and, in fact, in Greek mythology he was a highranking god whose essence captured the driving force of every phenomenon at the bottom of the sea or on its surface. Thus, he was instrumental in producing such upheavals as earthquakes, volcanoes, typhoons and seismic waves as the aftermath of earthquakes. His ability to create earthquakes earned him the title of Earth Shaker, a name that appears often in Greek literature. Poseidon was associated with dolphins, the horse, the bull and the trident, a three-pronged fish spear that was said to symbolize the third kingdom of the universe, namely, the sea.

Sailors relied on Poseidon to protect them and ensure a safe voyage. To guarantee a happy outcome, sailors often drowned horses as a sacrifice in his honor. Poseidon lived on the floor of the ocean in a place formed of coral and gems, and he drove a chariot fashioned from a shell and pulled by horses. He was often portrayed as a genial being—with a large powerful body, white beard and blue eyes—who, when in a good mood, created new lands and maintained calm seas. But he could also be angry and judgmental, using the trident to stir up the seas and trigger earthquakes.

Family Tree

Poseidon actually belonged to the power elite of Greek mythological hierarchy. Son of Cronus and Rhea, Poseidon was one of six siblings and one of the three who divided and ruled the divisions of the universe. His brother Zeus ruled the sky, his brother Hades ruled the underworld and Poseidon himself ruled the sea—both saltwater and fresh water.

Despite his reputation as a legendary lover, Poseidon was also a husband and father. He was married to Amphitrite, the sea nymph daughter of Nereus, the Old Man of the Sea. Together Poseidon and Amphitrite bore Triton who was a merman, half human and half fish. However, like his brother Zeus, Poseidon was not a particularly faithful husband and approached many goddesses and mortal women, often appearing in different forms such as a stallion, bull, dolphin or bird. For example, he transformed himself into a horse to appeal to the Gorgon Medusa and together they produced Pegasus, the flying horse. There were numerous other affairs as well, including one that produced the Cyclops (one-eyed giant) Polyphemus.

Dominion over Cities and Regions

At the time of the division of responsibility among the offspring of Cronus and Rhea, the gods decided that the earth would be jointly ruled with Zeus as king of the gods, Poseidon as king of the sea and Hades as ruler of the underworld. Despite the clear-cut division of authority, there were territorial disputes between Zeus, Poseidon and other gods and goddesses. Poseidon considered that as the god of land waters, creator of springs and controller of humidity and the fertility of the soil, it was part of his responsibility to found cities, tribes and nations; and he,

波 塞 冬

波塞冬,希腊海神(也称马神),掌管环绕大陆的所有水域。他有呼风之术,并且能够掀起或是平息狂暴的大海。传说他挥动三叉戟击打岩石,这样就有了人类第一匹马。

波塞冬最为人熟知的身份还是海神。实际上,在希腊的神话故事里,他占有很高的地位,掌管着所有的水域,控制着地震、火山、台风,有着呼风唤雨之术。"地震"之名也由他而来。提起波塞冬,自然就会联想到海豚、马、公牛和三叉戟,波塞冬是宇宙第三大神——海神。

海员们对波塞冬极为崇拜,希望他保佑他们航程顺利,因此水手们在出航前都向波塞冬祈祷,将马溺水致死,作为贡品敬供波塞冬。波塞冬大部分时间住在海洋深处他的灿烂夺目的金色宫殿里。他乘坐的战车就是用金黄色的战马所拉。波塞冬给人的大体印象是和蔼可亲,庞大身躯,白色耳朵,蓝眼睛。当波塞冬心情不错时,他会在海中建块陆地来平息风浪,当他心情糟糕时,他将会用三叉戟击打海底,引起海啸和地震。

家族

波塞冬属于希腊神话中强力精英人物。波塞冬是喀琅娜斯与洛伊之子,是他们六个子女中的老三。当初三兄弟划分势力范围,宙斯获得了天空,哈得斯屈尊地下,波塞冬就成了大海和湖泊的君主。

波塞冬娶了海神涅柔斯的美丽女儿安非特里特,后来他的妻子安非特里特给他生下半人半鱼的儿子特里同。波塞冬和宙斯一样好色,他有很多情人,常化身为马、牛、海豚和鸟以接近其他女神和凡人妇女。他曾变成一匹马,去追求美杜莎,并和她生了一个儿子皮格斯——飞马。诸如此类的事还有独眼巨人波吕斐摩斯特的出生。

掌管地域范围

在喀琅娜斯与洛伊的子女划分势力范围时,宙斯掌管大地和天空,成为全神之王,波塞冬掌管海洋和湖泊,成为海神,哈得斯屈尊地下,成为冥王。虽然海陆空看似是由三兄弟分管,但是内部势力范围并不均衡,波塞冬常与宙斯和其他各神发生冲突,争夺势力范围。尽管波塞冬掌管着陆地全部水域,控制着清泉,肥沃的土壤,能呼风唤雨。但是他不满足所拥有的权力,也想掌管陆地上的城市、部落及整个国家。

therefore, often competed for dominance over certain areas.

One of the best-known stories is his competition with Athena, the goddess of war, for the city of Athens. To demonstrate his power and benevolence, Poseidon struck the Acropolis with his trident, causing a saltwater spring to burst forth in three streams. Athena, on the other hand, planted an olive tree, which the Athenians felt was more useful than a spring of sea water. Thus, the citizens of Athens constructed the Parthenon as a temple to Athena.

Poseidon's Wrath

Although Poseidon could be benevolent and protective, he could also exact revenge against those who enraged him. A well-known story is the tale of the hero Odysseus, who blinded Poseidon's son, the Cyclops Polyphemus. This act of revenge is one of the episodes in the Odyssey, an epic poem by the Greek poet Homer. Cyclops were huge monsters with one eye in the middle of their foreheads. In Homer's story, a scouting party from Odysseus' ship discovered a large cave on the island of Cyclops. Entering the cave, the mariners ate the food they found there. The cave was the home of Polyphemus who returned, trapped the mariners in his cave and devoured several crew members.

Odysseus made his escape by plying the Cyclops with strong wine and then answering that he was No Man when Polyphemus asked his name. After the giant fell into a drunken stupor, Odysseus and his crew took the spit from the fire and gouged out the Cyclops'eye. Polyphemus' cries were ignored by his companions because he told them that No Man had blinded him. In the morning Odysseus and his men strapped themselves to the underbellies of the sheep as they were led out to pasture. Blinded, Polyphemus could not feel the men riding astride the sheep, and the crew escaped. As he left, Odysseus identified himself and Polyphemus appealed to his father Poseidon to prevent the Odyssey from returning home as a punishment for their deed. And Poseidon did, indeed, delay the hero's return home from the Trojan War, placing obstacles and setbacks to slow or prevent his progress.

In another story an angry Poseidon punished King Minos of Crete by placing a curse on the king's wife. Poseidon had bestowed the divine right to rule Crete by sending the king a bull from the sea. As part of the bargain, King Minos had agreed to sacrifice the bull in Poseidon's honor. When Poseidon sent the bull, however, the king liked the bull so much that he refused to sacrifice it. In retaliation Poseidon asked Aphrodite, the goddess of love to entice the king's wife, Queen Pasiphae, to fall in love with the bull. The result was the half man, half bull monster Minotaur.

At the same time, he displayed a benevolent and protective side when he chose and as a result was a popular god. His counterpart in Roman mythology was Neptune.

Resources

The Library of Greek Mythology (Oxford World Classics), Oxford University Press, USA, 1998. This is a primary source for Greek myths since it is based on the Library of Apollodorus, which was compiled in the 1st to 2nd century B.C.. The book provides a detailed history of the Greek myth, a reference source for ancient thinking and a view of how the Greeks originally viewed their myths and history.

Poseidon, Capstone Press, 2006. This book, aimed at children aged 4 to 8 years old, is an introduction to ancient Greek and Roman mythology. The author also explains how mythology influences thinking and literature today.

www.pantheon.org/articles/p/poseidon.html. History of Poseidon, his life, loves and the primary role he played in Greek mythology.

波塞冬经常与诸神交战，其中最著名的是雅典城的雅典娜争霸战。为了维护他的权力，波塞冬用三叉戟敲击雅典卫城引起海水的狂暴，导致形成三条河流。但雅典娜却在雅典卫城种上橄榄树，这比一河海水要有用的多。雅典人还在这里建了一座巴台农神庙以供奉雅典娜。

波塞冬的愤怒

尽管波塞冬平时显得平静，仁慈，但是如果有人惹他生气了，他也会报复那些人。如：希腊《荷马史诗》中《奥德塞》就有专门描写波塞冬愤怒的一节内容。波塞冬的儿子吕斐摩斯特是个独眼巨人。一天奥德修斯在海上航行时，他在侦察时发现独眼巨人岛上有一个大洞。水手们就走进洞里，发现有食物，就吃了这些食物，后来吕斐摩斯特回来时，将水手们全部围困在洞里，并吞食了几个人。

这时，奥德修斯劝吕斐摩斯特喝酒，想趁机逃走。后来吕斐摩斯特喝得大醉，问奥德修斯的名字，奥德修斯回答"没有人"。然后，奥德修斯和他的同伴们拿起火中的铲子，刺瞎了吕斐摩斯特的眼睛。他的同伴们没有理会吕斐摩斯特痛苦的尖叫声，因为他告诉他们"没有人"刺瞎了他的眼睛。第二天早上，奥德修斯和他的水手们把他们自己捆绑在绵羊的肚子下，骑着绵羊悄悄逃走了。吕斐摩斯特后来知道了真相，要求父亲波塞冬抓回奥德修斯，并处罚他。波塞冬应允，这样就使英雄奥德修斯不能从特洛伊战场上及时赶回家。

还有一个故事，克里特岛的米诺斯王惹怒了波塞冬，随后波塞冬就报复他。波塞冬准备赐给米诺斯王一头牛来统治克里特岛，国王米诺斯同意宰杀了这头牛祭祀波塞冬，但是，看到这头牛后，米诺斯王非常喜欢，就没有宰杀它。波塞冬很生气，就让爱神阿芙罗狄蒂劝说国王的妻子帕西法耶亲近那头牛并爱上那头牛，并生了一个半人半牛的怪物。

作为掌管水域的海神，他也有仁慈、友善的一面。需要提及的是，在罗马神话里也有与波塞冬相类似的海神——尼普顿。

相关资源

《希腊神话集》(牛津世界名著)，美国牛津大学出版社，1998 年。本书包含公元前 1~2 世纪的希腊神话故事，内容源自阿波罗多罗斯图书馆。本书详细记录了希腊神话的历史，以及希腊人怎样看待他们的神话及他们的历史。

《波塞冬》，角石出版社，2006 年。本书适合 4~8 岁的小读者，是一本古代希腊和罗马神话的入门书。此外，作者还阐述了神话对人的思维及当今文学的影响。

www.pantheon.org/articles/p/poseidon.html. 讲述波塞冬的历史、生活、爱情以及他在希腊神话中的作用。

Thirty-four

Robin Hood

Robin Hood was the legendary English outlaw who stole from the rich and gave to the poor. Subject of numerous ballads and stories dating as far back as the Middle Ages, Robin Hood became a symbol of independence from oppressive authority. The tales and songs all tell of a hero who treated the poor fairly and who fought corrupt officials who persecuted and mistreated those less fortunate.

According to the legend, Robin Hood lived with his band of merry followers—or outlaws, as some storytellers imply—in Sherwood Forest in Nottinghamshire during the 1100s. His friends and followers included the well–known Friar Tuck, Little John and Maid Marian. Friar Tuck was usually depicted as a fat, jolly priest while Little John, portrayed as a skilled archer, belied his name by being well over 6 feet tall. Maid Marian, of course, was Robin Hood's sweetheart whom he treated with elaborate courtesy.

Robin Hood's sworn enemy in many of the tales was the Sheriff of Nottingham, who abused his official position by levying unfair taxes, appropriating land without cause and persecuting the poor. Robin and his merry band often took the law into their own hands in order to undo the injustices committed by the sheriff. Typically, most of the stories and ballads show Robin Hood pursuing justice, fairness, generosity and egalitarianism while the sheriff and other figures of authority sought to undercut the rights of the poorer classes. Thus, Robin Hood became a hero of the common people and a thorn in the side of those in power.

Background of Legend

Some of the earliest references to Robin Hood appeared in the reports of legal or court cases of the late 1200s in which the term Robinhood was used as shorthand or a code word for felon or criminal. This type of usage continued throughout the Middle Ages and was still employed to convey treachery and sedition in reports of the Guy Fawkes' incident in 1605 when Fawkes and his followers attempted to kill King James I of England by blowing up the House of Lords during the opening of Parliament.

The oldest written reference to Robin Hood appears in the *Vision of Piers Plowman*, a long poem written by William Langland about 1378. Later around the mid–1400s a manuscript entitled *A Gest of Robyn Hood* collected several stories about Robin Hood and presented them in a continuous narrative form. Stories from this period usually introduced the various characters of Robin Hood's band of followers. What was interesting about these early versions was the fact that Robin Hood's famous sense of democracy and generosity were not featured in the stories. In fact, Robin Hood was often portrayed as greedy and power hungry. It was only in later versions that the well–known practice of taking from the rich and giving to the poor was described.

The first printed versions, usually based on *A Gest of Robyn Hood*, appeared in the 16th century after the introduction of printing in England. Although the actual legend was about a man from the Middle Ages, the stories and ballads from the 16th century actually provided historical context to the stories by connecting the story plots to historical events in the 1100s. For example, the stories illustrated the medieval themes of the vast gulf between upper and lower classes of

罗宾汉

在英国的传说中,罗宾汉的名字是极为响亮的,他是劫富济贫的英雄人物。有关罗宾汉的故事可以追溯到中世纪时代,他的故事也经常出现在民间故事及影视屏幕上,罗宾汉是劫富济贫、对抗昏君暴政的传奇英雄。

相传在公元12世纪时罗宾汉生活在英国诺丁汉地区的舍伍德森林,在那里,罗宾汉认识了法莱尔塔克、小约翰和玛丽安几个伙伴。法莱尔塔克是一位大肚皮的修道士,小约翰擅长箭术,玛丽安后来成为罗宾汉的心上人。

诺丁汉郡长是罗宾汉不共戴天的敌人。他滥用职权,横征暴敛,迫害百姓,非法没收罗宾汉的庄园和财产。为此,罗宾汉聚集了一帮好汉,对抗郡长的暴虐统治。很多故事和民谣都将罗宾汉刻画成维护公平与正义、行侠仗义的英雄人物。相反,将诺丁汉郡长描述为欺压百姓的君王。罗宾汉是家喻户晓的传奇英雄,更是统治者的眼中刺,肉中钉。

传奇背景

据介绍,13世纪后期,在一些法庭审理案件时就使用"罗宾汉"这一术语,指的是罪犯的一个代码,到中世纪时期这种用法还存在。1605年在盖伊·福克斯事件中,"罗宾汉"一词是"奸诈,阴险"之意。当时,福克斯想趁国会开会时,炸掉上议院,谋杀国王詹姆斯一世。

公元1378年左右,在威廉·兰格兰的《庄稼汉》这首诗中出现过"罗宾汉"这个词,这是有关"罗宾汉"一词的最早书面记载。15世纪中后期,《罗宾汉历险记》这本手抄稿中记载了很多关于罗宾汉的故事,这些故事都是以罗宾汉自述的方式叙述的。从那以后,有关罗宾汉及其兄弟的故事也有很多,有趣的是,罗宾汉在早期的很多故事中不是一位行侠仗义、追求平等的人物,而是一位贪婪的、迷恋权势的人物,只是后来的故事才将罗宾汉描述为劫富济贫的英雄好汉。

公元16世纪,印刷术传到英国,《罗宾汉历险记》成为第一部印刷版作品。罗宾汉的传说发生在中世纪时期,但16世纪创作的很多作品都以12世纪的历史事件为基础的,也反映了当时的社会状况。如:很多故事描写了中世纪时期上层社会与底层社会格格不入,贵族的贪婪,天主教的虚伪。与此同时,许多16世纪的文学手法把玛丽安也描绘为侠义人

society, the corruption and greed of nobility and the hypocrisy of the Catholic Church that was perceived by many to be sacrificing substance for ritual. At the same time, many conventions from the 16th century, such as the full characterization of Maid Marian as an object of chivalrous behavior, colored the tales.

Real or Legend

Did such a man really exist? No one really knows for certain whether or not Robin Hood is a fictitious character or someone based on a real person.

Over time many scholars have speculated about the actual identity of the real Robin Hood. Early on it was thought that a Robyn Hood served as a servant to King Edward II until he became bored and left for the outlaw's life. Later Robert Hood of Wakefield—near the home of the legendary Robin Hood—became involved in a rebellion against King Edward II but was pardoned by the king who was visiting Nottingham. However, there is no proof of either story.

Another well-known tradition claimed that Robin Hood was actually the Earl of Huntingdon, outlawed for his participation in Simon de Montfort's rebellion against King Henry III of England in 1265. After the rebellion, de Montfort became de facto ruler of England and called the first directly elected parliament in medieval Europe, thus establishing himself as one of the founders of modern parliamentary democracy. This bit of history connects de Montfort's values to the ideals perpetrated by Robin Hood, fictional or real. Again, however, this was never proved.

Over time, people who were interested in Robin Hood have researched many possible leads. Some have searched for information about people with the names Robin Hood, Robert Hood or similar variations who lived during the period the stories describe. Others have studied historical events that occurred in the same or nearby geographic locations described in the stories. People have identified Robin Hood as a nobleman whose land was taken over by opportunistic churchmen. Some tales tell of a man who, upon returning from the war, found his land appropriated by a corrupt and malevolent sheriff. Yet while some of the information seemed accurate and maybe even provable, there were never enough verifiable facts to establish a link between the legend and the persons or areas being studied.

In reality, most scholars believe that Robin Hood was a legendary figure, based on many stories, half-truths and folk tales. After all, he was credited with fighting for the downtrodden and what historical period has not had its downtrodden? Even though the means were questionable, even criminal, the ends nevertheless fulfilled the important goals of seeking justice and establishing what is right. When justice was done, the greed and corruption of the nobility, the rich or the powerful were the keys to their downfall.

What remains constant about the Robin Hood legend is that the stories change in context during each period of history. The legend of Robin Hood has been refashioned to reflect the values of each period and this persists even to modern times. The underlying themes of the legend— fairness and justice, robbing the rich to help the poor—have universal and timeless appeal; it is the details that change as history and social values change. Answering the question about whether or not Robin Hood was real is not really the point. What is important is how the legend is perceived and developed by each new storyteller.

Resources

Robin Hood: A Mythic Biography, Cornell University Press, 2003. As the title indicates, this is a biography about the mythical Robin Hood.

www.robinhood.info/robinhood/index.html. The worldwide Robin Hood Society.

物,增加了故事的传奇色彩。

真实还是虚构

罗宾汉存在吗? 没有人能确切地回答罗宾汉是虚构的还是真实存在的。

多年来,学者们就在推测罗宾汉的真实身份。早期的学者认为罗宾汉是爱德华二世的佣人,后来触犯了法律,被宣布为生命、财产不受法律保护的"法外人"。另一种说法是:住在罗宾汉家乡附近的威克费尔德镇的罗伯特·汉认为:罗宾汉反对爱德华二世而谋反叛乱,被迫逃到诺丁汉得到郡王的赦免。然而这些说法都无法考证。

另一种说法是,罗宾汉是亨廷顿的伯爵,1265年参与了西蒙发动的反叛亨利三世的叛乱。后来西蒙成为英国的国王,罗宾汉直接进入议会,这样,罗宾汉成为现代议会的创始人之一。将罗宾汉和西蒙联系在一起,参与谋反叛乱,是事实还是虚构?还是无从考证。

多年来,许多人都对罗宾汉的身份感兴趣。一些研究者还找到当时故事里描述的罗宾汉、罗伯特及类似名字的很多资料。还有些人研究了当时发生相关历史事件,这些事件的时间与地点都与罗宾汉有关的故事里描述的相同或接近。还有人认为罗宾汉是个贵族,他的庄园被教士趁机霸占。也有这说法,罗宾汉参加了战争,当他从战场返回家乡时,发现自己的庄园和财产被诺丁汉郡郡长没收。这些说法有些是真实的,有些甚至可以证实,但是这些说法与研究中谈到的人和地点是否存在关系,并没有充分的证据。

实际上,很多学者认为罗宾汉是一个虚构的人物形象。罗宾汉行侠仗义,反对统治者的暴虐统治,尽管手段不太妥当,甚至使用暴力,但是结果是维护公正、公平与正义。当公平得到维护,公平与正义得到体现,贵族、富人、强权者的腐败与贪婪就成了他们通向衰亡之路的钥匙。

不同的历史时期有关罗宾汉的说法不尽相同,但直到现在,罗宾汉作为一个劫富济贫、行侠仗义、维护公平与公正的形象并没有改变。随着时代的发展,社会价值观念的变化,有关罗宾汉传奇故事的细节可能也会有所变化,但罗宾汉是一个劫富济贫的英雄好汉,这一点不会改变。罗宾汉是确实存在的还是虚构的,这个问题不重要,重要的是怎样理解这个传奇故事,将来又怎样去叙述这个故事。

相关资源

《罗宾汉:神话传说》,科奈尔大学出版社,2003年。标题已做了解释,本书是一本关于罗宾汉的传记。

www.robinhood.info/robinhood/index.html. 罗宾汉学会网址。

Thirty-five

Salt Myths

Salt is such a basic necessity of life that it is inevitable that myths and stories about salt have existed for centuries. Chemically known as sodium chloride, salt, particularly sodium, is vital to basic chemical reactions within the human body. That is why human blood, tears and sweat all taste of salt.

Old Superstitions about Salt

Many of the early myths surrounding salt arose because, despite the fact that salt is one of the most common minerals on Earth, it was difficult to extract and transport in ancient times. Those who were able to mine salt and then carry it over river, sea or land routes became wealthy and powerful. Eventually salt became identified with money and value. As early as the 6th century salt was used as currency in Africa, and Marco Polo related that salt was used as a medium of exchange among several Asian cultures in the 13th century. Eventually, the word salt with its meaning of currency and value became part of the English language; the word salary comes from the Latin word salarium, which means salt.

Attaching these degrees of importance to salt also enhanced its mythical value. In many religions salt was bestowed as a blessing. In addition, salt was linked to sexual desire and fertility. And many even believed that salt drove away evil spirits. An example of a superstition that combined the value of salt with the evil spirits belief was the advice to toss a pinch of salt over the left shoulder whenever salt was spilled. Because of its worth, spilling salt was bad luck (some also believed that the superstition stemmed from the fact that Judas had spilled salt at the Last Supper). To ward off bad luck after a spill, you were supposed to toss a pinch of salt over your left shoulder where evil spirits supposedly lurked. As additional protection, you were supposed to use your right hand to throw the salt. Blinding the devil or evil spirits with salt prevented their retaliating.

Superstitions and myths about salt abound in various cultures and bodies of folklore. Some of the more common ones include the following:

· An old belief in Naples, Italy, states that an amulet of rock salt protects its wearer from evil spirits.

· In some cantons in Switzerland, inhabitants believe that carrying rock salt in each pocket fortifies one against spiritual enemies.

· In early Scotland salt was considered a charm and the saltbox was the first item to be moved into a new home.

· There is also a tradition among fishermen in Scotland that sprinkling salt over their nets will bring good luck.

· Salt and bread, symbolic of the basic needs in life, are the first items carried by Russian newlyweds into their home after the wedding.

· The Japanese view salt as an important preservative as well as a spiritual talisman and perpetuate a tradition of tossing a small quantity into a fire to prevent misfortune.

有关盐的神话

盐是人们生活的必需品，几个世纪以来，有很多关于盐的神话故事。盐(化学名氯化钠)是人体一种重要化学物质，这也是为什么人的血液、眼泪和汗液都是咸的。

有关盐的古代传说

盐是地球上最普通的物质之一。在古代由于科技不发达，提炼盐和运盐都很困难，所以关于盐的传说故事也很多。一些人开采盐矿，然后通过水路或陆路将盐运出去销售，赚了很多钱。后来，盐就成了金钱的代名词。早在6世纪时，在非洲，盐是充当货币使用的。马可·波罗说在13世纪的亚洲一些国家，盐是商品交换的媒介。在英语语言里，薪水(Salary)这个单词是来源于拉丁语的Salarium(盐的意思)，盐在英语里已成为货币或价值的代名词。

盐如此重要，使之变得更神秘。在许多宗教故事中，盐象征着福气。此外，也有人说盐与性欲(生殖能力)紧密相关，甚至很多人认为盐可以驱赶邪恶。有这样一种说法，如果盐被撒出，你就在自己的左肩膀上撒一撮盐。传说盐撒出去就会带来厄运(这种说法源于"最后的晚餐"，说犹大是最后一个进来参加最后晚餐的人，在吃饭时，将盐洒出了)。因此，为了驱赶厄运，你应该在左肩膀上洒一撮盐(传说邪恶就躲在左肩膀上)，最好是用右手撒盐，这样将邪恶和盐捆在一起，就会消除它们之间的报复。

不同的文化有关盐的神话故事说法不同，常见的有：

· 在意大利的那不勒斯，人们认为盐是护身符，你身上带着盐，就会得到保护。

· 在瑞士的一些州，人们认为口袋里装有盐，能驱赶邪恶。

· 在早期的苏格兰，盐是护身符，人们乔迁新居时，盐罐是最先放进家里的物品。

· 在苏格兰，渔夫们也相信，往渔网上撒点盐会带来好运。

· 在俄罗斯，盐和面包是生活必需品，婚礼后，新人要最先把盐和面包放进家里。

· 在日本，盐是重要的防腐剂和护身符，往火里撒点盐能驱除厄运。

Fables about Salt

Although there are many fables throughout folklore, two stand out because of their popularity. The first one, *The Merchant, the Donkey and the Salt*, is from the collection of Aesop's fables.

A merchant decided to increase his profits by importing salt from the seashore where it was cheaper. He loaded his donkey with salt and headed home. On the way the donkey accidentally stumbled and fell into a stream. The salt dissolved, lightening the donkey's load. The donkey happily traveled on. On the next trip, the donkey remembered the previous journey and deliberately fell to his knees in the stream in order to lighten his load. The merchant realized what was happening and decided to transport sponges—also cheaper by the seaside—in the future. On the next trip, the donkey, now loaded with sponges, again fell to his knees in the stream. This time, however, the sponges grew heavy as they absorbed water, and the donkey's load doubled in weight. Moral: What once seemed good may turn out to be bad.

The second fable grew out of a Roman folk tale. There once was a king with three daughters and he wanted to learn which daughter loved him the most. To satisfy his curiosity, he asked each daughter separately how much she loved him. The oldest answered: As much as bread. Since bread was basic to existence, he decided she loved him the best. His middle daughter answered: as much as wine. Again, the king decided that wine was almost as basic as bread and therefore, his second daughter loved him very much as well. His youngest daughter, however, answered his question by saying: As much as salt. The king was enraged, believing that she only loved him as much as the cheapest and most common condiment on the table.

The furious king sequestered the youngest daughter in a wing of the palace where she lived alone watching the activity in the palace's inner courtyard from her solitary window. One day she called to the cook who was washing vegetables at the fountain. She asked him to prepare a meal for her father without any salt. When the meal was served, the king refused to eat the tasteless food and called the cook. Explaining that since the king thought salt was worthless and cheap, the cook decided that it did not deserve to be served to the king. Therefore, salt was not used in the preparation of any of the food. Then the king understood the value of salt and the depth of his daughter's love for him.

This particular fable became so well–known that Shakespeare used its story as the basis of his play King Lear.

Today's Myths

Today salt has been linked to health problems. Salt is still basic to human health and cannot and should not be eliminated completely. Without enough salt, people can experience fatigue, dehydration and a host of other symptoms. Salt is essential to maintaining normal fluid balance and blood pressure in the body. On the other hand, too much salt can also cause disease and disorders, so the key is to establish and maintain a sensible balance. It should be used in moderation and with consideration of health issues.

Resources

www.saltinstitute.org. This Website, sponsored by the Salt Institute, a professional association supporting the salt industry, provides any and all information that anyone would want to know about salt.

Neptune's Gift: A History of Common Salt, The Johns Hopkins University Press, 1996. This book examines the significance of salt and its role in socioeconomic history. The book contains photographs to illustrate the history and science of the salt industry, including a breakdown country by country and historic period by historic period.

有关盐的寓言故事

世界上有许多民间寓言故事，较流行的有两个，《伊索寓言》中的《商人、驴和盐》是其中之一。

故事是这样的：一位商人为了牟取利润，从海边进了一袋盐，价格很低，然后让驴驮着盐赶回家。突然，驴被绊倒在河里，身上的盐遇水后溶化了，驴感到身上的重量轻了不少，很高兴地回了家。第二次，驴仍然记着上次发生的事，知道跌进水里后，盐就会溶化，身上就会轻很多，于是就故意跌入河里。后来，商人知道了这些情况，决定下次运海绵（海绵价格也很低），于是驴再次故意跌入河里，但这次情况不一样了，海绵吸水后，重量是原来的两倍。这个寓言的寓意是：福之祸所倚，祸之福所分。

另一个故事是罗马民间寓言：从前，有个国王，他有三个女儿，他想知道哪个女儿最爱他，出于好奇，他就一个一个分别问她们："你爱我有多深？"大女儿回答："像爱面包一样爱你，因为面包是人生存的必需品。"国王认为大女儿最爱他。二女儿回答："像爱酒一样爱你，因为酒和面包一样，也是人的基本必需品。"于是国王认为二女儿也很爱他。小女儿回答："像爱盐一样爱你"，国王听后大怒，认为小女儿爱他就像爱盐一样，而盐是人们餐桌上的调味品，是最便宜的。

后来，恼怒的国王将他的小女儿囚禁在皇宫的偏僻的地方，她感到很孤独，每天只能从窗户看到院子里的事情。有一天，她看到厨师在水池边洗菜，就将厨师叫过来，让他给她父亲做一顿没有盐的饭菜。饭菜做好后，国王不吃这样无味的饭菜，就将厨师叫来，说盐是最便宜的，不值钱的东西，为何饭菜不放盐？厨师听后决定不再为国王效劳。后来，国王餐桌上的饭菜都不放盐。这样，国王才理解了盐的价值，也懂得了小女儿对他的爱。

莎士比亚的《李尔王》就是以这个故事为基础创作的。

现代神话

今天盐已与人的健康问题息息相关。盐是人体健康的必需物质，缺少盐，人就会感到疲劳、缺水及其他许多症状。盐是保持人体正常的液体平衡和血压的必备物质。但是，吃太多的盐，会引起一些不适和疾病。我们应该每天摄入适量的盐，保持一个合理的平衡，以保证健康。

相关资源

www.saltinstitute.org. 食盐协会网。食盐协会是一个扶持盐工业的发展专业协会，该网址提供了人们想知道有关盐的所有信息。

《海神礼物：盐的历史》，约翰·霍普金斯大学出版社，1996年。本书讲述了盐的重要意义以及在社会中的作用，书内附有不同历史时期、不同国家的盐业发展史及盐业科学的照片。

Thirty-six

Legend of the Alligator in the Sewer

One of the most famous urban legends is the one about alligators living in the sewers of New York City. First reported in February 1935, the story has grown so much over the years that it is difficult to decide if these sightings were real or just hoaxes.

Sightings

This urban legend may have begun as early as the Byzantine Empire when there were reports of crocodiles living in the sewers of Constantinople. The Byzantine Empire, also known as the Eastern Roman Empire, existed from 395 A.D. to 1453 A.D. and occupied southeast Europe and southwest Asia centered around its capital, Constantinople.

More recently, stories of alligators or crocodiles in sewers have appeared in Europe but are more popular in the United States. In the 1930s, reports that construction workers discovered alligators in gullies and waterways in Mississippi circulated but were often dismissed as hearsay.

The New York City Sewer Alligators

The most common legend, however, is the oft-repeated story of alligators inhabiting the sewers of New York City.

The first sighting occurred in the mid-1930s and was reported in *The New York Times* on February 10, 1935. Three teenagers were shoveling snow into a manhole on East 123rd Street near the Harlem River. When there were signs of clogging below the street, one of the boys peered into the hole and saw an alligator struggling to break free of the heaped snow. After confirming the sight, the boys decided to help the alligator and ran to a nearby shop to get a clothesline. Fashioning a slip knot, one youth managed to snare the alligator and pull it to the street's surface. When the boys tried to loosen the rope, however, the alligator snapped its jaws. Switching from rescuers to executioners, the boys beat back the alligator with their snow shovels.

As soon as the alligator was dead, the boys dragged the animal to the shop and measured its weight and length (125 pounds, seven to eight feet). Eventually, they called the police who attempted to soothe neighbors by speculating that the alligator had fallen overboard from a passing ship traveling from the Florida Everglades to the Harlem River. Everyone further concluded that the alligator, seeking refuge from the cold river water, swam toward shore and entered the sewer's conduit. At that point a Department of Sanitation truck arrived to transport the dead animal away to an incinerator.

Later that year the Superintendent of Sewers, Teddy May, received reports of a colony of alligators living in the sewers beneath the city streets. May dismissed the reports, assuming the workers filing these reports were either mistaken or drinking on the job. When he learned that the sightings were possibly real, he investigated for himself. He claimed to be startled to discover that alligators, averaging about two feet in length, did live in smaller branches of the sewers where the water flow was apparently slower. His response was to order the alligators to be exterminated and in a few months the alligators were gone.

The Legend Grows

Over the years the legend has grown and various versions have been suggested. The best

下水道的鳄鱼

1935年2月10日，在纽约下水道里发现一条鳄鱼，这是世界上非常流行和知名的都市传奇之一。这个故事流传了很多年，是真是假，不太清楚。

发现

下水道里的鳄鱼这种说法要最早追溯到拜古庭帝国的君士坦丁堡。拜古庭帝国(公元395年~1453年)，位于罗马帝国东面，界于欧洲东南部和亚洲南部之间，首都君士坦丁堡。

近年来，在欧洲有很多关于下水道鳄鱼的传说，但流传最多的还是美国纽约下水道的鳄鱼。20世纪30年代，一群建筑工人在密西西比河畔下水道捉到一条鳄鱼。

纽约下水道的鳄鱼

纽约下水道的鳄鱼是世界上最流行的都市传奇。

1935年2月10日《纽约时报》刊出发现下水道鳄鱼的报道，当时三个十几岁的孩子在哈林河畔铲雪，他们把雪铲到123东大街的一个下水道入口处，雪快堆满时，其中一个小孩朝洞口看了看，发现鳄鱼在雪堆里挪来挪去。他们确定是鳄鱼后，想解救它，于是就跑到附近的商店拿了一根绳子，其中一个小孩将绳子打结，套住鳄鱼，将鳄鱼拉出洞。孩子们在解开绳子时，鳄鱼突然攻击他们，孩子们将鳄鱼打死。

鳄鱼死后，孩子们将它拖到商店称量，这条鳄鱼有125磅重，7英尺5英寸长。后来他们叫来了警察，警察说这条鳄鱼很可能是从佛罗里达的埃弗格雷斯港驶往哈林河的船上掉下来的(警察这样说主要是怕邻居们因此而恐慌)。人们后来认为由于河水太凉，鳄鱼为了生存，朝岸边游去，最后游到一个下水道里。后来，美国卫生部派了一辆卡车将鳄鱼运走去火化。

后来，下水道管理员泰蒂也听说下水道有鳄鱼出没的说法。泰蒂没有理会，认为排污工人们的说法是胡言乱语。后来，他得知这件事可能是真的，就亲自去寻查，确实发现了鳄鱼。这些鳄鱼体长约2英尺，生活在水流缓慢的狭长下水道里。结果，他要求派人清理下水道，捕获这些鳄鱼。几个月后，在下水道中的鳄鱼完全消失。

成为传奇

多年来，有很多关于下水道鳄鱼的传说。最流行的说法是，几十年前，鳄鱼就被当做

known version traces the origin of the alligators in the sewers to a fad that began many decades ago. It seems that it was trendy to own a pet baby alligator, either purchased in a pet shop or brought back from Florida vacations; however, once the pet grew too big to handle, the owners flushed the animals down the toilets. The flushed alligators ended up in the sewer system where they lived on rats, sewage and other offal in the pipes.

The alligators allegedly thrived and grew large and menacing. One version even explained that the alligators, deprived of sunlight at a young age, lost their eyesight and pigmentation, resulting in blind, albino alligators with red eyes traveling through the New York sewers. While albino alligators, in fact, do exist, they are seldom seen in the wild; because of their vulnerability to light and predators, albino alligators retreat from sight. This survival behavior fed well into the sewer legend: What could be a better retreat than a dark enclosed sewer?

Popular culture has perpetuated the legend. The 1961 novel V includes a character who has a job as an alligator exterminator in the New York City sewers.

The comic characters Batman and Spiderman both fight enemies who reside in the city sewers. And the Teenage Mutant Ninja Turtles originated as four pets who were dropped into a New York City sewer where they mutated into humanoid reptiles.

Fact or Fiction?

Although there may be some truth to the story in The New York Times in 1935—that is, an alligator may have fallen overboard in the Harlem River and eventually appeared in the sewer—most people, especially herpetologists (zoologists who study reptiles and amphibians), think that alligators living in the New York City sewers is an urban myth.In reality a sewer is not a good environment for alligators. Sewers are too polluted, too dark and too cold for alligators to survive.

Alligators and other reptiles are cold –blooded animals, which means that their blood temperature is determined by the temperature in the environment rather than by their own internal metabolism. Therefore, they need heat and sunlight to remain warm and alive. If alligators are too cold, they cannot digest their food, and they will die. Furthermore, without sunlight alligators cannot use calcium to build and maintain bones; therefore, their bones will become soft and the animal will eventually die. And if the cold temperatures and the lack of light do not kill them, the pollution in the sewers will.

One explanation of the sightings may be that what people see or try to capture are not really alligators but rather caymans (also spelled caiman). A cayman is a small reptile similar to alligators and crocodiles that is native to Central and South America. Some of the reports about small alligators may actually be sightings of caymans that may be abandoned pets. In fact, however, colonies of alligators do not live in the New York City sewers and most of the sightings can be attributed to the persistence of the folklore about abandoned alligators congregating in the sewers of the city.

Resources

The Big Book of Urban Legends, Paradox Press, 1995. This book presents common urban legends, including the alligator in the sewer story, in entertaining ways by a variety of writers and artists.

Urban Legends: 666 Absolutely True Stories That Happened to a Friend of a Friend of a Friend, Black Dog & Leventhal Publishers, 2005. This book is a collection, including the alligator in the sewer myth, of outlandish tales with themes that run from funny to frightening to humorous.

V, Harper Perennial Modern Classics. Reprint edition, 1999.

Legend of the Alligator In the Sewer

宠物饲养，人们要么去宠物店购买，要么去佛罗里达度假时带一条回来。但是，一旦鳄鱼长得体形过大，不再适合饲养，主人便将其冲入马桶，进入下水道。这些鳄鱼就依靠下水道里的老鼠、污物和垃圾生存。

传言这些被遗弃的鳄鱼长的体形过大，变的凶猛残暴。因为鳄鱼生活在暗无天日的环境，基因出现变化，失去了视力，眼睛变红，身体出现白化并游走于下水道中。这种白化鳄鱼确实存在，但在野外很少见。白化鳄鱼害怕阳光及一些食肉动物的攻击，却能在下水道生存。对白化鳄鱼来说，呆在黑暗的下水道生活可能更好。

通俗文化使这则传说更加流传长远。1961年，小说《V》问世，书中有一角色其任务就是搜捕纽约下水道里的鳄鱼。这些滑稽的角色就像蝙蝠侠和蜘蛛侠，他们与住在下水道中的敌人斗智斗勇。另外，传说"忍者神龟"最初是四只宠物，后来被扔进纽约的下水道，他们就变成了类似于人的爬行动物。

事实还是虚构

1935年《纽约时报》报道的下水道鳄鱼的故事，有些或许是真实的。比如：鳄鱼可能是从船上掉进哈林河的，然后再逃到下水道里的。大多数人特别是爬行学家(研究爬行动物和两栖动物的动物学家)认为纽约下水道的鳄鱼是个都市传奇。实际上，下水道并不适合鳄鱼生活，下水道污染严重、黑暗、寒冷，鳄鱼很难生存。

鳄鱼和其他爬行类动物都是冷血动物，这说明他们它们的体温是受外界环境影响，而不是靠自己的新陈代谢。因此，鳄鱼适合生活在温暖、有阳光的地方，如果气温太低，就无法消化体内的食物而死去。另外，没有阳光的照射，鳄鱼也不能生存，因为太阳发出的紫外线可以帮助鳄鱼体内产生钙。而缺少钙，鳄鱼的骨头会变松软。即使鳄鱼可以在低温和黑暗的环境生存下来，但下水道污染严重，鳄鱼也很难生存。

另一种解释是：他们所见到或捕捉到的鳄鱼不是真正的鳄鱼，而是一种凯门鳄。凯门鳄是一种类似鳄鱼的爬行动物，生活在美国的中南部地区。有些关于小鳄鱼的报道可能就是被人们遗弃的宠物——凯门鳄。实际上，纽约的下水道并没有大量鳄鱼，关于纽约下水道有鳄鱼出没的说法可能还是民间传说。

相关资源

《都市传奇》，茅盾出版社，1995年。本书包含了许多作家及艺术家创作的有趣的传奇故事，纽约下水道鳄鱼的故事是其中之一。

《都市传奇：发生在朋友身上的666个完全真实的故事》，黑狗和利尔撒尔出版社，2005年。本书收集了一系列传奇故事，有趣味型、恐怖型和幽默型，下水道鳄鱼的故事是其中之一。

《v》，哈珀·柯林斯，现代图书，重印本，1999年。

Thirty-seven

Shangri-La

Shangri-La, for most people, is a much generalized condition of ease and peace. It is a concept which is synonymous with a life without tension and conflict. In some ways, it is an old-fashioned term popularized in earlier generations but used frequently throughout literature, the movies and other media. The very word itself was capable of conjuring up an immediate image of a mysterious, long-forgotten location. Whatever it is, in theory it is an actual, physical place.

Shangri-La is a mystical utopian place, isolated in the Himalayan Mountains, whose inhabitants live in peace and harmony governed by moderation. Thus does British author James Hilton describe the earthly paradise in his 1933 novel, *Lost Horizon*. Since the publication of this book, scholars, explorers and others have searched for the real geographical location of this place, the name of which has come to symbolize the triumph of good over evil, harmony versus discord and hope for a better world over the reality of a dream sought but never realized.

Lost Horizon

Lost Horizon is a novel classified as utopian fiction or fantasy. The setting is an earthly paradise located high in the Himalayan Mountains where wise Lamas (Buddist priests) safeguard the noblest manifestations of modern culture whilst renouncing violence and evil. This novel is definitely a reaction to the times in which it was written. It is important to place the book in its historical context and to understand both the plot and the imagery within this setting. In 1933 the world had just endured the slaughter of World War I and its catastrophic economic and political aftermath. Militarism and dictators were emerging—Hitler in Germany and Mussolini in Italy, for example. All signs pointed to another global war with even more cataclysmic effects. As a result, the concept of a safe, peaceful and beautiful haven removed from the realities of the real world was appealing and this contributed to the immense popularity of Hilton's book. In addition, the famous film director Frank Capra turned the book into a successful movie.

The basic story of *Lost Horizon* tells of the evacuation of 80 white residents in Afghanistan during a revolution. Among the evacuees is Hugh Conway, British consul to Afghanistan. The plane carrying the evacuees flies over the mountains into Tibet where it crash lands. As he lies dying, the pilot advises the travelers to seek shelter at the nearby lamasery of Shangri-La. A postulant from the lamasery leads the party to his home where eventually the travelers decide to stay. The High Lama receives Conway who learns that the lamasery was built in the early 18th century and since has become a sanctuary for others traveling into the valley. The High Lama explains that those who join the group in Shangri-La no longer age as quickly, but if they leave the valley, they age quickly and die. Eventually, the High Lama informs Conway that he is dying and that he wants Conway to lead the lamasery.

Lost Horizon became a bestseller. Many scholars believe that Hilton was partly inspired by travel reports published in *National Geographic* by Joseph Rock, an explorer and botanist. Rock made expeditions to Yunnan and Sichuan in China, taking photographs, making maps, collecting plants and recording the activities of many ethnic groups living in remote areas.

香格里拉

在大多数人眼中"香格里拉"就象征着安宁、和谐。很早以前"香格里拉"这个字眼就开始在文学作品、电影电视屏幕上出现,提及"香格里拉"一词,一片宁静、祥和的世外桃源景象便自然在人们脑海中浮现。不论香格里拉是什么样的,从理论上说,确实有这样的地方。

香格里拉,位于喜马拉雅山深处的一块神秘的理想之地,那里的人们奉行适度的原则,过着宁静、和谐的生活。香格里拉是1933年英国小说家詹姆斯·希尔顿在小说《消失的地平线》中所描绘的一块土地。小说出版后,吸引了无数学者、探险家和其他一些人来探寻这片祥和、永恒、和谐、宁静的理想乐园。

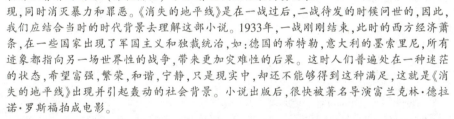

《消失的地平线》

《消失的地平线》是一部幻想小说,小说以喜马拉雅山深处某个神秘的地方为背景,那是一个宁静、祥和的人间天堂,在那里睿智的喇嘛(佛教僧侣)护卫着现代文化最高贵的表现,同时消灭暴力和罪恶。《消失的地平线》是在一战过后,二战待发的时候问世的,因此,我们应结合当时的时代背景去理解这部小说。1933年,一战刚刚结束,此时的西方经济萧条,在一些国家出现了军国主义和独裁统治,如:德国的希特勒,意大利的墨索里尼,所有迹象都指向另一场世界性的战争,带来更加灾难性的后果。这时人们普遍处在一种迷茫的状态,希望富强,繁荣,和谐,宁静,只是现实中,却还不能够得到这种满足,这就是《消失的地平线》出现并引起轰动的社会背景。小说出版后,很快被著名导演富兰克林·德拉诺·罗斯福拍成电影。

《消失的地平线》描写的是在阿富汗大革命时期80个白人被疏散的故事。故事的主人公康韦——英国驻阿富汗的领事,是被疏散者之一。飞机载着那些被疏散的人员进入西藏境内时突然坠毁,当康韦奄奄一息时,飞行员建议他们去香格里拉的喇嘛庙附近找一个地方避难。后来,喇嘛庙的一个人将他们全部带往庙里照料。一位高僧收留了康韦,康韦也决定留在此地。康韦后来得知喇嘛庙是在18世纪早期修建的,后来一直成为旅游者的避难所。高僧还说,在这里生活的人都能长寿,要是离开这个地方,就会很快衰老,寿命也短。最后,高僧临死前对康韦说希望他接管这个喇嘛庙。

《消失的地平线》是世界上最畅销的小说,很多学者认为他的小说素材来自洛克的探险照片、日记和记录。洛克是美国的一位植物学家和探险家,应《国家地理》杂志的约稿来到中国的云南和四川进行研究,他拍摄了很多照片、绘制了地图、收集了很多植物标本并记录了当地多样的民俗活动。

Where Exactly Is Shangri–La?

Although Hilton is vague about the actual location of Shangri–La, he does describe the fateful flight as flying in the wrong direction into the Himalayans, supposedly somewhere in or near Tibet. Assuming he was inspired by Joseph Rock's *National Geographic* articles, many turn to Rock's descriptions of locations for clues to the actual geographical location of Hilton's Shangri–La. For example, Hilton's description of the sacred mountain of Karakal is quite similar to Rock's depiction of the Konkaling mountain of Jambeyang, now part of the Yading National Nature Reserve northeast of Zhongdian in Yunnan Province. In fact, in 2003 Zhongdian County in northwestern Yunnan officially renamed itself Shangri–La County because of its claim that it was the inspiration for Hilton's novel. On the other hand, other mountains, such as Mt. Kailash in the western part of Tibet, have been designated as the inspiration for Karakal. Yet another name mentioned in Rock's reports is Mt. Kawakarpo in northwest Yunnan and many scholars believe that the similarity of the name Kawakarpo to Karakal is significant.

The High Lama in *Lost Horizon* is a former French cleric, Pere Perrault. Joseph Rock, in his article about Kawakarpo tells how he met a French priest in a remote village called Cizhong in Yunnan below Mt. Kawakarpo. In another report, however, Rock describes Muli, a monastery town that sits high on the hillside of the Litang River valley in Sichuan. Rock portrays Muli as a peaceful, isolated place in the midst of chaos and crime in western China. The inhabitants, too, are naive and cut off from the real world, believing that natural phenomena such as thunder or lightening are supernatural occurrences.

While there are many parallels between Joseph Rock's facts and James Hilton's fiction, no one knows with any certainty the actual location of Hilton's Shangri– La. Many places in China resemble the Shangri–La that Hilton described, but in reality Shangri–La exists only in James Hilton' imagination.

Shangri–La as a Symbol

In recent times the term Shangri–La is used more as a figure of speech or metaphorical reference than as a destination. The term may represent the search for perfection, love, happiness or contentment. Shangri–La is often used in the same way as the Garden of Eden or the Fountain of Youth—to signify a form of perfection that may be hidden from or forbidden to human beings.

In keeping with James Hilton's perception of his Shangri–La, the concept of Shangri–La today is a spiritual one. Like Hilton's vision, Shangri–La represents utopian values, that is, a place founded upon ideals envisioning perfection in social and political organization. Shangri–La is idealistic and visionary. It is an imaginary place symbolizing personal quests for the ideal in a reality far from perfection.

Resources

Lost Horizon, Harper Perennial, Reprint Edition, 2004. Also available as a book on tape from AudioFile, Portland, Maine.

The Siege of Shangri–La: The Quest for Tibet's Sacred Hidden Paradise, Broadway, 2002. Written by a contributing editor at National Geographic, this book documents the history of both the geographic and spiritual exploration of Tibet's Tsangpo River Gorge.

The Last River: The Tragic Race for Shangri–La, Three Rivers Press, 2001. This book examines the expeditions into remote areas of Tibet, including the Yarlung Tsangpo. Considered one of the most remote places on Earth, this river valley has been reported as the source behind the myth of Shangri–La.

香格里拉存在吗

希尔顿本人并没有到过香格里拉,他的小说取材于洛克探险时的照片和记录。但他想,在西藏的附近或境内确实有这样的地方。后来,很多人依据洛克的描述作为线索寻找希尔顿小说中的香格里拉。例如:希尔顿在小说中提到的神圣山脉——卡拉卡尔与洛克在《国家地理》杂志中描述的Konkaling山脉类似,现在这里已经成为云南省中甸西北部的亚丁国家级自然保护区的一部分。受希尔顿小说的启发,2003年云南西北部的中甸县被更名为香格里拉县。另外,西藏西部的凯撒拉山也与希尔顿小说中描述的卡拉卡尔山脉大体一致。也有人认为云南西北部的卡瓦格博(又称梅里雪山)山脉类似于卡拉卡尔。

希尔顿在小说中提到卡拉卡尔山脉与小说《消失的地平线》中的人物高僧以前是法国的一个牧师——皮埃尔佩罗,洛克在他的有关卡瓦格博山脉记录的文章曾提到他当时在云南偏远的山村——茨中遇见过一位法国牧师。另外,在洛克的探险记录中有关于四川理塘河谷附近的小镇——木里的描述。木里位于中国西部,是一块祥和宁静的世外桃源之地,那里的居民还过着原始的生活,认为雷电是一种超神灵的自然现象。

希尔顿小说中描述的很多内容与洛克在探险记录中描述的非常类似。在中国有很多地方,都与希尔顿笔下的香格里拉很相像,但是没有人知道香格里拉具体位置,香格里拉只是存在于希尔顿的想象中。

香格里拉的象征意义

近年来,"香格里拉"代表的不仅是一片风景,而是一种意境。"香格里拉"是"伊甸园、理想国、世外桃源"的代名词,是宁静和谐的象征。

与希尔顿笔下的"香格里拉"一样,今天香格里拉已经成为人们理想中的国度,是一块宁静、和谐、人与人、人与自然和谐相处的理想乐园。

相关资源

《消失的地平线》,哈珀·柯林斯,重印本,2004年。该书磁带版有售。

《香格里拉的四周:寻找西藏的神圣世外桃源》,百老汇出版社,2002年。该书由国家地理杂志资源编辑所著,记录了西藏雅鲁藏布江地理和人文探险的历史。

《最后的河流:艰难走进香格里拉》,三河出版社,2001年。该书记录了有关探险西藏及雅鲁藏布江的情况。雅鲁藏布江被认为是地球上最神秘的地点,雅鲁藏布江河谷被认为神秘香格里拉的源头。

Thirty-eight

Shroud
of Turin

The Shroud of Turin is a linen cloth that many believe was wrapped around the body of the Jesus Christ after his crucifixion. All four Gospels of the New Testament cite accounts of Jesus' followers wrapping his body in a burial cloth (Matthew 27:59, Mark 15:46, Luke 23:53 and John 19:40). The shroud is so named because it is kept in a chapel in the cathedral of St. John the Baptist in Turin, Italy.

Description of the Shroud

Measuring 14 feet long by four feet wide, the cloth bears a faint image of the front and back of a man who was whipped, beaten and crucified. The actual markings on the cloth match the details of Jesus's beatings and torture as described in the Bible. For example, there seem to be wounds around the hairline, consistent with the biblical description of the crown of thorns that Christ was forced to wear. There are also images of stripe–like injuries extending from the shoulder to the legs, corresponding to tales of the wounds Jesus received when he was beaten. And a chest wound appears on the cloth, matching the description of the piercing of Jesus's chest.

History of the Shroud

The first historical mention of the shroud appeared in the 16th century when the shroud was first brought to the cathedral in Turin. Supposedly, the shroud was originally discovered in Turkey during one of the Holy Crusades in the Middle Ages. In fact, some scholars believe the shroud is actually the Mandylion, an Orthodox Christian term referring to the Image of Edessa. First appearing in Edessa (now Urfa) Turkey in the 500s, the Mandylion is a piece of cloth that bears the image of a man's face. Its connection to the Shroud of Turin lies in the fact that the image of Christ's face on the shroud closely resembles artists' copies of the face on the Mandylion. The Mandylion was taken to Constantinople (Istanbul) in the mid–900s and disappeared in 1204 during the Fourth Crusade when the Crusaders sacked Constantinople and carried off many of its treasures to Western Europe.

The Shroud of Turin turned up around 1355 in the possession of Geoffrey de Charny, a French nobleman. In 1453 the House of Savoy, a royal family of Italy, acquired the shroud and took it to Chambery, France, where it was damaged in a fire in 1532. In 1578 they took the shroud to Turin.

Authentic or Fake?

Scholars and theologians have been studying the Shroud of Turin for decades—centuries, in fact—in an effort to authenticate the claims that the shroud is indeed the burial cloth of Jesus. The results have been inconclusive because of research methods, technological changes and the credentials of the researchers.

In 1389 the bishop of Troyes, France, claimed the shroud was a forgery painted around 1355 when Geoffrey de Charny first exhibited it. In 1898, however, the first photographs of the shroud seemed to disprove this theory because the negatives of the photographs revealed a positive image that was much clearer than the image on the shroud. Therefore, it was speculated that the shroud is a negative image. If this is true, experts conclude that no medieval artist could have painted

都灵尸衣

都灵尸衣,一块古代的细麻布,人们认为它是耶稣的寿衣。《新约四部福音》(马太福音27:59,马克福音15:46,路迦福音23:53和约翰福音19:40)中说耶稣在十字架被钉死后,他的追随者用一块尸布裹着他的尸体,这块尸布现在存放在意大利都灵圣·约翰的教堂里,因此得名都灵尸衣。

关于尸衣的描述

都灵尸衣,长14英尺,宽4英尺,尸衣正面有暗淡的图案,背面绘有人的头像(耶稣被钉在十字架上抽打)。尸衣上的这些形象与《圣经》中耶稣被酷刑折磨而死相吻合。例如,尸衣上的形象头部有伤,这与《圣经》上说耶稣头上戴有棘刺的王冠一致。另外,尸衣上的形象从肩膀到脚,都有伤痕,这也与民间故事里描述的一样(耶稣受到严刑拷打,伤痕累累),还有胸部有伤痕,这点也是吻合的(耶稣的胸部被刺伤过)。

尸衣的历史

有关尸衣的历史记载最早可以追溯到16世纪意大利都灵的大教堂。传说,在中世纪十字军东征时期,在土耳其就有关于尸衣的说法。一些学者认为尸衣实际上是一块印有基督圣容的方形的布。Mandylion一词源于基督教,最早出现在公元5世纪土耳其的埃德萨(今乌尔法),有"埃德萨形象"之意。画家绘制在Mandylion上的形象与耶稣基督的形象极其相似。这块印有基督圣容的方形的布于10世纪中叶被带到君士坦丁堡 (今伊斯坦布尔),后于1204年失踪了。当时正值十字军第四次东征,他们占领了君士坦丁堡,大量文物被掠取到西欧。

查尼·乔佛瑞,一位法国贵族,于1355年获得了尸衣。1453年,意大利的王室家庭,萨伏衣公爵获得了尸衣,将尸衣保存在法国的善贝里,此地于1532年遭火烧毁。1578年,尸衣又被带到意大利的都灵。

真的还是假的

几个世纪以来,许多科学家和学者一直在研究都灵尸衣,他们想找到尸衣确实是耶稣的寿衣的证据。但或许是研究方法、技术手段及一些研究者提供的证据材料等原因,目前没有充分的证据能够证明尸衣确实是耶稣的寿衣。

1389年,法国特罗亚的主教在一封信里解释说:1355年,查尼·乔佛瑞第一次在教堂里陈列的尸衣是伪造的,这块尸衣是由画家绘制的。1898年,有位摄影师拍摄了尸衣,但惊讶地发现,尸衣上的影像竟然呈现出阴片的效果。因此,专家们得出这样的结论:在中世纪没有任何画家可以绘制这样的影像。

such an image.

During the 1970s and 1980s, scientists performed many tests on the shroud. In 1988, for example, the Vatican permitted teams at Oxford University, the University of Arizona and the Swiss Federal Institute of Technology to date the cloth and each reported the shroud as originating in the medieval period around 1350. However, scholars who believe in the shroud's authenticity claim that a fire damaged the shroud in the early 16th century, which distorted the carbon dating of the shroud. Other scientists dismiss this idea, saying that fire damage would not change the outcome of scientific carbon dating processes. On the other hand, tests have also shown that the material tested in the carbon dating analysis was cut from a patch woven into the shroud to repair the fire damage. In this case, the actual fabric tested would have, indeed, been from the medieval period.

Putting the questions about the carbon dating procedures aside, in 1978 a team of researchers found that the stains on the cloth appeared to be human blood. In contrast, another group of scientists have found that the stains on the shroud contain traces of chemicals that were used in common artist's paint—red ochre and vermilion—during the 14th century. This brings the scientists back to the claim of the bishop of Troyes, France, that the image on the shroud was painted in 1355. In addition, the stains are red–like paint whereas dried aged blood is black.

Final Analysis

The final analysis about the authenticity of the Shroud of Turin is that there is no final analysis. There are those who firmly believe that it is actually the burial cloth of Christ and in many cases they point to scientific research to support their belief. Conversely, others can point to equally convincing research to refute the shroud's authenticity.

Unfortunately, to date, carbon dating, chemical analyses and historical research have not led to a definitive answer to the question of the shroud's authenticity. The shroud itself, however, carries enough historical, religious and scientific interest so that research will continue. As technology improves, perhaps there will be a breakthrough in the present inconclusive evidence and someday the debate about the Shroud of Turin will be resolved.

For believers, Catholics in particular, whether the shroud is actually authentic is, in some ways, missing the point. One motivation with the whole concept of relics, much as one would keep a locket of hair from a deceased friend or relative, was to make faith and the religious experience real and concrete to the believing public. Remember that universal education is a very recent concept and that most Christians in the early centuries were neither literate nor sophisticated. Relics of all kinds were tangible reminders of the good life lead by a person (a saint) officially recognized by Church. The shroud, as a relic, is similarly valued as a concrete symbol of the life and suffering of Jesus. Many true believers will readily step aside of the authenticity argument and see the Shroud for what it is intended: a symbol of holiness.

Resources

The Mysterious Shroud of Turin, Lulu, 2007. This short book discusses the shroud without making a case for its authenticity. The book examines all of the facts in an attempt to present an unbiased overview of the topic.

www.shroud.com. The Shroud of Turin Website.

20世纪70~80年代,科学家们用了很多方法来鉴定尸衣的真伪。如1988年,英国牛津大学、美国亚利桑那大学及瑞士联邦技术学院的专家们来到梵蒂纲,鉴定尸衣的起始年代,他们都认为尸衣是始于1350年左右的中世纪时期。然而一些学者,他们相信尸衣不是伪造的,但认为尸衣在16世纪早期已遭火焚坏,用碳测年法测定尸衣的起始年代不准确。另外一些科学家则认为尸衣即使遭火焚坏,并不能改变科学的碳测年法得出的结果。况且,碳测年代分析法所测试的材料就是取自当年修补尸衣破洞的那块布,结果确实证实尸衣是始于中世纪时期。

关于碳测年法测定过程的疑问这一点暂且不去争论。1978年一组研究者发现尸衣上有两点血渍,好像是人的血液。相反,另一组科学家发现尸衣上的血渍含有化学物质,在14世纪,这些赤红和朱红色的化学物质是用作绘画颜料。这一点使科学家们认同了法国特里亚主教当时所说,尸衣是1355年由画家绘制的。此外,尸衣上的血渍像一种赤红色的绘画颜料,而人的血渍,多年后应该是黑色的。

最终分析

有关都灵尸衣真实性的最终分析是:没有最终结论。一些人认为尸衣确实是耶稣的裹尸布,并在很多方面提供了科学证据来支持其观点。相反,另一些人也同样出示了很多有说服力的证据来证实都灵尸衣是伪造的,并不是耶稣的寿衣。

很遗憾,都灵尸衣是否是耶稣的寿衣,就这一问题,无论是碳测年法、化学分析法还是历史研究都没有给出确定的答案。都灵尸衣本身带有历史的、宗教的及科学的色彩,因此,有关尸衣的研究还将继续。随着科学技术的进步,或许将来可以找到有说服力的证据来证实都灵尸衣的真实性,关于都灵尸衣的争论或许会最终得到解决 。

对一些信徒,特别是天主教信徒来说,尸衣是否真实并不重要,他们将尸衣视为宗教遗物,就像死者的亲戚和朋友保存先人的一盒头发一样。因为遗物是看得见摸得着的有形物体,看见遗物就会想起先人生前的生活。都灵尸衣作为宗教遗物,上面印有钉十字架基督的形象,象征着耶稣复活。关于尸衣真实性这一问题,许多虔诚的信徒不准备去争论,只要看看尸衣是用来做什么的——神圣的象征。

相关资源

《神秘的都灵尸衣》,露露,2007 年。本书提供了很多相关尸衣的资料,探讨了尸衣的真伪,试图给出一个公正的判断。

www.shroud.com 都灵尸衣网址。

Thirty-nine

Six Degrees
of Separation

Six degrees of separation is a theory that anyone on the planet Earth can be linked to any other person on the planet with no more than six links in the chain.

Background History of the Theory

The idea first surfaced in 1929 when a Hungarian writer, Frigyes Karinthy, published a volume of short stories, one of which was entitled Chains. Karinthy believed that because of modern advances in communication technology the world was shrinking and people were becoming more and more interconnected. He further elaborated the idea by speculating that the number of connections in each link in the chain grew exponentially so that eventually only a few links would be necessary to connect everyone on the planet. This was one of the original ideas that led to the field of network theory. For this reason, some credit Karinthy as being the originator of the six degrees of separation theory.

Meanwhile in 1967 a Harvard social scientist, Stanley Milgram, devised an experiment to determine the social networks in the United States. Calling it the small world problem, Milgram chose people from several U.S. cities to send postcards to people in Boston and a city in the Midwest. Simultaneously, the participants sent copies of the postcards to Milgram's researchers so that they could keep track of the chain.

The final results reinforced the original idea of six links in a chain. In Milgram's experiment, the average chain was six links; therefore, the researchers concluded that on average people in the United States are separated by six people, that is, it took six steps for a postcard to reach the destination person using only personal contacts to form a chain.

Modern Follow-Up

Milgram's experiment had some flaws: It was a small sample size and only included participants in the United States. Yet nearly 40 years later, the Small World Research Project conducted by researchers at Columbia University in New York City, yielded similar results. This time, the researchers turned to the Internet to send the messages and the experiment covered the entire world. The object is the same as the goal in the Milgram experiment: To see how many links appear in a chain from one person to another.

The first stage of the experiment was finished in 2003 and the outcome was very interesting. More than 60,000 people from 166 countries participated and out of approximately 24,000 initial chains, 384 were completed. From these statistics, researchers estimated that people were separated by five to seven degrees and the chains between people living in the same country were even shorter.

This experiment is still going on. Researchers are still trying to pinpoint factors that people consider to be links between themselves and others. The researchers are looking at geographic proximity, professional links, family ties and personal friendships. The first phase of the experiment showed that most people chose friends as the connecting link, but in reality professional ties were more likely to forge a successful chain. This experiment has also shown that the Internet has not really changed the way human beings forge links to one another, that is, it has

39

六度分隔理论

六度分隔理论简单地说就是在这个社会里,任何两个人之间建立一种联系,最多需要六个人,无论这两个人是否认识,生活在地球的任何一个地方,他们之间只有六度分隔。

理论的历史背景

1929年,匈牙利作家Frigyes Karithy的短篇故事集出版,他在《链接》这篇文章中第一次提出了"六度分隔"这个概念。Karithy认为随着通讯技术的发展,世界正变得越来越小,人与人之间的联系更加紧密,几乎在成幂数级增长。但在这无数的人际关系网中,要结识任何一位陌生的朋友,这中间最多只要通过几个朋友就能达到目的,这就是网络理论的起源。因此,也有人认为Karithy可能是六度分隔理论的创始人。

1967年,美国哈佛大学的社会心理学教授斯坦利·朱尔格兰姆想要描绘一个连接人与社区的人际联系网,做过一次连锁信实验,结果发现了"六度分隔"现象(又称为"小世界现象"small world problem)。他从内布拉斯加州和堪萨斯州招募到一批志愿者,随机选择出其中的300多名,请他们邮寄一个明信片,明信片的最终目标是朱尔格兰姆指定的一名住在波士顿的人和中西部城市的人。同时朱尔格兰姆要求每一个转寄明信片的人都回发一个明信片给朱尔格兰姆实验的研究者以便跟踪观察。

最终结果表明:大部分明信片在经过六个步骤后都抵达了他所指定的人,也就是这些明信片经过的中间人的数目平均只有6个。因此,可以说在美国人与人之间平均是被6个人分隔,米尔格兰姆的这个实验进一步证实了"六度分隔"现象。

理论的进展

朱尔格兰姆的实验有很多不足之处,如:被检测人数太少且仅限于美国。大约40年后,哥伦比亚大学也开展了"六度分隔"理论的验证工程——"小世界研究计划"。他们通过因特网向全世界发送邮件,目的与朱格尔姆的实验相同,就是测算两个陌生人通过多次连接,才可以相互认识。最终,研究者们得出了与朱格尔姆相同的结论。

实验的第一阶段于2003年完成,结果出人意料。166个不同国家的6万多名志愿者加入了这项研究,他们一共发了24,000次信件,其中有384封成功地抵达指定的接收者。从这些数据来分析,世界任何两个人之间建立一种联系,平均只需要5~7个人,也就是说,他们之间只有5~7度分隔,在同一个国家,甚至更少。

实验仍在继续,研究人员正试图找到这方面问题的答案,如:人们联系的方式究竟有多少种,信息究竟是如何传播的,是因为地理位置接近(邻居关系)建立联系的、还是通过职业关系、家庭关系(亲属)和个人友谊(朋友)建立联系的。第一阶段实验表明,大多数人是通过朋友与其他人建立连接关系的,但实际上,通过职业关系(同事)可能更容易与别人建立连接关系。实验也表明,因特网的发展并没有真正改变人际沟通的联系手段,并没

not brought people closer together. No matter how the messages are sent, postal or via Internet, the links in the chain still average around six.

Anyone can sign up to participate in this ongoing experiment. Visit *www.smallworld.columbia. edu* to log in and take part.

Popular Culture

Although this idea plays an important role in mathematical and statistical network theory, it has also become a popular notion among ordinary individuals. John Guare's 1990 play, *Six Degrees of Separation* and the subsequent film in 1993, has brought this idea to the attention of the public. The play and movie are based on the true story of a man who conned his way into Manhattan high society by claiming to be the son of a famous actor. This same type of plot has also been developed into a television series entitled *Six Degrees* and the six degrees of separation theory is one of the premises of the popular TV series *Lost*.

In addition, the theory was popularized by the game *The Six Degrees of Kevin Bacon*, which connects actors to each other through their appearances in films with Kevin Bacon. One version of the game was invented in 1994 by two students at Albright College in Pennsylvania who used the game to link any actor to Kevin Bacon using no more than six connections. Another version of the game is an example of the blending of sociological research and pop culture; this form of the game was published as a computer game on the University of Virginia's Website in the section on the small world problem. Dubbed by *Time* magazine as the Oracle of Bacon at Virginia, the University of Virginia game used an Internet movie database to display connections between different actors.

Applications of the Theory

Despite the popular games, movie and television shows based on this theory, scientists and researchers are looking for ways to study the small world problem in order to define the social and physical networks in the natural and manmade worlds. Current research is centered on developing network models for various social and educational purposes. Knowing how a social network operates helps scientists determine the spread of infectious diseases, for example.

Others want to explore network theory to increase or improve their networking across the Internet. Engineers and social scientists want to examine the small world networks found in nature to apply their concepts to such networking systems as power grids, sociological clusters and housing and food distribution. And, of course, everyone is interested in enhancing communications.

While tinkering with adding or subtracting elements from networks intrigues scientists and other scholars, there is also work to be done on the problems that can arise from manipulating networks. For example, although adding a few connections to a cellular phone system or the Internet can speed transmission and communication, it can also overload systems, resulting in a breakdown of the network system. These issues have to be addressed when advocates start tinkering with networks.

It is easy to see therefore, that even though the notion first occurred in a short story in the 1920s, there is much work yet to do to discover and understand all of the uses and disadvantages of the small world network theory,much work remains to be done to learn how to use this fact to everyone's advantage.

Resources

John Guare's Six Degrees of Separation: A Study Guide, Gale Group as a PDF in Adobe Reader, 2002. This e–document contains a plot summary; character analysis; author biography; highlights of the play's themes, style and historical context; study questions; and bibliography.

Six Degrees, Vintage, 2004. This book moves beyond the six degrees of separation into the field of network theory.

有使人的关系变得更近。不论通过什么方式发送信件，邮寄还是因特网，信件要到达最终收信人，平均只要经历6个人左右。

对这个实验有意者，请登录www.smallword.columbia.edu.

流行文化

六度分隔理论广泛应用于数学和统计学领域，现在也走进人们日常的文化生活。1993年约翰·贵尔的剧本《六度分隔》描述的是一个真实的故事，主人公声称自己是一位著名演员的儿子，通过欺骗手段进入曼哈顿的上流社会，后来，以这个故事为素材创作了电视剧《六度》，电视剧《失踪》也是依据六度分隔理论而创作的。

六度分隔理论也被应用于网络游戏，《凯文·培根的六度分隔》就是一例，讲述了游戏中的玩家们如何认识凯文·培根。1994年，宾夕法尼亚州的阿尔布莱特学院的两名学生开发出游戏的一个版本，即任何一位演员最多只需要六个人就可与凯文·培根建立联系。另外一版是电脑游戏，作为社会学研究和通俗文化的混和物，出版后挂在"小世界研究计划"的弗吉尼亚大学网站上，后来《时代周刊》杂志进行了报道，弗吉尼亚大学网站上的奥雷克尔数据库是专门的网络电影数据库，讲述的是不同玩家之间建立联系的故事。

理论的应用

六度分隔理论广泛应用于游戏开发与影视创作。现在，很多科学家和研究者们试图寻找研究"小世界现象"的新方法，目的是验证自然界中的物质链及人的社会关系网。出于各种社会目的及教育目的，当前以开发网络模式为研究中心。知道社会关系网是怎样建立的，可以帮助我们理解病毒是怎样传播的。

还有一些人想用"小世界网络理论"来改善网络传输服务。工程师和社会学家们验证"小世界网络理论"并使之应用于网络系统开发，如：电力网、社会生物群、住房、食品流通。如何通过自己的关系纽带互相交织，继而形成一张庞大复杂的人际关系网，这当然是大家关心的。

由于网络操作过程带来的一些问题，一些科学家和学者们也开始关注网络维护这一领域。如：加强移动电话网络的连接或者提高网络传输速度，但这也可能导致网络负载过大，造成网络瘫痪。我们不得不面对这样的问题。

尽管"六度分隔"这一概念最早是在19世纪20年代的一篇短篇故事中出现的，如何探索、理解"小世界网络"理论，如何运用这一理论服务人类，仍有很多工作要做。

相关资源

《约翰·格尔的六度分隔：学习手册》，盖尔集团出版公司，PDF格式，需借助 Adobe Reader 阅读器浏览，2002 年。这是一本电子图书，内容包含剧情介绍、任务分析、作者传记、剧本主题、剧本风格、历史背景、学习思考题及参考书目。

Sports Illustrated Curse

The *Sports Illustrated* Curse, also know as the SI Cover Jinx, has grown out of the perception over the life span of the magazine that misfortunes seem to happen to people soon after they appear on the cover of *Sports Illustrated*.

The *Sports Illustrated* cover jinx began with the very first issue of the magazine. In August of 1954, Atlanta Braves third baseman Eddie Matthews appeared on the first cover of the new *Sports Illustrated*. One week later Matthews suffered an injury to his throwing arm that forced him onto the disabled list for seven games. In retrospect, this was the beginning of the Sports Illustrated cover curse.

History of the Magazine

Sports Illustrated is the largest and most widely read sports magazine in the United States. Launched in August of 1954 by Henry Luce, publisher of the news magazine *Time*.

Two magazines entitled *Sports Illustrated* were started in the 1930s and 1940s, but each failed because there was a general feeling that sports was not important enough to warrant the attention of serious journalists and that the public had little interest in reading about sports. In the early 1950s Henry Luce, however, thought the time was ripe to capitalize on the public interest in spectator sports. After all, post–war times were prosperous so potential readers who had endured the hard times of the Depression and World War II were now economically secure enough to indulge in spectator sports. In addition, the widespread availability of television brought spectator sports to the attention of everyone who owned a TV set.

The immediate success of *Sports Illustrated* proved Henry Luce was right. Nevertheless, it took some time for Sports *Illustrated* to find its niche; the early issues featured stories about upper class activities, such as yachting and polo. Eventually, however, Luce and his advertisers realized that there was a huge lucrative market in average sports fans.

Innovative Publishing

From early in its production, *Sports Illustrated* adopted practices that seemed innovative for a specialty magazine about sports. The editors sought and encouraged good writers and in–depth reporting. There were scouting reports and previews of sports events that preceded and enhanced television coverage of the events. The magazine included features on promising high school players and unknown athletes. Gradually, *Sports Illustrated* became the authoritative voice of the sports world.

Graphically, *Sports Illustrated* was also ahead of its time. The editors used a great many color photos, and when printing technology advanced to allow overnight color printing, the editors were able to include color photos with each story on a weekly basis. *Sports Illustrated* was well known for its color photography.

The Cover Curse Endures

Regular readers probably remember many of the following jinxes, many of them tragic:

·MVP quarterback Kurt Warner was the cover star on the October 9, 2000, issue. The next weekend he broke a finger and missed five games.

40

《体育画报》不吉利

《体育画报》不吉利(也称《体育画报》封面不吉利),谁上画报封面谁倒霉,这一厄运从创刊开始。

《体育画报》1954年8月推出第1期,选择了亚特兰大沃基士队著名棒球选手马休斯作为封面人物。一周后,马休斯在比赛中手臂骨折,被迫错过了7场比赛。这似乎预示着《体育画报》的封面将成为无数后来者的"百慕大"(不吉利)。

画报的历史

亨利·卢斯,《时代周刊》杂志的发行商,于1954年8月创办的《体育画报》,是美国发行量最大的,最具影响力的体育专业杂志,在全球拥有广泛的读者。

二十世纪三四十年代,曾出现两本体育杂志,都冠名为《体育画报》。但当时很多运动项目没有普及,很少有人去阅读体育杂志,《体育画报》也很难吸引到撰稿人,因此,这两本杂志很快就夭折了。五十年代,美国经济繁荣,很多人开始喜爱体育运动,亨利·卢斯认为重新创办《体育画报》杂志时机成熟。毕竟,很多人在经历了二战及经济大萧条后,现在生活水平大大提高,完全有能力担负得起体育运动的支出费用。另外,随着电视的普及,有更多的人关心体育运动。

《体育画报》推出后,立即风靡全国。早期的《体育画报》主要报道的是上流社会那些人喜爱的一些体育项目,如帆船和马球。后来,《体育画报》也提供有关大众体育项目的报道,卢斯及他的广告商们意识到这一领域也有巨大的潜在市场。

画报改版

《体育画报》从创刊之日就试图改版成为专业体育杂志。杂志编辑鼓励优秀作家撰稿。画报主要有追踪报道栏目、今日观察栏目、热点聚焦栏目以及新面孔栏目(主要是报道一些有前途的中学运动员及普通的运动员)。因此,《体育画报》逐渐成为体育界的权威代言人。

《体育画报》杂志大量采用精美的彩色图片。随着彩色印刷技术的出现,《体育画报》杂志每期的每个故事都附有彩色照片。《体育画报》也因这些精美图片而风靡全球。

不吉利封面

普通读者也许还会记得以下的一些倒霉事件:

· 2000年10月9日,身价最高的球员圣路易斯公羊队四分卫库尔特·华纳的照片被登在了《体育画报》的封面,但一周后,他就在比赛中手指骨折,被迫错过了5场比赛。

· Michael Jordan's celebrated return to the NBA merited his photo on the January 15, 2002, cover. Up to that time, Jordan had appeared on 42 covers without any repercussions. His 43rd appearance, however, was followed by his wife filing for divorce the very next day.

· On October 13, 2003, there was a double curse: One of the regional covers of the baseball playoffs portrayed Kerry Wood of the Chicago Cubs, the other regional cover featured a photo of Pedro Martinez of the Boston Red Sox. As many expected, both teams lost in their League Championship Series.

· The jinx did not figure in on the issue of January 14, 2002, although everyone though it could become a problem because the featured sports figure would be posing with a black cat. MVP Kurt Warner of the St. Louis Rams declined to appear on this cover, he had not forgotten his first cover shot after which he sat out five games with a broken finger. Thus only a black cat appeared on the cover under the headline.

Speculating about the Cause of the Jinx

The magazine staff has investigated more than 2,000 covers of which they found more than 900 so–called jinxes. This has translated into a decline in performance or a misfortune following a cover appearance approximately 37 percent of the time. The investigators were able to further refine the type of sport likely to be jinxed; golfers were cursed almost 70 percent of the time and tennis players 50 percent of the time; boxers, however, were affected only around 16 percent of the time.

So far, there are only three answers that people have been willing to consider:

1. The jinx is a self–fulfilling prophecy. Because of the legend, those who appear on the cover are under extreme pressure to live up to their reputation or to exceed their previous records. The pressure leads to poor performance or injury.

2. The jinx is subject to statistics. To be on the cover an individual or a team would have to excel and perform above average. Mathematically, these individuals would then have to move backward toward the average, and the curse simply occurs during this statistical regression to the mean.

3. The jinx is a hoax, perpetrated to sell more magazines. How else to explain the majority of covers with photos of people or teams who went on to perform well or exceed previous records.

While no one can identify the cause of the curse of the Sports Illustrated cover, it is safe to say that the legend adds interest to each week's issue. One of the biggest problems athletes, teams and owners face is whether or not to enjoy the prestige of being on the cover of Sports Illustrated or to decline the honor for fear of an unfortunate aftermath.

Resources

Sports Illustrated 50 Years: The Anniversary Book, Sports Illustrated, 2004. This book, divided into six parts, highlights the best of the magazine from its first 50 years.

Sports Illustrated for Kids: The Amazing World of Sports, Sports Illustrated, 2006. This book, aimed at children aged 9 through 12, is filled with amazing sports photos by renowned photographers. Each photo has a detailed caption, a fun fact and a sports trivia question.

· 著名篮球运动员迈克尔·乔丹已上了42次封面,在返回NBA后,于2002年1月15日再次成为《体育画报》的封面人物。可是,第二周,他就与妻子离婚了。

· 芝加哥俱乐部的棒球明星伍德2003年10月13日成为《体育画报》棒球专版的封面人物,而波士顿红袜队的马丁尼兹的照片也同样出现在专版封面上,像人们预料的那样,在当年的决赛中,这两个队都以失败而告终。

· 2002年1月14日出版的《体育画报》的封面上,破天荒地以一只猫作为封面人物。当时,圣路易斯公羊队四分卫库尔特·华纳拒绝再次成为封面人物,他不会忘记上次成为封面人物后发生的事情。这次只有一只猫作为"封面人物"。

不吉利的原因

《体育画报》的资深工作人员曾对以往2000多位封面人物的命运做了详尽细致的资料搜集和分类。统计数字表明,在2000多位封面人物中,很快出现状态下滑和遭遇不幸的为900人,约占封面总人数的37%。研究者按照运动类型分类,高尔夫球员遭遇不幸的差不多占70%,排球运动员差不多占50%,而拳击运动员大约只有16%。

目前,仅有三种解释值得参考:

1. 骗局:预言会实现。因为一直有这样的说法:谁上画报封面谁倒霉,所以运动员一旦上了画报封面,便产生巨大的心理压力。他们想获得成功,超越他们以前的体育成绩,这种压力便会导致状态下滑或者身体受伤。

2. 骗局:容易受统计数字的影响。运动员或者运动队一旦成为封面人物,人们便认为他们很优秀。如果运动员状态不好,体育成绩下降,从数字角度看,数字也就下降,这时不幸即被认为出现。

3. 骗局:促销杂志的骗局。如果说谁上了封面,谁就倒霉?那么又怎样去解释那些成为杂志封面人物的运动员,他们的体育成绩超越了先前的记录这种情况呢?

没有人知道所谓不吉利现象的真正原因,但可以肯定地说,《体育画报》封面不吉利的说法确实使画报更有趣味性。而运动员及运动队所面临的最大问题是:你是把成为该杂志封面人物视作无上光荣的事情,还是恐惧"谁上封面谁倒霉"而拒绝成为封面人物。

相关资源

《体育画报五十年:50周年图书》,体育画报,2004年。本书共分6个专栏剪辑。

《儿童运动画刊:不可思议的运动世界》,体育画报,2006年。本书适合9~12岁的读者群,书内有很多著名摄影师拍摄的运动照片,每张都有标题、详细的文字说明及运动方面应注意的小问题。

Forty-one

Stonehenge

Stonehenge is an ancient monument of huge stones set in circles on the Salisbury Plain in Wiltshire in southwestern England. While its purpose or use is one of the biggest mysteries of the monument, scholars believe that ancient tribes built Stonehenge and used it at various times as a gathering place, a religious center or a cremation cemetery.

Stonehenge belongs to a classification of monuments known as henges. A henge, derived from a word in Old English, is a circular earthwork composed of a ditch and a bank with a level plain or plateau in the center. The soil dug out of the ditch is used to construct the bank. Technically, a henge does not have to enclose a stone circle, but many, including Stonehenge, do.

Who Built Stonehenge?

Despite the mystery surrounding much of Stonehenge, scholars are fairly certain they know who built it. Most agree that a different tribe built each stage. The first stage was built by a Neolithic tribe called the Windmill Hill people. Windmill Hill is an earthwork near Stonehenge. The tribe was an early agricultural community who revered circles and symmetry. They buried their dead in communal tombs encased in stone and often connected to a hill–top mound.

The second group arrived on the Salisbury Plain from Europe around 2000 B.C.. Because they buried beakers or pottery cups with their dead, archeologists call them the Beaker People. They did not use mass graves but instead buried their dead in individual graves with beakers and weapons. The Beaker People had an organized social system based on communal living with a chief or tribal leader. Scholars believe that they also worshipped the sun and developed religious rituals based on the winter and summer solstices. This period may be the origin of the astronomical alignment of the Stonehenge stones.

The third group who worked at the Stonehenge site is called the Wessex People, who enter the picture around 1500 B.C. during the Bronze Age. This was an advanced, intelligent tribe who developed and controlled trade routes. Their highly organized culture was reflected in the precision of their calculations at the building site.

Recent Excavation

In late 2006 archeologists studying the monument excavated a small village located at Durrington Walls about two miles from Stonehenge. The archeologists have uncovered eight houses and a wooden replica of Stonehenge. It is interesting that the wooden replica is oriented to face the midwinter sunrise and midsummer sunset while Stonehenge is oriented to face the midsummer sunrise and midwinter sunset.

Using carbon dating techniques, the scientists pinpoint the origin of the village to around 2600 B.C., during the first stage of Stonehenge. Artifacts at the site, which may contain at least 25 houses, indicate that the village was residential and was connected to the Avon River and to Stonehenge by paths called avenues, thus indicating a pattern of movement between the two sites.

How Was Stonehenge Used?

The purpose of Stonehenge is probably its most mysterious question. Since its origin is so ancient, there are no written records about its use, but researchers have speculated for centuries

巨 石 阵

巨石阵位于英格兰西南部威尔特郡索尔伯兹里平原,是古代著名的环状巨石遗址。学者们至今仍不能断定当初建造此"巨石阵"的真正目的,而只是推测这是早期的部落集会或举行宗教仪式的地点,或用做墓地。

巨石阵又称Henges,是著名的古遗址。Henges在古英语中是"圆形石结构"之意,其外围是环形土沟,内侧是圆形坑。从技术上看,当时人们不可能将这些巨石围城石圈。

谁建造了巨石阵

尽管巨石阵至今是一个特大的谜题,大部分学者认为巨石阵的建筑期经历了三个阶段。第一阶段是由新石器时代的Windmill Hill人建造的。Windmill Hill人当时生活在巨石阵附近的村落,他们精通数字,他们在山上建墓地(墓的四周用石块砌成)。

公元前2000年左右来自索尔伯兹里平原的Beaker人是巨石阵第二阶段的建筑者。因为他们喜欢将酒杯和陶瓷用作陪葬品, 因此, 考古学家称他们为Beaker人 (酒杯之意)。Beaker人喜欢群居生活,他们也是太阳的崇拜者,而巨石阵具有天文观象的功用(不同石块的位置与夏至或冬至时候的太阳的位置相吻合)可能就源于此阶段。

大约公元前1500年(青铜器时代),Wesses人是巨石阵第三个阶段的建筑者。当时的Wesses人很聪明,他们掌握了精密的计算方法。

最近发现

2006年, 考古学家在离巨石阵两英里外的著名的杜灵顿垣墙附近发现了一个村落,有八座房子和一块木桩。有趣的是,这块木桩,他的主轴线指向冬至太阳升起和夏至日落的方向,而巨石阵恰好与它相反。

使用碳测年法,科学家推测这小村落建于公元前2600年左右(巨石阵建造的第一阶段)。从现场发现的遗物来推测,这个村落当时至少有25户人居住,还有一条叫做"林荫道"的小路,这条路直接通往埃文河和巨石阵。

巨石阵的用途

几个世纪以来,没有人真正知道这巨石阵的用途,因此才有许多关于巨石阵的猜测。很多人认为是德鲁伊人建造了巨石阵,是用作祭祀的场所。然而,碳测年法表明巨石阵在

about its purpose.At one point, many believed that it was a religious monument built by the Druids for holy ceremonies and sacrifices. However, carbon dating has proved that Stonehenge existed almost 2,000 years before the Druids appeared. Other researchers decided that it may have been a cemetery for influential and wealthy people, but that was hard to prove from studying the cremated remains found in some of the mounds.

The most prevalent theory is that Stonehenge was built as a physical calendar to mark astronomical and seasonal events, such as the solstices, lunar and solar eclipses and the equinox. Since many early religions were tied to astronomical phenomena, Stonehenge was probably used as a religious monument at various times in its history.

Myths and Legends Surrounding Stonehenge

There are several myths that persist about Stonehenge. One concerns the Heel Stone, a large stone that has stood at the northeast entrance to Stonehenge from its earliest stage. A 17th century legend claims that the Devil built Stonehenge, having stolen the stones from a woman in Ireland. After the Devil magically transported the stones to the Salisbury Plain, he bragged that no one would ever discover how the stones were carried to the Plain. A friar challenged the Devil who retaliated by throwing one of the stones at him, striking him on the heel. The stone became known as the Friar's Heel or the Heel Stone.

Another myth states that Merlin of King Arthur legend built Stonehenge at the command of King Ambrosias Aurelianus to commemorate the nobles who died battling the Saxons and were buried on Salisbury Plain. Merlin advised the king to move Stonehenge from its home in Ireland to Salisbury, so the king sent Merlin, Uther Pendragon (King Arthur's father) and a squadron of knights to Ireland to retrieve the monument. When the knights were unable to move the heavy stones, Merlin magically transported them to England.

Modern Stonehenge

Over the centuries inhabitants of the area broke off and removed or carried away the stones from the monument to build homes, bridges and roads. Only about half of the original stones are intact today, but there are ongoing attempts to preserve Stonehenge as a national monument. In 1922 the British government took over the preservation and restoration of Stonehenge and has replaced some of the scattered stones.

Today Stonehenge is a major tourist attraction, averaging more than one million visitors each year. The sheer numbers of visitors can cause deterioration of the site and damage to the stones. So visitors are now prohibited from walking within the circle of stones and are directed to a pathway near the stones.In addition to the average tourist, the monument has become a pilgrimage destination for neo-Druids and pagans, they performed rituals at the site.

Resources

Brief History of Stonehenge: One of the Most Famous Monuments in Britain, Carroll & Graf, 2007. This book highlights the history of Stonehenge and includes chapters on the beginnings of Stonehenge, Bluestones, the Great Circle and the Altar Stone. There are also appendices of ancient words and carved motifs in Britain and Ireland. The book includes a bibliography and index.

Stonehenge: A History in Photographs, English Heritage, 2004. This book traces the history of the photography about Stonehenge from the earliest known photo in 1853 to modern thermal imaging shots. What is revealed in the photographs also portrays the cultural history of Britain from 19th century picnickers to RAF bomber planes parked behind the monument in World War I .

德鲁伊人出现前就已存在2000多年了。还有些研究者认为巨石阵是富人用来作墓地的,但是从古墓出土物的检测来看,这种说法证据不充分。

最普通的说法是,巨石阵可能是远古人类为观测天文现象和季节变化而建造的,如:冬至、夏至、日食、月食、秋分及春分。早期的宗教也与这些天文现象有关,巨石阵也可能是部落举行一些仪式的地点。

有关巨石阵的传说

有很多关于巨石阵的传说,"黑尔"石柱就是一个例子。"黑尔"石柱是早期巨石阵里的一个巨大的石柱,位于巨石阵的东北面。传说,17世纪,"恶魔"从爱尔兰的一位女士那里偷来了许多石头,然后运到索尔伯兹里平原,在那里他建造了巨石阵,他夸口说没有人知道这些石头是怎样运到索尔伯兹里平原的。后来,一位修道士出于报复,搬起一块石头砸向"恶魔",恰好砸在脚后跟,"黑尔(Heel,脚后跟的意思)石柱"因此得名,也称修道士石柱。

另一个说法是,梅林建造了巨石阵。梅林曾建议国王安伯罗瓦士将他的家乡爱尔兰的巨石搬运到索尔伯兹里平原,然后国王就派遣梅林·潘德瑞根(梅林的父亲)和一些骑士到爱尔兰去搬运那些巨石。骑士们都搬不动那些巨石,而梅林却神奇地将这些巨石运到了英格兰的索尔伯兹里平原,在那里建造了巨石阵,目的是纪念在撒克逊战场上牺牲的埋在索尔伯兹里平原的将士们。

现代巨石阵

几个世纪以来,有些石块已经被搬走去建造房子、架桥和修路了。目前,只有一半左右的石块还在原地。1922年英国政府接管巨石阵,并对其进行修复,准备将其列为国家历史文物。

今天,巨石阵已经成为英国主要的旅游景点,每年都有从世界各地100多万人前来参观,石块也遭到一定程度的破坏,因此,现在已经在石块周围修建了道路,禁止游客们踩踏石块。除了普通的游客们来这里,巨石阵也成为新德鲁伊教和其他宗教教徒的朝圣之地,他们来这里举行宗教仪式。

相关资源

《巨石阵的历史:英国最著名的遗址之一》,卡诺尔·格拉夫,2007年。本书重点讲述了巨石阵、青石、石圈及圣石的历史。本书附有英国及爱尔兰的雕刻画图片,一份词汇录、参考书目和索引。

《巨石阵:图片史》,英国遗产,2004年。本书描述了有关巨石阵图片的历史,涵盖了从1853年最早拍摄的照片到现代利用热成像原理拍摄的照片。这些照片本身就是一部19世纪至一战期间的英国的文化史。

Forty-two

Curse of United States Presidents Elected in Years Divided by 20

There is a widespread legend that every U.S. president elected in a year divisible by 20 has died while in office or within the first year of his being elected to a 2nd term. In addition, each of these ill-fated presidents was involved in an unfortunate war culminating in a very narrow victory.

Origin

It all began with Tecumseh's curse. Tecumseh, a Shawnee Indian chief, had been involved since his youth in the various battles and wars among the Native American tribes, the French, the British and the American forces in the Northwest Territory in the late 18th and early 19th centuries. The Northwest Territory was made up of what is now Indiana, Ohio and part of Michigan. As the Native Americans fought to save their land from the newcomers, they often encountered a U.S. army officer, William Henry Harrison.

At one battle in Greenville, Ohio, in 1795 Tecumseh refused to sign the Treaty of Greenville and began to build a Native American resistance unit. To accomplish this goal Tecumseh and his brother established their own settlement at Prophetstown in 1808 along the Wabash River in Indiana near present-day Lafayette. Prophetstown became a military training camp for Shawnee warriors.

Later in 1811 while Tecumseh was away recruiting new warriors for his resistance forces, General William Henry Harrison marched on Prophetstown, hoping to destroy it. Tecumseh's brother ignored Tecumseh's admonition to avoid fighting the U.S. Army and attacked Harrison's forces. Harrison soundly defeated the Indians and burned Prophetstown, thus ending Tecumseh's hope of a united Indian nation. This battle, taking place at Tippecanoe near Prophetstown, eventually became the slogan—Tippecanoe and Tyler, too—for William Henry Harrison's presidential campaign in 1840. (John Tyler was the vice presidential candidate running with Harrison.)

But it also marked the beginning of the end of the Native American resistance movement. Tecumseh eventually joined the British forces and was killed in one of the last battles of the War of 1812. Before his death, however, he supposedly cursed the American presidential office, prophesizing that every 20 years the president would die and that the nation would be wracked by divisiveness and war during that president's term.

Has Tecumseh's Curse Come True?

The prophesy or curse has, indeed, affected every American president elected in the so-called zero years, starting in 1840 when Tecumseh's nemesis William Henry Harrison was elected to the presidency. Harrison died of pneumonia shortly after his inauguration and every 20 years thereafter the American president has either died while in office or within the first year of his second term. Each of these 20-year presidents has also dealt with war or some sort of political turmoil. Look at the following historical facts:

· In 1860 Abraham Lincoln was elected to the presidency. During his term the country divided and erupted into civil war. Forty-two days after his inauguration for his second term, Lincoln was assassinated on April 15, 1865.

特科抹的
诅咒

传说美国所有在能被20整除的年份当选的总统都会在在任期间或第二任期的第一年内死掉。另外,这些总统在位时候,都会卷入到战争且都没有取得决定性胜利。

起源
所有这些是源于特科抹咒语。年轻的特科抹,肖尼印第安人的首领,驰骋疆场多年。18世纪末19世纪初期,在美国西北部一带(今天的印第安纳州,俄亥俄州及部分密歇根州)他经常与印第安人、法国人、英国人及美国人交战。特科抹为了从占领者手里收复失地,他经常在战场上遇见一位美国军官,威廉·亨利·哈瑞森。

1795年,特科抹拒绝签署《格林维条约》,并组建印第安反抗联盟。为了实现这个目标,1808年特科抹和他的兄弟在印第安附近的瓦伯许河畔的Prophetstown(今天的老佛爷)建立了印第安人居住地。Prophetstown成为萧尼战士的军事训练营。

1811年,当哈瑞森行军到Prophetstown时,特科抹正在招募一批新兵,知道这些情况后,哈瑞森决定消灭这支军队。特科抹的兄弟没有听从特科抹的忠告,直接与哈瑞森的部队交战。最后,哈瑞森在Prophetstown附近的Tippecanoes大挫特科抹的部队,并焚烧了Prophetstown。这也让特科抹的印第安民族统一梦想破灭。后来,"Tippecanoes and Tyler, too"成为1840年哈瑞森竞选总统的口号。(John Tyler是其竞选伙伴,副总统。)

但是,这标志着印第安抵抗运动的结束。后来特科抹加入了英国部队,在1812年战争的一场战争中战死沙场。他在临死前许下了一个咒语:美国每隔20年总统都会在任期内死掉,国家在这些总统任期内会发生分裂和战争。

特科抹诅咒实现了吗
从那时起,每到结尾数字是0的年份当选的总统都印证了特科抹诅咒。哈瑞森首当其冲,1840年他当选总统,上任后一个月死于肺炎。此后每隔20年,美国总统要不是死在任上,要不就是在第二任期的第一年里。而且这些总统也要面对战争或政治动乱。请看看以下历史事实:

· 1860年当选为美国总统的林肯,面临国家分裂,爆发美国内战,在第二任期刚42天,即1865年4月15日遭到暗杀。

·In 1880 James A. Garfield was elected and took office on March 4, 1881. On September 19, 1881, Garfield was shot and died from his wounds. Although the nation was not at war with any other countries, there was internal turmoil between the United States government and the Indian Nations. The Battle of Little Bighorn had taken place only 4 years earlier in 1876, and although the Indians achieved a decisive victory over the American Army, retaliation against the Indians was swift and complete.

·In 1900 William McKinley began his second term, 2 years after the end of the Spanish–American War, which had begun during his first term. McKinley was shot on September 6, 1901 and died on September 14.

·In 1920 Warren G. Harding was elected president only 2 years after the end of World War I. His presidential campaign was marked by controversy and infighting over the issue of the United States' joining the League of Nations. Three years into his term, Harding died of a heart attack on August 2, 1923.

·In 1940 Franklin Delano Roosevelt broke with tradition and ran for a third term. During this term the United States entered World War II on December 7, 1941. In 1944 Roosevelt again defied his advisors and tradition and ran for a fourth term. He died suddenly after a cerebral hemorrhage on April 12, 1945, during the 2nd year of his fourth term.

·In 1960 John F. Kennedy was elected president with a narrow margin. His term was marked by political upheaval as he dealt with the Cuban missile crisis and the burgeoning conflict in Vietnam. On November 22, 1963, Kennedy was assassinated on a visit to Dallas, Texas.

·In 1980 Ronald Reagan was elected during a period when the United States was again divided after the Vietnam War. In addition, the Iran hostage crisis created a problem for Reagan's predecessor, Jimmy Carter, but helped Reagan win the election. On March 30, 1981, Reagan was the victim of an assassination attempt, but he survived the shooting. Many observers think that Ronald Reagan may have broken Tecumseh's curse because he did not die in office.

·In 2000 George W. Bush was elected president and has survived into his second term. On September 11, 2001, simultaneous terrorist attacks on the World Trade Buildings in New York City and the Pentagon in Washington D.C. launched the Bush administration'War on Terror. The attack in Washington D.C. was supposed to have also targeted the White House and the president, who was originally scheduled to be home on that day. Instead, Bush was in Florida on the morning of September 11. On October 7, 2001, as a response to the events on September 11 in New York and Washington, the United States attacked Afghanistan in an attempt to quell the terrorists, capture their leaders and eliminate their support. On March 20, 2003, the United States invaded Iraq, again to conduct the ongoing War on Terror.

It remains to be seen whether or not Tecumseh's curse has been broken after 160 years. Although neither Ronald Reagan nor George W. Bush died in office, both of their administrations were marked by political turmoil, upheaval and foreign policy problems. We now have to wait until 2020 to see if the legend continues.

Resources

Presidential Fact Book, Random House, 1998. This book contains details and facts about every U.S. president from George Washington to Bill Clinton. The book is divided into two parts: The first part contains individual profiles of each president with information on birth, family, education and details about each one's personal and political life. The second part provides information by subject or topic to enable the reader to compare presidents according to their original occupations, religion, education and other information.

· 1880年共和党人加菲尔德当选总统,1881年3月4日宣布就职,1881年9月19日被枪击并因伤而死。仅管国家没有与任何其他国家发生战争,但是在国内美国政府与印第安民族之间却有骚乱发生。而在4年之前的1876年,爆发了小大角羊战争,虽然印第安人取得决定性胜利,大挫美国军队,但对印第安人的报复却迅速而全面的发动。

· 1900年,美西战争结束2周年,麦坎尼连任总统,当年9月6日遭刺杀,于9月14日死在任上。

· 1920年,第一次世界大战刚结束2年,哈丁当选总统。他在任期间,国内爆发了美国加入国际联盟的争斗。他任期的第三年,1923年8月2日死于心脏病。

· 1940年,罗斯福第三次当选为总统,1941年12月7日,美国卷入第二次世界大战,1944年罗斯福再次连任,在他第四任期的第二年,1945年4月12日,罗斯福突然死于脑溢血。

· 1960年,肯尼迪当选总统,他在任期间,爆发了古巴导弹危机,和越南发生冲突,1963年11月22日遇刺身亡。

· 1980年,由于伊朗人质危机事件,使里根在竞选中挫败卡特获得成功,成为美国第40位总统。随后,爆发了越南战争,美国再次面临分裂。1981年3月30日遇刺,身负重伤大难不死,是唯一逃过咒语的总统。

2000年,小布什当选总统,并于2004年连任。2001年9月11日,恐怖分子袭击了纽约的世界贸易大厦和华盛顿的五角大楼,他因此发动了一连串的反恐战争。恐怖分子袭击华盛顿,其实目标是布什总统,而那天早上,他恰好在佛罗里达州。2001年10月7日,他发动了以铲除恐怖势力为目的的阿富汗战争,推倒了塔里班政权及其支持者,接着他在2003年3月20日,发动了伊拉克战争。

尽管里根和小布什总统都遇险,但幸免于死。然而,他们在任职期间都爆发了政治动乱和外交危机。特科抹诅咒是否还存在,需等到2020年,看这种传奇是否还会延续。

相关资源
《总统概况》,兰登书屋,1998年。本书记录了从乔治·华盛顿到比尔·克林顿时期,美国历史上每一位总统的详细资料。本书分为两部分,前半部分关于每位总统的生平介绍,包括出生、家庭、教育以及他们的总统生涯和政治生活,后半部分提供了一些主题及话题,以便读者根据每位总统的职业、宗教、教育及其他信息对其比较和分析。

Forty-three

Vampires

The term vampire most commonly conjures up a vision of a dead person rising from the grave at night to seek out living victims while they sleep. According to most legends, every vampire was once a living human being who, after being bitten by a vampire, died and then rose from the grave as a vampire.

Technically, vampires are the living remains of deceased persons who have reinvigorated themselves by consuming blood. For this reason, vampires are often called the undead. They can, however, move undetected among the living because they themselves appear normal and healthy. In fact, they may even appear to be attractive and desirable, seducing their victims before sucking their blood. They also do not cast a reflection and they possess superhuman strength.

The legend of the vampire has become a symbol of the human desire to defeat death and achieve immortality. Vampires are usually considered to be immortal since they rejuvenate themselves with fresh blood each night. However, they do have some vulnerabilities. Vampires can be destroyed by fire, direct sunlight, beheading or a stake through the heart. They can also be warded off by a crucifix, holy water or garlic.

Vampires In Ancient Cultures

Four thousand years ago the ancient Babylonians and Assyrians of Mesopotamia feared a vicious demon goddess named Lamastu who was believed to steal or kill babies. These ancient peoples attributed what is now called sudden infant death syndrome to this goddess. In fact, ancient peoples often used vampires, along with other monster figures, to explain away the unknown or negative events.

Lamastu seemed to evolve into Lilith, a child-killer in ancient Jewish folklore. She, too, was described as a demon that killed unborn babies and young infants. Lilith was also often portrayed as a seductress, seducing men at night.

Bloodsuckers In Real Life

Vampirism exists in the animal world in the form of the vampire bat. Actually, vampire bats do not kill their prey but do feed on their blood. In reality, vampire bats are rather tame animals that pose no threat to human beings.

In certain parts of Central and South America there are stories about chupacabras, literally translated as the goat sucker (see Chapter 5). These are vampire-like creatures that suck animal blood for sustenance.

The ancient Greeks had their own demons, one of which was named Lamia who had the head and torso of a woman and the lower body of a snake. As a lover of the god Zeus, Lamia incurred the wrath of Hera, Zeus' wife, who compelled Lamia to eat her own children. When she realized what she had done, Lamia became a monster, sucking the blood of young children because she was jealous of their mothers.

Similar figures appear in Asian mythology, including Indian demons that preyed on children and Chinese undead, corpses who arose from their graves and attacked the living at night.

In addition, throughout history many cultures have engaged in the practice of drinking blood to overcome death and to satisfy their deities. For example, some Native Americans, including the Aztecs, ate the hearts and drank the blood of captives in order to please their gods and gain

吸血鬼

所谓吸血鬼,可以理解成夜间从坟墓出来的死尸,在成为吸血鬼之前,他们都是人。只要被吸血鬼吸食了鲜血后,被吸食人就会变成吸血鬼。

吸血鬼,在英文中Vampire意思是僵尸,靠吸食人的血液为生。吸血鬼是被遗弃的世界里出来的恶灵所附的身体,他们的力量远大于常人,而且拥有常人无法获得的异常能力。他们有思想,四处走动,往往能诱惑别人并在不知不觉中夺取他的生命。

吸血鬼传说已成为人类渴望战胜死亡、获得永生的象征。传说,吸血鬼每天晚上吸取人的新鲜血液,他们会变得年轻美丽。很多资料认为吸血鬼害怕的东西很多,比如:怕火,怕阳光,怕圣水,怕大蒜和十字架。

古代吸血鬼

4000年前,古巴比伦人,美索不达米亚的亚述人害怕一个叫拉玛什的邪灵。传说拉玛什会偷走或杀死婴儿,因此,古人将小孩突然死亡这样的情况归咎于这个邪灵。古人对一些无法作出解释的自然现象也归咎于吸血鬼或其他怪物。

在古犹太民间故事里,魔鬼莉莉斯相当于拉玛什,是专门捕杀还未出生的孩子或婴儿的恶魔,拉玛什也被认为是勾引男人的女妖。

古希腊神话中的幽灵拉弥阿,长有女人的头和躯干,下半身像蛇(称有翼半蛇人),是宙斯的情人。宙斯的妻子赫拉嫉恨拉弥阿,逼迫她吃自己的孩子。拉弥阿知道这些后就变成了专门吸食小孩血液的怪物。

在亚洲也有类似的神话,如:印度的恶魔专门吸食小孩的血液;在中国,传说鬼魂经常从坟墓里出来袭击人。

在很多文化中,都有吸血能够延长寿命、长生不老的说法。如印第安人,包括阿兹特克人,他们吃人的心脏和吸食被停者的血液,目的是取悦神灵,获得长生不老。基督教的

immortality. Even the Christian communion practice of transubstantiation of wine into the blood of Christ may have had its origin in ancient blooding and drinking religious ceremonies.

The Vampires of Eastern Europe

The vampires of Transylvania (now Romania), Moldavia and Wallachia were called strigoi from an ancient Greek word that meant demon or witch. Later the word vampire evolved from the Russian word upir. In many cases vampires were believed to be the undead of those committing suicide, criminals or victims of violent death. The presence of vampires was supposedly signaled by objects flying around a house, sudden unexplained deaths, holes in the earth near a grave or a person refusing to eat garlic.

Modern Vampires

By the 17th and 18th centuries, the mythology of eastern European vampires had spread to Western Europe. Bram Stoker, an Irish novelist, latched onto the vampire phenomena spreading through Europe and developed a character named Count Dracula. Researching vampirism, Stoker set his novel in Transylvania and based his character on Eastern European folk tales.

Stoker's character, both in name and reputation, grew out of his research about a real person, Prince Vladislav Basarab who ruled Wallachia in the 1400s. His father was called Vlad Dracul, meaning Vlad the Devil and the young prince was often referred to as Vlad Dracula. Vlad the son had a reputation for being cruel and inhumane and he was often named Vlad the Impaler because of his habit of impaling his enemies on long wooden stakes.

Stoker's character captured the imagination of 19th century Europe and became the prototype vampire of today. In 1927 the play *Dracula* and later the film adaptation, starring Bela Lugosi, portrayed the count as a sophisticated gentleman living a life of luxury. While this characterization did not match the original ugly man described by Stoker, it did become a popular representation of the modern vampire in numerous stories, films and television programs.

Many of the vampire legends that are popular today have come to public attention through books, stories, dramas, films and television. Starting in 1966 and running into 1971, *Dark Shadows*, the first daytime drama featuring a vampire named Barnabas Collins (Jonathan Frid) brought the world of the supernatural into homes throughout the United States. Although this show also featured a beautiful witch named Angelique and a handsome werewolf named Quentin Collins among other creatures and ghosts, it was the character Barnabas Collins that appeared in more episodes than any other character—594 out of 1225 episodes. During his appearances, Jonathan Frid played the role of an intelligent, mysterious (possibly appearing so due to a form of stage fright) vampire with a sympathetic side towards others. This series presented a vampire that could be seen as having a humanlike character. Devotees to this show included Johnny Depp and Madonna.

Once presented and accepted in mainstream television, numerous other series featuring vampires started to appear, such as *Forever Knight*, *Buffy the Vampire Slayer* (a spinoff of the movie), *Angel, Blade (another movie spinoff)* and *Moonlight*. Each one of these modern vampires appear as everyday working people—except for Buffy, who was a high school cheerleader that hunted and killed vampires—holding jobs as police detectives or private investigators. Over time, each of these vampires have evolved to enter and interact with the general population. *In Forever Knight*, the lead character, Detective Nick Knight worked the night shift and satisfied his thirst for blood by drinking red wine. In *Angel*, a spin off of *Buffy the Vampire Slayer*, the lead vampire is a private detective named Angel and is described as a vampire cursed with a soul.

Hollywood was not far behind in the modernization of vampires. One of the most popular

圣餐也是源于此(圣餐葡萄酒和面包变成的血,喝了耶稣的血可以长生不老)。

现实生活中的吸血鬼

在动物界,也有吸血鬼——吸血蝙蝠。吸血蝙蝠只是吸食俘虏者的血,不会夺取他们的生命。实际上吸血蝙蝠是很温驯的动物,不会威胁人类。

在美洲东南部地区,也有很多关于吸血山羊的故事。这些动物很像吸血鬼,以吸食动物的血液为生。

东欧神话——吸血鬼

川索凡尼亚(今罗马尼亚)、摩尔达维亚及瓦拉其亚这一带的吸血鬼称作斯泰格。斯泰格源于希腊语,有"恶魔,女巫"之意。而"吸血鬼"一词源于俄语词汇"Upir",凡是自杀、犯罪、不寻常死亡的人都会成为吸血鬼。吸血鬼出来活动前,也有一定的征兆,如不明物体在房子周围飞过、不寻常的死亡、墓地附近突然发现一个小洞以及有人拒绝吃大蒜。

现代吸血鬼

在17~18世纪期间,东欧的很多吸血鬼故事流传到西欧。当时的爱尔兰小说家史托克以东欧民间故事为基础,以川索凡尼亚这一带的环境作为小说的背景,创作了小说《德古拉》中的主人公"德古拉"的形象。

史托克在小说《德古拉》书中的主人公"德古拉",在历史上是真有其人。他的全名弗拉德·则别斯·塔古拉,是15世纪瓦拉其亚公国的公爵。他的父亲弗拉德·塔古拉极其凶残,喜欢将他的敌人钉死在木桩上,也被人称作弗拉德暴君,因此,弗拉德有"恶魔"之意。

史托克小说中的主人公"德古拉"是以19世纪欧洲大量有关吸血鬼故事而塑造的,也是现在我们常见的吸血鬼形象。1927年,剧本《德古拉》问世,随后被拍摄成电影,由贝拉·卢·戈西主演。影片中的"德古拉"是一位诡辩的绅士,过着豪华奢侈的生活,这与史托克小说中丑陋的、残暴的吸血鬼形象不一样。但现代很多故事及影视节目中描述的吸血鬼形象就是这样。

现在关于吸血鬼的故事的书、剧本和影视节目有很多。在1966~1971年期间的就有:《黑影》,第一部戏剧,主人公巴那巴斯·柯林斯(由乔纳森·弗瑞德主演)。讲述一个具有超自然神力的吸血鬼巴那巴斯·柯林斯的故事。尽管剧本还刻画了两个幽灵人物:年轻貌美的女巫——Angelique和英俊潇洒的狼人——昆廷·柯林斯,但主人公巴那巴斯·柯林斯出现的频率很多,在1225幕中高达594幕。乔纳森·弗瑞德饰演一位聪明、神秘的且富有同情心的吸血鬼形象,把吸血鬼的感情完全人性化。这也吸引了很多人关注,其中还包括约翰·德普和麦当娜。

关于吸血鬼的电视剧有很多,如《永远的游侠》《吸血鬼猎人巴菲》(由电影改编而成)、《天使》《刀锋战士》(由电影改编而成)和《月光》。在这些吸血鬼中,巴菲与其他的吸血鬼有所不同,她是一个中学拉拉队的队长,也是一位侦探,她独立对抗吸血鬼,同各种吸血鬼及恶魔斗争。《刀锋战士》主人公尼克·奈特,是一个半人半吸血鬼的角色,他晚上上班,喜欢喝红酒,以满足吸食人血的渴望。《天使》中的吸血鬼"天使"与《吸血鬼猎人巴菲》中的角色一样,也是一位侦探。

recent releases was *Blade*–starring Wesley Snipes. Known to his fellow vampires as the Daywalker, this character was actually half human and half vampire. This occurred when Blade'mother is attacked and killed by a vampire while pregnant. The attack was so severe, that she died while giving birth to Blade, but managed to pass the vampire virus to her new born. By being half human, Blade was able to endure sunlight, hence his name. His calling in life was similar to that of *Buffy the Vampire Slayer* in that he hunted and killed vampires, while treating his desire for blood with his own serum. The movie proved popular enough to allow for two more sequels and a televisions series sharing the Blade name.

Anne Rice has popularized vampires with the Vampire Chronicles, a series of 10 books. Two of these books, *Interview With The Vampire and The Queen of the Damned* were made into movies. *Interview* did its best to make the vampire an visually acceptable creature by having the lead roles filled by leading Hollywood actors. In the movie, *The Queen of the Damned*, Queen Akasha is awakened by the singing of the vampire Lestat after he awakens from 65 years of sleep. The character Lestat, while appearing in the previous two movies, is also part of the Vampire Chronicles with his own book *The Vampire Lestat*. Although it has not been made into a movie, it has enjoyed a very successful run on Broadway.

For the true believer, or for those wishing to learn more about the lifestyle of vampires, it should be noted that there is actually a vampire code of ethics, also called the *Black Veil or The 13 Rules of the Community*.

The 13 rules consist of the following topics:

- Discretion
- Diversity
- Safety
- Control
- Lifestyle
- Family
- Havens
- Territory
- Responsibility
- Elders
- Donors
- Leadership
- Ideals

These topics, with a detailed explanation of their meaning to vampires, can be found at www. apocalypse.org/~hilda/blackveil.html. The topics themselves appear very human–like in their scope. After examining the detailed explanation, you might be surprised at its simplicity as well as its seemly high morality. Once you remove the concept of vampirism from its content, you realize that this code of ethics has very serious applications for those of us going through our lives as plain, ordinary mortal beings.

The myth of the vampire, from the beginning of history until the present time is unfortunately a negative metaphor: The vampire symbolizes a creature that defines and sustains itself by destroying others—in other words, a parasite. No matter how exciting the story, vampires will always be associated with death.

Resources

Vampires: Encounters with the Undead, Black Dog & Leventhal Publishers, 2006. Wide–ranging collection of vampire stories. Each story includes a commentary by the editor, embellishing the story and examining the vampire obsession in folklore, literature and popular culture. The book includes more than 200 illustrations, including vintage engravings, film posters and detailed drawings.

Hollywood Gothic: The Tangled Web of Dracula from Novel to Stage to Screen, Faber & Faber, 2004. This well–researched book outlines various 19th and 20th century interpretations of Dracula as he appeared in various media forms. The book includes numerous illustrations.

www.vampires.monstrous.com. A good source of information about Dracula, Bathory and other blood–sucking monsters.

好莱坞影片中也有很多关于现代吸血鬼的描述。如最近热播的大片《刀锋战士》,韦斯利·斯奈普斯在该片中饰演一个半人半吸血鬼的角色。该片讲述"刀锋战士"的母亲在怀孕时遭遇一名吸血鬼的攻击,然后她生下了"刀锋战士",由于吸血鬼的血液也传到了他的体内,这样"刀锋战士"就成了半人半吸血鬼的模样。他的母亲也因为被吸血鬼吸食血液,受伤严重,很快就死亡了。"刀锋战士"并不惧怕阳光,他与巴菲一样,同各种吸血鬼及恶魔作斗争,猎杀其他吸血鬼。另外,他也喜欢吸食自己的血液。现在《刀锋战士》又有两部续集。

安妮·莱丝,她的吸血鬼系列小说共十本,统称为《吸血鬼年代记》。能看到改编而成的电影版本的有两部:《夜访吸血鬼》和《天谴者女王》。《夜访吸血鬼》由很多好莱坞明星出演,可算是吸血鬼电影中的神作。《天谴者女王》讲述女王阿可奇沉睡了65年后,由于听到吸血鬼黎斯特的歌声后被唤醒的故事。吸血鬼黎斯特在先前的两部电影中也出现过,也是《吸血鬼黎斯特》这本书的主人公。尽管《吸血鬼黎斯特》没有被改编成电影,但这本书在好莱坞影视城中很受欢迎。

无论是对吸血鬼的忠实信徒来说,还是对那些想了解吸血鬼生活方式的人来说,"吸血道德守则"又称"黑面纱"或"群体十三条守则",都值得一看。
"十三条手则"有如下关键词:

裁量权	多样性	安全	控制
生活方式	家庭	避风港	领土
责任	长老	捐助者	领导
理想			

有关这些守则的详细解释,请登录 www.apocalypse.org/bilda/blackveil.html 查询。你了解这些守则的含义后,或许会感到惊讶,这些守则如此简洁,且道德含义如此深刻。如果你把这些守则的含义与吸血鬼故事分开的话,你就会发现这些守则对我们普通人也很适用。

从历史开始的时候到现在,有关吸血鬼的传说一直带有反面的和恐怖的色彩。吸血鬼是靠攻击别人,吸食他们的血液维生。换句话说,吸血鬼就是寄生虫、是食客。无论以后吸血鬼的故事有多么生动,只要谈到吸血鬼,人们总是联想到死亡。

相关资源

《吸血鬼:遭遇吸血鬼》,黑狗和利尔撒尔出版社,2006年。本书收集了一系列的吸血鬼故事,探讨了民间传说,文学作品及荧屏中吸血鬼的形象。并附有编辑的评论,本书还附有200多幅插图、古雕刻画、电影海报及图画,使故事更加生动。

《好莱坞哥特:德古拉从小说走向舞台,走向荧屏》,法贝尔出版社,2004年。该书描述了19~20世纪各种作品中德古拉的形象,可供研究之用。书内有大量插图。
www.vampires.monstrous.com 该网址主要内容有德古拉、巴斯瑞及其吸血鬼的有关资料。

Forty-four

Moon Landing

On February 15, 2001, Fox TV network aired a program called *Conspiracy Theory: Did We Land on the Moon?* The hour–long program featured guests who argued that NASA technology in the 1960s was not up to the task of a real Moon landing. Instead, eager to win the space race against the Soviet Union in any way it could, NASA acted out the Apollo program in movie studios. Neil Armstrong's historic first steps on the Moon, the Moon buggy rides and even Alan Shephard's arcing golf shot over Fra Mauro were all staged.

The program's guests concluded that NASA filmed the entire program in the Nevada desert.

Evidence of a Hoax?

According to the guests on the conspiracy theory program, NASA produced photographs that proved the Moon projects were a hoax. For example, pictures of astronauts transmitted from the Moon do not include stars in the dark lunar sky-supposedly an obvious discrepancy from reality. However, as every photographer knows, it is difficult to capture something very bright as well as something very dim on the same piece of film. Astronauts walking across the bright lunar soil in their white sunlit suits presented a dazzling scene. Setting a camera's exposure to accommodate the glaringly bright suits would render background stars too faint to see.

Another photograph questioned by the conspiracy advocates was a picture of the astronauts planting a flag on the Moon. The flag in the photograph appears to be unfurled and rippling and bending. That would be impossible on the Moon, given that there are no breezes on the Moon to ruffle the flag. This can be explained by the fact that the flag was mounted on a pole with a horizontal bar inserted through a placket in the top to unfurl the banner. In addition, the astronauts rotated the flag pole back and forth in order to better penetrate the lunar soil; this action in itself created a slight breeze and accounted for the rippling of the flag.

In photos of the lunar module landing, there is not a deep blast crater. Conspiracy theorists claimed that a rocket landing on the lunar surface should have carved out a large crater. But these theorists forgot that the rocket had a throttle, and the astronauts throttled down to about 3,000 pounds of thrust as they landed. Furthermore, the exhaust from a rocket disperses over a large area in a vacuum like the Moon's atmosphere. In contrast, in the Earth's atmosphere the air funnels the thrust of a rocket into a narrow configuration, resulting in tongues of flame and columns of smoke that blast out a crater. That does not happen on the Moon, so there is not going to be a large crater at the landing site.

Many of the questions about the photos revolved around gray shadows in the pictures. If the Sun is the only source of light, then the shadows should be black. Yet there is evidence that the Sun is not the only source of light. The lunar dust on the Moon itself reflects light back in the direction of its origin. Thus, the lunar surface is reflective enough to lighten the shadows of vertical objects.

NASA's Rebuttals

According to NASA, the best rebuttal to allegations of a Moon landing hoax is common sense. First of all, one dozen astronauts walked on the Moon between 1969 and 1972. Most of them are

登　月

2001年2月15日，美国霍士有线电视网拍了一个访谈节目"阴谋理论"，探讨美国航天员是否真的曾登上月球。接受采访的嘉宾认为在20世纪60年代，美国的航空航天技术还没有成熟，不可能登陆月球。因为美国和苏联当时是死对头，相互开展太空争夺，美国渴望在太空争夺中赢得某些优势，所以美国航空航天局就拍摄了阿波罗登月这一节目。美国航天员阿姆斯特朗历史性的迈出了第一步，首次登上月球，并在月球上漫步，甚至还有艾伦·谢波德在毛罗打高尔夫球这一镜头。

接受采访的嘉宾认为电视上播放的美国登月这一幕是美国航空航天局在内华达州的沙漠拍摄的情景。

登月骗局

依据"阴谋理论"节目的嘉宾的说法，从美国航空航天局拍摄的照片是来证明这是登月骗局。如：宇航员拍摄的登月照片没有星空，这明显是不符合实际。有拍摄常识的人都知道，很难拍摄到非常明亮或者昏暗的景物。而宇航员当时穿着白色耀眼的宇航服，在月球表面上行走，而月球上的星空是很暗的，在这样的拍摄环境下，只要调整好相机的曝光组合，完全可以拍摄出群星闪烁的夜空照片。

阴谋理论还提出另一个疑点就是宇航员在月球上插上的美国国旗，松手后国旗仍会摆动，这在月球上是不可能的，因为在月球上没有风，不可能造成国旗摆动。可能的解释是：当时旗杆上方是有一个水平支架，使国旗自然垂下。另外，由于月球地质较硬，要用力扭动才可以把国旗插上，这样也会产生微风，便造成国旗的摆动。

阴谋理论还质疑称：登月飞船降落时，应吹起大量粉尘，可照片上的陆地表面却平静如常。但是在月球上，由于岩石具有节流作用，登月飞船着陆时，只会产生大约3000磅的冲击波。另外，由于月球是真空环境，不存在气流的影响，飞船降落时的喷射物不会把周围的粉尘吹走。相反，在地球上，由于空气气流的作用，飞船着陆时，会产生舌状火焰，柱状烟雾。这些在月球上都不可能。因此，登月飞船降落时，不会产生强大气流，周围粉尘不会被吹起。

大多数的疑点聚焦在照片上的灰色阴影上：既然在月亮上，太阳是唯一的光源，登月照片内所有物体的影子应该是黑色的。但是，月球表面本身具有反射作用，这样照片上所有竖直物体的影子就变淡了。

来自美国航空航天局的反驳

美国航空航天局宣称，认为登月是个骗局的人简直是无知。首先，有多位宇航员于1969年和1972年之间登上月球。现在他们中的大部分人都还健在，可以证明自己的

still alive and can testify to their experiences on the Moon.

Furthermore, the astronauts brought back evidence of their journeys. Apollo astronauts carried back more than 840 pounds of Moon rocks. Moon rocks are unique and cannot be found or duplicated on Earth. For example, lunar rocks have almost no water trapped in their crystal structure, and substances commonly present on Earth, such as forms of clay soil, are not found in lunar rocks. In addition, NASA scientists have found particles of fresh glass in Moon rocks that were produced by explosive volcanic activity more than 3 billion years ago. The presence of water on Earth rapidly breaks down volcanic glass in only a few million years, so it is obvious that the rocks must have come from the Moon.

Moon rocks have tiny craters from meteoroid impacts, which can only happen to rocks from a planet with little or no atmosphere. These meteoroids are microscopic specks of comets that travel through space at 50,000 mph or faster. They disintegrate in the air above Earth's stratosphere and so do not strike rocks on Earth. The Moon, however, does not have a protective atmosphere, so these tiny specks strike Moon rocks, forming miniature craters.Cosmic rays also bombard the Moon and Moon rocks. Moon rocks contain isotopes—created by nuclear reactions with high-energy cosmic rays—that are not normally found on Earth. Earth is spared from this type of radiation bombardment because of its protective atmosphere. So there is no way they could be fabricated to create a hoax.

Finally, almost 40 years after the Apollo 11 Moon landing, NASA and the National Science Foundation are still conducting an Apollo science experiment. About one hour before the end of their final Moonwalk on July 21, 1969, Neil Armstrong and Buzz Aldrin placed a lunar laser ranging retroreflector array—that is, a small panel studded with 100 mirrors pointing at the Earth—on the lunar surface. This device allows scientists on Earth to bombard the Moon with laser pulses that the array sends back directly to their origin on Earth. This allows scientists to precisely measure the Earth-Moon distance. The device also permits scientists to evaluate the Moon's orbit and to test theories of gravity. The lunar mirrors require no power source and have not been covered with moondust or pelted by meteoroids. There is no sign that the 40-year experiment cannot continue forever.

The array testing has revealed some fascinating facts:

·The Moon is spiraling away from the Earth at a rate of 38 cm per year. Scientists believe the Earth's tides are responsible for this.

·The Moon probably has a liquid core.

·The laser tests confirm Einstein's theory of relativity, that is, Einstein's equations can predict the shape of the Moon's orbit as accurately as the laser ranging can measure it. However, many scientists believe that Einstein's theory may have a flaw and they are eager to use the laser ranging test to detect that flaw.

Were the Moon landings hoaxes? The consensus among reputable scientists, even some who are critical of NASA's space flight program, is that there is overwhelming physical evidence that human beings did, indeed, walk on the Moon.

Resources

Moon Landings: Did NASA Lie?, Carnot USA Books, 2003. The author of this book presents interpretations of NASA photographs and reports and invites the readers to arrive at their own conclusions about whether or not the Moon landings were faked.

www.hq.nasa.gov/alsj/frame.html. This Website presents the transcript and commentary of the Apollo 11 crew on their journey to the Moon. The Website includes photographs.

登月经历。

　　此外，宇航员还带回了重达840磅的月球岩石。月球岩石是独一无二的，现有的技术手段无法人为制造出具有这些特征的岩石。例如：月球岩石不可能有被水冲刷的痕迹，周围也不可能有泥土。美国航天航空局的科学家还发现月球岩石周围有一些玻璃般的粒子，这些粒子是3亿年前火山爆发形成的，而地球上的这些粒子是一亿年前火山爆发形成的，而且有被水冲刷的痕迹。显然，这些岩石是来自月球。

　　月球表面没有空气，这些宇宙尘埃以每小时5万英里的速度撞击月球，甚至更快，因此，月球岩石其表面布满了饱受宇宙尘埃撞击留下的微小的"陨石坑"。地球由于有大气层的保护，免受宇宙尘埃的入侵，因此地球岩石不具有这些特征。月球岩石还受到高能宇宙射线的撞击引发核反应，产生的特殊同位素元素，而地球由于有大气层的保护，免受高能宇宙射线的撞击。因此，登月不可能是骗局。

　　最后，在"阿波罗11号"登月成功后的40年来，美国航空航天局和美国国家科学基金会一直在做"阿波罗"科学实验。1969年7月21日阿姆斯特朗和艾德灵在月球上放了一块由100面镜子组成的激光反射镜。这块反射镜以高速粒子撞击月球产生脉冲，然后直接传回地面，这样科学家可以测算地球与月球的轨道距离，可以验证相对论。因为反射镜不需要电力，也不会受到尘埃及高速粒子的撞击，它可以一直工作下去。

　　已经验证的事实：
　　·月球以每年38厘米的速度远离地球。科学家们相信地球上的潮汐现象与这有关。
　　·月球上可能有水。

　　·证实了爱因斯坦的相对论是正确的。通过爱因斯坦的方程式测算的月球轨道形状与反射器测量的完全吻合。科学家们认为爱因斯坦的相对论也有不足，希望通过激光反射器的测试找到那些缺陷。
　　登月是个骗局吗？很多权威科学家，甚至曾经对美国航空航天局的太空飞行计划持批评态度的人，一致认为有充分的事实依据证明人类确实登月成功。

相关资源
　　《登月：美国航空航天局在说谎吗？》，美国卡诺图书，2003年。本书作者提供了美国航空航天局拍摄的照片及相关报告，然后让读者自己判断是否骗局。作者在书中就美国航空航天局拍摄的登月照片提出了很多疑点，但并没有解释为什么航空航天局要说谎。
　　www.hq.nasa.gov/alsj/frame.html 该网址提供了很多阿波罗11号飞船登月的实况报道及相关图片。

Forty-five

Weather Myths

Is the old saying: Red sky at night, sailor's delight; Red sky in morning, sailor's warning—true, or is it just an old wives' s tale?

Answer: Within limits, there is truth in this saying. And the saying has appeared in different sources for a long time. Shakespeare wrote a variation of this weather prediction in his play *Venus and Adonis* in the 16th century. *The New Testament* of the Christian Bible also contains this adage

Weather lore has been around since people needed to predict the weather and plan their activities. Sailors and farmers in particular have relied on weather to navigate ships and plant crops. But it is important to remember that weather sayings based on someone's specific observations are not necessarily accurate. Furthermore, a weather observation in one location may not be true in another, because weather patterns and conditions differ throughout the world.

For example, in order to understand why "Red sky at night, sailor's delight; Red sky in morning, sailor's warning" can predict the weather, it is necessary to understand the interaction of the atmosphere and the colors in the sky. Usually, weather moves from west to east, blown by the westerly trade winds. This means storm systems generally move in from the west.

The colors seen in the sky are due to the rays of sunlight being split into colors of the spectrum as they pass through the atmosphere and ricochet off the water vapor and particles in the atmosphere. The amounts of water vapor and dust particles in the atmosphere are good indicators of weather conditions. They also determine which colors are seen in the sky.

During sunrise and sunset the sun is low in the sky and it transmits light through the thickest part of the atmosphere. A red sky suggests an atmosphere loaded with dust and moisture particles because red wavelengths (the longest in the color spectrum) are breaking through the atmosphere. The shorter wavelengths, such as blue, are scattered and broken up.

Red sky at night, sailors delight. A red sky at night means that the setting sun is sending its light through a high concentration of dust particles. This usually indicates high pressure and stable air coming in from the west. Basically, good weather will follow.

Red sky in morning, sailor'warning. A red sunrise reflects the dust particles of a system that has just passed from the west. This indicates that a storm system may be moving to the east. If the morning sky is a deep fiery red, it means high water content in the atmosphere. So, rain is on its way.

Can Animals Predict Weather?

Some people, particularly those who work with animals, claim that animal behavior is a reliable predictor of weather. As a matter of fact, most animals and insects are more attuned to changes and variations in air pressure, humidity and temperature than are humans. Birds flying low may indicate that air pressure is dropping. Falling air pressure may also affect the digestive process of cows, encouraging them to lie down rather than to go pasture to graze. The hairs inside a cow's ear may respond to changes before a rain storm, so a cow scratching her ears may foretell rain. Similarly, a cow brushing her hide with her tail may be reacting to the static charges of electricity that raise the cow's hair before a violent thunderstorm. Variations in air pressure,

天　气

"晚上天色红,水手乐呵呵;早晨天色红,水手急煞煞。"这句古谚语正确吗?还是无稽之谈?

答案:在一定的范围内,这句谚语是正确的。这句谚语在很早以前就有了,16世纪在莎士比亚剧本《维纳斯和阿多尼斯》中就有类似的说法,圣经中的《新约》也提到这句谚语。

水手们要依靠天气出航,农民们也要依靠天气耕作。人类在耕作、航海等活动中,不断总结天气变化经验,这也有一定的科学依据。但需要记住的是,根据人们观察和经验而得成的谚语来判断天气,这不一定正确。依据人们长期观察总结的规律来判断天气变化,这不是适用所有的地方,要因地而变。

例如:要理解"晚上天色红,水手乐呵呵;早晨天色红,水手急煞煞"这句谚语,我们必须懂得观察天象,观察气流的运动和天空的颜色。俗话说:"云是天气的招牌"。若低云由西向东移动,又受到刮来的西风影响这说明阴雨系统在东移。受到空气中水汽及微粒的影响,就会形成波长不同的光线,这样就会产生不同的天色。空气中的水汽及尘埃的含量,决定着不同的天色,通过观测天色,可以预兆一定的天气。

天空中色彩各异的颜色是在不同的气象条件下,阳光在大气层中的散射所引起的。我们所看到的天空的颜色,受空气中水汽及微粒多少的影响,是大气层散射的光线的颜色。

日出、日落时,太阳的位置较低,阳光穿过大气层中最厚的部分,空气中水汽及尘埃较多,红色波长(光谱中最长的)就会穿透大气层,而短波像蓝色就被分散开,这样天空就会变成红色。

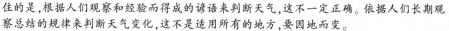

晚上天色红,水手乐呵呵。因为晚上天色红,就是日落时阳光穿过尘埃较多的大气层,这样就意味着空气中气压高,气流稳定,晴朗天气即将来临。

早上天色红,水手急煞煞。因为早上天色红,西方有云,阳光照射在云上就散射出彩霞,这表明空气中水汽充足,预示着有雨。

动物能预测天气吗?

一些人,特别是与动物打交道的人,认为很多动物都有预测天气的本能,根据动物的行为也可以判断天气将要发生的变化。实际上,大多数动物和昆虫对气压、气流和温度的变化相当敏感。食虫的鸟类,如果飞的很底,通常意味着气压很低,暴风雨要来临。如果牛呆在牛棚里,不愿意去牧场吃草,或用尾巴刷屁股,或甩耳朵,则预示着阴雨将来临。雷雨来临前,由于气压及温度的变化,一些动物容易觅食,不愿意归巢,而有的动物会选择高处掘新窝,更好的防御雨水的袭击。这是为什么几个世纪来,人们能通过观察动物的行为变化来判断天气的变化的原因。

increases in wind or changes in temperature may propel animals to eat more or to seek shelter to protect themselves from an approaching storm. That is why for centuries human beings have relied on observations of animals to predict a change in weather.

Birds

Many people turn to birds as reliable weather soothsayers. A bird's feathers trap air for insulation, so they will feel changes in air pressure, temperature and humidity before a storm. Therefore, there is a saying that if a rooster crows at night, rain is in sight. Or chickens who scratch in the soil together are expecting a storm later in the day.

Insects

Insects, too, are sensitive to weather changes. Insects may fly lower than usual before a rainstorm because their wings are weighted down with humid air. In many instances they seem to be swarming before a storm. Similarly, cicadas cannot vibrate their wings when the humidity is high, so a silence from cicadas may mean a rainstorm is approaching.

Bees, in particular, are sensitive to changes in heat, humidity and air pressure. When humidity increases before a rainstorm, bees tend to stay near their hives.

One of the more interesting insect forecasting methods is counting cricket chirps in order to determine air temperature. Counting the number of cricket chirps in one 14−second period and adding 40 will equal the air temperature to within one degree accuracy. This has been proven to be true 75 percent of the time.

How Reliable Are Weather Myths?

As a general rule, weather lore based on scientific proof and principles are reliable. Myths based on the activities of animals are more subjective, primarily because animals, birds and insects are affected by weather that is actually occurring and not by weather that may be approaching. In addition, some myths that may actually appear to be accurate are not universally true in every location. Weather myths from the Bible or from old tales from Africa may not apply to the terrain and atmospheric conditions of the Western Hemisphere. So it is always a good idea to exercise a little skepticism when quoting weather proverbs.

Still, some myths refuse to die, and continuing repetition has made them a part of modern folklore. Below are a few weather myths that will probably persist whether or not they can be scientifically explained:

- A ring around the Moon means rain or snow is coming.
- If March comes in like a lamb, it will go out like a lion.
- The blossom of a morning glory opens when the day is sunny and closes when rain is coming.

Resources

Encyclopedia Weather and Climate, Facts on File, 2007. More than 3,000 alphabetically arranged entries explain how the atmosphere works and how weather forms.The book is well illustrated with photographs, maps, drawings and charts.Bibliographies, timetables and comprehensive indexes are included.

www.members.aol.com/Accustiver/wxworld_folk.html. Weather folklore page—filled with weather folklore sayings and weather wits.

鸟

鸟对天气的变化十分敏感,在雷雨来临前,鸟对气温、气压及空气温度的变化很敏感。因此,有这样的谚语:公鸡叫,雨来到或鸡宿迟,兆阴雨。

昆虫

昆虫对天气的变化也很敏感。在暴风雨来临前,空气中温度高,昆虫飞得比平常低。在暴风雨来临前,许多昆虫会集结在一起。蝉的叫声是由它腹部的薄膜振动而发出的,在下雨前,它的发音薄膜潮湿,振动不灵,因此,蝉是不叫的。

蜜蜂对温度、空气温度及气压的变化也十分敏感。暴风雨来临前,空气湿度大,蜜蜂就喜欢呆在蜂箱附近。

更有趣的是,蟋蟀的鸣叫声可以当温度计使用。先数清蟋蟀在14秒内鸣叫的次数,然后再加40,这就是当时的华氏温度。这种测温法据说准确率达75%。

天气神话可靠吗

基于科学依据判断天气是可靠的。

而依据动物的行为变化判断天气带有主观性,因为鸟和昆虫确实对天气的变化很敏感,但并不能断定那种天气肯定会出现。另外,有关天气的神话故事或许在某个地方是适用的,并不是在任何地方都适用。源于圣经故事或非洲民间故事的天气谚语或许并不适用西半球的情况,因为西半球的地形、地貌和大气状况与东半球不尽相同。因此在引用天气谚语判断天气时,不能完全相信。

今天,仍然有很多有关天气谚语的民间故事及神话,下面几条不知是否有一定的科学依据。

- 月亮附近有圆环则意味着雨和雪。
- 若3月初的天气像雄狮般严峻,那么月底的天气就像羊羔般温顺。
- 有雨天边亮,无雨顶上亮。

相关资源

《天气百科全书与气候》,档案出版社,2007年。该书以字母顺序编排,3000多词条包括天气的很多内容。本书附有很多照片、地图、绘画及图表,还包括参考书目、时刻表及完整的索引。

www.members.aol.com/Accustiver/wxworld_folk.html. 天气故事网址,主要内容是天气谚语、天气传说及天气知识。

Forty-six

Wedding Myths

True or false: The tradition of throwing rice at newlyweds as a symbol of fertility and prosperity as they depart for their honeymoon is no longer acceptable at modern weddings? The answer, unfortunately, is not a simple yes or no. The prohibition of rice is thought to be supported by churches and reception halls who find rice difficult to clean up as well as a hazard on hard, slippery floors.

The rice tradition is only one of many age-old wedding traditions and customs whose origins have been lost in time. Here are a few traditions—along with a description of their original meaning—that can be observed at almost any wedding.

Something Old, Something New...

Something old, something new, something borrowed, something blue. This old saying originated in the Victorian era, but the original symbolism remains the same today.

Something old symbolizes the bride's link with her past. A bride may choose to wear family jewelry or her mother's wedding dress. Something new represents good luck and success in the bride's new life. In many cases, the wedding dress is something new. Something borrowed signifies that a bride's family and friends will support her in her new life; the borrowed item may be a treasured piece of jewelry from a friend. Something blue is a symbol of good luck and faithfulness and dates to Biblical times when blue represented purity. Often a bride's garter is blue.

The Ring

The wedding ring is a symbol of endless love, since the ring is an unbroken circle with no end. The ring has been worn on the third finger of the left hand for centuries because ancient cultures believed that a vein ran directly from that finger to the heart. The first rings were generally woven from grasses or later fashioned from leather or metal. The tradition of a diamond engagement ring, although originally a sign of wealth among royalty and the well-to-do, did not really become widespread until the 1930s and 1940s when the South African diamond company DeBeers tried to boost sales by promoting diamond engagement rings in movies and among film stars.

The Wedding Day

There is an old poem that spells out the significance of each day of the week when it comes time to plan a wedding:

Monday for health,
 Tuesday for wealth,
Wednesday the best of all.
Thursday brings crosses, and Friday losses,
But Saturday—no luck at all.

婚　礼

在传统的婚俗中，撒大米代表嫁出的女儿是泼出去的水，父母再也不过问女儿以后的一切，并祝女儿事事有成，有吃有穿。在现代婚俗中还是这样吗？答案不是"是"或"否"这样简单。但是，在很多地方，特别是教堂和宴会厅，撒大米这种婚俗被禁止，因为在那些地方撒大米，地面很难清扫，也容易使地面打滑。

撒大米这种习俗仅仅是许多传统婚俗的一种，起源于什么时候已经记不清楚了。除了这种习俗外，还有许多传统的婚俗仍在沿用。举例如下：

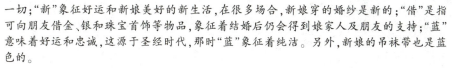

婚礼时有旧、新、借、蓝

婚礼时有旧、新、借、蓝，这个古谚语起源于维多利亚时代，至今含义并没有变化。

在西方国家中，婚礼时有旧、新、借、蓝等习俗。"旧"代表着新娘的过去，她可以穿戴母亲传下来的婚纱或首饰，代表承受美好的一切；"新"象征好运和新娘美好的新生活，在很多场合，新娘穿的婚纱是新的；"借"是指可向朋友借金、银和珠宝首饰等物品，象征着结婚后仍会得到娘家人及朋友的支持；"蓝"意味着好运和忠诚，这源于圣经时代，那时"蓝"象征着纯洁。另外，新娘的吊袜带也是蓝色的。

婚戒

婚戒是圆的，没有起点，没有终点，代表永恒的爱。根据习俗，婚戒一般戴在左手的中指上，古人认为这个手指的血管直接通往心脏。最早的戒指是用玻璃制成的，后来是用皮革或金属。二十世纪三四十年代，南非的钻戒公司（戴比尔斯公司）通过电影或电影明星大力促销钻戒。自那以后钻戒不仅被视为财富的象征，钻戒也是永恒不渝的爱情象征。

结婚日

下面这首诗给一周的每一天赋予了一定的意义，以便安排婚礼之用。

星期一象征健康
星期二象征财富
星期三象征一切顺利
星期四预示着灾难
星期五预示着破财

Obviously, no one today attaches such meaning to the days of the week, since most weddings occur on Saturday.

Many consider a rainy wedding day will predict many tears during the marriage. Others think that a rainy day foretells of many children born to the couple. Most people, however, prefer a rain–free wedding day because that symbolizes good luck and prosperity.

Wedding Clothes

There are many traditions about the wedding clothes, particularly the wedding dress. Many believe that a white wedding dress symbolizes the innocence and purity of the bride. Yet, contrary to popular belief, the white wedding dress did not come into fashion until the middle of the 19th century when Queen Victoria decided to wear white for her marriage to Prince Albert. Up to that time, a white dress was considered an extravagance because white was an impractical color that could not be worn more than once without laundering. Women who married in white implied that they were wealthy enough to afford a dress that would only be used one time.

It was and still is considered unlucky for the groom to see the bride in her wedding dress before the ceremony and it is also bad luck for the bride to try on her dress more than once after the alterations.

The Bridal Veil

The bridal veil, particularly the part covering the face known as a blusher veil, symbolizes virginity. Therefore, only brides being married for the first time should wear it. In some cultures, the veil was used to hide the bride's beauty and ward off evil spirits. In cultures where marriages were arranged and the couples did not meet until the ceremony, a blusher veil supposedly prevented the groom from calling off the wedding if the bride was not attractive to him.

The Wedding Garter

At one time, it was traditional for male members of the wedding party to escort the bridal couple to their bedroom and compete to retrieve the wedding garter—representing faithfulness and good luck—from the bride'leg. Whoever seized the garter gave it to his favorite lady as a symbol of good luck. Because this festivity often became unruly and offensive to the bride, the new wife began tossing the garter to the male members of the wedding party to identify the next man to become engaged to be married. When this did not curb the disorderliness, the bride took to tossing her bouquet to the women in the party.

This tradition of tossing the garter survives to the present, except that today the groom tosses the garter to the men in the group while the bride still throws the bouquet to the women. The garter is still traditionally blue, the color that signifies good luck for the bride, groom and lucky individual who catches it.

The Wedding Party

There is an old tradition that the bridal couple should be surrounded by other people of the same age and dressed in similar clothes so that evil spirits cannot pick out the pair getting married. That is why bridesmaids were dressed alike. Today's couples do not necessarily adhere to this custom. The relationships of the wedding party members to the

星期六没有任何运气

显然,今天没有这样的说法,因为大多数的婚礼都是安排在周六。

很多人认为婚礼那天碰上雨天,则意味着未来的日子里会遭受更多痛苦;还有一些人则认为雨天象征着多子多福。但大多数人还是喜欢在晴天举行婚礼,因为这样会带来好运。

礼服

有关婚礼服的说法很多。许多人认为白色礼服代表着纯洁。19世纪时,维多利亚女王决定穿着白色婚纱与阿尔波特王子举行婚礼,自那时起,白色礼服才开始流行。也有这样的说法,穿白色礼服是富裕的象征,因为白色的礼服只要洗一次就不能再穿了,新娘穿白色的婚纱是富贵的象征。

现在仍有人认为,新郎在结婚仪式前是不能见新娘的,否则会带来厄运。另外新娘也不能多次试穿婚纱,这样也会带来厄运。

面纱

最初,新娘的面纱象征着忠贞和纯洁,因为只有第一次结婚的新娘才可以带白色面纱。在一些文化中,面纱可以用来遮掩新娘的美貌,也可以驱赶邪恶。另外,在婚礼前,新郎是不能够见新娘的,如果新郎提前揭去了新娘的面纱,发现新娘不漂亮,就有可能取消婚礼。

吊袜带

吊袜带是系在新娘腿上的蓝色带子,象征忠诚与好运。从前,有这样的习俗,参加婚礼的男宾客必须护送新娘入洞房,然后去争抢吊袜带,谁抢到吊袜带就会给他带来好运。在结婚这样喜庆的日子里,新娘向参加婚礼的男宾客抛吊袜带,谁抢到吊袜带,就表明他是下一个要结婚的人。在抛吊袜带的同时,女宾客们也会凑热闹,所以新娘也会向她们抛花束。

今天,仍然还有抛吊袜带的习俗,新郎向男宾客抛吊袜带,而新娘向女宾客抛花束。吊袜带依然是传统的蓝色,因为蓝色代表着好运,对新郎、新娘及抓住吊袜带的人都会带来好运。

婚宴

古代婚俗中有这样的说法,结婚时要举办婚宴,邀请一些年龄一般大的人参加婚宴,在婚宴上他们穿与新郎新娘类似的衣服,这样可以驱赶邪恶,因为恶魔无法辨别谁是新郎新娘。今天,没有必要遵守这样的风俗习惯。男女双方邀请谁参加婚宴取决于他们自己。

couple take priority.

The custom of having a best man began in the time of marriages–by–kidnapping—that occurred when the father of the bride did not give his blessing for the marriage. The best man's job was to watch for the opportunity to capture the bride–to–be and then help with the kidnapping.

The Honeymoon

The tradition of taking a honeymoon also began with the marriage –by –kidnapping practice. Obviously, after the kidnapping the couple was forced to flee to avoid the rage of the bride'father. It was customary for the couple to hide for as long as it took the moon to complete a lunar cycle, about 1 month. In addition, it was believed that drinking a concoction made from mead and honey during the first month of a marriage would ensure fertility. This is the origin of the word honeymoon.

Resources

A Bride's Book of Wedding Traditions, William Morrow, 1995. This book provides a vast collection of wedding traditions that span cultures and centuries. In addition to describing the traditional customs of modern Western cultures, the book also covers wedding traditions from the Victorian era as well as from African–American, Native American, Asian and other ethnic cultures.

Timeless Traditions: A Couple's Guide to Wedding Customs around the World, Universe Publishing, 2001. This book combines time–honored traditions, folk rituals and unusual observances from all cultures.

The Knot Guide to Wedding Vows and Traditions: Readings, Rituals, Music, Dances, and Toasts, Broadway, 2000. The book presents traditions related to the wedding ceremony itself. Drawing from religious ceremonies and folklore rituals, the book explains the cultural traditions behind wedding and marriage rituals.

50 plus one Tips to Organizing a Successful Social Event, Encouragement Press, 2007. This is a wonderful book which assist almost anyone planning a wedding or other major event–whether you believe in wedding myths or not!

www.yourwedding101.com/wedding–basics/wedding–myths.aspx. The meaning behind the myths.

伴郎也起源于古时抢亲的习俗。男女双方自由恋爱有了感情,但说亲时女方父母不同意,这时伴郎就是要寻找机会,帮助新郎抢走新娘。

蜜月

度蜜月起源于古时抢亲习俗,因为新郎抢走了新娘,他的岳父很生气,新婚夫妇就在婚后一个月内直到月缺时要躲藏起来。在度蜜月期间,还要喝蜂蜜发酵制成的饮料以增强性生活的和谐,这就是"蜜月"的来源。

相关资源

《婚俗》,威廉·莫罗,1995年。本书涵盖了不同时期不同文化中的很多婚俗习惯,如:维多利亚时代、美国黑人、印第安人、亚洲人及其他文化群体。此外,本书还描述了现代西方文化中的传统婚俗。

《永恒的传统:世界婚俗介绍》,万卷出版社,2001年。本书包含有传统婚俗,民间婚俗介绍以及特殊婚俗介绍。

《婚礼必读:婚礼证词、仪式、音乐、舞蹈和祝酒》,百老汇出版社,2000年。本书讲述了婚礼上的一些婚俗习惯,有教堂仪式和民间仪式。此外,本书还解释了婚礼背后的相关文化习俗。

《成功组织一项活动的50加1条建议》,鼓励出版集团,2007年。不管信还是不信婚礼神话,这都是一本好书,可以帮助你组织好婚礼或其他重要活动。

www.yourwedding101.com/wedding-basics/wedding-myths.aspx 该网址提供了婚礼神话背后的含义的相关信息。

Forty-seven

White Buffalo

White buffalos are sacred to several Native American groups and therefore carry spiritual significance as well as a presence in their religious ceremonies and rites.

The white buffalo is especially sacred to the Cheyenne, Sioux and other nomadic tribes of the northern plains of the United States because these peoples once depended on buffalo for sustenance—food, clothing, housing and other daily necessities. Part of the mystique of the white buffalo for Native American tribes derives from the fact that American buffaloes or bison are normally brown in color, and white buffalos are extremely rare. According to the American Bison Association, the odds of a white buffalo are at least one in a million.

Biologically speaking, there are several reasons a buffalo may be white:

· The buffalo may be born lacking normal coloration because of genetic factors. In these cases, the animal may have white fur and blue eyes or white fur and pink eyes. The latter type is called albino and these animals remain without coloration throughout their lives. They may also have vision and hearing problems.

· Some buffalo are born white but become brown within a year or so as they mature.

· A white buffalo may be a bison–cattle crossbreed, also known as a beefalo and may inherit white coloration from its cattle ancestors.

The Legend of the White Buffalo

Long ago the seven councils of the Lakota Sioux gathered in the sacred Black Hills of South Dakota to discuss their plight. The people were starving because there was no game for food and the sun was relentless and hot.

Two young warriors went out to hunt for food and saw a large white body moving toward them. It appeared to be a white buffalo calf and as it approached them, it transformed itself into a beautiful Indian girl dressed in white. The two warriors were awestruck and one of them desired to touch her. Unknown to the warriors, this woman was a sacred image and could not be disrespected. The young man who desired her was suddenly overcome by fire and smoke and reduced to a pile of bones.

The second warrior fell to his knees in prayer and the young woman instructed him to return to his people and tell them to prepare to receive her and a sacred bundle in 4 days. The tribe prepared for her arrival and in 4 days a cloud descended, revealing a white buffalo calf who became the beautiful young woman. She carried the sacred bundle and presented it to the tribal leaders.

The White Buffalo Woman spent 4 days among the people and taught them the meaning of the sacred bundle, including seven sacred ceremonies that, if remembered and performed, would entitle the tribes to remain caretakers and guardians of their sacred land. The seven ceremonies were:

白色水牛

对一些土著的美洲居民来说,白色水牛是件圣物,象征着精神方面的非凡意义,在他们的宗教典礼或仪式上不可或缺。

对于夏安族人、苏族人以及美国北部平原的其他游牧部落来说,白色水牛尤为神圣,因为这些民族曾依靠水牛来满足衣、食、住及其他日常必需品。美洲土著的部落为何视白色水牛为神物呢?部分原因就在于,美洲的水牛或野牛通常呈棕色,因而白色水牛就显得异常珍贵。据"美洲野牛联合会"统计,白色水牛的出现比例是百万分之一。

从生物学上讲,以下几个原因可能致使水牛出现白色:

· 基因方面的因素可能导致水牛出生便缺乏正常的颜色。在这种情况下,水牛的皮毛呈现白色,眼睛是蓝色或者粉红色。后一种情形称之为白化病,这样的水牛终身白色,而且可能出现视觉和听力障碍。

· 有一种水牛一出生是白色,但大约7年过后逐渐成熟,就转变为棕色。

· 还有一种白色水牛,可能是野牛和家牛杂交而成,也叫做皮弗娄牛,它能够从家牛先祖那儿遗传到白颜色。

白色水牛的传说

很久很久以前,拉科塔部落苏族人的7支分族在南达科他州神圣的黑山碰头了,要商讨彼此之间的誓约。当时人们忍饥挨饿,没有可以食用的猎物,而太阳把一切都烤得酷热难当。

两名年轻的士兵出去寻找食物,突然看见一具庞大的躯体向他们靠过来。那是一头白色的小水牛,向他们越走越近,竟变幻成一位美丽的印第安少女,身穿白色的衣裙。两名士兵又敬又怕,其中一个恣意妄为,竟然想抚摸她。他们不知道,这位少女其实是个神女,不可不敬。妄为的年轻人突然间遍身烟火,立时化为一堆枯骨。

另一名士兵跪下来祈祷,神女指引他回到家园,并让他们做好准备,迎接她和一个神圣包裹在4天之后到来。整个部落准备好迎接神女,4天之后,一朵祥云飘落下来,现出一头白色小水牛,继而化身为那个迷人的年轻少女。她提着圣包,并把它交给了部落首领。

白牛神女和人们相处了4天,传授他们圣包的价值所在,也提到了7种神圣的仪式。他们如果能够牢记这7种神圣的仪式,并认真执行,那么整个部落就能够继续掌握并守护他们的圣地。这7种神圣的仪式分别是:

1. The purification ceremony or the sweat lodge;

2. the naming ceremony or child naming;

3. the healing ceremony;

4. the adoption ceremony or the creating of relatives;

5. the marriage ceremony;

6. the vision quest ceremony; and

7. the ceremony for all of the nations or the sundance ceremony. (To commemorate the White Buffalo Woman, a mature and universally respected tribal woman is often given the honor of representing the White Buffalo Woman at the sundance.)

Teaching the ceremonial songs, rituals and traditional ways, the White Buffalo Woman informed the tribes that as long as they performed the seven ceremonies they would never die and would always possess their land. And, in the myth, after the White Buffalo Woman's departure, great herds of buffalo appeared so that the Lakota and the other tribes could survive.

When it came time for the White Buffalo Woman to depart, she walked off into the distance, stopping and rolling over four times. Each time she rolled, she changed color: first into a black buffalo; second into a brown buffalo; third into a red buffalo; and finally into a white buffalo.

Miracle

Miracle, a white buffalo born in Janesville, Wisconsin, in 1994 has received so much attention. Miracle was born white but has changed colors from white to black to yellow brown as predicted by the legend of the White Buffalo Woman.

In addition to the color changes foretold by the legend, Miracle's timing seems to coincide with improved economic stability among the Native American tribes (similar to the return of the buffalo herds in the original legend), thanks to profits from legal gambling and gaming establishments of Native American nations. Furthermore, the Wisconsin buffalo has stimulated interest in the legend and in Native American legends and rituals. Several nations have established their own buffalo herds and reinstated old rituals and ceremonies. Best of all from the standpoint of cultural awareness, Miracle's birth has interested the young people in learning their native languages and discovering their spiritual heritage.

Resources

Eyes of Wisdom: Book One in the White Buffalo Woman Trilogy, Atria Books, 2006. This first book in the trilogy presents a narration of the life and ceremonies of the plains Native Americans, based on the legend of the White Buffalo Woman.

Painted Earth Temple: Book Two in the White Buffalo Woman Trilogy, Atria Books, March 2007. This second book in the trilogy continues the exploration of the Native American culture through the vehicle of the White Buffalo Woman.

Lying Down Mountain: Book Three in the White Buffalo Woman Trilogy, Atria Books, July 2007. This conclusion of the trilogy offers additional stories from the history of the Native Americans and includes photos of the author's artwork.

1. 净化仪式或蒸汗屋仪式(有重生的意思);
2. 命名仪式;
3. 拯救仪式;
4. 收养仪式或建立亲属关系;
5. 结婚仪式;
6. 探求希望仪式;
7. 各族庆祝仪式(为了纪念白牛神女,通常从部落里面挑选出一位成熟而广受尊敬的女性,在仪式上代表白牛神女)。

白牛神女向他们传授仪式上的歌曲、礼仪以及传统的方法,并告知他们,只要他们认真执行这7种神圣的仪式,他们就可以永生,并永远占有这块土地。

在神话中,神女离开后,大批的水牛出现了,拉科塔及其他部落才得以生存下去。

神女离别之际,走向远方,曾有4次停下来转身向后看。每次转身,都会变色:第一次变成黑色水牛;第二次是棕色水牛;第三次成了红色水牛;最后变为白色水牛。

奇迹

1994年,威斯康星州出生的一头白色小水牛"奇迹"颇为引人注目。"奇迹"一生下来是白色的,但后来由白色转为黑色,又转为黄棕色,正符合了传说中白牛神女的预言。

不仅仅局限于传说中预言的颜色变化,"奇迹"的出生也恰逢美洲土著部落的经济稳步增长时期,这还多亏了美洲土著民族建起合法的赌场,并从中获益。更进一步,威斯康星的"奇迹"激发人们对传说产生了兴趣,尤其是美洲土著的传说和礼仪。数个民族建起了自己的水牛群,并恢复了古老的仪式和典礼。从文化意识的观点来看,最好的情况莫过于"奇迹"的出生,使得年轻人对学习本族的语言、发现本族的精神遗产有了浓厚的兴趣。

相关资源

《白牛神女三部曲之第一册:智慧之眼》,阿特利亚图书,2006年。这是三部曲的第一册,以白牛神女的传说为基础,讲述了美洲土著平原上的生活和典礼。

《白牛神女三部曲之第二册:漆画之庙》,阿特利亚图书,2007年3月。这是三部曲的第二册,以白牛神女的传说为载体,继续探索美洲土著文化。

《白牛神女三部曲之第三册:卧倒之山》,阿特利亚图书,2007年7月。这是三部曲的结局部分,提供了美洲土著历史上的其他故事,并包括了作者所持有的艺术品的照片。

Forty-eight

White House Ghosts

The presidential mansion in Washington D.C., commonly called the White House, is haunted by ghosts of dead presidents and others who have had a direct connection to the building.

History of the White House

Construction of the White House began in 1792 on land donated to the government by David Burns, who owned 263 acres of land in the heart of the designated federal district. The location of the country'new capital had been selected by George Washington, who also plotted out the federal district. The cornerstone of the White House was laid on October 13, 1792, one day after the celebration of Christopher Columbus?300th anniversary of his first trip to the New World.

By November 1800 the White House was ready for its first occupants, President John Adams and his wife Abigail, although the building was not completed until after 1801 when Thomas Jefferson moved in. At that time the president's residence was called the Presidential Palace.

During the War of 1812, during which James Madison was president, British troops stormed the mansion and set fire to the building. After the War of 1812, the mansion was repaired and the building was whitewashed to cover the smoke marks from the fire set by the British. From that time on, the mansion has been called the White House.

Ghosts of the White House

Historical institutions like the presidency are bound to have mysterious happenings or ghosts. And the White House is no exception.

Arguably, the oldest ghost to haunt the White House is David Burns who donated the land on which the building stands. During Franklin Delano Roosevelt's administration, both a guard at the mansion and FDR's personal valet heard a voice claiming to be David Burns.

Abigail Adams, the first First Lady to occupy the White House, is said to have been seen floating through the halls of the White House looking as though she were carrying something in outstretched arms. During her residency in the White House, Abigail found the building to be drafty and damp except for the East Room where she decided to hang the laundry. Her ghost today is assumed to be carrying laundry toward the East Room.

Dolley Madison, the occupant of the White House when it was burned by the British, may also be a ghost. When the wife of Woodrow Wilson lived in the White House, she undertook a redesign of the Rose Garden that Dolley Madison had planted more than 100 years earlier. The gardeners fled when Dolley's ghost appeared to chastise them for disturbing her garden.

白宫闹鬼

华盛顿特区的总统官邸通常称为"白宫",这儿常常有已故总统或其他与白宫密切相关人员的鬼魂出没。

白宫历史

白宫的建造始于1792年,土地是由大卫·伯恩斯捐给政府的,他在国家规定的联邦政府区域中心地带拥有263英亩土地。美国的新首都由乔治·华盛顿指定,政府区域也是由他规划出来的。白宫于1792年10月13日打下基石,前一天正是纪念哥伦布初次发现新大陆300周年的日子。

1800年11月,白宫已经基本修建完成,迎来它的首批住户:约翰·亚当斯总统及其夫人阿比盖尔。不过彻底完工是在1801年托马斯·杰弗逊入住以后。当时这所总统的住宅叫做"总统宫殿"。

1812年战争期间,詹姆士·麦迪逊任总统,英国军队强攻白宫,并在白宫放了把火。1812年的战争结束后,白宫重新修葺,墙壁刷成白色以掩盖英国人纵火留下的烟熏痕迹。从此以后,人们称它为"白宫"。

白宫鬼魂

像总统府邸这样年代久远的机构,总会有些神秘的事件甚或鬼魂。白宫也不例外。

可以说,最早在白宫出没的鬼魂就是那个捐献建房用地的大卫·伯恩斯。富兰克林·德拉诺·罗斯福当政期间,白宫的一名卫兵和罗斯福的一名私人仆从都曾听到有个声音自称大卫·伯恩斯。

阿比盖尔·亚当斯是首位入住白宫的第一夫人。据说有人曾见到她飘过白宫的厅堂,双臂前伸,手里似乎抱着什么东西。她在白宫居住时,发现房子里通风良好但比较潮湿,除了"东室",于是她决定把洗好的衣服挂在那儿。因而人们猜测,直到现在她的魂魄还在把衣服送往"东室"。

白宫遭到英军烧毁之时,里面住着多莉·麦迪逊,她可能也成了一个鬼魂。伍德罗·威尔逊的夫人生活在白宫时,重新设计了100多年前多莉·麦迪逊种植的玫瑰园。多莉的鬼魂现身,责备园丁弄乱了她的花园,吓得他们转身就跑。

The Busiest Ghost: Abraham Lincoln

Abraham Lincoln is, by far, the busiest ghost in the White House. He is the most commonly seen ghost at the White House and is said to return when national security is at risk. On those occasions, he paces up and down the second floor hallway, knocks on doors and pauses by certain windows clasping his hands behind his back. Grace Coolidge, wife of President Calvin Coolidge, reportedly saw Lincoln standing at a window in the Oval Office with his hands clasped behind his back staring out toward the battlefields of the Civil War across the Potomac River. He has also been spotted in what is now known as the Lincoln Bedroom; during his occupancy he used the room as his personal office and the Cabinet Room.

During Franklin Delano Roosevelt's administration, Lincoln was seen in the Lincoln Bedroom on numerous occasions either sitting on the bed to pull on his boots or lying on the bed. Mary Eben, Eleanor Roosevelt's secretary and other staff members during that time also reported seeing Lincoln in the bedroom at various times.

In fact, Lincoln seemed to be the busiest during Franklin Delano Roosevelt's terms of office. Throughout the 13 years the Roosevelts occupied the White House, there were many reported sightings of Lincoln. Eleanor Roosevelt used the Lincoln Bedroom as her study and she often mentioned having a sense of being watched, although she never personally saw Lincoln. Other residents of the White House during this period reported several sightings of Lincoln. This may have been part of the legend that Lincoln always visited the White House when the security of the nation was at risk, as it certainly was during World War Ⅱ.

No matter when he visited, however, Lincoln seems to have been unfailingly polite. He never entered a room without knocking. In fact, Presidents Theodore Roosevelt, Herbert Hoover and Harry Truman, in addition to Queen Wilhemina, all reported knocks from Lincoln on their doors.

In more recent years occupants and guests at the White House have reported seeing Lincoln, although there have been fewer sightings since the building was extensively renovated in 1952. Nevertheless, stories about Lincoln's ghost persisted.

Some people speculate that because Lincoln's son, Willie, died in the white House at age 11, Lincoln still haunts the building. Others claim that Lincoln was subject to supernatural thoughts and premonitions and therefore, was likely to return to the place where he had experienced momentous events.

Resources

www.whitehouse.gov/ghosts. This Website includes five videos that describe the ghost stories associated with the White House.

Ghosts of the White House, Simon & Schuster, 1998. This book, aimed at ages 9 to 12 years, presents facts about the White House in a fictional framework. A young girl, Sara, on a field trip to the White House is pulled away from her group and taken on a tour by the ghost of George Washington. The first president takes Sara into different rooms of the White House and introduces her to former presidents who tell her about each of their accomplishments while in office.

最为忙碌的魂魄：亚伯拉罕·林肯

迄今为止，亚伯拉罕·林肯是白宫里面最为繁忙的魂魄，被人们见到的次数也最多，而且据说一旦国家安全出现危机他就又回来了。这样的情况下，他就会背着双手，在二楼的走廊踱来踱去，偶尔地敲敲门，或在某扇窗口停下来。据说，卡尔文·柯立芝总统的夫人格蕾丝·柯立芝曾看见林肯背着手，站在椭圆形办公室的一个窗前，双眼注视着波托马克河对岸内战的战场。还有人见到他出现在现在的"林肯卧室"中，当年他住在白宫时曾以这个房间作为私人办公室，也用来召开内阁会议。

富兰克林·德拉诺·罗斯福当政期间，有人多次在"林肯卧室"见到林肯，他要么坐在床沿穿靴子，要么躺在床上。当时埃莉诺·罗斯福的秘书玛丽·爱本以及其他工作人员也汇报说曾多次见到林肯出现在那间卧室。

事实上，罗斯福执政期间林肯似乎尤为繁忙。

罗斯福入主白宫的13年间，好多次有人汇报见到林肯。埃莉诺·罗斯福将"林肯卧室"作为她的书房使用。她虽然没有亲自见到过林肯，但她常常觉得有人在看她。这一时期，其他居住在白宫的人曾多次报告见到林肯。这也许就符合了传说中提到的情况：每当国家安全出现危机，林肯就会造访白宫，二战期间当然如此。

不过，林肯无论何时前来造访，总显得那么彬彬有礼，进门之前总要敲门。事实上，西奥多·罗斯福总统、赫伯特·胡佛总统、哈里·杜鲁门总统以及威廉明娜女王都说，林肯曾敲过他们的门。

1952年白宫大规模翻新以后，人们见到林肯的次数就减少了，不过近些年里面的住户或者来宾也曾几次报告又见到他。无论如何，林肯魂魄的传闻仍然屡见不鲜。

有人推断，林肯的儿子威利仅仅11岁就在白宫夭折了，因而林肯还在白宫徘徊。另外一些人则认为，林肯相信超自然，相信预兆，因此很可能重返白宫，毕竟他在那里历经众多国内外大事。

相关资源

www.whitehouse.gov/ghosts　该网址包含了五个视频，描绘的是与白宫相关的鬼故事。
《白宫鬼魂》，Simon & Schuster，1998年。本书以9至12岁的儿童为读者群，以小说的框架讲述了白宫的一些事实情况。一个名叫萨拉的小女孩正参加一次白宫之行，突然乔治·华盛顿的魂灵将她拉离队伍。这位首任总统带着萨拉参观白宫内各个房间，还将她介绍给前任总统们，而他们则告诉她各自执政期间的功勋。

Forty-nine

Wizard of Oz Hanging

The *Wizard of Oz* is one of the all-time classic movies. Based on a book by L. Frank Baum, the movie was filmed in 1939. The story centers on Dorothy Gale, played by Garland, who is blown away by a tornado from her home in Kansas to a magical place, the Land of Oz. Here she meets the munchkins, who inhabit the land, and makes both friends and enemies as she searches for the Wizard of Oz who supposedly can help her find her way home. Accompanying her on her journey to the Wizard are three of her new friends, the Scarecrow, the Cowardly Lion and the Tin Man, each of whom is hoping the Wizard can fulfill his wish—the Scarecrow wants a brain, the Lion seeks courage and the Tin Man desires a heart.

The Legend

One of the rumors surrounding the film was the hanging theory. Supposedly, an actor portraying one of the munchkins hanged himself because of an unrequited love affair with a female munchkin.

An alternative theory claimed that a clumsy stagehand became tangled up in his cables and wiring and accidentally hanged himself. Both theories stipulate that the hanging took place on the set while filming was in progress.

The so-called suicide occurs at the end of the scene in which Dorothy and the Scarecrow meet the Tin Man. While plucking apples off the talking apple trees, Dorothy and the Scarecrow encounter the rusted Tin Man and stop to help. After oiling the Tin Man so that he is again able to move, the three encounter the Wicked Witch of the West who tries to set fire to the Scarecrow. The Tin Man puts out the fire with his hat as a gesture of friendship for the Scarecrow. After the Witch leaves, the three new friends head down the yellow brick road in search of the Emerald City and the Wizard. With their backs to the camera, the three skip down the road, which winds its way through a dense forest. To the left of the road far back in the trees, something moves in the shadows. This is the alleged hanging. In the film's original print, there appears to be a small shadowy figure hanging and moving. The image is so small and remote that the three actors prancing and singing as they move down the road give no indication of having seen anything off in the forest's shadows.

This story possibly originated after the re-release of the film for the movie's 50th anniversary in 1989. At that point, the film was heavily promoted, and home videos allowed viewers to watch the movie over and over, pausing to study the scene or rewinding to review it again. At the same time, the image was so tiny and indistinct on a small television screen that many people decided that the video perhaps did, indeed, reveal a hanging on the set.

Fact or Fiction

Despite the fact that this suicide myth continues to fascinate the general public, the actual story is just that—a myth.

210

《绿野仙踪》上吊镜头

《绿野仙踪》是一部盛况空前的经典影片,摄制于1939年,以弗兰克·鲍姆的小说为基础,这个故事主要讲述多萝西·盖尔(伽兰饰)在自己的家乡堪萨斯州被一阵龙卷风吹到一个神奇的地方——欧兹国。在这里,她见到了当地的居民曼奇金人。听说国内有个巫师能够帮助她找到回家的路,她就出发去寻找巫师,沿途结交了朋友,也结下了仇敌。一路上陪伴她的是三个新朋友:稻草人、懦弱狮子和铁皮人,他们也各怀希望,希望巫师能帮助他们实现愿望——稻草人想要一个会思考的大脑,狮子寻求勇气以壮胆,而铁皮人则渴望一颗跳动的心。

传说

围绕影片传出了一些谣言,其中之一就是上吊之说。据说,一名扮演曼奇金人的演员爱上一名曼奇金姑娘,却得不到爱的回应,结果上吊自杀了。

另一种说法则是,一名舞台工作人员笨手笨脚的,居然把自己缠在缆绳和电线之中,出人意料地将自己吊死了。两种说法都明确表示,自杀发生地点是在片场,而且当时影片正在拍摄中。

所谓的自杀事件,就出现在多萝西和稻草人遇见铁皮人那一幕场景的边上。当时多萝西和稻草人正在从那棵会说话的苹果树上摘苹果,突然看到生了锈的铁皮人,就停下来帮忙。他们给铁皮人上了油,于是他又能动了。三个人一起碰上了那恶的西方女巫,她竟然妄图一把火烧死稻草人。铁皮人挺身而出,用自己的帽子把火扑灭,表达了对稻草人的深厚友谊。女巫走后,三个新朋友沿着黄砖路继续走下去,寻找翡翠城和巫师。三个人当时背对着镜头,沿途蹦蹦跳跳,脚下的黄砖路蜿蜒穿过茂密的森林。路的左边,远远地从树丛间,可以看到阴暗处有什么东西在摇晃。这就是传闻中的上吊镜头。在影片的原始胶片中,确乎有个模糊的小影子垂挂着摇来摆去。但这个身影太小了,而且那么远,三名演员沿途又唱又跳,根本没有注意到森林深处的阴影里面有任何异常。

这个传说大概起源于1989年,当时为了纪念影片发行50周年,将这部影片重新发行。那时,《绿野仙踪》已经备受瞩目,而且有了家庭影院,人们可以一遍又一遍地观看,也可以暂停下来研究一下场景,或者倒回去再看一遍。况且,那个影像在电视屏幕上播放出来又小又模糊,很多人都认为,这部录像说不定揭露出当时片场上有人上吊了。

事实还是虚构

虽然这次自杀传闻不停地令大众着迷,事实的真相却是:那只是一个虚构的故事。

To give the indoor movie set of an outdoor scene more realism, the set designers for the *Wizard of Oz* borrowed or rented more than 300 birds from the Los Angeles zoo. Among the birds were pheasants, an African crane, peacocks and a South American toucan. A few of the birds escaped their confinement and wandered throughout the set. A peacock, for example, can be seen strutting around the Tin Man's hut while Dorothy and the Scarecrow are revitalizing the Tin Man with oil. When the suicide scene is viewed on the large screen, it is apparent that the moving figure in the background is one of the larger birds, most likely a crane or a stork, flapping its wings and pecking at the ground. For much of the time this same bird appears to be tethered near the house on which the Wicked Witch of the West perches. When the scene is studied in slow motion and on a large screen, the bird is quite clear.

Additional refutation of the munchkin suicide theory is the fact that all the forest scenes in the *Wizard of Oz* were filmed separately from the scenes with the munchkins. Therefore, no munchkins were present on the set during the forest scenes.

Aside from the facts that there were large birds roaming the set and that no munchkins were present during the filming of the forest scenes, common sense is also a factor. How could a suicide take place without anyone noticing it—especially after the fact? None of the actors reacted to the movement to their left on the set. And in later years when Judy Garland and other actors discussed the movie on television talk shows, no one mentioned anything about a suicide or unusual death at the time of the filming.

Most important of all, why would MGM permit a suicide scene to be left in the released film?Yet a suicide or any death on the set of the movie would involve a police investigation and report, not to mention a great deal of publicity. Since neither occurred, it is highly improbable that a suicide of a munchkin or a stagehand took place on the set of the *Wizard of Oz*.

Resources

The Annotated Wizard of Oz, W. W. Norton, 2000. This is the annotated book on which the 1939 musical film was based. This book is a facsimile color version of the first edition of the children's classic written in 1900 as a fairy tale. The book points out that several sequels followed this book and there were many stage adaptations that predated the well-known 1939 classic. The annotations clarify some of the discrepancies between the book and the film and there are commentaries by such well-known writers as Gore Vidal and Salman Rushdie.

The Wizardry of Oz: the Artistry and Magic of the 1939 MGM Classic, Revised and Expanded, Applause Books, 2004. Published on the 65th anniversary of the release of the 1939 film, this book discusses the stagecraft behind the film, including the construction of the sets, the make–up, the special effects and the costumes. The book features includes illustrations, blueprints and photographs as well as interviews with Oz's cast and crew.

　　为了要让摄影棚内的户外场景看起来更加写实，《绿野仙踪》的片场设计师向洛杉矶动物园或租或借了300多只鸟，其中有野鸡、孔雀、一只非洲鹤和一只南美犀鸟。有几只鸟从笼子里逃出来，在片场四处乱窜。比如说，多萝西和稻草人给铁皮人上油的时候，一只孔雀就在铁皮人的小屋附近昂头蹀步。所谓的自杀一幕在大屏幕上放映，很明显就能看出，背景上摇摆动荡的身影，其实是一只体型较大的鸟，很有可能是鹤或者鹳，正拍打着翅膀在地上啄食呢。很多场景中，这只鸟都被拴在西方女巫栖息的房子附近。如果在大屏幕上播放慢镜头，这只鸟还是蛮清楚的。

　　针对曼奇金人自杀一论，另外还有反驳的观点就是：《绿野仙踪》中所有的森林场景和曼奇金人场景都是分开拍摄的。因此，在森林场景中根本就没有曼奇金人出现。

　　片场有很多大鸟在到处乱走，拍摄森林场景时根本没有曼奇金人出现——除了这两个事实，人类的常识也是辩驳的一个理由。有人自杀了，怎么可能没人注意到？更别说自杀发生以后了。当时片场上没有一名演员对此作出任何反应。数年之后，朱蒂·伽兰和其他几名演员在访谈节目中说到这部影片，也没人提起拍摄过程中关于自杀或者非正常死亡的只言片语。

　　最重要的是，米高梅电影制片公司(MGM)怎么可能放任一部含有自杀场景的影片在市场上流通呢？如果在片场有人自杀或者去世，警方势必前来调查并作出报告，更别说有那么多百姓正在关注此事。既然什么也没发生，那么最有可能的就是，《绿野仙踪》的片场根本就没人自杀。

相关资源

《绿野仙踪(附有注解)》，W.W.诺顿公司，2000年。本书带有注解，其实是1900年成书的儿童经典之作的翻版，1939年的音乐剧就是以此为蓝本。书中指出了故事的几种后续结局，还有好几处改编成剧本，比著名的1939年经典影片还早。注解部分指明了书本和影片的一些差异，另外还选登了著名作家的评论，如郭尔·菲德尔和萨尔曼·孺西迪。

《绿野仙踪：1939年MGM艺术和魔幻的经典之作》，重新修订版，掌声图书，2004年。本书于1939年的影片发行65周年纪念之际出版，探讨了影片幕后的舞台艺术，包括场景的搭建、化妆、特效以及服装。书中诸多特色，主要有插图、设计图、照片以及对演员阵容和工作人员的采访。

Fifty

Yeti

The Yeti, also called the Abominable Snowman, is a creature that supposedly lives in the Himalayan Mountains range that straddles the borders of India, Nepal and Tibet(China) in Asia. Reports of sightings of this creature have come from Nepal, Tibet (China), and Siberia.

According to legend, the Yeti is a large hairy animal with an apelike body and a face that appears to be human. The hair is generally black to dark brown in dim light and red in bright sunlight. Its arms are long, reaching to its knees and it walks erect on thick massive legs.

The Origin of the Name

The name Yeti comes from the term metoh kangmi, the Tibetan name for animal, which can be loosely translated as dirty snowman, wild man of the snows or magical creature, depending on who is doing the translation. The Sherpa people of Nepal actually gave the animal the name Yeti and to the Sherpas that name probably meant all−devouring demon creature. The various peoples in the Himalayan region also use other terms that do not translate exactly the same way but do conjure up images of legendary and mythical animals. Some terms refer to man bears, wild man, monkey−like animal or Himalayan red bear. Many of the terms are tied to regional dialects and to legends surrounding the mythical animals.

The term Abominable Snowman was coined in 1921 by a Western journalist who may have mistranslated metoh kangmi. More likely, however, the Western newspaper staff wanted to use a name that would impart a sense of fear and terror to their readers as part of the mystery and sensationalism surrounding the stories.

Expeditions

Expeditions into Asia in the early 19th century mention accounts of unidentified creatures, but in most cases these were stories told by the guides of the explorers. In 1832, for example, native guides of the explorer B.H. Hodgson described a sighting of a large apelike animal and although Hodgson published an account of the story in the Journal of the Asiatic Society of Bengal, he assumed the creature was an orangutan. Toward the end of the century, the explorer L.A. Waddell wrote about his guide's sighting of a large apelike animal that left huge footprints. Waddell could find no proof of a specific animal matching the guide's description so he concluded the prints were those of a bear.

Later in 1925, N.A. Tombazi, a Greek photographer working as a member of a British geological expedition in the Himalayas, spotted a large animal near a glacier on a lower slope about 1,000 feet away. The animal disappeared before Tombazi could reach the slope, but the photographer found and photographed some large footprints in the same area.

In 1951 the British mountaineer, Eric Shipton, discovered and photographed a set of fresh footprints on the southwestern slope of the Menlung Glacier that lies between Tibet

夜　帝

夜帝,也称为"可恶的雪人",是一种生物,通常认为生活在印度、尼泊尔及中国西藏交界的喜马拉雅山脉一带。夜帝的目击报告一般来自尼泊尔、中国的西藏以及西伯利亚。

根据传说,夜帝是一种体型庞大的动物,浑身长毛,身体像猿人,面部接近于人类。毛发在暗光下一般介于黑色和深棕色之间,有强光照射时则呈现红色。手臂很长,可以够到膝盖,用两条粗壮的大腿走路。

称谓由来

"夜帝"这一称谓源自藏语中动物一词的说法metoh kangmi,不同的翻译人员随意地把它译成了"肮脏的雪人"、"雪中的野人"或"魔幻生物"。其实是尼泊尔的谢范人给这种动物起了夜帝的名字,对谢范人来说这个名字可能意味着鲸吞一切的魔鬼生物。喜马拉雅地区的各族人民也用别的说法来给它命名,精确的翻译虽然不尽相同,但都可以勾勒出传说中神奇诡秘的动物形象。这些名称当中,有的指人熊、野人或者某种跟猴子差不多的动物,也有的说是喜马拉雅红熊。很多名称与本地方言密切相关,和围绕着这种神秘动物的传说也有着千丝万缕的关系。

"可恶的雪人"这种说法产生于1921年,是因为一名西方的新闻记者把metoh kangmi译错了。不过,也许更有可能的情况是:西方报业挖空心思才想出这么一个噱头,为新闻报道营造出神秘而又哗然的氛围,能让读者产生一种又惊又怕的感觉。

深入探险

19世纪初,深入亚洲的探险活动记载了不少不明生物的报告,不过大部分都是导游讲述的故事而已。比如1832年,英国探险家霍奇森雇佣的当地导游描述了他所见过的一种体型巨大、很像猿人的动物。霍奇森由此在《孟加拉亚洲社会杂志》上发表了一篇报道,但他还是认为,那种动物应该就是猩猩。19世纪末,英国探险家瓦代尔在作品中写道,他的导游曾见过一种体格庞大、类似猿人的动物留下了巨大脚印。瓦代尔找不出哪种动物符合导游的描述,因此他认为那些脚印应该是熊留下的。

1925年,希腊的摄影家汤姆巴兹正参加英国地质探险队在喜马拉雅山的工作,突然发现大约1000英尺之外的一处低坡上,冰川旁边有一只大型动物。汤姆巴兹还没来得及赶到那处斜坡,动物就不见了,不过他还是在现场找到一些大脚印,并且拍了下来。

1951年,在西藏和尼泊尔之间的门龙冰川西南坡上,大约海拔2万英尺处,英国登山

(China) and Nepal at an altitude of 20,000 feet. Many scientists reviewed the photographs but could not pinpoint any animals that may have made them. Nevertheless, only 2 years later in 1953 Sir Edmund Hillary and his guide Tenzing Norgay also reported seeing unusually large footprints while scaling Mount Everest. Later, however, Hillary dismissed the photographs as inconclusive. Later in 1960 Hillary set out with explorer Desmond Doig to collect and analyze evidence of the Yeti. He tested an alleged Yeti scalp, but the results indicated that the hair came from a Himalayan antelope.

Other explorers on Himalayan expeditions during the latter part of the 20th century continued to seek evidence that the Yeti existed. In addition, a Japanese mountaineer embarked on a 12−year linguistic study that concluded in 2003 that the word yeti was actually a corruption of a regional term meaning bear.

Myth or Real?

Despite the numerous expeditions, treks, reports and linguistic studies, no one yet has come face to face with the Yeti. Many of the stories and sightings are hearsay, and some of the so−called evidence is based on sounds or shadows. No one can prove that the large footprints so carefully photographed are anything more than distorted footprints of large animals known to be living in the region.

Some scientists, however, speculate that the sightings could be actual animals that evolved from the extinct giant ape known as Gigantopithecus who retreated into the Himalayans more than 500,000 years ago. Most, however, think that the Yeti could be one of two existing animals. The first is known to the Sherpas as the dzu teh and to the rest of the world as the Tibetan blue bear. These are extremely rare large shaggy animals that attack cattle. The second animal is a gibbon, a type of large ape that is known to live in the Himalayan area.

Although there is no concrete evidence to support the existence of the Yeti, there is also no firm proof that such a creature does not exist.

Resources

Field Guide to Bigfoot, Yeti, & Other Mystery Primates, Harper Perennial, 1999. This book is a comprehensive study of the mysterious apelike and humanoid animals that are reported as sighted throughout the world today. The book includes range maps and typical footprints for each type of creature as well as eyewitness accounts of the sightings.

Monsters and Water Beasts: Creatures of Fact or Fiction? Henry Holt and Co., 2007. Each chapter of this book discusses one creature that has been sighted but has not undergone scientific scrutiny. One chapter has been devoted to Yeti and Bigfoot.

家艾瑞克·谢普顿发现一组新鲜的脚印并将之拍摄下来。很多科学家研究了这组照片,但没人能够确定究竟是什么样的动物留下了这些脚印。然而,仅仅两年之后,也就是1953年,新西兰的埃德门·希拉里爵士及其导游滕森·诺给也报告,在攀登珠峰的过程中看到了非比寻常的大脚印。不过,希拉里后来却说仅凭这些照片是无法推断出结论的。到1960年,希拉里偕同探险家黛斯蒙德·道伊格一起出发,去收集夜帝的证据以作分析之用。他测试了一块据说采自夜帝的头皮,但试验的结果表明,上面的毛发来自一只喜马拉雅羚羊。

20世纪后半叶,还有一些探险家继续在喜马拉雅山脉寻找能够证实夜帝存在的证据。此外,一名日本的登山爱好者从事一项语言研究长达12年之久,他在2003年得出结论:"夜帝"这个词汇,其实是当地一个已经废弃的说法,意思就是"熊"。

是真是假?

虽然人们进行了不计其数的探险、考察、报告以及语言学研究,却仍然没有任何人曾和夜帝面对面过。大部分的报道和目击不过是道听途说,而所谓的证据多半也是声音或阴影而已。那些仔细拍摄下来的大脚印,也许是生活在当地的某种大型动物所留下,只不过有点变形罢了,对此,谁也无法举证辩驳。

然而,有些科学家推断,人们见到的也许真是某种动物,它们是从已经灭绝的古代巨猿演变而来,在50多万年前退居到了喜马拉雅山。不过大部分人认为夜帝可能是两种现存动物当中的一种。其一,谢范人称之为祖岔,而世界上其他地方人称之为西藏蓝熊的动物。这种动物非常罕见,体型庞大,毛发浓密,经常袭击牛群。其二,生活在喜马拉雅山区的一种大型猿猴——长臂猿。

尽管没有具体可靠的证据证明夜帝确实存在,可同样缺乏有力的证据证明这样一种动物的确并不存在。

相关资源

《大脚印、夜帝及其他神秘动物指南》,Harper Perennial出版社,1999年。本书对类似猿人又具备人类特征的神秘动物进行了综合研究,这样的动物在全世界范围内都曾有目击报道。本书包括各种地图、每种动物的典型脚印以及目击者的报告。

《怪物和水兽:真正的生物还是虚构?》,亨利·霍特出版公司,2007年。书中每个章节探讨一种生物,都是有人见过但未经科学证实的。其中一章就专讲夜帝和大脚印。